The Missing Boy

Rachel Billington

The Missing Boy

First published in Great Britain in 2010 by Orion Books,
an imprint of The Orion Publishing Group Ltd
Orion House, 5 Upper Saint Martin's Lane
London WC2H 9EA

An Hachette UK Company

1 3 5 7 9 10 8 6 4 2

A CIP catalogue record for this book is
available from the British Library.

ISBN (Hardback) 978 1 4091 1137 5

Typeset at The Spartan Press Ltd, Lymington, Hants

Printed in Great Britain by Clays Ltd, St Ives plc.

The Orion Publishing Group's policy is to use papers that are natural,
renewable and recyclable products and made from wood grown in sustainable
forests. The logging and manufacturing processes are expected to
conform to the environmental regulations of the country of origin.

Extract from 'Sonnet XVII' by Pablo Neruda, from
Essential Neruda. Translation copyright 2004 by
Mark Eisner. Reprinted by permission of City Light Books.

Extract from 'Poem' by Dylan Thomas, from
Selected Poems. Copyright 2000, Orion Publishing Group.
Reprinted by permission of David Higham Associates on behalf of
the Trustees for the copyright of the late Dylan Thomas.

While every effort has been made to trace the owners of
copyrighted material reproduced herein, the publishers would
like to apologise for any omission and will be pleased to incorporate
missing acknowledgements in any future editions.

www.orionbooks.co.uk

To Kevin

The Day Breaks not, it is my Heart
JOHN DONNE

PART ONE
The Runaway

CHAPTER ONE

The car was not a car: it was a limousine, one of those drawn-out white vehicles with darkened windows you see swimming through London streets. The boy had imagined them filled with pouting blondes on their way to film premières or veiled dark-eyed beauties taking a break from their sheikh owner. The word 'limousine' was identified with glamour, sex, money.

He took a step closer. He shivered. This limousine lay in the far corner of a field, just outside a broken-down shed littered with old farm implements, disguised by nettles, brambles and bulging bales of straw.

How are the mighty fallen! He remembered that line from somewhere. He might have read it, although it was the sort of thing Eve would say. He shivered again. He wasn't cold. The sun was shining. It was fear of the strangeness of everything and now this car. It was also excitement.

He climbed over the gate, which was padlocked with a rusty chain, and began to walk towards the car. He didn't want to think about his mother. It felt like days since he'd left home. As if he'd gone on the longest plane trip in the world and landed up on another planet. Actually, he'd travelled by train that morning and it was still afternoon. Just look how the sun glinted off the limo's chrome even though the body of it was bog filthy.

His backpack was beginning to feel heavy so he unhitched the strap from each shoulder and let it fall to the ground. In a moment of glee, he thought there was no one to tell him where to put it or ask him what was inside it.

In fact, he could hardly remember what he'd put into it. His leaving had been so sudden and had so disturbed him that his exit from the flat had been carried out in an emotional haze, noises too, strange vibrations in his head as he dashed about the house grabbing whatever seemed like a good idea. He did remember throwing in a large jar of Marmite because he'd heard explorers in the Himalayas took it for its vitamins.

Once again, the boy advanced on the car. He had to trample down an army of nettles, which he did with some relish, before he could reach the door handle, which had a kind of push-in button. He pressed it without much hope of anything happening but, to his surprise, it swung slowly open, creakily, and only halfway, but still enough for him to peer in.

Not too bad. It smelt of damp, and a shiny trail of some animal or other, slug or snail, he supposed, criss-crossed the seat. It would clean up. He put his head in further and was beginning to form a plan when there was suddenly an enormous bellowing, which gave him such a fright that he came out too quickly, cracking himself painfully on the head.

He stood upright, rubbing the place. He'd also been stung on his hand, a cluster of red bumps. The noise wasn't repeated but he wasn't crazy enough to have imagined it.

He moved cautiously round the car and saw, on the other side of a hedge, a whole gang of cows or bullocks. Anyway, the sort of animal that could moo in a bellowing sort of way. So this wasn't such a forgotten corner after all. Someone must look after them. Of course, nowhere in southern England was remote, he knew that, but the abandoned car and the derelict shed beyond had given the impression that no one ever came to this little bit of the world.

Perhaps they didn't. Not just here. The hedge was thick, backed up by a barbed-wire fence. Still cautiously, because of course he must be trespassing, he headed for the shed.

That really was in a bad condition, the corrugated-iron roof rusty and pitted with holes. The earthen floor was uneven, damp in some places, dusty in others. A trail of feathers led into one corner where the remains of a largish bird lay ransacked.

The boy came out again quickly, blinking in the sunlight. He preferred the limousine. The back of it was facing him now, the word 'Lincoln' marked out in silver letters. So that was what it was. He'd always liked cars. Eve said all boys liked cars because they wanted to drive away and escape. Too right! Annoying that he was quoting her again.

All the same it was funny to think this 'Lincoln', all six doors, stretched length of it, wasn't going any place soon. He kicked a black tyre as flat and wide as a puddle. Not ever.

From the back it looked roadworthy. It still had number plates. And another smaller name: 'TownCar'. That really was funny. Bird muck on the roof, cow pats under the wheels. The name would have suited him well, though: 'TownBoy'. Born and bred. In a foreign world now: the countryside. Perhaps that's why he was clinging to this car.

He walked round to the front and only then noticed there was no glass in the windscreen. Heaving himself half on to the bonnet, he stared down into the dark interior. The front seats were mouldy and unwelcoming, as he'd already noticed, and there was some kind of barrier – perhaps the back seat raised up – so that he could only partly make out the interior but it seemed much cleaner.

He slithered down again, stood staring at the darkened windows for a moment before realizing that, as he'd opened the front door, he could most likely open the back. What a loser!

He leant forward, pressed the button on the handle and swept the door open – as if he was a doorman at a grand hotel, he thought, pleased at the image. He even gave a little bow before sticking his head in.

Just as he'd hoped: dry and relatively clean. One seat had been turned forward, making the barrier; the other, black and spongy, was just where it should be. Without hesitating, he eased himself inside and half sat, half lay on the cushions. Pity they weren't leather but beggars can't be choosers. He smiled to himself. To his right was smart polished wood – bottle holders with three champagne bottles – empty, guess what. Above them dangled a row of wine glasses, quite clean. They might be useful.

The boy put his feet up. A great weight of tiredness almost overwhelmed him; he longed to shut his eyes. He hadn't slept properly for weeks – months, even. He let out a long breath. He'd hardly taken a relaxed one since he'd left home – or longer than that. The silence was awesome; he'd never heard silence like it.

Half dreaming, he imagined he'd known about this limousine-in-a-field all along and had been running towards it. It had been waiting for him.

Forcing his eyes open, he stared at the golden light beyond the open door. The sun was shining from that direction, which must mean it was south or south-west. He looked at his watch: four thirty. He continued looking at it. Somehow it seemed different out here among all this greenery, all this grass and hedges and trees, all this nature. It seemed out of place. Too urgent. Too demanding.

He felt very tired again. At night when he couldn't sleep, he'd look at the luminous dial every few minutes, sometimes for a long while. Sometimes it seemed like a comforter, sometimes an enemy, racing along, pushing forward to the next day before he'd dealt with the night. Yet he wanted the day to come. Out here under this quiet sky, the watch seemed insignificant, cheaply man-made. After all, it wasn't the watch that kept him awake.

Time had stopped. He could breathe now. He opened his mouth wide and took a deep gulp of air, then let it out slowly from his nose.

The sensation was good but something niggled at him. Of course! It was Eve again, one of her stupid exercises before her drama lessons.

Abruptly, the boy began to walk, almost to run across the field. Squeezing himself through a broken barbed-wire fence and a straggly hedge, he continued across another field that sloped steeply upwards. At the top there was a further thicker hedge. He stopped there, panting, and turned round.

Immediately his mood changed. In front of him spread a gentle pattern of green fields, rough land and wooded areas. Not a house to be seen and the only road the little lane, partially surfaced with rubble and old bits of tarmac, that he'd walked along. There was a stone barn and a couple more sheds further away but, apart from the cows he'd seen earlier, there were no other signs of man.

He couldn't even see the car because it was hidden below the curve of the land. It was nice to know it was there, though. His base. Everybody needed a base. Soldiers, mountaineers, explorers in the jungle, Shackleton, Fiennes, Ray Mears on the TV. He was linked to an intrepid lot who pushed through normal boundaries.

Unconsciously the boy, who was skinny and too tall for his weight, straightened his shoulders. This was the first day of his growing up and he was doing it on his own. No bossing, bullying, cajoling, caressing, competing, pretending, disagreeing. Just himself deciding what to do next. Or to do nothing next.

He could do with a drink. It had been yet another hot day. His eyes followed the lines of the terrain in front of him. The lane was at the bottom of the valley, which then rose up steeply. Before it did so, there was a line of shrubs and small trees that could easily hide a stream. He imagined water sparkling in the sun, cascading over shiny stones.

He'd bought a bottle of Fanta on the train, empty now. He could fill that and drink from the champagne glasses. That'd be a laugh. Faces of boys at school whom he didn't usually enjoy thinking about – they were the daring ones, never him – hovered admiringly.

He'd lounge in that spongy seat in the back of the car, sipping now and again, laughing, between sips, at the world he'd left behind.

CHAPTER TWO

Eve was doing the thing that most excited her: taking a group of difficult inner-city kids and impressing them with her personality. Very few teachers could do that and it was the only way you'd get them to listen. Make them follow you like the Pied Piper – not too PC an image, that – make them forget all their competitiveness and self-consciousness, grudges and misery and think of nothing but her. It was a kind of falling in love – not really, of course, she couldn't ever let that happen, although some boys, and girls too, got a bit over-obsessed. That was a small risk for the prize: children who suddenly found confidence. She was their stimulant, their source of energy, their paradigm (for the girls), their escape route from their own disastrous lives, their enabler, although she didn't like the word.

As a drama teacher, words were her business, true, but attitude, appearance and behaviour were much more important. That was why she dressed as she did: flamboyant, spectacular, eccentric. Every other drama teacher in the world wore black. It was the kids who were supposed to shine. She saw the point, all right, but she wanted to give the kids something to look at, make fun of if they liked, but that didn't last for long. No surprise that the Piper was called 'Pied', meaning he wore a multi-range of colours.

Today she had her long blonde hair in a tumbled, waterfall look, kept in place by an orange and turquoise scarf, which echoed her turquoise T-shirt, and gold bangles up her arm. She liked the clatter as they slid down. Let's see how this lot reacted to the traditional flat hand in the air for quiet and attention.

Eve looked assessingly at her students scattered about in the room. All except one were on their mobiles or pretending to be. The age group was fourteen to sixteen, her usual, ten of them, all English speakers – she'd insisted on that – but from various ethnic groups, three white and one of those Irish by his white skin and orange hair. Pity about the acne. Most were in trouble, permanently excluded from regular schools or dubbed at risk. Made it a bit different for her.

Question was how quickly she laid down the ground rules: no mobiles, iPods, drugs or knives. Didn't think she'd have a problem with the second two – these kids hadn't been forced to come. Usually she'd go heavy straight away but with these kids she'd been taking it a little easier. She didn't want them making a mass run for the exit. In the end is the beginning. She'd done OK with the two groups in the morning. Charisma. Get them on your side.

Her regular job was as drama teacher in the high school – the one she was standing in now, except it was holidays. Ten years at the same school gave her a few rights, like using one of the rooms for this initiative. She'd raised the money herself, taken her nearly three years so this was a big day – surprised the mayor wasn't here celebrating. *Get the kids off the streets* was the way her backers were thinking, but she had higher ambitions. The school had chipped in too, knowing she knew they had left-over money going begging.

'OK, guys!' she called suddenly, in her rich, deep voice. She'd trained as a singer and done very well until her vocal cords had let her down. That was when she and Max had decided to get married. Otherwise she might have become seriously depressed. So she'd trained to be a drama teacher. Brilliant! Absolutely brilliant. Hooray for her dud vocal cords.

'OK, guys,' she said again, because nobody except a couple of girls had reacted – but, then, she hadn't expected them to. 'It's lying-down time.' A boy sniggered, setting off a couple of others. So they had been listening.

'Lying on the floor, Miss?' mumbled one of the girls. 'It's fucking dirty.' 'Chelsea Jane' was scrawled on her name badge. They hated wearing them but she'd insisted. Just till she got them straight in her head.

'Health and safety, Miss,' complained the sniggerer – Ibou – managing to sound outraged.

'Then get the mats out of the cupboard.'

'Fucking cupboards're locked,' said—

Eve peered at his T-shirt, just near the line 'Suck shit': Louis.

Of course they weren't. She opened one herself and took out a mat. Ostentatiously, she lay on it. This gave them a problem. The boys playing bad would instinctively want to kick someone who was lying down, defenceless.

Around her, she heard nervous laughter, swearing, shuffling; a mobile phone rang with a line of rap. She'd deal with that later. So far it wasn't out of control. At least the boy turned it off. These kids were supposed to be mad keen on acting.

Two mats arrived on either side of her. Two figures, couldn't tell if they were boy or girl, struggled to lie down. After all, a teenager spent his time trying to hold himself together. It felt like giving up, letting go, making yourself vulnerable.

Out of the corner of her eye, she watched them contort their bodies into non-lying-down shapes while lying down.

'Do you want us right down?' shouted a girl, which kicked off a chorus of 'Fucking sleep time' and 'Acting, my arse'. She'd have to get on to the swearing too.

Time for her to stand up. 'Right, I want total relax. Then we'll start the exercise.'

It made her sad to watch them. How could anyone live with so much embarrassment? The girls were as bad as the boys. In particular, a fat one – Carla – was hating the way her flesh fell all over the mat.

The boys had their willies to think of too. One was lying on his face, partly to be clever but partly to hide – who knew what?

'Lie flat on your backs with your arms stretched out – make sure you're not touching anyone.' She waited for more giggles. 'Legs straight. Good. Fine. Louis, shut your mouth.' More giggles. 'Ibou, open your eyes. We'll be shutting them later. Good. Very good. Now you're going to concentrate on each part of your body, starting at the feet. Bottom to top.'

Dirty laughter and a different mobile went off playing. She'd have to deal with the mobiles. Nothing would be too hard now she'd got them on the floor on their mats. She'd got their curiosity, that was the most important thing.

The girl whose phone had rung got up and walked to the back of the room. You had to remember with kids like these that it could be something important. No one took responsibility for their lives. It might be a baby sister needing help or a sick mum. Even so, she needed to have them turned off now.

They made surprisingly little fuss, almost as if it was a relief to be out of touch for an hour or two. They were the first generation who never had a moment's peace, day or night. No wonder they made bad decisions, got into trouble.

She had them lying down again in no time. Most of them were already better at letting go and some of the girls were thinking they looked pretty neat on the floor with their breasts perking upwards.

'Work up your body. Fingers stretching and relaxing. Mouths opening, shutting, breathing in and out.' Some of them were really going for it. 'Eyes. I want you to focus on your eyes. Scrunch eyes and release.'

In a day or two she'd have them do their whole routine without thinking. Now she'd got them on their feet, a shambling lot, shoulders hunched, eyes glazed as if they were afraid of seeing too clearly. So much self-protection!

She'd break down all that and give them something better. That was the buzz of it. Not the money. She wanted to see them stand straight, filled with real confidence, not the sham stuff they put on. 'We're into Speed Dial. Anyone know what that is?'

Of course not. It sounded easy enough. 'Kids' games,' a girl muttered scornfully. True in a way: walking from slow to fast, one to five, and not bumping into anyone else or making any noise. She held up the number of fingers.

There were a couple of boys and at least one girl who had real charisma, with swagger that was more than the usual nervous disguise.

'Number one is slow, very slow, Louis.'

She tried not to favour the bright ones but, with any luck, it lifted the level of the rest. Unless they were recalcitrant. More 'at risk' because of their talents.

After this she'd get them on to Freeze Frame. Harder still but more like acting. They'd enjoy that. Put them in groups and make them give her an image for something or other. 'Lost in the Woods' was one of her favourites.

She had five fingers up and they were all careering around like mad horses. But they were silent, that was tops. Now she'd cool them down.

'That's right, Carla. Drop your shoulders.' She was the fat one. A bit sad. She had a sweet face, though, and had taken trouble with her hair. First it was plaited close to her head in a pattern of lines like a spider's web and then allowed to spurt out in little fireworks of black curls.

'Pretty,' said Eve, lightly touching her head, although she shouldn't, going by the rules. The girl smiled. Perfect white teeth.

Shit! Two girls pushing each other about in a corner. But at least they stopped when she got there. Chelsea Jane was clearly one to watch. Long, streaked hair and far too much makeup for a fourteen-year-old. Not that she would ban that. This was the holidays.

'Two groups of five. Ibou, Louis, Carla, Dave, Jade.'

'I'm the leader, am I?' Ibou punched a fist.

'No leaders.' But she needed him on her side. That he was showing off to her meant he cared.

'Don't we ever get to speak? Or sing or something?'

'When you know how to move.'

Of course they all wanted to sing – rap, pop, musicals. Whatever would make them rich and famous.

Eve moved among them, watched the two groups, made them watch and listen to each other.

'Now we're going to breathe from our diaphragms,' she allowed a pause for a few sniggers, 'and produce a supported sound on "Ooooh".'

'Ooooooooh.' Silly sounds.

The kids' concentration was slackening, reflecting her own tired-ness. The backchat was starting. Someone – Andy – had picked up his mobile.

'Deeper breathing, Ibou. Louis. Think *X Factor*.' She showed them how to do it by placing her hand on her own diaphragm. They were quick learners. She wasn't a singing teacher. Just all-round drama. But why not? Who's telling her what to do?

'OK, guys, on your feet and in a huddle.' She needed a bit of bonding here. She used to find it strange that kids who thought of nothing but sex could hardly bear to touch each other. Now she knew it mattered too much to be easy.

'Arms out and round each other's shoulders. Heads down. Right. I'm going to say a word and you pass it round.' Heads moved up and down, bodies swayed. They didn't seem a bad group. She could work with them. If they turned up.

'Cross-legged on your mats.'

They sat, boys' legs every which way. You'd think they had three or four. Then she let them up, told them to jump to the sky like a jack-in-the-box – a modern reference. But they jumped. Whooped. End with a bang not a whimper.

'Games over. See you tomorrow, guys.' Nice that guys did for girls as well, these days.

Eve sat on the one plastic chair in the room. She hadn't made the kids put away the mats; that was bad. Bad practice. Everything needed ritual, good manners.

For the first time since she'd left her home, she thought of her son. Dan hadn't been out of bed, of course. First Monday of the holidays. He was a nice, sensible boy. A bit too quiet but, then, she was a bit too noisy. Eve began to feel more herself. She'd left him money to buy himself a sandwich for lunch but she'd cook them a hearty supper, pasta and chicken. Boys were always so hungry, she thought indulgently.

She stood up and did a few stretching exercises. It was satisfying the way she could place her hands flat on the floor, legs straight as a soldier's.

On the whole she would not think of her stupid husband. He would come back to her. Briskly, she gathered up the mats and slapped them into the cupboard. She picked up her coat and bag.

The Polish caretaker, Stefan, was peering through the glass panel in the door. His pale face was distorted.

She waved cheerfully. 'Just leaving!' Why had his face given her a turn? She put her hand to her heart theatrically. It seemed to be beating too loudly and too fast. He'd looked like a ghost, full of anguish. Nothing was wrong. She'd just had a hard day. The sort of day she liked, she reminded herself, and banged the door behind her.

CHAPTER THREE

Max was chatting up Alison in her office. It was hardly more than a cupboard, filled with a desk, chair, computer and files. She had lured him in – something to show him on the Internet – so now it was difficult to avoid their flirtatious routine. It had been going on almost since the first time he'd visited her bookshop about five years ago. He was striking, tall and dark and rugged; she was small and fair. Their behaviour towards each other was inevitable, dogs sniffing, meaningless. It led nowhere, nothing more than the smallest touch, the look exchanged, the what-might-be-if-we-let-ourselves-go. It spiced the day a little, more for her than him, he thought.

It was business for him. She ordered more books from him than from other reps. Not that he would have behaved any differently if he'd had nothing to gain. He'd been very young when he realized women admired him. Even as a boy he'd been handsome. Girls hadn't cared what was in his head. He hadn't particularly liked it then and still kept a core of resentment.

He was also flattered, played along as expected, followed the easier route. What was inside his head soon became his business.

'See?' Alison pointed at the screen. She was sitting on the chair, he was bent over her. He smelt the freshness of shampoo.

'The book's not on the database. It was really embarrassing when the author came into the shop.'

'Local authors.' Max smiled. 'The scourge of the independent bookseller.'

Alison turned round to smile back but she was reproving too. 'He's right, in this case. It really isn't recorded.' She was wearing a rather low-cut T-shirt, and as she moved, her breasts squeezed together making a long crease in her skin. A small medallion hovered on the edge. Max thought of a photograph he'd seen of the Grand Canyon and a light aeroplane.

'I'll try to get it sorted.' He moved away a little, which meant he was partly out of the door. He felt the sun slanting in over his shoulder and turned round so that he could look across the shop and into the street beyond. The brightness gave him a sense of yearning mixed with hunger. He'd left London at seven and not taken a break for lunch. 'I think I'll have a sandwich at that pub round the corner.'

'The Rose and Crown.' Alison followed him out of the office into the shop. Her assistant behind the till, a well-educated young Irishman called Dermot, whom Max actually liked more than Alison, was watching them. 'I haven't eaten yet either.'

So, Alison would come with him. This had happened a couple of times before. Last time, over half a pint of lager (he drove in the afternoon too), he'd told her about his poetry. Maybe that had been a mistake, seeming to her like a chat-up line – 'I am at heart a poet' or 'The publisher's rep you've seen over so many years is not the real me.'

Max felt his heart squirm with embarrassment. It had been a mistake. He had talked to her like a bookish friend, not a woman with soft breasts that squeezed together. Now she would want more, more intimate talk, revelations. She might even ask about his wife. His marriage was the last thing he wanted to talk about at the moment – ever.

Max and Alison strolled across the road together, Dermot still watching, probably the whole small town watching.

When they sat down, outside at a grubby wooden table, Max looked at his watch. 'Twenty minutes,' he said uncompromisingly. He felt the sun warm his face.

'Absolutely,' agreed Alison, putting on sunglasses.

Despite his fears, she seemed in no hurry for a conversation. They both sipped their drinks, Diet Coke and a coffee.

He thought of a poem he was working on. It was about the sun; too ambitious for him. Donne dared far more, making the sun villain, an interruption to love. *Busy old fool, unruly sun,/ why dost thou thus,/ through windows, and through the curtains call on us?* His poem would be more conventional: the sun as healer, yet never to be relied upon. As he thought this, Alison took off her dark glasses. They were in shadow. A cloud or the light moving.

'Quite a summer we're having.' She smiled.

'We'll be heading for autumn soon.' Max knew a lot about the weather. His job involved hours of driving each day so he saw a lot of it. Heading west in the evening, the sun pierced his eyes in golden shafts; heading east in the morning, it got him again, although paler and less penetrating. He drove in heavy rain when the car seemed like a snake under water, and through high winds when the car moved from under him and he thought of Dorothy's house twirling up to the sky. The weather made his job interesting.

'Don't say that.' Alison looked mournful at the thought of autumn. People often did. Max pictured leaves scattered across his windscreen: dark green, lime green, lemon yellow, butter yellow, orange, ochre, scarlet, crimson, copper brown.

'Oh, you've got a couple more months.' He could see Alison was a summer girl. Her skin was tanned to a soft gold. He felt tolerant and rather patronizing at his imagined simplicity of her needs.

'Do you mind if I tell you something?' Her sunny look had waned.

'Be my guest.' He did mind. Why did women want to tell him things? Why did they trust him?

'I've just got divorced. It's all right, I'm not upset. It's been a long time coming.' But tears were filling her eyes. 'It's not a come-on. I know you're married.'

She knew nothing about him.

'I just needed to say it.' She made an attempt at a smile. 'I needed it out in the open and you being almost a stranger but someone I like makes it easier.'

'Yes,' said Max. He felt sorry for her, although he could see she didn't want pity. All the same, 'Yes' was an inadequate response. He wondered whether she had children but didn't want to encourage her to further intimacies. 'You're very pretty,' he said.

'Thank you.' She looked serious, as if he'd complimented her on her sales figures, then relaxed. Complimenting women on their appearance was always the right thing to do.

Max said, 'On my way here, I saw two buzzards on the horizon.' This was true; it had been an exciting vision of freedom and the nearest he could get to returning the conversation to the weather.

'This summer the countryside's been full of buzzards. Maybe it's something to do with the heatwave. People keep spotting a buzzard here and a buzzard there. Naturally, I haven't seen any.'

Max liked her again. He felt light-hearted watching her generous pink mouth chewing her sandwich. Eve had that same warm physicality. It was very strange what had happened between Eve and him. Bewildering. Even more so that this wasn't the first time.

Sometimes he felt it wasn't his decision at all, that the sisters called the shots and handed him backwards and forwards in a pass-the-parcel game, each of them unwrapping a layer. He might have examined the analogy further but realized that Alison was wearing the face of someone expecting a response. Women often wore that look in his company.

'Sorry. What did you say?' He daren't risk a generalization. The sun had come out again, lighting up her fair hair, naturally fair, pale down on her cheeks.

'I should get back to the shop.'

She wanted nothing more from him, then. Not till next month. 'Yes. I must get on the road.' Obscurely, he was disappointed. As they walked together, he took her arm just above the elbow and felt her bare skin respond. She desired him. She knew he knew. He felt a rising attraction.

They said their goodbyes in the street and talked a bit of business. He reminded her of a soon-to-be-published thriller. She renewed her commitment to order five, a good amount for the small shop. He promised to investigate the matter of the local author who wasn't on the database.

Max walked back to his car in the town car park. A large pigeon sat looking at him from a small maple tree. It was a warm late-July afternoon, very little wind. A nice time for love-making, he thought. Making love without strings in an anonymous room with the sun warming two naked bodies. The girl would be devoted and afterwards she'd let him lie quietly and turn over words in his head.

Instead, here he was driving off to another town, to another bookshop, another manager, this one a man. An interesting man with a passion for waterwheels and W.H. Auden, but all the same . . . Perhaps he'd divert over Salisbury Plain and see if they'd cut the corn yet and built noble straw towers as they had last year.

CHAPTER FOUR

Martha had been called to a man's cell. The story was he'd tried to strangle his cellmate. He hadn't pursued it but the attacked man had made such a racket, swearing and shouting, that the other prisoners on his wing had reacted, not particularly on either man's side but in an agitated way. If things weren't sorted out quickly, so the wing officer had told her, there could be real problems.

She was accompanied by four male colleagues, big men. She'd leave them outside the door because she trusted the alleged would-be strangler not to hurt her. He was called Lee and she'd been working with him closely for eighteen months now. She was his personal officer. He was due out of prison very soon. 'Hi, there, Lee.'

He was sitting on his bed. No sign of his cellmate. No sign of trouble either here or on the wing. The men had gone to work. Either the story had been exaggerated, even invented, or, as was so often the case, it had been quick to rise and quick to fall. A lot of prison life was spent protecting against potential problems.

Lee hadn't answered her or acknowledged her arrival. He was a good-looking lean man in his late thirties, been in and out of prison since he was fourteen. His last sentence had run for thirteen years. It could have been ten but at eight he had seriously assaulted another prisoner, which had got him an extra six of which he'd served three. Numbers get counted in prison.

Martha stayed by the door. He needed his space. 'What happened?'

At last he looked up. She could see him checking whom she'd brought with her. She hoped the burly officers would stay in the corridor. He put a hand to his head. His hair was prematurely grey, cut short, his face heavily seamed and pale like most prisoners', but his eyes were a clear blue. He hadn't used drugs or drunk alcohol since she'd known him. He looked older than his age, but healthy. He'd told her he was preparing for the out.

'Nothing. Nothing happened.' He still talked with a Glaswegian accent, his home town – not that he'd ever had much of a home.

'I'm glad,' said Martha. She'd rolled up the sleeves of her white uniform shirt and now pushed them further up her arms. It was warm in the cell. 'Was the man hurt?'

'That cunt. He'd know it if I put a hand on him.' It was true that, although slim, Lee worked out regularly and his T-shirt was shaped with his muscles. He looked at the floor scornfully, then seemed to decide she deserved more. 'I lost it. That's all.'

Martha could have said that 'losing it' had put him where he was now and kept him there beyond his sell-by date. But she'd been working with him to create a real future and she believed in him. 'You were shouting.'

'Verbals. Just a bit of verbals.' He didn't sound angry, more resigned.

Martha heard noises in the corridor. 'I'll see you later.' She left the room with relief and confronted the officers outside. She walked them a little way down; they'd been prepared for a bit of physical, one or two of them looking forward to it. Their faces were not exactly thuggish but they had controlled any sensitivities.

'No problem,' one suggested.

She agreed. There was no problem for the prison. Business as usual. But what would or should she write on Lee's report? His release date was due any time now. The Parole Board had given him the all clear. With overcrowding the way it was, it could be weeks or even days. A hostel knew he was on the way. He'd jumped through all the necessary hoops: anger management, victim awareness, enhanced thinking. Actually, some of them more than once.

Martha had an urge to turn round and take another look at him. How could you ever fully understand another person? When Lee was twenty-four, he'd killed a man. OK, it was in a fight. Technically, he wasn't a murderer. Man slaughterer, if there was such an expression. Some people said anyone could kill, given the right circumstances.

'Blotted his copybook, has he? Your chosen one?' Bob was one of the friendlier officers. They drank coffee together. Once they'd joined in a charity run. Martha enjoyed running, pushing her body till it trembled and poured with sweat.

'I don't know. It doesn't seem much. And he's not my "chosen one".'

'When's he out?'

'Tomorrow. Next week. Two weeks.'

'Oh, yes?' Meaning: is that such a good idea? Bob was in his fifties, old to be a heavy but he was fit and brave. Kinder, too, than many. He decided to say more. 'Nervous about what he might do?'

Martha didn't answer except to say she had to go. She was suddenly angry at the weight of doubt Lee had to break down before he could start again. The man was in a nervy state, even fearful. Who wouldn't be after half a lifetime in prison?

Over the months they'd worked on so many of his problems, but men didn't like to admit to fear. Not macho men like Lee. It was a strange relationship the personal officer had with her prisoner. She was supposed to find out everything about him, help him enter society on a better footing while giving away nothing about herself – nothing about her attitudes, her family, friends, hobbies. They became on close terms but he knew absolutely nothing about her. Or wasn't supposed to. He knew she was fit because she ran most days. She couldn't help letting things drop sometimes, without meaning to. She believed in security too. Once he was out of prison, she expected never to see him again. That was the rule. A good rule.

All the same, it felt weird. Perhaps because she'd come late to the service she couldn't take it quite for granted. How could there be trust between them when she kept her life secret?

Martha made up her mind: she'd record the incident but she'd downplay it as far as possible. Lee had shouted at his cellmate. What was new?

For the rest of the day this decision made Martha feel vaguely elated, as if she'd stood up for liberty, not to say fraternity and equality. Somewhere Bob's 'chosen one' comment rankled – was that the prison gossip? But mostly she felt elated.

Men, she thought, when she had a moment, are not as strong as women. They operate on a denial basis, which makes them vulnerable to emotional impulses. This made her think of Max who had come to stay with her. She didn't care to work that one out: why he'd come, why she'd let him stay, why Eve hadn't demanded him back. Presumably they both loved him, although even that wasn't certain. Sometimes she knew she didn't believe in love.

Martha was walking down corridors and unlocking doors as she thought this. Some of her colleagues complained about how much time was spent in walking, unlocking, locking, but she liked it. She liked the moments alone, the moving along and, conversely, the people you met, jockeying round the doors, hurrying, deferring, joking – always bad jokes.

Lee was waiting for her, standing in the middle of his cell. He had recovered from whatever had gone on in the morning. When he looked at her like this, defiant but a little humble too, he reminded her of Max, even though he was physically quite different. Perhaps that was what Bob had picked up, her 'chosen one'. For a woman working in a men's prison, it was surprising how little of this sort of thing (what sort of thing? Flirting, sexual games) went on. It did go on, officer or prisoner shipped out to another part of the system, but not much.

Was she attracted to Lee? No, definitely not, except in an entirely appropriate way: she believed he was worth helping. Was he attracted to her? Who's to know? Sometimes she thought so.

'I'm good.' He was answering her calmly.

'You went to work?'

'I went to work.' He was not tall, five inches smaller than Max, but there was something powerful about him. A watchfulness that she had found disconcerting in her first dealings with him. She felt it strongly now.

'Not much to report, then.' She knew he would understand what she was saying but her earlier elation was edged with uneasiness. She needed something from him. Reassurance.

'I'm waiting for my date of release. I hadn't slept. It got to me. He's a cunt. It won't happen again. No harm done. I'm sorted.' He curved his thinnish lips in a not very convincing smile.

There you are. He'd given it to her. Then why did she feel uneasy as she said goodbye? Her shift was ending. It had started early. She'd go home, shake off the job. She was tired. She must remind herself it was only a job.

Max would come back later. He was sleeping in her spare room. Said he needed space. That was what she should be thinking about. And Dan. No one paid enough attention to the boy.

CHAPTER FIVE

Dan leant over the stream and let his fingers drift through the cool water. It was clear but shallow, running over small stones. It must come from further up the hillside. He walked, following its course until it disappeared under a tangle of brambles and nettles. The ground sloped steeply, and as he grew closer, he heard the sound of gushing water; he guessed there was some kind of waterfall – just the place to fill his bottle.

He stood back and looked around him. The sun had darkened, glowing from above the hill behind him on to the face of the hill in front so that it turned amber red. The only sound came from a dark grove of trees some way off where a whirl of birds, black dashes from where he stood, cawed restlessly. It looked as if they were competing to find a place in the trees.

Apart from the birds, the scene was static, peaceful. Evening was coming, followed by night. He didn't allow himself to think of this. The sun was still shining. Besides, he had no idea how dark country darkness was. He literally couldn't imagine it so he got on with the job in hand. He was supported by his constant awareness of being alone. He didn't remember ever being truly alone before.

The answer to collecting water turned out to be simple: remove shoes and socks, roll up trousers and wade slowly up the dim tunnel made by the brambles. As he advanced, the water become colder and fierce thorns snatched at his clothes, parted his hair. He felt as if he was being tested, a game of courage, and soon he was rewarded by bright sunlight spattering through the tunnel's roof, lighting up a tumble of glittering water.

Bent almost double, bony white toe magnified, he held out his bottle. It was not at all like filling it from a tap. The drops danced around the narrow top of the Fanta bottle, refusing to go in.

'Fuck,' said Dan, as his hand and arm were splashed after an attempt to thrust the bottle into a stronger, deeper flow. Blood from scratches he hadn't even noticed mingled with the water and dripped off him in pinkish rills. 'Don't want to be drinking my own blood.'

His voice sounded eerie, childish, too, and whining. He felt claustrophobic, unable to stand, feet colder by the minute, thorns poised to get him if he moved too quickly. The bottle filled eventually and he backed out as patiently as he could. Even so, he felt a thorn nick his ear. He'd have to find an easier way of collecting water. Thinking of this, he didn't think the word 'tomorrow'. Determinedly, he lived every moment in the present.

Outside finally, he stood on the edge of the stream and breathed deeply. The light had changed again, glowing even more richly on one hillside and only just topping the other. Very probably his limousine was already in shade. He rubbed his feet dry with his socks and put on his trainers. Walking quickly, he was surprised by the warmth of his feet as the blood circled around. Summer time, yes, that was what it was. In the city he'd hardly been aware of it, except to be irritable if the buses or tubes were too hot. His classroom, with its large glass windows, was often too hot.

Reaching the limo – it had not been a mirage as he'd half feared – he zipped open his backpack and rummaged around, throwing some things out on to the grass. He needed food; he was starving, ravenously hungry, pleased to be so. Sometimes he didn't want to eat at all, unless you counted Mars bars and Snickers.

There was his jar of Marmite, a packet of digestives. No harm in putting them together. He even had a knife. With excitement, he realized he could use it to cut away the brambles. He hadn't done badly with his packing: Marmite, two packets of biscuits, a lump of cheese, a fruit cake, a bunch of bananas, bacon, sausages – he'd have to think how to cook them. At least he had matches so a fire wasn't out of the question, although he had no frying-pan.

Once Martha had taken him camping. She was part of everything that was wrong now but he'd trusted her then. She'd listened to what he said, not like Eve. Funny they were sisters, so unlike to look at. In every way, actually. At least, he used to think so.

What else was there? No iPod. But he didn't want it now anyway. He was getting used to the sounds of the country. The iPod was part of what he'd left behind. Weird he'd brought no books. Usually he hardly moved without something to read.

Eating, that was the main thing. The boy, Dan, sat in the limousine and ate Marmite, cheese and biscuit sandwiches, accompanied by spring water (as he thought of it) in a champagne glass or 'flute' – the word sprang to mind. Afterwards he ate a large chunk of cake; it was filled with nuts and red cherries and raisins, which, he guessed, were very nutritious. That had been a good choice too. He suspected he was a natural adventurer.

He put the empty glass in its holder and lay back. The car was quite dark now, although outside there was still light spreading down the hill. Dusk, he thought. You don't get dusk in cities. Then he remembered walking along pavements and peering into other people's houses and thinking how cosy they looked, small children in high-chairs eating boiled egg and soldiers, bigger children with homework spread across a table, a woman attentive near them. That was probably at dusk just before she drew the curtains and kept their cosiness for themselves. There was always more than one child in those families.

The dusk was creeping along now, settling into shadowy corners. He'd better get his torch and the other things inside, organize himself for the night. He crouched forward ready to get out of the car.

The moving shape beyond the window, only just visible, scared him so much that he froze, scarcely able to breathe. Fear scorched his gut. Without realizing it, he shut his eyes. He forced them open.

He made out two shapes, not one, about five metres from him, standing quite still, animals, not humans. Tentatively, he began to breathe again. Slowly fear loosed its hold.

One of the animals took a few delicate steps closer. It was a deer. No horns, brownish-coloured. Both deer advanced. He could see their wide, curious eyes, their pretty nostrils. Of course they couldn't see him, behind the glass. They snuffed and snorted a bit, edged nearer. They were curious about the limo, just as he had been.

Dan wanted to pet them, touch their soft noses and sleek coats. He was surprised at himself because he didn't take much interest in animals. When Martha had suggested buying him a dog, or a cat if he preferred, he'd been disapproving. Who wanted some stupid, smelly, time-consuming pet?

But the two out there in the growing darkness were wild animals, part of this alien but real world he'd discovered. They were part of *his* world, choosing to keep him company as he faced the night ahead. They were friends, spirits of the countryside.

All this was silly, Dan knew, but if he wanted to believe that, he would, for the same reason he'd come out here in the first place. Very gently, he eased the door open.

The tiniest creak and his new friends were off, bounding so high that they were silhouetted against what little light was left in the sky. Two blobbish tails, almost phosphorescent in their whiteness, bounded with them.

Dan laughed at the sight. He didn't mind them going: it was their nature to be nervous and he knew they were still out there. He opened the door fully and felt the air cooler and fresher on his face. Already a little damp. Above his head a dark shape crossed slowly. This time he didn't start. When it was a little further away, it hooted, surprisingly loudly. Somewhere on the other side of the valley, perhaps from the tall trees where he'd seen the black birds earlier, another owl replied. He felt the countryside was filled with activity, even at this ending of the day. In the city, he often felt overwhelmed by the number of people around him, all busy, all leading complicated patterns of life that seemed to threaten his own puny attempts. Here, in this place where he understood even less, he felt joyous at their activity.

He shook his head, unable to puzzle out these thoughts. Instead, he gathered up his food supplies. There was no hurry, he told himself. At long last he'd given himself time. There was no hurry, just the black night and the soft seat at the back of the limo, and in the morning, dawn.

His heart beat fast at the thought of all this newness. When he considered Eve for a brief moment, it was to picture her in her exuberance and strength, her vibrant voice, her bouncing, brightly coloured hair, her firmly planted feet. She wouldn't worry about him.

CHAPTER SIX

Martha let herself into her small house with a sense of joy and of foreboding. Ever since Max had arrived, she'd been torn between these emotions. When he was actually there, joy predominated; when she was alone, as she was now – she knew he wouldn't be back for at least a couple of hours – foreboding took over.

People fled from Eve, that was the trouble. Her sense of knowing what was right became too much; it diminished those close to her. Her energy sapped the will of those around her. Max had said he couldn't live in the same house as Eve. What he meant was that he couldn't write his poetry.

That was why he'd come to her, begged her to let him stay. He wasn't looking for a lover, he was looking for a refuge. 'She's your wife,' Martha had pointed out, and she'd seen the weakness and guilt in his face.

He hadn't gone, though, and she had been the weak one. She showed him the spare room, told him he could be her lodger for a short time while he got his act together. She'd been business-like, attempting to hide her feelings for him, which was utterly pointless because they both knew all about them, but had made her feel slightly better, as if she were behaving like a responsible sister-in-law instead of the loveless widow she was.

If she'd truly wanted to talk him out of it, she'd have mentioned his responsibilities to his son. Truthfully, that hadn't even occurred to her. This made her weak and guilty too, perhaps even cruel.

Martha dropped her bag and went up to the bedroom Max was sleeping in. This had become a habit over the two weeks he'd been staying, started because she wanted to check if he'd left in her absence and continued as a kind of sentimental pilgrimage.

They had become lovers, inevitably, as they had once before. He was the sort of man who expected women to say yes and they did. It was not just his astonishing good looks – astonishing her afresh every time she saw him – but his confidence as a man. He had no confidence in anything else, certainly not in his poetry, which might not be any good for all she knew; he had never shown it to her.

But when he came into her bedroom and stood above with a gleaming look of sex about him, it had been – it was – impossible to say no. He was such a good lover too, unselfish and gentle when gentleness was needed. Ridiculously Martha felt herself blushing.

It had to stop. She would tell him so tonight. After their love-making – or sex, as she suspected he thought of it (three times since he'd arrived) – he went back to his room, and for the rest of the time he behaved as if nothing had happened. Men could do that, Martha thought painfully, as she tried to harden her heart: box up things and deny their existence.

Martha walked slowly down the stairs. Tonight she would tell him he must leave, find another house, if need be with another woman who was not his wife's sister.

She opened the door to the kitchen and stopped there. He was making her feel like a whore. She would tell him so.

With a mixture of the adrenalin pumped up for the day's activities and tiredness, Eve began to cook supper. She must get herself in synch, she thought. She wondered briefly where Dan was, then contemplated the following day. It would be easier than today because she and the kids would know more what to expect. There'd be a few drop-outs. She could guess which ones, even if she couldn't remember their names. She must study the lists later.

She turned her attention to the tomato sauce – her speciality: real tomatoes, tomato paste, olive oil, fresh basil, mushrooms, plenty of garlic, salt, pepper, sugar, a dash of wine now that Dan was older.

It was odd for him to be out. Had she forgotten some plan he'd told her about? If Max had been here, she would have asked him. Not that he'd have had a clue.

Eve half sat down at the table and then stood up again. She cried easily, just the way she was made, but she wasn't in the mood for it tonight. She'd concentrate on work, anger, practicalities, chop the basil fine – there were always plenty of practicalities for those with a bit of go. She put her left hand up to her bunched curls and loosened them round her face. She liked the way they bounced on her shoulders.

Max had always been weak. Why else had she been able to snatch him from all those voracious girls at college? They'd all wanted him but she'd got him. They were married a year after they'd graduated, when her vocal cords failed her. His best man had read one of his poems and her father had commented too loudly, 'It's not Shakespeare, I must say.'

Since Max had gone, she'd thought of him as little as possible. His departure had been mentioned only in the most casual way between her and Dan. Dan could think what he liked but they both knew Max would be back; that was the point. Least said, soonest mended. In her heart of hearts, Eve suspected she knew why he went. When he lived at Martha's he could kid himself he was a young man again, no responsibilities, no failures reflected in his wife's eyes.

Martha should have more self-respect. Of course they didn't sleep together – she could never have forgiven that. She had her pride. But sometimes she allowed herself to think it was better Max took a break with Martha than with some of those other girls. Gave the marriage leeway.

Anyway, Martha knew Eve and Max were soul-mates. Mates for life, that was what she'd always told him. She wasn't interested in any other man; she *loved* him. He'd never find anyone who loved him as much as she did.

Now she was thinking about him, it all came in an overwhelming rush. Without being aware of what she was doing, she turned off the gas under the sauce and sat at the table. It wasn't only his extraordinary beauty. That attracted everybody. It was the *need* she felt in him, a yearning he tried to express in his poems. Without her, he became a drifter, dangerously at sea in a predatory world that saw his extreme physical manliness as a reflection of his inner soul while, in fact, it was a contradiction. She'd sometimes thought he'd be happier if an illness reduced him to something in a minor key, more in line with his inner self.

She was his confidence. She believed in him. Every day she told him so. Yet he had left her. And for her sister. 'I need a break.' Those were his words. He'd assured her it was not to do with love. He was tentative because neither of them liked to use the 'love' word very much; it had become debased, they agreed, often meaningless. 'Love' made most sense in poems, he said, although he didn't use it much there either. One thing was sure: he didn't 'love' Martha in any way.

He'd said she gave him too much; she didn't allow him to be himself. But what was his self without her? He'd said his happiest times were in his car, looking at the weather. Well, that was crazy.

Despite all her resolutions, Eve began to cry. She told herself it was not for herself who had been abandoned (however briefly) but for Max, a grown man but still a little boy, alone and staring at the clouds.

After a while Eve went in search of tissues. The tears had given her a headache and her adrenalin had been drowned out of existence.

She hadn't cried so hard when her father had died. He'd been fairly old, of course. Martha and she had sat holding hands in the waiting room of the hospital. They'd been told an operation would give their father a fifty-fifty chance of new life. He'd been unlucky.

The sisters hadn't invited their husbands. She and Martha had always been a close unit since their mother's death when they were children.

Their father had been an Anglican priest who'd taught them about duty and loyalty and that it wasn't a sin to be unhappy. Not that they'd thought themselves unhappy. On the contrary, they'd had carefree childhoods being spoilt by the parishioners in a Sussex village. They were secure children, used to the idea of helping others less fortunate. They were well cared for by their father, healthy, properly educated and almost resentful that people made such a fuss about them being without a mother. Women usually, they eventually decided, who wanted to marry their father.

Martha would never want to hurt her. She had probably convinced herself that she was helping the marriage by having Max to stay. They were as close as sisters could be. Eve pictured Martha in her running gear, slim and taut, sweat rolling down her white skin. Max liked softer, more feminine women. She had to trust Martha because she couldn't do without her, and Max would come back.

Eve decided to run herself a bath. Again she wondered about Dan but, looking at her watch, she saw it was still only seven. The last thing Dan needed was a fussing mother. Independence was what children of his age craved, plus a comfortable home and plenty of food. She could remember what she'd been like at thirteen. Their father had always been careful not to impinge too far on their lives.

The bathroom filled with the odour of lavender oil and scented soap – a present from a grateful pupil. It would be three weeks before she knew how her kids had done in their A levels. Finlay had real star quality and Gina, with all that Italian style and passion, had given her the soap. Eve allowed the faces of last year's pupils to run in front of her closed eyes. They'd bonded. It always happens but she'd grown particularly fond of this lot. They'd promised not to lose touch – a likely story. Eve smiled to herself. A teacher had to learn to let go. Like a parent.

Gradually, the water began to cool, and the room, cleared of steam, seemed harder-edged and less relaxing. Eve realized that she was listening for the key in the door. Although the flat had three bedrooms, it was not very large and she was used to hearing the slight scuffle before the door, a little stiff, was pushed open. They had lived in the flat since Dan had been born, a luxury to have an extra room, or perhaps preparation for the other child who never came.

Neither Max nor Dan called when they came in. She called out to them, welcoming. If it was Max, she kissed him, asked him about his day, made sure his head had come out of the clouds. She knew not to do that with Dan. If she tried, he turned his head away and she got a bony skull.

She supposed if she wasn't there they went to their rooms silently. At least, she couldn't imagine them chatting across the kitchen table. To be honest, she couldn't imagine them without her.

Eve smiled at herself as she towelled her body vigorously.

Max let himself into Martha's house. He put his bag down on the hall floor with great care even though it contained only a few books and papers. He wished she was out or, better, away for a few days. If he'd had more money, he'd have been staying in a hotel. Alone. Much as he liked and respected Martha, he did not want to be with her. It had been the easiest escape route, born out of panic that if he stayed with Eve one more moment she would envelop him as a snake would a mouse. Now he would have to run away again, causing more confusion.

As he stood uncertainly, wondering whether he could sneak upstairs for a momentary break on his bed – he was tired too, quite exhausted – an image of Alison came into his mind. That sunny, golden look of hers as they sat outside sipping their coffee and she confided in him, without self-pity, about her divorce. They had been companionable, he thought, forgetting his fears that she would become more intimate. Both Eve and Martha were too intense to be companionable and they worked too hard to have skin warmed by the sun.

'Oh! I didn't hear you.'

Martha stood in front of him. He found himself staring at her with surprise. She was still wearing her prison officer's uniform – white shirt, dark trousers, heavy shoes and a large key-ring at her waist. There were no keys hanging from it but it reminded him of her role as gaoler, locking men in and letting them out, then locking them in again.

'Sorry.' His gaoler. Yet at the same time he was aroused by the sight. His mistily romantic image of Alison contrasted sharply with Martha's tough appearance, resulting in an erotic charge.

'I'm eating.'

He suspected she knew what he was thinking. He followed her into the kitchen where two places were set.

'I wonder how long you're staying?'

It was obvious she had planned the question, perhaps even staying in her uniform to give herself more authority. No place for the libido here.

'I don't know.' He joined her at the table. 'Do you want me to go?'

'Yes, I do.'

She was blushing, her pale skin suffused with pink all the way down to her neck. The same thing happened when they had sex. 'I see.' There was no need for either of them to say more. If she had decided to turn him out, then he would go quickly, although where was not so obvious.

'Will you go back to Eve?' Martha was still blushing and he felt sad to witness her emotion. He would have preferred to discuss things over the telephone.

'I don't know.' He owed her more. 'I'll think about it tonight. That is, if I can stay till tomorrow?'

'Of course you can.' Her eyes were big but she was trying to hide the appeal in them.

He remembered when her husband had died, a disagreeable, self-satisfied solicitor who took cancer as a personal attack. Eve had told him that Martha had often thought of leaving him but when he became ill, she had given up her job in his office to look after him. After his death, she'd trained as a prison officer, a total change of career. She was a strong-minded woman.

'Anyway, eat something.'

He ate obediently, although not hungrily. He wanted to say something to make her happy, to make the situation happier, but all he could think of were sad love poems from Marvell to Neruda. *I don't love you as if you were the salt-rose, topaz/or arrow of carnations that propagate fire . . .'* Perhaps not sad.

It would have been nice to tell her that he loved both sisters but in fact he loved neither of them at the present moment – and, anyway, even if she'd believed him, it would have made her no happier. He assumed they both knew it was Eve who held them together and that Eve would always be first in his life. He could tell her she was right to send him away so he did, with a little irony to show he suffered too. She answered they were ships in the night and tomorrow morning it would be time for them to part.

He liked the image. He saw the dark vessels each with a single light, finding each other in a turbulent sea and linking up across the waves. He told her she thought like a poet and she smiled. At least, it was nearly a smile.

After a long silence, during which he finished his food and was considering whether he could go to his bedroom, she began to tell him about a prisoner.

'He's our sort of age. Nothing's gone right for him. He's caused so much harm, to others, of course, and to himself.'

At first Max presumed this story related to his own failings, an attempt, perhaps, to put him in his place as a minor sufferer in the context of the big world, more particularly the world in which Martha worked. He listened attentively and soon understood that she was merely sharing a day of trial and indecision. She needed someone to talk to outside prison. She was helping this man. It was her job. But perhaps she was getting things wrong.

'Could he be dangerous?' Max asked, as he tried to reconcile inner turmoil with a passion that affected others. He had never been violent.

'He has been.' Martha seemed reluctant to explain further. She looked up. 'I'm only a prison officer, quite a junior one. How should I know?'

'But you said something about . . .' he hesitated, '. . . risk assessment?' There was no risk assessment in books or poetry. His life felt flaccid compared to Martha's. His infinite capacity for self-deprecation undermined his curiosity.

Martha began to explain the process that preceded a prisoner's departure from gaol but he didn't really listen.

The sisters' strength made him feel tired. He remembered a book of poems he'd bought on his third call of the day, *Lyrics from Elizabethan Song Books* published in 1887. One poem he'd glanced at began, *Arise, my Thoughts, and mount you with the sun* . . . He imagined reading them in bed and had stood before realizing Martha was still talking.

'. . . a leap of faith.' She finished her sentence and frowned up at him. 'You're off.'

He searched for something to say. 'I admire you.' It was true enough.

She dropped her head. She knew he hadn't been listening. 'Goodnight, Max.'

He left then, his hunger for the new poems overwhelming anything further he might have said.

CHAPTER SEVEN

Eve was lying in bed. She felt feverish. Dan still hadn't come home and she knew he'd gone to Martha's. The idea made her so angry that she couldn't think straight. He'd done it before but not when Max was there. How could Martha steal the two people she loved most in the world? Once she'd have called Martha the third.

The double bed was very wide, enough room for her legs to thrash about and her body to turn from one side to the other. Tomorrow she had a long, difficult day. How could they do this to her? If she wasn't on form it would be the children who suffered, kids who already knew too much about pain and adults failing them.

For the last two hours she'd been fighting the urge to ring Martha. But if she rang her, she might easily get Max and she didn't want to speak to him. He'd taken the decision to leave and he must take the decision to return, with no prompting from her. She wasn't so desperate. That was one reason not to ring.

The other was more shameful: she would shout, she would scream, she would lose her rag, and that would give Martha the upper hand. Martha was always controlled. Always had been. Like their father. She, Eve, was like their mother.

Eve threw off the duvet and swung herself around so she was sitting on the edge of the bed. The room was boiling. Martha should have rung her or made Dan ring her. She was his mother. She might have been worried. She *was* worried.

Eve reached for the telephone yet again and stopped yet again. She needed sleep, not a row. It was never a good idea to discuss difficult things in the middle of the night.

She looked at her watch: one a.m. Outside a motorcycle startled her with the immensity of its roar. The traffic seemed aggressively loud, despite the hour. She had to be up by seven a.m. at the latest. It was too late now to risk a sleeping pill.

'Dan!' she cried suddenly, as she thought she heard a sound. But she *knew* he was with Martha. And Max. Let's not forget Max.

'Oh, God. Oh, God.' Bundling herself into the duvet with a mixture of rage, anxiety and despair, Eve tried once more to shut herself down.

A minute or so later, she flung back the bedclothes again and sat upright. She'd ring the police, that would show them. A missing child. Horrible thought. Eve shivered. The police would go round to Martha's neat little house and demand Dan's return. She would be taken to the police station, Max too, accused of kidnapping.

Eve rubbed her aching forehead. What was she thinking of? Martha was her sister. The police would think her quite mad, accusing her own sister.

The only thing to do was to make that call, have that row. If she went on like this any more she would go mad. And then how would she manage those kids?

Dan woke up suddenly. His heart was beating so hard it felt like it would pump itself right out of his skin. Sweat broke out, prickled his scalp. He could feel his eyes were bulging and rolling and staring. It was so utterly dark he could see nothing, just depths of blackness. He'd never seen (or not seen) anything like it before. In his room in London there was always some light coming through the curtains, whatever the time.

He put up his hand and felt his face, almost for comfort as if it belonged to another person. His heartbeat slowed. He knew where he was and he knew he'd been dreaming and that the dream had woken him. It was the dream – nightmare actually, with the same voice – he'd been having for a year. He'd hoped it wouldn't follow him out to the countryside.

He shifted his position on the seat a little and breathed in the cool, only slightly musty air. He was quite comfortable, his head on the backpack, his jacket and sweater piled over him. He reached for his watch still face down on the floor somewhere. The luminous dial, glaringly bright, told him it was just after two – several hours till dawn.

Now that the drumming of his heart and the clamour of his dream had settled down, he was amazed by the silence. The noise in his London bedroom never stopped. It was quietest at three o'clock in the morning but, even then, he'd hear a taxi or a lorry or a police siren, sometimes shouts from the pavement below. By five it was revving up, and at full throttle when he got up.

Dan relaxed back and decided he liked the darkness and silence. There was nothing out there to threaten, only animals like the two deer, as keen not to be seen as he was. He supposed that by now Eve might have noticed he was not around. He knew her thinking processes so well it almost made him smile: she would assume he had gone to Martha's, and because they weren't on speaking terms, she wouldn't want to ring. Typical! And quite funny. Brilliant, on his part.

Maybe he'd stay awake now to watch dawn come up. That should be a sight, rising over the hill behind the stream. He tried to remember what time it happened; as he was further west it would be a bit earlier then at home. Before six anyway. A long time. Perhaps he'd shut his eyes and let himself drift off. On the other hand he didn't want the dream to come back.

He should have brought a torch but he hadn't known about country darkness. He felt a flare of excitement in the pit of his stomach as he remembered he'd run away. He was independent, the maker of all choices. Impatiently, he wanted the day to start immediately.

This limo was a bit of luck. He wouldn't have wanted to sleep on the grass, it had been soaking wet with dew by the time he'd gone to bed. The old barn might have done but it smelt of dung and was probably overrun with rats. That didn't appeal. He'd read *Nineteen Eighty-Four* and it had scared the life out of him. The rats bit.

He shifted about. Not quite so comfortable but not fearful, still with that fizz of excitement. He allowed his hand to travel where it wanted, down inside his trousers. He'd loosened the waistband so it was easy enough. His fingers were cool like little silver fishes stroking the warm skin. He'd never quite gone the whole way, inexpert as at most things. But the feeling was good: the stiffening gave him a sense of powerfulness.

He lay back, fingers moving, waited to see how far he could go.

CHAPTER EIGHT

When Max arrived in Martha's bed, his beautiful heavy body naked and desirous, she determined to push him away. The whole idea was impossible, absurd, obscene. They had agreed to part only a few hours earlier. But his very weightiness defeated her. She felt unlike her usual self, small, weak, helpless. The night supported his determined maleness and reduced her to subservience. 'No,' she whispered, as if such a softly spoken and insignificant word could reach him.

Then the telephone rang. He didn't hear that either. He was crouching above her. The bleak image of Nebuchadnezzar turned him old and ugly.

She pushed him off with all her strength so that he toppled on to the floor. It was ridiculous, ridiculous, she thought despairingly, as she searched for the telephone. At last she had it in her fingers. It could only be Eve.

Below the bed, Max must be crawling. She could hear the rumbling noises on the wooden floor but he hadn't risen. Perhaps he'd sleep there, catch a cold, die. She felt vicious, against Max, on her sister's side. Why had he come between them?

'Hello.' There was only silence. 'Eve? Is it you? Evie?'

The silence turned into choking sobs. Words intervened, although she could hardly understand them.

'I'm sorry, Eve. So sorry. I told him he must go.' But she would hate that. Max should make his own decision.

'Fuck you, Martha.' The first words she could properly understand. She found herself surprised that she should care quite so much. She'd never heard such venom in her sister's voice, or such misery in the sobs. Max was Max, after all, and she would never

38

imagine they were sleeping together – *not* sleeping together tonight. Never sleeping together again.

The bedroom door opened and Max's naked body, now upright, was silhouetted against the landing light as he left. His lack of curiosity was just a form of self-protection. Like her, he would have known it was Eve on the phone, on the warpath.

'He doesn't want me.' She tried again. 'It's just a quiet space for him.'

'Fuck Max.' More sobs and sort of muted shrieks, which, in the turmoil of the moment, reminded Martha of when they were both girls and Eve wanted to shriek but didn't want to disturb their father. Nostalgia glowed and saddened.

'He's coming to you tomorrow.' Of course, she didn't know if that was true. Max could go anywhere but the odds were on him returning home.

The sobbing and shrieking increased. Martha could imagine Eve's poor red face and puffy eyes. How often she had consoled and comforted her! How had they reached this point? How had she let it happen? What a horror. A horror.

'Oh, Eve. Please. Please. I'll come to you.'

More unintelligible words and then some she could hear. 'It's not Max I want, it's Dan. I want Dan!' Now the shriek had risen to a wail, a lament.

Martha sat back in the bed and pulled the duvet over her. 'What do you mean?'

'Dan! Dan! Dan!' Eve pronounced the name over and over as if Martha wouldn't understand who she was talking about.

'I don't understand.'

'You can have Max for all I care but Dan's my son. Just because you haven't got one, you want mine. Always trying to make him turn to you, giving him special care and understanding, taking him off on adventure holidays, buying him presents . . .'

This was an old rant. Martha felt confused. 'Are you suggesting Dan's here? With me?'

'I'm not bloody suggesting! I know where he goes for TLC, his perfect, perfectly controlled aunt who never makes a fuss . . .'

'Evie, he's not here.'

It took Eve a few moments to halt her juggernaut of rage and reproach.

Martha heard rumblings and splutterings and she added, 'I haven't seen him for ages.' She didn't say 'since Max came' although that was true.

'But he isn't here. Where else could he be?' Eve's voice was faint.

'With a friend?'

'He never stays with friends. He always goes to you.' There was the echo of the reproach but now with a different meaning: was Martha trying to prove her wrong about her son?

'Perhaps there's some school thing.'

'I work at his school.' Eve's voice had risen again. 'I know what goes on there. *I*'m the only thing going on there. And, as a matter of fact, I offered him a place on the drama course I'm running but he declined.'

Martha decided this wasn't the time to investigate why Dan might not want to join a course run by his mother for children at risk. Clearly they needed to stay calm and find Dan. 'I'll go down and see if he hasn't turned up on my doorstep,' she said. He'd done that a few months ago. She'd found him huddled in the doorway. She kept giving him a key but he kept losing it.

'You do that.' Martha thought Eve was eager for someone else to take responsibility.

She rang off and went downstairs. There was no sign of Max. She supposed she should knock on his bedroom door and say that his son hadn't come home. Possibly that was the normal thing to do. But things didn't seem normal at the moment. Besides, she and Eve managed most problems arising over Dan without his father's help. Also, Dan would be back. Of course he would. With relief, she decided not to disturb Max.

She stood at the front door and peered out. This was a quiet time of the night. She lived on a busy road not far from the prison. Now only the occasional night bus passed, the odd lorry or car. A bus was coming now, its eyes wide and glowing. Since Dan had not been on the doorstep – she imagined him there, leaning against his tatty old backpack – she pictured him on the bus, ready to get off as it stopped a few metres down the road. She took a step or two towards it but no one appeared.

She called softly, 'Dan! Dan, are you there?' A bird trilled briefly from above her head. She remembered hearing that day birds were tricked by the brightness of streetlamps into singing at unnatural times.

She shivered. The air was cooler and damp and she was naked under the coat she'd grabbed in the hallway. A car went by and then a minicab, the drivers, probably on night shifts, going to work, coming back from work. She did that sometimes. A prison never closes.

It was stupid to stand there hoping Dan would appear, out of a bus, a car, just walking along, his face pale in the light of her door. He had always been an anxious child.

Not that she was seriously worried. Definitely not. Eve never had a clue what was going on in Dan's life. Which didn't mean she didn't love him or that she didn't boss and control him. She made too much noise to hear him.

Where was he? It was perfectly possible Eve had overlooked him in the flat somewhere. Martha turned briskly and went into the house. Still no sound from Max. He must be asleep. She thought of him driving those long hours out of London, through countryside, villages and towns. Every day on the move.

She picked up the telephone in the living room. Eve began talking as she picked up the phone. 'You've been so long. Where did you go? You said the doorstep but you could have got to Piccadilly Circus and back. Have you found him?'

'I'm afraid not,' said Martha. She wondered if Eve was truly upset or whether it was still about the reproach. She suspected the latter. Eve was good at allowing the reproach to obfuscate the matter in hand. Perhaps she had too much emotional energy. It made her brilliant at her job, Martha knew, where she was the one and only utterly top dog. Martha pulled herself back. This was childish thinking, going the same way as Eve. 'Are you sure he hasn't bedded down in some corner of your flat?'

The answer was a squeal of rage. 'Do you think I'm crazy? I've searched everywhere, including under the beds. This isn't an object I've lost, Martha, it's my son!'

Putting me in my place, thought Martha, but at the same time she got up to peer into an alcove off her living room. Then she realized it was absurd and sat down again. 'He must have some friends. He has to be with a friend.'

'You know he has friends. He just doesn't like staying with them. He's a very private boy, in case you hadn't noticed.'

'Maybe he's changed. It *is* the holidays. Are you sure he hasn't left a message?'

'I'm not blind.'

But by the tone of her sister's voice, Martha knew she hadn't looked for a written message and she felt a sudden light-heartedness.

'I'll look,' said Eve, grudgingly.

While she was gone, Martha made a cup of tea and noted that it was still dark outside. Yet dawn couldn't be far away. The traffic was increasing. Soon she wouldn't notice as it became a continual roar.

The telephone rang.

'There's nothing. Nothing.' Eve's voice had changed as if the act of searching and finding nothing had turned anxiety and annoyance into real fear. Martha immediately felt protective. She was the elder sister, always had been.

'Who is the friend he's closest to?'

'But we can't ring in the middle of the night!'

'It'll be morning soon. We need to know where he is.' Eve would respond to her tone, calm, sensible.

'Yes. Yes. I'll try and find some numbers.' She paused. 'Do you think I can call now? He doesn't have any really close friends.'

Martha thought for a moment and while she thought, her eyes raised to the room. She saw her mobile on the side table where she'd left it the night before. She gasped, had to take a little breath of hope before speaking. 'Eve, we've forgotten his mobile! Have you rung his mobile?'

'His mobile!'

Martha could hear her wonder. Here was the simplest form of connection. How could they have forgotten? Why else were children given mobiles? 'The kids in my class drive me crazy with their mobiles,' Eve said.

Both sisters were filled with the same delight. They would have hugged each other if they'd been in the same room. They loved each other.

'You ring,' said Martha, knowing her place. She did not admit she knew the number by heart when Eve said she'd go and find it.

There was no answer, of course. Neither of them was too upset. It was not yet five o'clock. He would have switched it off.

'Anyway, you've left a message for when he wakes up.' Martha had heard the message, a mixture of all the emotions felt by an anxious mother plus a few special to Eve: self-dramatization, 'You know how hard I find it at the start of a new course'; irrelevant detail, 'I was planning to cook you an especially nice supper'; side-swipes, 'You're not a child any more, even if this behaviour makes you seem like one.' There was loving stuff too – of course Eve loved him – and a message so long that eventually the answer-machine cut her off. That was always a problem. No sense of when to stop.

Afterwards, however, she became calm and organized, as if the problem of Dan's absence had been solved, at least by her, at least for the time being.

'I must get a couple of hours' rest, even if I can't sleep.'

Martha understood she was planning to go to work. It was typical. Possibly admirable. 'My shift doesn't begin until one tomorrow. I could ring again if he hasn't responded.'

'Oh, Martha darling, would you?'

But the move to Martha's role introduced Max into the arena. Martha could hear it in Eve's silence. 'I'll tell Max,' she said, 'before he leaves.'

'Yes.' The single word of agreement made it clear that Eve was not to be deflected from her present purpose, which was to continue her life.

There seemed nothing more to be said. They were both exhausted.

After Martha had put down the receiver she realized it was Dan's fourteenth birthday in a few days' time. Neither of them had mentioned that.

CHAPTER NINE

The sun pierced through the windscreen of the limo in a thin beam and focused on Dan's nose. Aware of something disturbing, he twitched a little. As the beam dropped to his chin, a couple of flies came to join it, whirring about his face and, now and again, like naughty, teasing children, touched down, then buzzed off again. He guessed the scratches from the brambles had attracted them.

After his long period of wakefulness in the night Dan had plummeted into a deep and dreamless deep.

He opened his eyes to the feeling of readiness, slightly nervous as he saw where he was but fully alive to possibilities. He batted the flies away, stretched, yawned, tried to guess how long he'd slept and what time it was without looking at his watch. He thought it could probably be worked out from the angle of the sunbeam but he needed a pee too badly to spend time on sums.

He leant forward to put on his trainers. Outside he could hear birds. Slowly, he pushed the door open; it creaked loudly. The freshness outside told him about the smelly fug inside. He got out and two big black birds shot away over his head. A flurry of smaller birds fussed about near the hedge.

He watched them as he peed. Their tails were long in proportion to their bodies and wagged about energetically. Little fusspots, he thought, enjoying the word.

The sun was warm on his face, well over the opposite hillside, moving round already from east to south. All these bits of information pleased him, set in his locality, in tune with the birds and the sun.

He looked further and saw, very high in the sky, two dark specks. They had to be birds, although they were unmoving in a way he found disconcerting, almost threatening, as if they were watching, spy planes looking out for enemies.

He turned away, eyes watering from screwing them up against the sun and suddenly desperately hungry.

It was hard not to think of Eve as he pulled the food out of his backpack. She'd have gone to work by now, all done up for the day, bright makeup, rings on her fingers, bells on her toes. At some point she would find out he'd really gone, not just to Martha. Perhaps this evening. He had a day, then. Off duty. A day just for himself.

He'd start with a couple of bananas. He'd jammed them back into his bag so they were rather squashed but eatable all the same. Sportsmen ate bananas. He'd never be that. Not that he'd had much of an opportunity to try. Every now and then Eve jollied him to some weirdo club or to judo or *t'ai chi* or wrestling, or something for losers who couldn't make out in regular sports.

That was how he'd got to know Rufus, Ru. He'd known him by sight from school – he was in the year below, small and plump, not obese or anything like that, just a bit soft-looking. Dan could just about bear to think of Rufus in the morning. They'd been made wrestling partners, two oddballs: he'd been skinny and a head taller. Ru had been mixed race, which was nothing unusual in their school, although you didn't get many of his particular mix – Chinese with West Indian. Chinese mum. Once Dan had asked him where his weird name came from and the answer was 'A book'. His mum read all the time. She was proud, too, she could do her *r*s.

Anyway, they pretended to wrestle, promised never to hurt each other and became friends – just for that time in the week, not at school. They told each other things. Ideas. Stories. Ru liked writing best and he liked reading. Sometimes they made up a story, each taking turns with a sentence.

Dan finished the bananas and threw the skins towards the hedge. It was fun throwing them but he didn't like the look of them splayed out on the fresh green grass. The little gossiping birds had risen in irritation and swirled off to a point further down the hedge.

After retrieving the banana skins, he straightened up and took a long breath, sucking in deep the sweet summer air. Over the hedge and some way distant, the cows that had frightened him moved slowly across the field. Bursting with energy, he grabbed the Fanta bottle from where he'd chucked it the night before and set off for the spring. Just in time, he remembered the knife. He didn't want to add to his collection of stinging scratches. Pity he hadn't thought of bringing some Savlon.

But what a day! He couldn't remember ever having felt so full of life. It was as if the whole beautiful countryside, sky, hills, hedges, trees, was laid out especially for him. As if he owned it. In front of the furthest skyline, there were smaller hills – 'Tumuli,' he said to himself, remembering a book he'd read recently – or maybe a burial ground of Viking ships. They were like big waves in a green sea of grass. The idea made him think – annoyingly – of Max. This must be the sort of thing poets, even so-called would-be poets, imagined.

He began to run, enjoying the pounding of his heart, the blood rushing to his face. I'm alive! he exulted, and forgot for a while to be guilty.

The knife was pretty useless at cutting the brambles, but he persevered. In the end he'd made a hole so that he could lean over quite easily and fill his bottle. Later, when the air was warmer, he'd have a wash, although it worried him a little, using the same water for drinking and washing. Go downstream for the washing, he supposed. He felt pleased with this piece of good sense. After he'd had some more to eat and tidied things up a little, he'd explore further afield, see what lay beyond him over the skyline or perhaps set off in the other direction, although that seemed less wild, more cultivated, more likely to contain people.

Supported by his brimming good humour, he allowed himself to think about Eve. He was still confident his absence would be causing her no anxiety – it just wasn't her style – but what if it were? Would he care? When he thought of the anguish he'd hidden from her, protected her from, a tiny bit on her side wouldn't be so unfair. But he didn't want to hurt her deliberately. At least, maybe a fraction of him did. Really, he just needed a day's peace. Not something she could ever understand.

Enough! Dan swigged the cold, clear water and the good times were back. Then, one more hesitation. His mobile. He could leave a message on hers. She was always leaving messages on his, about the only person who did. She told him where she was, how she was, what she'd cooked, when she'd be home. All about *her*. He'd call her later. He might even go back later. You never knew. He could do what he liked, with no one watching him, that was the thing. What was it Ru had said? 'They tell you they love you but how can they when they don't know who you are?' Something like that. At the time Dan hadn't taken it seriously.

He didn't want to be thinking like this. Especially not about Ru.

He raced himself back to the limousine, filled his pockets with biscuits, deliberately left his watch beside the glasses. He was hot, sweat prickling on his nose. He thought of lying in the cold stream but that would keep. He folded his jacket on to the seat, tidied the rest of the food into the backpack and was about to leave when, on impulse, he pulled out his mobile. It was turned off. He considered a moment, then put it back in the front pocket and zipped it up.

He looked up. That pair of birds was back, not the two that pecked around on the grass but the spy planes so high up you could hardly see them. They were a bit lower now and circling slowly, then hanging still. In the silence, he thought he could hear a faint mewing sound, but it could have come from anywhere. He didn't know why they unnerved him. Birds of prey – that was probably what they were, looking out for a baby rabbit or some other, even smaller, animal. Nothing to worry him.

Firmly turning his back on them, he started up the field behind him.

CHAPTER TEN

Martha had lost count of how many times she'd rung Dan's mobile. There wasn't even a recording of his voice. Just an automated lady. Perhaps it wasn't his number. But she knew it was. She looked at her watch – she'd done that a million times too. The sleepless night had affected her in ways she knew well. When Adrian had been dying, she'd spent weeks without grabbing more than a few hours. Adrenalin had kicked in giving her an operational energy admired by those who saw her. But she'd known that underneath her brain was scattering, her thoughts losing logic and control. Now after only one sleepless night, she felt almost the same.

Should she ring the police? That was one question. But she couldn't do that without telling Eve. So, should she get Eve out of her school? Of course Martha had left messages, which presumably Eve would pick up at lunchtime. Which led to another question: should she call the prison and say she couldn't get in today? What reason would she give? They were short-staffed already and her absence would mean some prisoners were locked down.

Then there was Max. She replayed in her head their morning conversation. He had come down to the kitchen at seven o'clock, looking refreshed and ready to go. (Go where was another matter.) She was on her third cup of coffee, unwashed, undressed, unmade-up. Not that he had looked at her as he efficiently made himself coffee and toast.

She'd had to open the conversation.

'Eve rang in the middle of the night. She was worried. Dan hadn't come home.'

He'd taken his knife out of the marmalade jar. He'd seemed bewildered. 'What do you mean?'

'We rang his mobile but of course it was turned off. We left a message.'

'We,' Max had repeated, spreading the marmalade.

'Eve made the call.' Martha thought she knew Max's complicated feelings about her and her sister. 'This is about Dan.'

'Yes.' He'd begun to eat quickly as if he was in a hurry to be off. 'You've left a message for him. So he'll ring back.'

'Eve says he never stays away.'

'Eve likes him under her thumb even when she's not there.'

Years ago Martha had decided that the reason Max made so little effort with Dan was nothing to do with his continual travelling but because he didn't want to be in competition with Eve.

'What else is Eve planning to do?'

'She's going to work.' Martha had realized this was a mistake because Max had visibly relaxed. She'd added quickly, 'I'm on a lunchtime shift so I said I'd help.' But it was too late. She understood Max's thinking. He would take his lead from Eve: if she was unworried enough to go to work, then he would do the same.

He'd left soon afterwards, thanking her politely for having him to stay – as if those visits to her bedroom had never happened. At the door, he turned. 'Keep me in touch about Dan.'

A braver woman would have slammed the door in his face. She said nothing. She was the responsible sister-in-law, the older sister, the aunt. She was also a prison officer. She knew about people going missing. She knew about the police. As a personal officer over the last four years, she knew how easy it was for a man to disappear in London if he wanted to. Sometimes Probation and the police lost an ex-offender for days. But, of course, that would be an adult, off on a drinking spree or a drug binge. They would turn up eventually, picked up after a fight or a burglary. At the very least they would have breached the conditions of their parole and duly arrive back in prison.

But Dan was a child. Not a young child. Old enough to get himself around. Not the usual age or sex for a kidnap victim. Now she was thinking seriously, as if he really were missing, and she was frightened enough to want to cry, 'No! No!' But that wouldn't do. The best thing was to calm herself down, take a shower, dress, then consider the options. A senior prison officer had advised her when she joined the service, 'If in doubt, take action,' but she'd often found the opposite true: 'If in doubt, do nothing.'

On her way upstairs, she passed her laptop, shut since the day before. Despite her earlier resolutions, the urge was irresistible. Still standing, she switched it on, found Google and typed in 'missing children'.

A flood of information massed on the screen. 'One hundred thousand children go missing each year'; 'One in nine children runs away overnight'; 'One in eight begged or stole to feed themselves'; 'One in twelve was hurt while they were away.' These pieces of more precise information came from a report compiled by the children's charity called Still Running.

Feverishly now, irritated by the slowness of her computer, she brought up the charity, which seemed to deal with a multitude of problems, and eventually found the report. It was far too long to read or even scroll through in her present state. Now she was only just stopping herself dialling 999. 'One in six children slept rough.' What did that mean in London? A sleeping-bag under the arches at King's Cross or Waterloo? An open invitation to predators? Had he taken a sleeping-bag? What had he taken, come to that? If he had taken things, it meant he hadn't been snatched.

Abruptly abandoning the computer, Martha hurried upstairs. In the bathroom she stared at her pale, shocked face in the mirror and reminded herself that she was the steady one, Eve the bundle of emotions. That had been established for ever when their mother had died.

At this very moment Dan could be at home, making himself the huge bowl of cereal teenagers seemed to live on. At the same time she realized that, although she'd rung his mobile constantly, she'd never tried the landline in the flat. Eve had been gone for a couple of hours now. They'd talked before she'd left, and she'd already rung a couple of Dan's friends but one was away on holiday and the other seemed surprised that she would think he'd know anything about Dan's whereabouts. Neither could he suggest anyone else likely to help.

Martha hesitated on the stairs. The picture in her mind of Dan eating hungrily was vivid and she went back into the living room and made the call. When Eve's throaty actor's message came on the line, she was more angry than anything.

Giving up the idea of a shower, she dressed hurriedly and made two more calls, to Dan's mobile, where the recorded voice had begun to seem dismal and far away, and to Eve's. 'We need to speak urgently,' she said, the anger returning. *What was Eve doing at work?*

Then she rang her supervisor and, to her own surprise, found she was explaining the situation in some detail. Clearly she needed to talk to someone she trusted. 'I need advice, Gerry. I know I'm only his aunt but I've always been involved in his life and I love him dearly.'

'Make all the calls or get his mother to make them.' He sounded serious. 'Police, Missing Persons, ChildLine. You can get the numbers off the Internet.' Martha hadn't told him about the scary encounter she'd already had with her computer. 'I know it's the holidays but get any school friends on the job too. They may know things the family don't. No one's going to be too worried yet. He's not a girl or a cute little boy. He doesn't drink or use, as far as you know. He's a street-wise Londoner, not one of those boys who come from somewhere else and haven't a clue what's what. He'll almost certainly walk back in, Martha, but none of this is a bad idea. Boys that age get themselves in a twist. I know.'

Martha remembered that Gerry had three or four children, one, she thought with problems. 'I don't really know much about boys,' she said humbly. 'Not having any, never working with children, being one of two sisters, going to an all-girls grammar school.'

'You're telling me!' interrupted Gerry.

Martha could hear the smile in his voice and allowed herself to relax a fraction. 'He seemed all right to me. Quiet. Contained.' She paused. So far she hadn't allowed herself to think of the reasons Dan might have run away (if that was what he'd done). Presumably the police or another service might ask.

'So, let me know how you get on.' Gerry's tone was designed to be comforting, similar to the voice he used when she was having difficulty with a prisoner. That reminded her of her job.

'Keep an eye on Lee,' she said. 'He was a bit on edge yesterday.'

'I saw it in your report. "Leaving troubles", you called it.'

'Yes.' Martha added nothing more. A personal officer was duty bound to record anything noteworthy about her charge but the emphasis was up to her. Yesterday she'd been exhilarated at her decision not to cause Lee further aggro; today it seemed unimportant.

They said goodbye, and as soon as Martha put down the phone, it rang. She picked it up, cheeks flushing. 'Hello?'

It was Eve.

'There's no need to leave me three messages. You knew I'd ring you as soon as I could.' Eve felt harassed, put upon, getting older. The first set of kids had been great, really motivated, made strides from the day before. But they'd been demanding, each one wanting all of her attention all of the time. She'd seriously wondered if she needed a helper. Then one of the brightest girls, Shamana, had insisted on talking to her right through the break between the two classes. She'd been entered for a TV talent show and wanted tips. It was impossible not to be excited and give her some time. Then it was straight on to the next lot, who'd shrunk into a smaller, biddable group since the day before.

'Sorry,' said Martha.

Eve knew that tone of voice. Nothing was ever hidden between sisters. Of course she was incredibly worried about Dan (and annoyed): he'd been in the back of her mind all morning, even though she'd assumed the messages would say he was back. 'What now?' she said. She looked round the small, grey room she was sitting in on a plastic chair: not a picture, not a speck of colour; in need of a thorough clean. Usually inhabited by the night security guard, it was the only place other than the studio that the school authorities had allowed her to use. There wasn't even an outside window. It was hard to be so unappreciated. Eve felt like bursting into tears.

'I think we should report him missing,' said Martha.

Under her sister's competent manner, Eve could sense the trembling that unnerved her. Martha had to stay strong. 'Do you think so?'

'Yes. Why don't you call the police and I'll do the rest?'

'The rest?' asked Eve. She looked at her watch. She could feel what energy she had draining away. She was hungry but she couldn't think of eating. Dan wasn't the sort of boy to get into trouble. The kids she was working with today, repeat truants, drug users, thieves, violent some of them – at least when it was dark and they were in the majority – were the kids who didn't come home. You couldn't blame them, with homes like theirs.

'Missing Persons Helpline, that sort of thing.'

'That sort of thing,' Eve repeated, as if she couldn't understand the words. She thought this was the most horrible conversation a mother could have and felt deeply sorry for herself. She tried so hard – with Max, her work, with Dan. 'Do you think we should be really worried, Martha?' Martha would know that appeal, over the years: big sis, tell me it'll be all right.

'I don't know,' answered Martha, wearily, warily. 'But I think it's right to take action now.'

'Yes,' agreed Eve, obediently. She supposed that doing the right thing was some comfort. 'Will you come round this evening?' The invitation was heartfelt. It overrode whatever was going on with Max. Martha had said he'd left.

'I'll be in touch.' Martha cut the line.

Eve knew Martha could never let her down. With nervous dread, she realized she'd promised to call the police. Last time she'd had any contact was when a boy threatened her with a knife. He was one of her pupils but it happened in the street, not even very near to the school, so she'd gone to the police station.

On the whole it had been a pleasurable experience. She'd been a victim – or, at least, a near victim. She'd been upset and the policewoman behind the desk sympathetic – the uniform had done her curves no services. After she had taken the boy's name, it was clear that not much else would happen. Eve hadn't minded. She'd told the school too and the boy would be watched.

She and Martha had been brought up to despise physical fear. Their father had briefly been an army chaplain and had learnt to admire his men's courage. She'd felt nicely heroic as she'd smiled goodbye to the policewoman.

But now she'd be contacting them with failure. 'I've mislaid my son.' Only bad mothers mislay their sons. The police, she imagined, would be brisk, perhaps even critical. She might begin to cry. But she didn't want to cry; she wanted Dan to be back. She didn't even want to admit he was gone. Probably she should be at home now, checking if he'd taken anything with him.

CHAPTER ELEVEN

Dan had walked a long way. He'd set off in the opposite direction from the stream, up behind the limo. He'd crossed several grassy fields, then a couple with stubble where a crop had been recently cut – there were still some big rolls of straw left.

He jumped on to one and surveyed his kingdom. The sun was high; the sky blue. He celebrated his freedom with a whoop or two, then encouraged the bale to roll down the slanting ground. He tried to ride it, like a cowboy on a charging bronco but it picked up speed and threw him off.

The ground was hard but he lay there as comfortably as if he'd been on a feather mattress – not that he'd ever seen, let alone lain on, a feather mattress. He laughed at himself and, after a bit, sat up and swigged from his bottle of spring water.

Somewhere the stillness was broken by a banging sound, irregular and fairly close. After only twenty-four hours away from London, he'd got used to the idea of being the only human around and felt offended that someone else should be in his world. All the same, he was curious so he set off in the direction of the noise.

It was further than he'd guessed. The land became rough, nettles and thistles among the grass, some prickly bushes with the remains of yellow flowers he didn't know the name of. Instead of hedges there were walls, big stones piled haphazardly one on top of another, sometimes covered with all kinds of growths, bright yellow, silver green, garlanded with weeds and ivy.

In one case the ivy was so thick it had pulled down half the wall and sprouted triumphantly with layers of greenish flowers on top. He stopped to look, attracted by something odd, a quivering aliveness. Trying to avoid the nettles at his feet, he stepped closer and saw that the ivy flowers were topped with a mass of butterflies:

bright red and orange and black, spotted and striped, several different kinds. He began to count them but stopped for the pleasure of watching as they fluttered from flower to flower.

It was like a natural art installation, he thought to himself, remembering a trip to Tate Modern. Red Admiral, that was certainly one. Although so beautiful, they were very busy and he'd always identified beauty with stillness. There was that poem they'd studied at school, about a Grecian urn. Their English teacher had a thing about old poetry. Most of the kids had messed about in his classes but Dan had liked it: *Thou foster-child of Silence and slow Time.* But these butterflies never stopped, moving from one flower to another. He supposed they were sucking the honey, like bees. It was a great sight, that was the point. It gave him a funny warm feeling in his stomach.

After a while he heard the banging again, quite a bit nearer. He walked across the uneven turf towards the sound. He was hot, the sun beating hard on his head and making everything wavery, the lines of field and sky and walls. He climbed over a padlocked gate, foolishly, his legs too weak and undirected. As he landed on the hard-baked earth, he saw the man: he was lifting a stone above his head.

For a dizzy moment, Dan thought the man was going to throw it at him. He flinched, even ducked but, as his eyes focused better, he saw him lay the stone gently on top of a wall. He was building it. He was also, although tall, with long legs and wide shoulders, old. His face was turned away, intent on his work, but Dan could tell by his belly, the stoop of his back and his thick white hair.

The man stood back, surveyed the wall, stretched, found a handkerchief and wiped his face. He was hot too.

It was strange to be staring at a man so intently. In London he'd never behave like that: you never knew what stunt they'd pull. But this man seemed unthreatening, not just because of his age – he was strong enough to heave rocks about – but because he seemed part of the stillness of the countryside. The air was so warm and quiet that Dan felt dopily only half awake, a bit like being in a dream, a good dream for once.

The old man turned, saw him. He waved. He seemed pleased at the sight of someone else. Dan walked towards him. His steps seemed to float above the rough ground; he felt happy.

The man smiled. 'A hot day.' He drawled his vowels. Dan liked the sound.

'Very hot. Hot to be building a wall.'

'Ah.' The man looked at his wall again. Dan understood that he talked and thought and moved more slowly than people he knew in London. 'Time for my dinner,' he said eventually. He went towards a canvas bag leaning against a part of the wall that was finished.

Dan watched as he took out a Thermos, a rough-looking cheese sandwich and an apple, bright red and not very big. Not the sort you bought in shops. He sat on a stone and leant against a wall.

'You can lean against that bit?'

The old man munched on his sandwich, making Dan feel even hungrier. 'These old walls fall down as soon as you look at them. In the rain most times.'

'It's lucky it's dry, then.'

'Ah.'

Dan saw he was having trouble with his false teeth and the bread and wondered if he usually took them out to eat.

'Dry-stone walls, aren't they?' He laughed and tried to swallow a bit of cheese. His eyes were very blue. He looked at Dan kindly. 'They didn't give you a packed dinner at the farm, then?'

Dan realized the old man thought he knew where he'd come from. 'I left too early. Didn't know I'd be gone so long.' He was talking at the old man's speed.

'Here.' He held out the other half of the sandwich. 'Boys your age are always famished.'

Dan took it and ate greedily. The man nodded, pleased. 'I've not the appetite I used. Not since my Gwen passed on.'

Passed on? Died. Dan felt embarrassed. He looked away and mumbled, 'Sorry.'

The old man didn't seem to notice. 'You have a name do you, young man?' he asked.

'Dan.'

'And I'm Silas Chaffey. Si to you.' He paused. 'They take too many young folk at the farm. Not enough to do, now harvesting's done. So early this year. With all the sun. Never known it so early.' He paused and eyed Dan assessingly. 'You're on the Maize Maze, I shouldn't wonder.'

'Yeah,' replied Dan, having no idea what Si was talking about. He walked away a bit and took a last gulp of his water. It struck him he shouldn't have given his real name, not if he wanted to stay secret, but the old man seemed so alone, that was the thing, as if he lived on this hill and never talked to anyone. 'Do you often build walls?' he asked.

Si paused in slicing his apple. 'Always been good with stone.' He took a bite and chewed slowly. 'Did the walls for the farmer when I worked there. Did all sorts for him. I used to be a big strong lad.'

Dan guessed he was thinking, Not like you, skinny and pale.

'So when I retired, he told me, "You keep an eye on the walls, Si, put them up when they fall down and I'll see you right." Of course, it's his son now, mean young bugger, but he gives me something when he remembers. He's let the land go. Shocking. Gwen said she didn't like to walk up here any more, so many thistles and ragwort. She hated ragwort. That yellow and poisonous. Mind you, it didn't kill her. It was the illness did that.' He ate another slice of apple. 'The way it is there's no reason for people to come up here.'

'No,' agreed Dan. He didn't think he was much of a person. 'I like how you've built that wall. As if each stone was special.'

Si laughed and threw away the remains of his apple. Dan saw that once he got talking he wasn't so quiet, although he still paused between most sentences. 'The wall falls down. So many stones come down, so many stones go back up. It's a puzzle, see, fitting them back up. Other folk do crosswords, this new thing, Sudoku. I do walls.' He looked up at Dan. 'Go on, now, you choose the next stone.' He indicated a pile on the ground of every shape and size.

Dan walked over. The centre of the fallen part of the wall was still quite low. 'I suppose you use the biggest stones at the bottom?'

Si shook his head, smiling. 'Nothing so simple, Dan.' He got up, creakily, and came over. 'Here we are. She's a nice one. Let's see where you put it.' He picked up a stone and handed it to Dan who placed it awkwardly in the wall, making Si smile again. He took it down and placed it a few feet along where it immediately sat comfortably, as if it had always been there.

'That's clever,' said Dan.

'Give you fifty years and you could do it same as me.'

They worked together after that: Dan hauling up stones, which were rejected or accepted and then, after a good deal of hesitation, placed in the perfect position. It was like a puzzle, built vertically.

Dan had enjoyed making puzzles when he was younger but he'd never been able to impress Eve. 'Lovely, darling,' she used to say, without even looking. She probably found them boring.

Dan handed over another stone and watched Si as he inspected it carefully before turning back to the wall. 'They don't keep you too busy at the farm, then?' He seemed less curious than making conversation.

'No,' said Dan.

Si surveyed Dan rather as he did the stones. 'You need fattening up. You're as thin and white as a sheet of paper. When did you arrive?'

Dan put a hand to his face before answering. It felt different. 'I think I've caught the sun already.'

'What you need is a hat. Skin like yours burns easy.'

They began to work again, not talking much. The sun moved from above their heads and a shadow was cast by the wall. Dan walked away a few paces and picked up a round stone that caught his eye.

'Look. I've found a fossil!' he cried, like a delighted child.

Si straightened up. 'You're standing on a sea bed. You know that?'

'But we're high up.' The fossil was perfect, an ammonite, about four inches in diameter. The most beautiful thing he'd ever seen. How old was it? He tried to remember. He'd seen a programme about fossils a few weeks ago. The animals they came from first appeared 450 million years ago, he remembered that, and disappeared when the dinosaurs went, about 65 million years ago. The fossil in his hands was about 200 million years old. 'Awesome!' He stared down, almost unbelieving, at the circular stone.

Si came over to have a look. 'Nice one, that. Being high up makes no odds. Once you find one, you'll find more.'

While Si went back to the wall, Dan bent again, moved a few paces and found another fossil and then another. Neither was so perfect nor so large, one a semicircle with jagged breaks at either end. He looked more closely and found three more, one an oyster shell.

Si stopped working. 'The sea's twenty miles away now.'

Dan imagined waves rushing over the hill and fishes swimming round his trainers. He wondered if his stream had fossils too. When he got back there, he'd take off his clothes and lie down in the cold water.

'Well, that's it for the day. I'll be going on.' Si looked up at the sky. 'No rain tomorrow. Are you back to the farm?'

For an anxious moment, Dan thought Si was going to the farm himself or lived near it, and he would be discovered. 'Not yet,' he mumbled.

'No. Not your dinnertime yet. I go in the other direction.' He came over and looked at the collection of fossils. 'My Gwen used to like picking those up. We've got stacks of them all round the house. Seeing as we had no children, I teased her they were her family. We had the dogs, of course, but one died and then the other and then Gwen. I didn't have the heart to start again with training a puppy. Lonely without, though. Everyone tells me a dog is what I need. I'm not saying they're wrong. It's been nice having a bit of company, I'll say that.'

'Will you be here tomorrow?' asked Dan, squinting into the sun. The old man looked big and solid. He didn't want to be alone again.

'If I'm spared.' He smiled and became more animated. 'Ever gone dowsing?'

'What's that?'

'Looking for water.'

Dan nearly answered, 'There's enough taps in London.' Instead he said, 'No. Never.'

'That's what we'll do, Danny lad. With a string and a pebble.' He stumped off then, with a backward wave.

Dan stood for a while, watching him go, wondering what to do about the fossils. He wanted the big one but it was heavy. In the end he put a smaller one in each pocket. He'd be back tomorrow for the other. Si's dark figure merged into the fuzziness at the horizon and disappeared. He felt extraordinarily hungry, enough to go searching for the bit of apple Si had thrown away. He brushed off the dirt and gulped it down. It was a long walk back to the limo. Home. The word plucked an uncomfortable string in his heart so he peed boldly into the air, except there wasn't much pee because he was so dried out.

He started walking and soon felt better again. There were many more birds around; whole flights rose from the stubble of one field he crossed, weaving around his head before settling. The sun was behind him, warming his neck and back. His shadow went before him, not very long, a friendly shortened version of himself. It kept him going in the right direction – into the sun on his way to the wall, away from the sun heading back home.

He fell into a dreamy state, aware of his rumbling stomach and the flies and other insects that collected periodically above his head, but without any real thoughts. He might almost have been asleep. This was his dream: the warm countryside, the taut feeling on his exposed skin where the sun had caught it, his feet pressing down on soft grass, hard stubble, springy weeds, half-buried stones. The fossils weighted his pockets. Now and again he put in his hands and curled his fingers round them, noting the curves and ridges, the dimpled middle.

It was still warm when he reached the limo so, only stopping long enough to grab a handful of biscuits, which he stuffed immediately into his mouth, he carried on towards the stream.

By now he had lost awareness of anyone else in the world so he had no hesitation in throwing off his clothes and sliding into the still water. It only just covered him but his arrival had set up little floats of sediment. Sandy earth, brownish leaves, twigs gently settled on his pale body, then slid away again, carried off by a rippling eddy he could hardly feel. He lay with his whole head back, resting on a stone not unlike a pillow. His willie floated up, like a pale underwater plant. Not a bad size, he thought, pleased with himself. The sky above him was slowly changing colour, as it had the evening before. He must remember the damp and cool that followed the going down of the sun. He didn't want to think of the night.

Because he had no towel, he chose the brightest patch of sun and vaguely rubbed at himself with his underpants. Then he threw them in the stream. They could do with a wash and would be dry by morning. It didn't strike him that the hot weather would end. He dressed, filled his water bottle, wrung out his pants and started back.

The limo was in shadow. He shivered and went to find his sweatshirt. It was very warm inside the car with a sweetish smell he didn't remember. His backpack was on the seat. Vaguely, without giving it too much attention, he thought he'd left it on the floor. He looked for his watch to find out the time but it wasn't where he'd thought, by the champagne glasses. He reminded himself he told the time by the sun now and didn't bother to look for it. Must be about seven thirty. A day and a half since he'd left home. He thought again it was odd he hadn't brought any books. But books were instead of living life and now he was living.

Carefully, he set up his two fossils beside the glasses. Two hundred million years old and they were still around.

Then, a little guilty, he turned to his backpack. If he didn't call Eve soon, his mobile might run out of juice. He slipped his fingers, cool now, into the front pocket. Nothing. He usually put it there but not always. He tried the side pockets. Nothing. He heard a high whining noise inside the car. A mosquito. He swatted and the noise stopped, then started again. He put his hand up to his neck and scratched. He could feel the bumps where the mosquito had bitten him. Not very nice on top of his sunburn. Lucky it wasn't the equatorial jungle, he thought, or he might be already infected with some death-dealing fever.

It was harder to search the main body of his backpack. He had to take out all the food first and that made him hungry and more inclined to eat than to keep looking. The mobile had probably fallen out on the floor somewhere but it was quite dim inside the car, and to look properly he'd have to take out the seats and, well, it could wait till the morning.

Eve wouldn't worry too much. She wanted to know everything about him when she was there but half the time she was somewhere else and he was the one waiting. If she'd really wanted to know things about him, she'd have found out about Ru, his nightmares.

There was his dad. He was all right. When he was around. He used to take him swimming. Male bonding time, Eve had said. It never struck either of them that they might have bonded better over books. The swimming only lasted two or three sessions, Anyway, the so-called 'dad' was off with the so-called aunt.

He felt his willie stirring. That was sick, wasn't it? Not that they owned up to anything like that. 'Going for a break from your mum,' he called it. He used to do the same himself. He put his hand down inside his trousers and felt his willie getting harder. Excited. Maybe this was the time.

Disgusting, though, to be thinking about his dad with his aunt. Boys thought of Mariah Carey or Cheryl Cole. All the same, he undid his trousers and carried on touching himself and it was different than it had ever been before and, by the time he'd finished, with wet on his fingers, it was definitely not the moment to crawl about trying to find the mobile and, even if he found it, why ever would he call his mother? He was a man now, he thought, his body still buzzing with satisfaction. More or less a man. He was alone, on an adventure. He'd rest a bit, eat a lot, and prepare for the night. Life was cool. He smiled into the darkness.

CHAPTER TWELVE

Eve arrived back in her flat at the end of her working day and for the first time truly took in that Dan had disappeared. Not only Max, but Dan. That thought, she knew, was a diversion. Max's leaving was periodic and explicable, even if she didn't want to understand the explanation.

She walked into Dan's small, neat bedroom (unnaturally neat for someone of his age) and flung herself onto the (hard) bed. But since there was no one to see her there sprawled in desolation – *O all you hosts of heaven! O Earth! What else? And shall I couple hell?* – she got up again quickly. This was a drama in which she was not the principal actor, or certainly in no way she wished to confront.

She came back into the sitting room and, still standing, began stripping off her jewellery and dropping it onto her chair. Did Indian widows going to the funeral pyre discard their jewellery or add more? She didn't know. Her lack of knowledge was profound, she thought. Probably that was why she acted, dealing with form and taking on other people's information.

She sat on a small chair, ringless hands dangling. The reason she'd been able to work all day, giving, giving, giving to those brutish sods dubbed children, tragic kids – baby goats baaing incomprehensibly, butting their stupid heads – was because she'd expected, no, *demand-ed* that Dan would be back on her return.

It was, in fact, almost unbelievable that he wasn't. He had never done anything to challenge her before. He was a good, obedient boy. He was her son. She loved him without mercy. Was he playing a trick? Where was he? He was not stupid. A dreamer, but not stupid. For the first time ever it struck her that he was more like Max than her.

She brought up her hands to her face and they were grey and cold, wrinkled like an old woman's. Her curls, too, which usually garlanded her face with such vivacity, hung dry and lifeless. Could this be happening to her? Unwillingly, she found herself recalling the day that she and Martha were told of their mother's death – not by their father: he was too upset. She had felt the same ageing and withering take place. Then she had been a child. Martha had put an arm round her.

The jab of the telephone startled her so much she had to take a few deep, actorish breaths before she could move. Immediately a huge sense of surety and release swept over her. She lifted her head; her skin glowed. They'd found him! He'd found himself. He'd found her. All's well that ends well.

'Hello.'

'It's me. I'll be coming over in a minute.' Martha paused, her practical tones changing to a lower level. 'Any news?'

'No,' said Eve.

'You reported it to the police?'

'Yes,' said Eve. 'They weren't very interested.'

'Ah,' Martha sounded practical again. 'We must pursue them.'

'Pursue?'

'Yes. We pursue them so they pursue him.'

The ridiculousness of this sentence silenced both women until Martha asked, with what Eve recognized as forced naturalness, 'Have you heard from Max?'

'No-o,' said Eve, making the short word move from a wan littlegirl-lost to a defiant so-what's-it-to-you.

'Well, I'll be over and I'll bring some food. We'll plan our next steps.'

'Good,' agreed Eve who heard the 'our' with more pleasure than anything else that day. Martha was her soldier, her knight in shining armour – at least, she was when she wasn't harbouring Max. But that, she reminded herself, meant nothing. Max always told her so, or implied it was so, and Max, a man of letters and a poet, prided himself on his inability to lie – although he called it unwillingness.

The point was that she would never find a better soldier to fight her battles than her older sis. She had her downside: soldiers are bluff fellows, keen to confront the worst, size up the enemy, define the opposition before girding their loins. In other words, Martha would make her think hard about Dan, about his problems, his

64

weaknesses, his needs. It would not be enough for her to proclaim love and sorrow. Martha would accept her feelings, even sympathize, but also discount them. She would be on the trail of a solution. She would question Eve: When did you last see him? Did he take anything with him? What was his mood? What did he usually do in the day when you were working? She would ask questions that the police had not asked and she, Eve, would feel her bravura shrivelling, squeezed to a dry husk, until there was nothing left of the self she had constructed. Nothing but a sad little person with not a jot of personality.

Martha was not cruel, however. She would not leave her like that. After the torturing process had ended, she would become gentle, treating Eve softly, allowing her to inflate gradually, like a balloon filling slowly with warm air. But the process, oh, what agony it was! The twisting, the wrenching, the prodding, the sucking.

Eve went back to the same small chair she'd scarcely sat in before and put her head into her hands. Martha would help her find Dan. Until this moment she had managed to avoid picturing him but now he was inside her imagination, a year or two younger than he actually was, not so tall, not so thin, not so slouched. What was he saying? Something about going out, meeting a friend. The friend *needed* him. That phrase had lodged with her. Not a thing boys usually said. Which friend? She hadn't asked. She didn't know. And it was some time ago. Last year, even.

Martha would be here soon. Martha would take her through everything. Best not to think too much till then.

Was she overreacting? Martha came out into the warm summer evening and wondered whether she was wrong to be so filled with anxiety, terror even – controlled, of course. Why had she not gone to work? Their father, the good vicar, had taught them that nothing was as valuable as duty fulfilled. Which was not the reason Eve had gone to work. Her work was an extension of herself, not something she performed outside her personal life as with most people, as with herself. Like their father, she had lost her partner to an early death. Had this darkened her view, dented for ever her sense of a benign world?

The road and pavements were busy. The continuing heatwave was taken for granted now, as if London had turned into a southern city. There were more shorts than trousers, more strapless, sleeveless, backless halter tops than regular T-shirts. Many of the younger girls had smooth golden tans, perhaps from a can but very convincing. London had put on the appearance of a holiday city.

Martha was dressed in a cotton shirt and skirt. Since joining the prison service she had grown comfortable with the dark trousers and white shirt as a kind of protective clothing and found herself uneasy, or at least unsure, in ordinary clothes. Her skirt, for example, seemed too insistently patterned, yet she saw much bolder around her. Her toes, revealed in their sandals (relatively sensible as they were), seemed alarmingly vulnerable and out of place. They were much better kept hidden in her heavy work shoes.

For a moment it struck her that both she and Eve preferred the ease of disguise. She quickly discounted the idea: she and Eve were mainly remarkable for the dissimilarity of their outlook. A shared background was what they had in common.

She was walking now, heading for her car, her skirt swinging round her bare legs. She could have put on jeans, instead she'd chosen this optimistic skirt, bought years ago when Adrian was still alive. Another world. Perhaps she'd go back and change into jeans. Perhaps she'd go for a run and not see Eve at all.

Impatiently she shook her head. This was all fanciful. In a moment she'd tell herself, like those poor deluded souls (there was one in the prison), that she was a man in a woman's body. Of course the prisoner, being a man, thought vice versa. She was a woman, all right.

She thought of Max's body poised above hers. The only time he was certain, and then so certain. Did Eve suspect? Would she and Eve have to talk about Max?

Where was Dan? She reached the car as a black sense of guilt rushed over her like sickness. She bent, held her stomach, then straightened and opened the door. There was no future in being cowardly. At least she had sent Max away before she known about Dan's disappearance. But Dan knew. Children always knew everything, someone had once told her. He would have run away to her if Max hadn't been there already. Once again the pain hit her stomach and she bent double.

*

66

The two sisters sat in the stuffy living room of Eve's flat.

'Can't we open a window?' asked Martha, irritably.

Eve seemed surprised at the idea. She'd reattached to her person her abandoned jewellery, increasing its volume with a bangle or two, and applied dark makeup round her eyes.

'You look like a clown,' muttered Martha, as Eve wrenched at the window.

'I'm just trying to keep up my spirits.' She turned back. 'Incidentally, Max rang.'

'That was good of him.'

'He certainly thought so.'

'Where was he?' Martha tried to make this sound casual.

'He's gone back to some bookshop he visited yesterday. In the West Country. He had to fix a computer blip. I don't know. I wasn't really listening.' Eve came back, but before she sat down she prepared herself a gin and tonic, complete with ice and lemon.

Martha declined. The ice was in a bowl, the lemon neatly sliced. Perhaps it was her second gin. 'What did he think about Dan? Max is a man, after all, and once a boy.' She guessed Eve had primed herself for this conversation.

'He said I was right to report it to the police.' Eve played with a strand of her hair. 'Then he said that Dan wasn't at all adventurous and not very attractive so he didn't see how he could be at much risk. He seemed amazed when I told him Dan had never stayed away with a friend – not for years anyway. I said, "You should know, you're his dad," so he became sulky.'

'That was it?' Martha found herself longing for a gin and tonic but refused to have one on principle. 'How could he say that about Dan being unattractive?' She puffed with indignation. 'It's cruel and not true and unnatural and . . .' Eve was staring at her: this wrath was not her style. '. . . inappropriate.' She finished, and went to pour herself a gin and tonic after all.

'Oh, Marth,' Eve raised her clown's eyes sympathetically, 'I expect you love him nearly as much as I do.'

For a crazy, heart-stopping moment, Martha thought she was referring to Max. 'He's my nephew,' she said, recovering a little dignity. She sipped at the gin. It helped. It definitely helped. 'I'm so sorry, Evie.' The sisters looked at each other. Could they live with this situation? How much did Eve want to know? How much could Martha hide?

'You shouldn't let him use you.'

'I know.' Martha dropped her eyes. They would manage. They always had and now there was even more reason to do so.

Eve stood up. 'I'll get you a pad and paper.'

'Good idea.' Martha knew she was notorious for her lists but usually Eve rebelled. She was trying to recover their equilibrium. 'We could do it online.' She raised her voice so that Eve, who had left the room, could hear her.

'The laptop's there.'

As she switched it on, Martha remembered the research she'd done earlier. She'd show it to Eve but first they must get things in order. She typed 'Dan'. It glowed a brilliant yellow on the blue screen. She added 'Friends', then 'Interests', 'Habits', 'Contacts', 'State of mind', then 'Places frequented' and 'Last seen'.

Eve had curled up on the sofa. Martha read out the list. 'Who's this *for*?' Eve asked, in a firm enough voice although her eyes had filled with tears.

'Us.' Martha inserted 'Age' and 'Home address' before 'Friends'. 'So that we can answer questions properly. And look for him ourselves, of course.' Eve made no comment so she wrote in Dan's date of birth and the address of the flat.

'Are interests different from habits?' asked Eve.

'They might be.' Martha thought. Going swimming isn't the same as picking your nose.

'And what about hobbies?'

'More like interests,' suggested Martha, wearily. Max dragged at her like a heavy weight. He hung between the two of them but he belonged to Eve.

'I don't think he had much of any of them, actually.' Eve looked sadly at her empty glass. 'He liked reading.'

'Books, you mean?'

'Of course I mean books.'

'Sorry. These days . . .' Martha let the sentence trail away. She didn't remember Dan bringing a book with him when he came to stay. But perhaps she hadn't noticed. 'What was – I mean, *is* – he reading now?'

'I didn't *see* him read. He read in his room. He liked his privacy.' She looked up. 'I suppose that comes under "Habits"?'

Martha typed 'Reading' under 'Interests'. 'I think we should look in Dan's bedroom.'

'I've looked in it! Ten times! Twenty times!' Eve was passionate. Then resigned. She settled back in the sofa. 'You look. Be a detective. I don't think mothers are good detectives. Besides, I've programmed myself not to see what might be in his room, in any teenage boy's room – porn mags, sex DVDs, that kind of healthy I-am-growing-into-a-man stuff.'

'I'll look,' said Martha, standing up. Once outside, she sighed with relief, as at a danger past. Now she could concentrate totally on Dan.

She stood in the small bedroom, paying respect to the absent boy. If he walked though the door, she didn't want to be caught in any shameful act. She noted the blind, still lowered. The sun had set but light still came through in stripes, probably from streetlights. It was noisy, only three floors up and right on top of the busy road. She would have found it hard to sleep there. She reminded herself she was looking for a book and turned back to the bed. Some magazines lay on the floor – not porn. She leafed through a few, one about prehistoric creatures, a bit young for him, nothing out of the ordinary. An iPod was on the bedside table and several books, including the latest Dan Brown, a P.G. Wodehouse, *The Curious Incident of the Dog in the Night-time* and a book called *Bog Child* about a mummified body in Ireland. It seemed Eve was right about his reading.

There was a bookcase, too, behind the door so she only noticed it now. The number of books surprised her, arranged alphabetically: Boyne, DeLillo, Horowitz, Higson, Ishiguro, Muchamore, Pullman, Pratchett, Tolkien. She wasn't much of a reader herself and there were many names she didn't recognize but it seemed a mix between teenage-style adventure and adult fiction. On the bottom shelf, there were some biographies and a row of encyclopedias and dictionaries, several given by herself as birthday or Christmas presents. There was even some poetry.

She didn't know why she was surprised by the idea of Dan as a reader. After all, books were his father's profession, even if he aspired to be a poet, and the flat's spare room (supposed to be for baby number two) was entirely filled with them, mainly in boxes.

There was also a laptop, but on the floor as if it wasn't used all that much. Maybe he pulled it up to the bed.

She'd not found much time for reading after finishing university. Eve had read plays, of course. Beside the bookcase there was a small chest of drawers and on another wall a built-in cupboard.

She was beginning to feel increasing unease: you didn't turn over somebody's things unless they were suspected of a criminal act or dead. Nevertheless, she opened the top drawer and found a jumble of socks, underclothes. She put out her hand, then stopped abruptly, her action interrupted by an image of herself as prison officer entering a cell for a formal search. On those occasions she had the righteousness of Her Majesty's rules and regulations supporting her.

She went back into the sitting room where Eve seemed to have sunk further into the sofa. 'I was thinking,' she said dreamily, 'that if Dan doesn't return soon, we'll be glued to the TV, watching for news, being interviewed with tears in our eyes. These days, it's so difficult to believe in reality.'

'I don't know,' said Martha. Eve had never been much attracted to reality.

'Tomorrow,' Eve raised her arms above her head almost languorously, 'I have all these kids waiting for me to give them a break. Do you think Dan was jealous? Do you think he chose his moment?'

Martha saw she had misjudged her sister but also that Max had gone off the agenda. 'Possibly. You were right about his reading. So many books. I didn't know half of them.'

'Porn?'

'Not that I saw.' Martha sat down and pulled over the laptop. 'Shall we go on with the lists?'

'Of course, we're assuming he ran away.' Eve half shut her eyes and continued with eerie calm: 'He might have been kidnapped or, if he's not attractive enough for that — according to his dad — murdered, chopped in half for some African ritual. Or even just run over by a lorry filled with illegal immigrants. Or stabbed by a boy who didn't like the cut of his jib — or a boy who liked the cut of his mobile jib. In other words, he could be dead. We could be wasting our time with Interests and Hobbies and Contacts. He could be dead, Martha, and I really think we should face it. Add it to our list, as it were. Between Hobbies and Contacts: Dead.' Eve stood up.

'And now I'm going to get myself another gin.' She walked unsteadily to the table.

Martha knew Eve in this mood, apparently melodramatic but actually expressing a dizzying terror. More gin was not a good idea. She spoke in what she hoped was a comforting tone: 'In a minute we'll look to see if he's taken anything. Then we'll know he chose to go. Anyway, the police will find out if anything very bad has happened.' But Eve was up again, mixing herself another drink. Martha returned to the laptop. 'They have a program to match information.'

'I would say my son is a closed book,' Eve had returned to the sofa, watching her glass as she made it waft about in the air.

'If he read books, he probably went to the library,' said Martha, head bent.

'He probably did. Perhaps he had a friend there. Girlfriend, even. Perhaps they ran away together, like Romeo and Juliet.'

'We must be focused,' muttered Martha, without much hope.

'And where was his dad? I ask you. I ask the court. Where was his dad when all this running away or abducting or murdering took place? I repeat, where the fuck was his dad?' Eve suddenly stepped up on to the sofa, swaying, holding up her glass as if for a toast.

'Do you want me to leave?' Martha stood up too. So she'd been wrong. Max hadn't left the scene. It had just needed three more gins for him to reappear.

Eve stood down again carefully without spilling a drop of her drink. Martha assumed her actor's training allowed her to pull off such a feat when drunk and emotional. 'I'm just trying to face realities,' said Eve, sitting back on the sofa. 'I'm not accusing anyone of anything.' Her words were blurred. 'You should try the realities too.'

This was a role reversal that confused Martha. 'I'm trying . . .' she began, which was certainly not true. 'I think we should contact the police.'

'Once more unto the breach,' agreed Eve, as if it didn't really matter. Then she looked up. 'And ask about hospitals.'

But instead Martha got up and went into the kitchen. She had to get away from Eve. Dan was always hungry. She opened the fridge: almost empty. On the table there was a bowl holding one apple. Dan liked bananas. Perhaps he'd taken bananas. She looked round despairingly. There was no point in doing this without Eve.

'Evie!' she called. 'Eve!' When there was no answer, not even a drunken howl, she sat down at the table and put her head into her hands.

Max and Alison were in the same pub where they had drunk coffee outside the day before. The room was low-beamed and stained yellow by centuries of smokers. The last rays of daylight angled through small windows. They sat at a table and held menus.

'The food here is supposed to be good. Good for this part of the world.' Alison was nervous, deprecating, as if she didn't understand what they were doing there and, possibly, regretted it.

Max saw her point. He knew why he was there. He had nowhere else to go. Any port in a storm, particularly if she was pretty. But he didn't want her to be unhappy. 'It's kind of you to look after me.'

She relaxed a little, at least stopped looking out of the window as if for someone to rescue her. 'It's no trouble.'

'It seems pointless to trek back tonight when I have to go even further west tomorrow.'

'Have you stayed in the B-and-B before?'

'Oh, yes. It's fine.' This was a lie to make her feel more comfortable, that his visit was part of a working routine, not a predatory man moving in on a recently divorced and vulnerable young woman. 'A glass of wine?' he asked. Tomorrow he would go back to Eve. With any luck, Dan would be back too. He definitely wasn't the running-away sort. He decided to order a bottle.

Dan was like him. It was painful to admit that. He'd recognized their similarity very early on, when Dan was three or four, a lanky little boy, happy to play on his own. He pictured him always crouched over something, making Lego or studying carefully a piece of paper fallen out of the wastepaper basket.

He had found words early, both in speech and in books, but he hadn't let on. Being alike should have made them closer but it worked the other way. Max was frightened for him, instinctively knew him too well, so pulled away. Let Eve give him some of her obstreperous energy. So, they had lost touch. He was away too much.

'Do you have children?' he asked Alison.

They had already drunk a glass of wine each. Their food was on the table.

'No. Luckily.'

He wondered how old she was and whether her 'luckily' was the truth. Most women wanted children, with or without a husband. He had been propositioned to play the biological-father role more than once. A tribute to his looks.

It had been a surprise when Dan had turned out to inherit neither Eve's punchy blondeness nor his own rugged looks. He was most like Martha.

'We're quite worried about my son at the moment. He's gone missing.'

Alison seemed not to take this seriously and continued eating, fast and efficiently. She'd be out of the place in five minutes. 'Missing?' She looked up eventually.

'Yes. Since yesterday.' He wanted to hold her attention. She had lovely eyes, blue-grey, almond-shaped, though buried in too much makeup. She was unusual for the manager of a bookshop.

'How old is he?' Now she was concerned.

'Thirteen. It's his fourteenth birthday in a couple of days.' He announced this fact with pride. Often Eve had to remind him. But this birthday he'd bought Dan the *New Oxford Book of English Verse*. He'd bought it for himself it at the same age. For the first time he was struck by an acute pang of fear. What if Dan was really missing?

'With a friend, is he?' asked Alison.

'I don't know.' If he didn't come back tonight, it would be the second night he was away. He needed to ring Eve. Perhaps Dan had just walked through the door.

'How scary!' Alison leant forward sympathetically but Max suspected this was not what she'd expected or wanted. She'd hoped for an evening off from her own troubles and didn't need to swap them for someone else's.

'Excuse me.' He stood up and went into the hallway. There was no one there but neither was there a signal for his mobile. The pavement was empty too, the sky above the rooftops the ink-washed blue before night falls. But there were lights above his head.

Eve's number rang engaged. Without thinking too much, he rang Martha's but that was an answering-machine. He didn't leave a message.

He looked up at the sky again, trying to define the impression of emptiness and waiting. He rang Eve's number again but it was still engaged. A line came into his head: *Terrified by night, the pale sky lingers.* But it was crap. How did he know it was crap? Because all his poetry was crap. Shit hard. Shit pellets.

He strode back into the pub and interrupted Alison in the act of pouring herself a second (or was it the third?) glass of wine. She seemed resigned or maybe relieved. 'Have you got to go?'

'I'm afraid so.' He looked at her and, in order to avoid another failure, more hurting, sat down. 'There's still time to finish our supper.' He smiled. If you're given a devastating smile, why not use it? Business too.

As they continued eating, drinking, bookshop gossiping, he wondered if she would have slept with him if he'd stayed in that mythical B-and-B. Probably, yes. She was looking for a new life. On the other hand she might have drawn the line at a man who was scarcely more than an acquaintance. Married too. Although that could have been a plus if she wasn't ready for involvement. He thought of her almost with nostalgia, even though she was still sitting across the table from him, as charming as ever.

In his mind, he was already driving a hundred and forty miles, racing night across the empty sky.

But when he was actually in the car a new rhythm of fear took hold of his mind. Behind him chased Goethe's Erlking, threatening the child in his arms, ever closer, however fast he drove. *Mein Vater, mein Vater, und hörest du nicht, / Was Erlenkönig mir leise verspricht? . . .* My father, my father, canst thou not hear / What the Erlking whispers in my ear? / Be calm, stay calm, my child / 'Tis only the wind rustling in the leaves . . .

He drove to the boy's terror and Schubert's thunderous music.

CHAPTER THIRTEEN

When Max arrived back at his home the two women were still up.

Eve opened the door. She stared at her husband with anguish. While she had lain on the sofa, Martha had spent the previous couple of hours emailing and talking to helplines and friends. She had tracked down the headmaster (on holiday) and also various teachers (not yet on holiday). They had several pages of lists and the police had promised to do more if Dan hadn't turned up the next morning. They were also fairly sure he'd taken some bacon, biscuits and bananas.

Yet the doorbell had turned Eve into a joyful fairy. She'd flown down the short hallway and thrown open the door. Her heart beat a high-pitched drum of celebration.

'Can I come in?' said Max. He frowned. His face was gaunt. 'Even if I'm not Dan.'

Eve burst into tears, and dropped to the floor. It was a mixture of disappointment, relief (she wanted Max back – he should be here) and anger.

Max patted her huddled, sobbing form. Then, stepping more over than around her, he proceeded into the living room.

'Hello,' he said to Martha. Eve heard it from the hallway. It got her off the floor. She wasn't having those two, even though they were two of the three people she loved most in the world, spending time alone. Staggering, head down, a fairy with bedraggled wings, she joined the others.

She sat cross-legged on the sofa while Martha filled in Max. She wondered at her sister's calm as she pronounced the terrible words necessary: lost, missing, abducted. But she herself had spoken them earlier. Now they sounded like the tolling of a bell. She contemplated the idea of another drink but suspected that gin had done all it could for her. Besides, the ice had melted because she hadn't put the tray back into the freezer. The room was still warm, a warm summer night. She tried to make that seem hopeful. If Dan was sleeping out, he would not be cold, frostbitten, rain-soaked, buried under snow or ice. Then she thought it was not the weather he had to fear but other people. And this thought, which she'd been trying to avoid all evening, lifted her off the sofa.

'I'll get you some soup,' she announced to Max, interrupting whatever he was saying.

He stared at her and she saw in reflection just how bad she looked, the pinpoint eyes and black streaks, the shiny, mottled skin, the wet, uncontrolled mouth.

'That's all right. I had something earlier.' He stood up and put an arm round her. 'Why don't you lie down for a bit? We'll tell you if there's any news.'

Despite her earlier resolution, she was too weak to resist so she went to the bathroom and washed her face, then to the bedroom where she lay on her bed. Immediately she fell asleep but such a shallow sleep that she heard herself snorting and gulping and turning from side to side. Soon the dreams started. Dan, again younger than his present age and much smaller, was threatened by a group of kids. She recognized them as her students, Louis and Ibou and fat Carla. They were pushing him about, from one to another, then swatting and batting him like a ball. With horror she realized Dan had turned into a ball, a smooth yellow one the size of a football.

'Please, no!'

Martha's hand was on her forehead, making her open her eyes. She felt herself trembling but gradually the image of the ball and the players faded. She saw Max standing behind her sister. His solidity warmed her a little and the trembling eased.

'You had a dream,' said Martha, gently.

'I won't tell you about it.' When they were children, after their mother's death, they used to swap dreams but if either of them had a really bad one, they made a pact to keep it to themselves. Sharing would only spread the horror, they'd reasoned, and give it more of a life. All the same, Eve sometimes told Martha her nightmares. Martha never described hers.

'We've done so much this evening,' said Martha, 'and Max is here so there're three of us.'

Max stepped forward. The bedside light lit him from below, giving him a Mephistophelian glow. Eve liked it and put out her hand. He held it.

'We should all get a few hours' sleep.' His voice was so beautiful. She'd forgotten how beautiful. 'Would you like a sleeping pill?'

'I'd prefer a Valium.'

So they settled down and she was comforted by Max's large body beside hers.

Just before dawn when the night was still quiet but on the edge of waking, she found herself sitting up, convinced that Dan had returned. Softly – she would be the one to find him – she crept along to his bedroom. The door was half open, the light had been left on in the hallway. She stepped into the room and, with hardly any surprise, noted the curled-up form, a sprouting of brown hair showing above the duvet.

He rolled over slowly on to his back.

A murderous rage seized Eve. She held out her hands like claws as if she would tear apart her sleeping sister. Martha opened her eyes. 'I'm sorry,' she said at once.

Eve bowed her head. The Valium had softened her and made her inactive.

Martha got out of bed and held her. 'I shouldn't have been there.' She led Eve back to her bedroom. But there was no point in trying to sleep again. The day had started.

They sat drinking tea in the kitchen, listening to the traffic building by fits and starts to its early-morning roar.

They were too tired to talk, too disheartened.

CHAPTER FOURTEEN

The sun came up sharply, lighting the dirt and dust, the dead flies and spiders littering the floor of the limo. Dan scratched his neck and thought what he needed was a brush or Hoover or even a feather duster. There was a shop that sold pink and lime-green feather dusters on the corner. Not any corner round here, however. He smiled at himself. The night had not been so bad, only a few seconds of the nightmare. Poor Ru, hardly getting a look in now. As he thought this, he caught a flash of the horror, the rope, the tongue, the swollen cheeks, but he was able to dismiss it easily. It was the sad little voice that was worst.

The worst things at this moment were his bites and a terrific hunger. It felt more like an animal gnawing away at his belly than emptiness. The trouble was, most of his remaining food needed cooking and he hadn't worked out how. This could be the moment to show his mettle. He bent over for his trainers and only recoiled slightly as a beetle crawled out of their musky interior. Maybe he'd throw them into the stream, like his pants.

Outside the car, the air was thrillingly fresh. He breathed deeply and even touched his toes a couple of times – not his usual habit. He thought he was the centre of this world. The black and white cows on the other side of the hedge were quite close, moving slowly, heads down, in a line over the field. They reminded him of something. That was it: policemen searching for clues.

He turned away and peed. That was one thing about not eating much, no need to crap. He started towards the old barn, sure there'd be something there to make a fire, and then had the prickly feeling that someone was watching him – more than the regular birds and cows. He stopped, unconsciously, holding his breath, and looked round carefully.

At some distance two white tails lifted into the air; legs on springs carried the curious deer away. He let out a loud gasp of relief and stamped off to the barn.

Poking around, among a pile of rusty, mostly antiquated farm implements, he spotted something that looked remarkably like a barbecue. He pulled it out and straightened it up. Perfect for the job! Already his mouth was watering at the thought of sizzling sausages and bacon. Now for pieces of wood.

As Dan worked, he was conscious of the sun rising and warming the air. It must have been early when he woke – he still hadn't bothered to look for his watch – but now the day was set fair, all the misty dampness evaporated. He allowed himself to imagine London streets at this moment: the grey, grimy pavements coated with old layers of dog shit, spittle and food remains; the roads, disfigured with signs, commands, lights, cars, vans, bicycles, motorbikes, police cars, ambulances, fire engines, people. Just so much shit.

When he'd got his fire going, he went to his backpack and found the food. He knew he should look for his mobile again but he was just too hungry. Later.

He draped bacon and sausages across a wire grill made out of bits and pieces of wire. They smelt odd, a bit disgusting, but he'd cook them longer.

He was beginning to be impatient to have his meal and set off on what he thought of as the journey to the wall but, really, it was the old man, Si, he wanted to see, more than that, talk to. Not many words. Enough to reassure him. He needed to hear a friendly voice and his own in response. It surprised him, this need, because the whole point of leaving home was to be alone, find out who he was and how he'd get on. Well, he knew the answer to the second question already: he was fine, very well, thank you, particularly fine after last night's all-male experience.

The bacon was truly disgusting, however, even burnt black, and the sausages not much better. Actually, uneatable. He flung them over the hedge and went to see what other food he had left: a few biscuits, a piece of cake and two bananas. No point waiting for a loaves-and-fishes miracle. He ate quickly. Now for a refreshing drink of spring water.

He sat comfortably on the tufty grass by the stream where he'd cut back more nettles and, putting down the knife, drank the water with his eyes on the sky and the rising sun. It was deliciously cool, the sun hot, the prospect of the day ahead perfect. He jumped up with a whoop of happiness and set off immediately in the direction of the wall. He was a free spirit, wandering high and low, a hero of his time. Imitating the deer, he sprang across the fields.

Returning from a fast thirty-minute run, Martha dressed herself in the prison uniform with a sense of relief. Her house, too, was orderly. She was right to go to work – for all kinds of reasons. The job required her presence, and so did Lee, but Max and Eve didn't. This was hurtful, which was an understatement. She did up her shirt, checking carefully that each button was properly in its hole. Once, early in her training, she'd been more casual and the result was her front had popped open. First she'd noticed a prisoner was leering, well, commenting, 'Nice boobs, Miss', which had got them both into trouble. Him more than her, but that was the way of prisons.

She'd be glad to be back at work, steady herself with thoughts about a world outside Max and Eve and Dan. She'd done everything she could for Dan the night before. The contacts were made, the line to follow. Max could handle things all right, even Eve. She wondered if Eve would go to work, then stopped herself. None of her business.

She picked up her car keys and went to the door. Another hot day. She wouldn't know it in the prison. It was eleven o'clock, between rush-hour and lunchtime, and the roads were not too busy. Not so easy to park when she arrived, however. She'd worked at three London prisons now and all suffered from a lack of parking space. It still felt odd to her, circling round and round the barbed-wire-topped walls, trying so hard to get inside them when hundreds of men were longing to get outside. Of course, the cars belonged to the workers, governors, social workers, probation officers, lawyers, visitors, charities, medics, psychiatrists, teachers and artists. There was a whole world behind the wire. She liked the orderliness, perhaps the danger. Not that she'd seen very much. Occasionally a fight but, as a woman, she wouldn't be called in for that. Not in a men's prison.

It had been emphasized to her that many of the men were potentially dangerous and she supposed she believed that. The older officers certainly did. The younger ones were more like her, not averse to recognizing an edge of danger but not taking it too seriously. 'You've all turned into a bunch of wanking social workers,' an older officer had complained bitterly, after a skirmish with an angry prisoner who hadn't been shut down quickly enough.

It was true, thought Martha, as she took the place of another car driving away, that she looked on the prisoners as men first and criminals afterwards. But she knew the line. She wasn't silly, not a social worker in the way the old officer had meant.

As soon as Martha had clocked in, she went on the wing to find Lee.

'Looking for the bad guy, are you?' Reggie, an affable officer who tried to be amusing, accosted Martha.

'Seen him, have you?'

'Yesterday he was on teabag duty.'

'He wouldn't like that.' Martha wondered what was to follow. Counting out teabags and packing them in a box would definitely not be Lee's idea of fun.

'Let's say he's not doing it any more.'

'How did he manage that?'

'Said to Jimmy, who was in charge, "What if I put a slip of paper in each box saying murderers, rapists and violent gang members packed these teabags?" Got no answer from Jimmy but he isn't on teabag duty any more.'

Reggie waited expectantly but Martha decided not to laugh. This could be serious for Lee. Maybe he really wasn't ready to get out.

She went along to his cell. 'I gather you've been making trouble.'

He was lying on his bed reading a newspaper. She could see the headline: 'Warning from America: Reject the Big Idea'. She recognized the prison newspaper, *Inside Time*. Usually he read the *Sun* but sometimes she caught him with the *Guardian*.

'It was just a stupid line.'

'Got you off teabags.'

'Yeah.'

Martha knew she shouldn't be standing at the door while he lounged on his bed. Her lack of determination was due to weariness and anxiety about Dan. She was supposed to leave outside concerns at the prison gates. She found some energy. 'We need to talk.' She turned.

He followed her obediently. Unusually, she found a room where they could sit together. Normally, it would be two plastic chairs on the landing, braving the traffic of prisoners and officers.

Perhaps it was the privacy that encouraged the turn of the conversation from final arrangements at his bail hostel and plans for a job to wider issues. Even in her limited experience, 'wider issues' led to roads best not travelled. Worse, they led to questions.

'I suppose you live round here?' The oldest question in the prisoner's armoury but one he'd never asked before.

'Not far.'

'With your husband?'

'Yes.' She had lived with her husband before his death. It had been his house. It was an easy lie. Some officers told much bigger ones.

'And your children?'

'No children.' Why had she answered? Because it didn't matter? Or because she wanted to be honest? Or because she was thinking of Dan? Dan was the nearest she had to a child.

'I have a nephew.' She was volunteering information about herself. Against the rules. She remembered Lee had children in his past. No longer in contact with them or their mother. Two mothers, now she came to think about it. 'You don't see your children, do you?'

Those pale eyes stared at her appraisingly. Was he trying to work out whether this question was part of her job?

'My boy will be fourteen tomorrow. Soon he'll be old enough to choose for himself.'

Martha felt herself flushing. The coincidence was too great. 'Dan will be fourteen tomorrow.' She clenched her fist on her lap, then took a tissue from her pocket. She was afraid she was going to cry. She never cried. She should end this interview at once.

'Is that so? You're close to him, then.'

'Very.' Her voice was muffled.

'That's nice.' She guessed he was thinking how lucky she was, and her only an aunt. He didn't know the impossible truth.

'We don't know where he is at the moment.' Warning bells jangled in her ears but, with nervous determination, she overrode them. 'He disappeared on Monday.'

'So that's why you weren't here yesterday.'

'Yes.' She knew why she was telling him: because a runaway, or kidnap victim or something worse, seemed part of the world he knew more about than she did. A world where things go seriously wrong. Perhaps she was even idiotic enough to think he could help her.

'The police know?' He was pulling back. He knew the rules too. He'd been in prison a long time. He was scared of involvement.

'Oh, yes.' She tried to lighten things. 'I expect he's back now.' Of course she didn't expect that. Life had taught her that things never work out the easy way.

'I don't know where my lad is. In front of the TV eating his dinner or under a motorway being nibbled by rats.' As Lee spoke, his tones muted as before, he laid his hands on the table, fingers spread.

To avoid looking at his face, Martha stared down at them, slim, very clean. Prison clean: even the fingernails were white, at odds with his weirdly seamed face. She had to say something. 'That's terrible. I don't know how you bear it.'

'No choice. If you want my opinion, fourteen is the most important age for kids. Dangerous, too. I'd like to be there for mine. Boys need a father.'

Martha decided it would be insensitive to ask if there was a stepfather.

Lee continued, holding her eyes – she saw something fierce and slightly mad in his. 'Your boy's not lacking in love, I'd guess.'

He seemed to wait for an answer.

'No,' said Martha.

'He'll be all right, then. Make an entrance as and when.'

'Yes,' said Martha. She tried to feel more cheerful or, at least, appear it. They needed to walk out of this meeting with some semblance of order. There was a piece of paper in front of her, some form or other. She found tears blurring her vision.

'I'm sorry.' His voice was gentler, one layer of self-control removed.

She suddenly wanted to ask him about violence, losing control altogether, how it felt. Did he feel it seething inside him, only needing enough alcohol to relax his guard and set it free? Did he long for it or live in dread? She considered the members of the Parole Board, experienced men and women, ex-lawyers and -teachers, ex-policemen and -prison officers. They had judged him in control. It was not her business to do more than report. In her view, too, he was ready for freedom.

But how many men out there would never find balance? Until Dan had become unaccounted for the question had never worried her much. Now she had an image of a vulnerable boy lost in a jungle of unknown threats. She suspected another of her reasons for telling Lee about Dan was to bring to her side the unknown threats of which he was the closest and the one she knew best.

They were both standing now and he was watching her with the respectful expression that was never quite convincing. All the same, she respected him for getting his life back into shape, even liked him. Defiantly, she felt glad she'd told him about Dan. 'You're all set to go, then, when the call comes.'

'That's it.' He smiled. A rare occurrence. She wasn't sure what it meant: reassurance for her or heralding his brighter future.

Eve sat in her GP's waiting room. She could hardly stay still, however, continually badgering the receptionist. 'It's an emergency,' she repeated, nearly in tears. 'I have to be back at work.'

'I know, dear. Just sit down and I'll find you a doctor as soon as one's available.' Her manner made it clear that emergencies were two a penny from where she sat.

Eve fidgeted around, ignoring the chairs. The surgery was empty since it was officially closed at lunch. She longed to scream out, 'My son has vanished, disappeared, swept off the face of the earth,' but even without the Valium she could control that urge. The receptionist would probably have said in that same immovable manner, 'Bad luck, dear.'

Valium, or lack of it, was why she was there. It was typical she'd run out just when she needed it most. Of course, she'd upped her dose when Max left. Max was back now, and Max was in charge, that made a welcome first. Yet there was no good in being cynical about him. Poets were different. This morning he'd quoted Goethe at her. Now he was trying to be a responsible human being. He was at home. She was at work, except she wasn't: she was in this fucking surgery.

She slumped down in a corner. She must try to stop her mind jumping about like a gadfly. She put her hand to her temples, closed her eyes and tried to do calm breathing. It hadn't been too bad in the morning – the kids had been keen – but it had been building. That was why she needed the Valium.

She opened her eyes and her attention was caught by a screen in the far corner of the room. Two children, one black, one white, stared at her; above them, written large, www.missingkids.com, and below, their names, age, height and colouring. She could hardly read this because her eyes were blurring with tears.

It was impossible to restrain herself then. She squeezed her eyes shut and painful sobs shook her hunched figure.

She felt a hand on her shoulder. 'I'm sorry.' She recognized the receptionist's voice. What did she have to be sorry about, uncaring bitch?

'The doctor will see you now.'

But Eve found she couldn't stand. Nor could she stop crying. The receptionist, kinder now, patted her shoulder, then went away.

Another figure came to sit beside her. She didn't look up but she could tell it was a man. A man's voice: 'I'm Dr Khan.' Not her doctor. But, then, when did she see her doctor?

'Can I help you?' A gentle voice.

She looked up but could hardly see him through her tears. 'My son's missing and I need some Valium.'

'Let me take you to my room.' Between them, the doctor and the receptionist (now caring but it had taken Eve's collapse to make her so) led her to a small room. It seemed to be underground, like a burial place. They sat her in a chair.

In front of her Dr Khan's computer glinted. He was looking her up. Perhaps he would see Dan's notes too. In a muddled way, she pictured Dan's face coming up on his screen under that sign: www.missingkids.com. The doctor was giving her time to compose herself so she tried her best, although her thoughts seemed to fly away from her every time she got hold of them.

Then her phone rang. She scrabbled frantically in her bag, tears started again. Calmly, the doctor took the bag from her, found the phone and handed it to her.

'Hello.'

It was Max. His voice sounded distant, only just recognizable.

'What?' He was clearly asking her a question but her brain was failing to deal with it. 'What?'

He repeated the question.

'His toothbrush?' Where is Dan's toothbrush? Certainly, he had gone mad. She was mad herself so why not he?

'May I?' Dr Khan took the mobile from her. He listened gravely. 'The police are there. Nothing bad has happened. They have no news of any sort. But, as a matter of routine, they want an item belonging to your son from which his DNA may be taken. A toothbrush is usually suggested.'

'A toothbrush,' repeated Eve, helplessly. She pictured Dan's rather large white teeth. He had strong teeth.

'Yes,' said Dr Khan. 'Unfortunately your husband can't find your son's toothbrush.'

Eve felt this was beyond her. Where was Dan's toothbrush? In the bathroom. In his sponge bag. In the cabinet over the sink. It was impossible to take this request seriously. She might begin to laugh. It would be better than thinking about Dan's DNA.

The doctor seemed to understand her thinking because he spoke firmly into the phone. 'I suggest you wait for this information until your wife gets home.'

Soon he had turned off the phone and handed it back to Eve. She dropped it into her bag and sat up a little straighter, but how could she go back to work? On the other hand, who would tell the kids? There was no one. The panic that had only just subsided raised its head like a gleaming-eyed monster ready to sink in its teeth. 'I do need some Valium,' she whispered breathlessly.

'Yes. Of course.' He looked at his screen. 'I see you've been taking it for some years.'

'On and off.' He couldn't deny her. It was true she'd first started taking it as a teenager. About Dan's age, in fact. She'd been having panic attacks. Not able to breathe. Sweat pouring off. Her drama training had cured that eventually.

The doctor handed her a prescription. 'If there's any way I can help with your son . . . I presume he's one of our patients.' He was tentative, probably afraid she'd freak out again. But holding the piece of green paper had already made her calmer. Addict with a bottle.

'He'll probably walk back in.' She paused. The doctor was bent sympathetically towards her. He was handsome, his skin golden and unlined, his eyes golden, too, with thick black lashes. 'Last night on

86

the net we discovered that. One hundred thousand kids go missing each year. Most come back, sooner or later.'

'Sooner, I trust.'

Who were they fooling, him so polite, her so hopeful? She supposed it was civilization, better than screaming.

Weak at the knees but with some dignity, she hoped, Eve said thank you very much and she'd be in touch if she needed help but goodbye for now, and left the room. She went through the surgery, nodding thanks at the receptionist, mostly in order to avoid www.missingkids.com; people were gathering in the waiting area now, people with new emergencies.

Down the road, hot and noisy, and she began to think of her kids again, the boys and girls with recognized problems, a risk for others, at risk themselves. Perhaps she'd tell them about Dan. He was in their territory, dropping out of society. Although one part of her mind knew it was a crazy idea, she began to imagine they could find him. Much better than the police, better than anyone. Suddenly her work, which had seemed an impossible burden a few minutes before, appeared as the answer to her problems.

She was walking quickly, doing a little controlled breathing, swinging her arms. Ibou and Andy would get a line on Dan. Her mood soared to absurd optimism. She hardly needed the Valium, but she'd pick it up all the same. She'd need it for facing Max, if nothing else. Poet nothing. Bastard. Bastard! She entered the chemist so fiercely that her bag struck an old lady who tottered reproachfully.

'Sorry,' said Eve, but not too abjectly because she needed to sustain her new-found energy.

Max lay on the sofa, looking up at the white ceiling. He imagined clouds, silver-tinged with purple. The two policemen had been kind, informing him carefully of the procedures to be followed. Where was the missing boy's mother, they had enquired early on, with tactful, noncommittal faces. Perhaps they thought there was no mother or none in residence, yet she had reported him missing.

'My wife's at work.' He didn't explain further. He understood that they believed mothers had the answers to their questions. After all, he hadn't been able to find Dan's toothbrush. 'Perhaps he took it with him.' That was what he'd suggested but they'd made no comment.

Now he lay on the sofa waiting for Eve. He hadn't eaten all day and supposed he should go shopping for some supper. Earlier, he'd found the CD of Schubert's Erlking and played it several times before the reproach became unbearable. Silence seemed preferable, but it was the silence of a big city where millions of people lived in unknowing noisy proximity. Goethe's imagined father explained his son's terror with natural phenomena: a wisp of fog, some rustling leaves. He must contend with an urban conglomeration. So easy for one young son to be swallowed up in a world teeming with Erlkings, real and imagined.

The ceiling had changed colour, the sun outside reflecting washes of yellow and pink. No need to imagine clouds. It was beautiful with no help from him.

CHAPTER FIFTEEN

Dan was stupidly relieved when he saw Si up by the wall, stooping and placing the stones just as he had been the day before. It was stupid because he'd begun to fear, as he retraced his steps across the fields, that Si wasn't real, that he'd made him up, that there would be no one there – just a wall. No old man. Sun, wind, fossils, maybe, or perhaps he'd made those up. Stupid. But he'd become more and more jumpy, heart uneven, startled by birds rising out of the stalks, nearly petrified by a pheasant that had crashed out from some rough grass almost under his feet. Stupid. Mocked by bobbing and diving rabbits. Wanting, needing the old man. Stupid.

'Hi!' he shouted, and waved.

The figure continued in its same rhythm. All men of his age were deaf. Dan felt warmly towards him and approached closely. 'Hi!' he shouted again.

Si stopped working, turned and lifted a hand in salute. Dan remembered that he operated at his own slower speed.

'There you are, son.' The old man spoke slowly too, and Dan thought that these would be the first words this morning for both of them. Si hadn't smiled but Dan could tell he was pleased to see him.

'We've got the sun again.' Dan spoke cheerfully, his voice loud on the soft air.

'Another day or two,' agreed Si. He looked at the wall and then back at Dan. 'They've let you off early at the farm, then?'

'Nothing for me to do there.' True enough, thought Dan, unashamedly.

'Plenty to do here.'

'Yes.' It was a moderate answer for how Dan felt about being on the hillside, with the air like champagne and the golden wall and a task to perform properly with a friend. 'Harmony': that was the word that came to mind, harmony in his body, in his mind, between him and the old man, between him and the beautiful world around him. He wanted to shout, 'Harmony! I've found harmony!' Instead he scratched his bites.

Si had already turned back to the stones. He explained the likely ones he'd lined up and the approximate order he planned to use them. 'Got to slow down today. Heart.' He tapped his chest. 'Likes to let me know he's there.'

Dan didn't mind going slower. It gave him time to stop and look at the sky with a very few clouds stretched thin and far away. He felt his heart beat slowly in time with Si's. Once an aeroplane passed over, so high it made no sound. He imagined the passengers packed tight inside and felt sorry for them. The shadows fell the other way from the afternoon before. As the hour passed he saw them shrinking and thought that at midday they would disappear altogether.

Well before then, Si turned to Dan. 'You didn't think I'd forget the dowsing, did you?' He wiped his face with his hand. 'Tea break first.' He went over to his Thermos.

Dan stared down at the stone he was cradling; it was a big one, warm and rough, paler on the surface that had lain on the inside of the wall, darker on the outside with a greenish hint of moss or lichen. It must rain up here, thought Dan, unbelieving.

They shared the mug, Dan at first surprised by the sweetness of the tea, then liking it. He was hungry all the time and this lessened the need.

'Now let's find a likely place.'

The old man led off down the slope of the field. He'd unravelled from his pocket a piece of string with a small stone tied on the end. He balled it in his big hand and gave Dan an encouraging wink. 'Maybe we'll find the sea under our feet.'

After a few more minutes, he stopped, randomly as it seemed to Dan. 'You want a go?'

'You first.'

Si let the stone drop like an unwound yo-yo. It hung there, stilled by his fingers.

'Let's see.'

Very slowly at first, the stone began to swing. Dan watched the fingers holding it, delicately for such a large hand. He'd always enjoyed discovering a conjuring trick's secret; he was assuming this was a trick. He looked at the old man's face and something changed. Si's bright blue eyes in their web of lines and creases were fixed on the stone; his whole attention was absorbed by it but he himself was calm, unmoving. He was waiting to see what happened, waiting as an outsider.

The momentum of the swing increased but not by very much. Si pulled up the stone.

'Not much here. Or the water's deep.' He walked on, heading downwards, and Dan followed. Soon he stopped again. 'Your turn.' He handed the string to Dan.

Dan examined it, an ordinary piece of string looped round an ordinary stone. 'Go on, then. Let it drop. See if you get anything.'

Dan felt the seriousness of the occasion. He remembered adventure stories where the whole plot, life and death, hinged on finding water. He knew he was frowning and tried to imitate Si and become a calm channel for whatever might be under the ground. In his mind's eye, he saw the fossils he'd found the day before. They'd come from the ground millions of years ago, under the sea. He knew Si was watching him but he paid no attention, half shutting his eyes. The sun beat on his head.

He felt the weight of the stone, dangling lifeless. Then a small movement reached his fingers. He opened his eyes just to confirm that it had started swinging. It swung harder and higher. Dan felt as if its power could lift him into the air.

'There you are.' The old man's voice came from far away. 'You've got the gift. They say anyone can feel it but I say you need the gift.'

Dan guessed he was smiling like a maniac. At the peak of the swing, he grabbed the stone and threw it to Si. 'I did it! I did it!'

Si bent stiffly to pick up the stone, which had fallen at his feet, and pocketed it. He looked at Dan with approval. 'You're a good lad.' He started walking back to the wall. 'You should see some that come to the farm. Smoking, drinking. Don't want to know what the world looks like outside those computers of theirs.'

Dan didn't want to think about other people. He hadn't missed his computer one bit. *Sufficient unto the day.* The words came into his head from somewhere or other. 'Sufficient unto the day.' Repeated out loud, they were just as good. He began to run up the hill, overtaking Si, who smiled after the yelling boy. 'Sufficient unto the day! Sufficient unto the day!'

It was hard after such euphoria to return to the slow pace of wall building. After half an hour or so, during which Dan always had the stone ready for Si before he was ready for it, the old man stopped, wiped his sweating face with his hand and said, 'You go off for a bit. Use up some of that energy.'

Slightly disconcerted by his dismissal, Dan bounded away obediently and soon found himself in another large, sloping field with several left-over bales of straw. They were almost his height but he chose the nearest and scrambled on to it as he had the day before. 'King of the castle! Sufficient unto the day!' He stood up and spread his arms. Then it began to roll, gathering speed. Like some crazy circus performer, he tried to move his feet fast enough to keep pace but he'd never been a gymnast and once again he was thrown off on to the hard ground.

Winded, he lay back and looked at the sky. The brightness of the sun at full height was slightly shielded from his eyes by a veil of white. Then he saw two black specks, the spy-plane birds, directly above. As before, he felt a shiver of anxiety.

Slowly he got up and, picking off pieces of straw, sticking to him like burrs, he started back to the wall.

Si was sitting in the narrow shadow of the wall. He had his lunch out, although he didn't seem to be eating. 'What was that you were shouting out?'

'"Sufficient unto the day".' Dan sat down beside him. He was tired, could have gone to sleep. His body felt jarred and bruised from its impact with the sun-baked ground. He eyed Si's sandwich.

'Thought as much. We were brought up to learn our Bible. I don't expect you know the rest.' He recited, ' "Take therefore no thought for the morrow: for the morrow shall take thought for the things of itself. Sufficient unto the day is the evil thereof." '

The word 'evil' reminded Dan of the two birds, hovering above. He looked up for them but they'd gone.

'Have a sandwich,' offered the old man. 'I've no appetite today.' He watched as Dan wolfed it down. 'Go on. Have the other. It'll only go to waste.'

So Dan ate that too and felt much better. He decided to describe the spy-birds to the old man.

He listened in his careful way, nodded once or twice. 'Buzzards. There's a pair lives in these skies. Useful members of society, that's what they are. Scavengers. See a dead animal on the road one day, gone the next, that's the buzzards' work. Eyesight like a telescope. Pick off the living, too, if they spot the right kind. A weak lamb, baby rabbits on the run.'

'I don't like them,' muttered Dan.

'Sixty-inch wing tip to wing tip,' said the old man, admiringly. 'Don't always come off best, though. Had a ringside view once of a real ding-dong between a raven and a buzzard. Buzzard twice the size of the raven, but slower. You wouldn't think it the way they drop from the sky for a kill but that raven twisted and turned so as the eye could hardly follow. Like watching those wartime planes, dogfights they called them. By rights should have been birdfights.'

Watching Si's blue eyes brighten at the memory, Dan wondered whether to tell him how he had feared the watchful gaze of the buzzards. He guessed it would sound silly, childish. Instead he said, 'I'd like to have seen that,' which wasn't really true.

'Birds of prey,' continued the old man, thoughtfully. 'I used to have binoculars and watched all sorts. Knew all the names. *Buteo buteo.* That's the posh name for a buzzard. Doesn't sound like it somehow. More like one of those foreigners you hear on the radio, trying to sort out the world. Buzzard. A good English word.'

Dan wanted to stop talking about buzzards. The faint mewing cry he'd heard the day before must have caught in his ears because he could hear it now. He stood up.

'Want to get going, do you?' The old man stared up at him.

Dan thought he looked tired, older than before. 'I don't mind.'

'I tell you what. You have a go.' He added, as if to himself, 'I'm not so bright today.' He waved a hand. 'That's right. Pick up that big one on the top. She's a beauty.' He roused himself a little and watched as Dan placed it first in one part of the wall, then another.

'Just the job,' he said eventually. He advised a bit more as Dan lifted one stone after another. Soon he had more confidence – he'd watched the old man at it long enough – and a whole section grew under his hands.

When he next looked down, Si's eyes were closed, his mouth open. He was asleep, snoring gently. Although it was hot, Dan carried on, pleased with his achievement, looking forward to the old man's praise, 'Just the job.'

Now and again, he heard the old man's snores break their rhythm but on the whole it was a gentle background to the knock of stone on stone. After a while he stopped to study his hands, which were beginning to hurt; the skin was red and grazed in one or two places, not like Si's brown leathery palms, as good as gloves.

He glanced back at him and saw that he was sleeping so deeply he'd slipped sideways. It looked a bit uncomfortable.

'Si.' He went over, crouched down and touched his shoulder, expecting his eyes to open. In the heat, a cold terror made his vision blur. He'd been here before. Someone needing help. Only him to provide it. A nightmare deserved. The old man gave a snort but his eyes didn't open, and he slumped further.

Dan sat back on his heels and stared at him. 'Si,' he said again, but hopelessly. Something had happened to him. He guessed he was unconscious. What he needed was a doctor. Otherwise. Dan turned his head and stared round vaguely at the wide, empty field and above it the great blue sky, still thinly covered by a white veil of cloud. He half expected to see the buzzards floating above, waiting, but there was nothing.

Dan looked at the old man again. He was a great big chap, no way to carry or even drag him. And where would he drag him to? He needed help. What he needed was two men in green jumpsuits who leapt out of a chequered ambulance with a stretcher and life-saving equipment. Dan looked round the field again but this time more wildly before he got the answer: run back to the limo, find his mobile and dial 999. He should have done that before.

CHAPTER SIXTEEN

The boy felt like a scarecrow running across the fields, arms and legs too thin and uncoordinated. The faster he tried to move, the slower he seemed to go, once even tripping himself and falling into a bed of nettles. He knew he was in a panic. It was as if anyone he got close to – Ru, the old man – was at risk. And he couldn't save them. He ran faster and this time caught his foot in a rabbit hole. He fell heavily, twisting his ankle. One of his hands had been jabbed by a sharp stone; when he held it up, blood trickled down his wrist. He sniffed self-pityingly and felt like crying, except he kept seeing Si propped up against the wall.

Now he walked – or hobbled, as his ankle sent stabbing pains up his leg. He was hot, his T-shirt clinging damply to his back. It struck him that he probably stank, not having used any deodorant. His head felt boiled and itchy, itchy and dirty. He was a mess. But at least he could carry on, find that mobile, make that call.

Even though he was so hot, the air was cooling a bit; all kinds of birds had appeared, flickering and gossiping in the hedgerows. The scents of the ground and wild undergrowth were stronger. Once he trod on a puffy green plant that smelt like thyme – Eve liked using thyme – and once on a flaccid pale plant that whiffed of garlic, which Eve used most of all. A sweeter smell wafted from a ragged bunch of pale yellow roses growing out of a hedge. Gasping for breath, Dan stopped for a moment. He told himself that the countryside was still good and he was part of it. The old man was strong and part of the countryside too. Everything would be all right.

By the time he topped another hill and saw the limousine below, the shadows were longer and his legs were shaking as well as painful. His bites itched terribly. A few were bleeding where he'd scratched too hard. He scrambled down the hill, half blinded with sweat and the urgency to get there.

The door of the car was open already so he plunged in, an image of a badger into a hole. It seemed almost totally dark as he scrabbled round on the floor. He felt a nail break and heard himself mutter, 'Fuck. Fuck. Fuck.' His voice was hoarse and strange. His fingers had turned to claws, scrabbling among dirt, grit, bits of dead things. He felt wet on his cheeks and realized he was crying.

All the time he pictured the old man, alone against the wall he'd built. Perhaps he'd stopped breathing already. His image merged with another, the nightmare that tortured his sleep, a young boy hanging from a rope, eyes bulging, tongue protruding. Alone too.

'Where are you?' he screamed, meaning the mobile. He thought of home, his mum and dad.

'This what you're after?'

It was a nasty, mocking voice, which at first he thought was in his head. He backed up, hit the side of the car, pulled himself on to the seat, looked up.

A face outside the limo smiled, leered mockingly. A hand came up and dangled a mobile. 'Yours?' asked the voice. 'And this?' Another hand dangled his watch.

'Yes. Yes.' He didn't have time to be frightened or ask questions. He just needed that mobile. He lunged forward to grab it.

'In quite a state, aren't we?' The hand whisked away the mobile and the face, now attached to a man, young, dressed in jeans and a sleeveless T-shirt, jumped back.

'Please. I need it. A friend . . . a friend's ill.'

'Need. Need. Need,' returned the mocking voice. 'A friend. Whose friend? Not my friend.'

Dan managed to get himself out of the car. He didn't think of the tears running down his face or his filthy state or his agonizing ankle. He began to plead, eyes on the mobile, not on the man. Perhaps he could grab it and run but the man looked strong and fit.

'My friend's really bad. I need to get help quickly.'

'Dying, is she, your friend? What have you been up to? Naughty boy, are you? Gone too far with fun and games?'

'No. No. It's an old man.' He was almost on his knees. 'I think he's had a heart attack. He needs an ambulance. I need to dial 999.'

'Need. Need. Need. Here we go again. You need but what do I get out of it?'

Now Dan looked at the face and saw the small eyes and the big mouth and the greedy, stupid look. There were tattoos coming out of his T-shirt up his neck; snakes curled over his shaven head. 'It's my mobile,' he said, but his voice was weak and unconvincing.

'I'll tell you what.' The man was higher up on the slope of the hill and looked big as well as menacing. 'We'll make a bargain. I let you make your call and you get the fuck out of *my* limousine.'

'Yes! Yes!' Dan hardly listened to the bargain.

'Catch.' The man threw him the mobile and laughed derisively as it dropped at Dan's feet.

He picked it up, turned it on with trembling fingers and saw there was scarcely any charge left and almost no signal. He began to pray inwardly – he'd never prayed before in his life – *dear God let this work,* – and pressed in 999.

'Emergency Services. Which service?'

The efficient woman's voice threw him so that he was silent while she repeated her message.

'Ambulance,' he shouted. He tried not to shout. 'I need an ambulance.' He heard the man's laughter. He was sweating so much he could hardly hold the mobile. Despairingly, he saw there was no juice left.

'Ambulance. How can we help?'

'There's an old man. I th-think he's had a h-heart attack.' He was stuttering, hardly able to speak. The sound of his own jumping heart and the man's laughter was blocking his ears.

'What's the address?'

He almost gave up then. How do you describe a field in the middle of nowhere? All he knew was the name of the town where the train brought him.

'What address?' repeated the voice, an efficient man's voice this time.

'He's in a field.'

'A field?'

'Yes.' He felt frantic again. He named the town his train had arrived in. 'A few miles from there.' East, west, south, north? He'd looked at the sun often enough. He should be able to tell. He tried to

97

think back to his walk from the town and then his walk to the old man but it was all muddled in his head.

'Are you with him?'

'No. I . . .' How to explain? 'I had to come back for my mobile.'

'How old are you?' The voice was kindly enough. It made Dan feel like crying all over again.

He tried harder. 'Not far from a farm that has a Maize Maze. If you ask them.' Why couldn't he remember Si's surname?

'Or, if you stay put, we can locate you and you can lead us to him.'

'Locate me,' stuttered Dan, trying to grasp the implication. The police could find out where he was. He remembered it from movies. Big, safe men in uniform or pressed boiler-suits would rescue Si and him too. He would be found, taken home. It didn't seem such a bad idea.

At that moment, the phone was whipped from his hand. He hadn't heard the man coming. He danced around him, throwing up the phone and catching it, pretending to head it, drop it, kick it.

Weakly, Dan didn't even make an attempt to get it back, not even when the man came close and held it up to his face. He smelt of drink and cigarettes.

'You're no fun.' Bored of his game, the man glanced at the phone. 'You were having me on, weren't you?'

'What do you mean?'

'It's off.'

'It needs charging.'

'Still with your needs, are you?' Disgustedly, the man put the mobile into his pocket.

Dan wanted to sit down. He felt immensely tired. He wondered if the ambulance men would find Si. He knew he should be frightened of the man in front of him. In London, he was always aware of men like him, gave them a wide berth, assumed they carried a knife. What had happened to his own knife? Not in his pockets. Eve always said, 'Give them everything you've got. Whatever you do, don't stand up to them.' He'd followed her advice a couple of times. Lost two mobiles that way, a little money. He hadn't expected that sort of person in the countryside. It had unnerved him. He hadn't got his defences up.

'What are you looking at me like that for?'

'Nothing,' said Dan, avoiding eye contact. *Confrontation kills*: a policeman had come to school and told them that.

'So what are you doing in my limo?' asked the man, more aggressively. His accent was London, with something country too.

'Nothing,' said Dan. 'I've got to sit down. Take anything you want of mine,' he added, as an afterthought, and sat down.

'What do you think I am? A fucking thief?'

Dan thought of pointing out he had his mobile in one pocket and his watch in the other but knew it wouldn't be a good idea. 'Just sharing,' he said.

'Are you taking the piss?'

'No,' said Dan. His tiredness overwhelmed even his fear, although he was still shaking, he noticed. He half closed his eyes and pictured Si being lifted tenderly by four strong arms. He'd done his best for him.

The man went into the car. He returned with the backpack, shook it violently upside down till everything dropped out. 'Share,' he said, picking up the remaining banana, then dropping it again and jumping on it till mush squeezed out at either end.

Dan turned his head away. He saw the two fossils where the man must have thrown them out of the limo. The sun was dropping fast and the grass was already damp. He vaguely wondered whether he should go, leave his things, head back to Si and maybe join the ambulance men. The trouble was, his legs felt like jelly and something told him that running away from this gorilla – he said the word inside his head with relish – this gorilla wouldn't let him go. He had to wait him out, let him have his fun.

'What's this?' He was holding up the jar of Marmite.

'Marmite,' said Dan.

'Marmite, is it? I'd say it's more like a fucking grenade.'

While he was speaking and before Dan could duck, the man hurled the jar in his direction. There was a sickeningly loud crack as it hit Dan just above his right eye. The pain was immediate and devastating. He fell backwards clasping his face. Bright lights danced around him punctuated by wriggling black lines. He heard laughter and yodelling cries of triumph.

'Howzat? I didn't know my own strength, did I? Never taught to duck, that's certain. That'll teach you to come poking your nose into other people's business . . .'

His voice faded as Dan realized he was going to vomit. It came out in bitter strings of liquid. Some came out of his nose and his eyes ran.

'Disgusting, aren't you?' The man was standing over him.

Dan wondered if this was where he got finished off or, worse still, tortured, like in the movies he didn't want to watch but other boys talked about at school. His head ached dreadfully and he could feel a swelling starting round his eye. Maybe a bone was broken. He put his hands over his face and tried not to cry.

'So, what's your name? What are you doing here? And how did you fucking get here?'

'Dan. Walked.' It hurt to open his mouth. The man leant closer to hear him. His smell was powerful. He was sweating heavily.

'Dan, I'm Vinny.' He held out a hand, presumably in mockery. Dan put out his own hand with an effort. 'So why are you here, Danny boy?'

There was no answer to this one. Dan hung his head and tried not to think about being sick again.

'I know what. You're a runaway, aren't you? Left your mum and dad for a bit of freedom.' His voice, if not friendly, held a certain amount of understanding.

'Yes,' mumbled Dan. The pain was cracking his skull like someone was whacking him with a bat.

'Hey, that's some eye you're building.' He seemed pleased at the sight, no longer ferocious. He went back to the car and returned with a can of beer, some matches and another packet. Dan wasn't seeing too well. 'Share,' he said. 'Beer or spliff?'

'I don't feel well.'

'Make you feel better.' Vinny opened the beer and took a swig. He crouched on the grass. 'Be my guest.' He began to roll a joint. The air around them was damp and cool and sweet-smelling. And there was a new scent. After he'd puffed a bit, he handed the joint to Dan. It seemed to be an overture of friendship, as if he could afford to be generous after he'd established his superiority. Dan had never smoked dope but didn't dare say no. Besides, he'd read it took pain away. He puffed, coughed, which made his head hurt more, puffed, puffed again.

'Come on now, share.' Vinny took it back from him but not roughly. 'I know about runaways. I was one, see.' He said it confidingly. 'Not once but over and over.' He paused for several deep drags at the joint. 'How old do you think I am?'

'I don't know.' The joint had made him feel woozy. Better. He took another drag while Vinny turned his attention to the beer, pouring it into his open mouth from a height. 'Twenty-eight?'

Vinny laughed so hard that beer splashed out of his mouth. 'What do you think I am? Ancient? I'm nineteen years of age April past.'

'Nineteen,' repeated Dan, dragging deeply, head spinning.

'Nineteen it is. And how many times have I been inside?'

'Inside where?'

'Inside where? Inside, inside. You're a joker. And give me my smoke. Greedy bastard, aren't you?' He snatched the joint.

Prison. Inside prison, that was what he meant. So what? Dan felt his thought processes slowing down. He lay back on the grass. His fear, his anxiety about the old man, the anxiety he carried around with him all the time about what had happened to Ru seemed to be floating above him, not gone entirely but weightless.

'Eleven! Eleven times.' Vinny's harsh voice floated somewhere above him too. 'Now you may call me a liar but it's God's own truth, not that I believe in the fucker. Do you want me to tell you the establishments wherein I resided?'

'Yes,' said Dan. What he wanted to do was curl up in the limo and go to sleep while he felt okay, while he wasn't frightened. He wished Vinny would vaporize.

'First time I was thirteen, in care, not going to school, nicked a mobile phone once in a while, gave a bit of grievous . . .'

Dan stopped listening. Vinny, clearly interested in what he was saying, droned on, names and places and things he'd done, none of which seemed worse to Dan than throwing a jar of Marmite at a boy who was doing you no harm. He thought he was like that character in the poem, the Ancient Mariner who lies in wait to catch people as they come out of church and then bores them silly with history. *By thy long grey beard and glittering eye, / Now wherefore stopp'st thou me?*

'And Feltham! Feltham! Feltham!' This triple flourish seemed to be the finale to the speech. 'So, eleven times in six years. *Guinness Book of Records*, I'd say.'

'Yes,' said Dan, coming upright gingerly. He needed another drag of the joint but he could see it, just a stub on the grass. He supposed he might have been more impressed by Vinny's record if Martha hadn't worked in a prison. She had told him once that half of the men weren't bad enough to be there and the other half were mad so they shouldn't be there either. Then she took it back a bit, saying there were villains but not anything like as many as the papers said. Best not to tell Vinny about Martha. 'Can I have a swig?' He leant forward and tapped the can of beer.

'Fun-loving fucker, aren't you? Not planning to go home for a bit, then?'

Dan took this as permission to grab the can. Vinny watched him. 'Mind you don't chuck up again. Let's say I don't like you here. Do for now, a bit of sharing, best weed in the West Country, can't say I haven't been generous. Make up for turning you into a potato head. Bit of an apology. But this is my space, isn't it? Can't do nothing in the hostel, can I? No smoking anything rich, no booze, no fucking your girl. No life, you might say. No life at all . . .'

Dan understood Vinny had started on another speech. As this one seemed to concern him, he tried to listen but the words rolled over him.

'See, I got a shock yesterday, didn't I, when I saw someone had moved into my space? My home, dare I say it. So I nicked his mobile. Your mobile, in other words. I reasoned, he's passing through, he won't be stopping, not in my space, my home. So, fuck me, wasn't I surprised when I trot along today hoping for a bit of peace to enjoy my spliff – I might have had a girl with me, just get that scene – and there's his, that's your, things all still there and then, fuck me further, don't you come cheerily over the hill and bowl up to *my* limousine for all the world as if you had ownership when I knew I had prior claims? Prior claims!'

He almost shouted the last two words, causing Dan to look at his face, which he hadn't for some time. He was struck again by the aggressive stupidity and his fear began to trickle back. So did the headache and a pain in his wrenched ankle. 'Sorry,' he mumbled.

'Sorry isn't enough. Not enough and not the point. The point is, I want you out of here. Got it?'

'Yes,' said Dan. He tried to clear his mind. 'Do you mean now?'

'Now, meaning what?' Vinny had pulled another joint out of his pocket, ready rolled.

Dan watched fixedly as he lit it. He smoked luxuriantly. 'I mean, could I stay tonight?' He looked up at the far hill; only the very top still glowed in the rays of the setting sun.

'Tonight? You're asking me to validate rental of my property for one night, this night, when you've already taken two, at least two, without a by-your-leave?'

'I didn't know.'

'It's a question of whether you can afford to pay. One official night and two stolen, which makes a night and a half. Got much money?'

He didn't wait for an answer and Dan guessed he'd probably taken what he had anyway. Obviously, he was on to another riff.

'So, let's see. One illegal night, three for two illegal, which makes four. Hotel White Lincoln, fully equipped, scenically situated, running water en suite. I'd say fifty smackers per night, which makes a clean two hundred upfront with VAT and service additional as per usual. Yes, a grand total of £260.32p, which rounded up, makes a cool three hundred. Think you can afford it? Rich boy like you, no problem. You tell me.'

Dan was in no condition to tell him anything. Apart from the content of Vinny's speech, which was inexplicable enough – he seemed to be using some strange hotel jargon – he had delivered it in a pattern of stop-go, with long pauses where there shouldn't have been any and some words torn into two or even three with gaps in between.

'A drag?' pleaded Dan, reaching towards the spliff.

'Babies don't get second goes.' Vinny swatted him away easily. As he moved, Dan saw his expression change, something suspicious and dangerous in his eyes. 'What you doing here anyway? What are you doing?'

Suddenly he seemed angrier than he'd been since the beginning. He looked round wildly at the darkening fields. 'Got someone with you, have you? Up there? In that old barn? What's a boy like you doing here?'

'Nothing,' muttered Dan. How could Vinny be afraid of him? But that was what it seemed to be.

Vinny took hold of his shoulders, shook him roughly, then let him go equally abruptly. Dan held his head to try to stem the pain.

'You know what happens if they find me,' hissed Vinny, his face snake-like with venom. 'Inside. Bang up. No questions. Feltham, I'm on the way. Do you know what that means. Of course you know. You're a snitch, aren't you? Snitch.' He approached again and this time Dan tried to move away.

'No. No. I didn't. I don't.' There didn't seem to be any useful words in his head. To his relief, Vinny's expression changed again. Throwing the remains of the spliff on the grass, he turned away from Dan and began a jumbled conversation with himself.

'Got to get back. Go. Get back in time. What time? Don't want to be out late. After time. Bad news. Got to go. Now. Go.' He began to walk in a circle, head down, having apparently forgotten about Dan.

Through Dan's own muzzy brain passed the thought that Vinny had smoked the majority of two joints and that now he didn't know what he was up to. This was the moment to make his getaway. But get away where? Besides, he could barely stagger, let alone run. He had a raging thirst too. He stared at Vinny, who was like a mad dog chasing his tail. Then he was facing him again. His eyes bloodshot, unfocused.

'Got to go. See.' He straightened up and began to walk away from Dan, down the hill in the direction of the old lane that he himself had followed to the limousine. It seemed he was leaving.

Dan watched him till he was out of sight, then scrabbled round the grass till he found the stub of the joint and, by some lucky chance, the box of matches too. After he'd smoked it to his fingers, he sat back on the damp grass and tried to understand what was happening. But all he could think about was how thirsty he was and the soft seat in the back of the limo. Darkness was closing in. He needed to find his bottle and get to the stream, then back to the car. Vinny had gone, he told himself, gone to his hostel, and there was only night to fear.

He understood the sounds of the countryside: the birds returning to the trees, the hoot of the owl that had frightened him that first night but now seemed like a friendly watchman.

He bent over the stream and washed cool water over his trembling hands, his battered face and head, filled his bottle and drank the lot, filled it again, watched the running water. A calmness came to comfort him. Out here, hidden by undergrowth, he was alone and safe. Briefly, he considered the old man. With any luck he would survive. Thanks to him. This time he'd tried.

Dan walked slowly back to the limo. His head spun less but it ached more; so did his ankle. He needed sleep, nothing else. When he woke, he would decide the next step. Survival, commanded his brain. Sleep. Survival.

CHAPTER SEVENTEEN

Max felt happier on the end-of-day warm streets. Night had fallen as he walked but if anything the pavements had become more crowded. At first he'd felt a numb kind of despair, mitigated by relief at escaping the flat and Eve. Eve, he'd tried to remind himself, was a drama queen; Dan had only been gone two days. Two days was nothing, so the police had told him, hardly worth bothering about, certainly not worth them bothering about beyond routine. Thousands of children Dan's age went missing each day for all sorts of reasons, they continued cheerily, and almost all of them came back. Sooner or later. That was contributed by the second police-man, who had taken things a bit more seriously and asked for the toothbrush. That had been a concession when he'd insisted that Dan wasn't the running-away sort, more withdrawn and bookish. The idea of books had obviously amazed both of them. Then he hadn't been able to find his son's toothbrush, didn't even know what colour it was.

'In my experience, mums and dads don't know the half of what goes on in their kids' heads,' commented the first policeman, clearly implying that a dad who couldn't locate his son's toothbrush was well out of touch. Of course he hadn't told them he hadn't been home the last couple of weeks.

Towards the end of the interview, which lasted scarcely half an hour, when he was already beaten down by their attitude, the first policeman, already standing, said in a slightly more lively tone, 'Of course, if we have reason to believe there's any danger to the missing person . . .'

'What do you mean?' Max had interrupted, exasperated. 'A boy out in the streets must be in danger.'

'The super means specific, identified danger,' explained the second policeman soothingly, although he also stood.

'Like a note saying, "Hi, Dad, I've gone off with an axe murderer"?'

'Ha, ha.' The first policeman had laughed. 'That sort of thing. You'll be assigned a named officer. Let him or her know if anything comes up.'

'We're on your side, you know,' added the second policeman, before they both left.

Max knew they were. They were just trying to put things in proportion from their point of view. They'd come quickly, listened carefully and assigned him an officer. When Eve came back and started raving about all the things that could be done and hadn't been, like house-to-house searches and bulletins on the local radio, he'd found himself on the side of the police. 'I expect him to turn up at any moment,' he said, almost believing it.

Then he'd walked outside. House-to-house searches – what a joke! They were surrounded by blocks of flats with single houses filling the occasional gap and most of those had been turned into flats anyway. Eve was constitutionally incapable of thinking calmly. Now, if he could have had a word with Martha, they might get somewhere. However, since he didn't want to reflect on where they'd already got in the last ten days, it seemed best not to follow that line of reasoning.

In fact, as he looked at all the kids out on the street, bare-legged, bare-stomached, bare-chested, enjoying evening freedom, holidays from school, time off work, he began to be more seriously convinced by the police's argument.

Perhaps Dan had gone walkabout; in which case it would do him no favours to find him. He understood that. He did it himself. As a matter of fact, it was what he was doing at that very moment. 'Excuse me.' He stepped aside as two girls burst up on him. Eve's kind of girls, he thought wryly.

Sometimes a man had to escape and Dan was coming up to be a man. His birthday tomorrow. No one seemed to be talking about it and Eve would never believe he knew. Today he'd bought two more books for him. Seamus Heaney's version of *Beowulf* and the *Oedipus* plays. Dramatic stuff. He'd seen the books Dan read and knew he wanted excitement. Not that they talked about it. Not that they ever talked about anything important. Eve threw too big a shadow. Besides, he wasn't a good role model.

He'd reached a pub. Probably been aiming for it all along. The Tippler's Arms. Not that he was much of a tippler. He still prided himself on his powers of observation, noting the detail of people and places. It had become a habit at university when he believed he was destined to be a poet – a published poet, even acclaimed. Now, when he wrote so little, he enjoyed it as an exercise, like an old dancer who still does his pliés. Already his head was filled with pointillist material from this walk. Some he might note down later. He had not totally given up hope.

'Evening, Max, old chap.'

The bartender at the Tippler's Arms knew the names of all his regulars. He was a burly man, an ex-policeman called Larry, whose wife, Cherry, was an ex-singer. They were not your usual pub managers.

'Just a half, Larry.'

'Lucky I don't rely on you to keep me in business.'

Max settled himself at the bar. It was an old-style pub, dark panelling, dimly lit with coloured lights, which he assumed harked back to Cherry's days in the nightclubs. Several tables were filled but most people were drinking outside, enjoying the warm evening. Two young girls dashed in and out, serving them, but Larry stood, avuncular, behind his bar.

'I might need something stronger tonight.'

'How's that?' Larry was a listener, not a talker.

'My boy's gone missing. Third night. Can't be traced.'

Larry's expression didn't change, neither did he move, but Max felt sympathetic vibes coming from him. He heard replayed in his head the hideousness of his statement. A father who'd lost his son. Larry wouldn't read Goethe but he'd understand the feelings.

'A teenager, is he?'

'It's his fourteenth birthday tomorrow.'

'Celebrating with friends?' This was said without irony. Max tried to imagine Dan out on the town, cigarette in one hand, drink in the other, surrounded by his mates, sparky girls, lively boys.

'He's young for his age. Withdrawn.'

'A loner?'

'Bookish.'

'Now that is unusual!'

As Larry turned away to talk to one of the waiters, Max tossed back his drink. If he concentrated on Dan hard enough he might be able to work out what had happened to him. No hope of doing that with Eve around.

Larry returned. 'Break the habit of a lifetime?' He indicated the empty glass.

Max looked at it with surprise; he didn't remember drinking it. 'Why not? Tell me, what would you do in my position? You've had the experience – professionally, I mean.'

'Have the TSG been in?'

Max stared at Larry. His bland bonhomie seemed to have shifted to show something sharper or maybe it was the effect of the incomprehensible letters. 'TSG?'

'The search team. Specially trained. They're like ferrets – up the loft, down the drains. The tangles people get themselves into. You wouldn't believe it. Deviant sex more dangerous than horse-riding. Do you know, I once found a dead prostitute, chained to the bed by her client and no way to free herself after he had a heart attack? A young girl, died of starvation. You can imagine the scene.' He seemed about to launch on anecdotes of grisly deaths before recalling who he was talking to and slipping on his more normal face – mask, as Max now saw it. Did everyone's life contain monstrous experiences?

'Not your boy's category,' said Larry.

'No,' agreed Max. 'The police did search. Just to see if he was hiding, I suppose.'

'They want to find him alive.' Again Larry's face changed expression, this time to a look of nostalgia. 'Go into the bedroom of a missing person, you're searching for his soul. They used to talk about mapping the mind, but I liked to go further.'

Max thought that surely a parent would know better about their child's soul than a policeman off the street. But his confidence was so undermined, he wanted Larry to tell him more. 'Do you think they'll find him?' he asked impulsively.

'I wouldn't give you odds.'

Larry's instant reply punctured Max's tension – he realized he'd been holding his breath – so that he exhaled on a loud gasp.

'Just think of it,' elaborated Larry, leaning forward over the bar.

'There's CCTV everywhere he turns, mobile detectors, ways of finding his every computer message – they took his computer, did they?'

'Not yet.'

'On Facebook, is he?'

Tension began to build in Max again. 'No,' he answered, although he wasn't sure.

'Grooming. That's what they're looking for in the lab. Although it's not a quick or easy job. There's passwords and codes to crack and that's once you've reached the top of the queue.'

'What queue?' asked Max, weakly.

'In the lab. A boy like yours would come well behind a terrorist, for example. In my day, they weren't so bright at the technology but there weren't so many terrorists. Last time I heard it was a week to ten days' waiting.'

Max saw that Larry was getting off on being the police guru. He'd never heard him talk so much. 'You keep in touch, then?'

'Retirement at fifty. Just when you know what's what.'

Max was glad not to be talking about missing persons any more. If he was going to find Dan's soul, he'd better get started. He'd told Eve he'd gone out to look for Dan. But neither of them had mentioned his soul.

Martha and Eve sat in Eve's living room drinking pomegranate and nettle tea. Martha had brought it with her. The landline telephone, two mobiles and the open laptop were together on a table between them. Both of them were dazed with exhaustion, yet shared an air of expectancy.

They looked up as the door to the flat opened. 'Max,' said Eve, reluctantly.

Max came in slowly. He, too, seemed exhausted. He took in the two women's faces turned towards him. 'Nothing,' he said. Did they really believe he could pluck Dan off the street? 'I'm going to get something to eat.' He didn't offer to fetch them anything.

'I knew it was a waste of time.' Eve spoke when he was already halfway out of the room.

Max turned back. 'I had to try.' He went out, as Eve added, 'Dan never wandered about the streets. He had a home.'

Max shut the door behind him. However ridiculous, he would keep searching.

Martha recognized that the atmosphere had changed between her and Eve after Max had come home. They could be sisterly companions in distress when he wasn't around but the moment he came back they were cut off from each other. Max put a sword between them. Let's face it, hardly surprising.

'I'd better go.'

Eve looked up as if to protest, then shook her head. 'Are you going to work tomorrow?'

'It depends when the police want to do their search.'

'First thing – isn't that what they said? I'll tell Max – he can handle it.'

'They can't do both of us first thing.'

'I don't know why they want to do us again. Or you, if it comes to that.'

Martha thought Eve's grumbling, petulant voice brought a sense of normality into the room. She might have been complaining about a parking ticket. She wondered vaguely about the ways of expressing loss and dependency.

She stood up. 'Are *you* going to work?' They had already discussed this several times. Martha thought Eve's decision depended on whether she could get through the day rather than whether she should. In Eve's mind, Max's job, although better paid, was less important. Her kids needed her. Her job was a vocation. Her acting training made her strong, she'd told Martha, and Martha had agreed. The off-duty Eve who showed herself to her sister could no more control a bunch of teenage drop-outs than fly.

'It's just the panic attacks,' said Eve. 'I see his face.'

'Please, Evie,' Martha cut in hastily. Not tonight. 'I'll say goodbye to Max,' she said, as if asking for permission. Eve didn't react but allowed herself to be hugged.

Max was staring into one of the cupboards. He glanced round as Martha came in. She might as well have been Eve. 'I felt like toast and Marmite but there isn't any Marmite.' He pushed around jars and packets. 'Dan liked Marmite.'

'Yes,' agreed Martha. She remembered telling Dan on one of their camping jaunts that explorers took Marmite.

'The policeman asked me what he'd taken. I could do the backpack but I didn't know what was in it. Not really.'

'You suspect he might have taken the Marmite.' On the other hand, she thought, it might have been finished but not replaced while Max was staying in her house. 'We thought he'd taken bananas, bacon, maybe biscuits, which would mean he'd chosen to leave, gone prepared, not been kidnapped or had an accident.'

'I'll ask Martha.'

'You mean Eve,' said Martha. It was not often he mixed up their names. 'I'm going home now.'

Max turned to her. 'The chap who runs my local pub, a retired policeman, as it happens, told me a good policeman tries to understand a missing person's soul.'

'A bit presumptuous,' said Martha.

Max took a step forward, his face flushed. 'If it wasn't for the guilt . . .' He didn't finish the sentence.

Martha retreated. Did he mean guilt in particular because he had been with her when Dan disappeared? Or in general? She suspected the latter. She certainly wasn't going to ask.

'Martha, are you still there?' Eve called, from the sitting room. Her voice was querulous, like a bad-tempered old lady's.

'I'm on my way out,' Martha called back. Once Eve had been told about their mother's death, Martha had been the one to comfort her, to show her how to carry on. Her father had never talked about her mother again. It was not fair of him to make her forever the all-knowing, responsible elder sister. She put her head round the sitting-room door.

'Can I ring you at any time?' Eve asked, still curled up on the sofa.

'Yes,' said Martha. As she left the flat she wondered if her desire for Max was a way of stating her independence from Eve. But by the time she reached her car, she was inclined to think exactly the opposite: it was her way of getting closer to her sister. She thought she wouldn't like to be telling this to a therapist.

Instead, she began to look out for Dan. There were so many boys his kind of height and lanky build, hunched shoulders, in loose

T-shirt and jeans, pale face and fine brown hair. After she'd nearly run a set of lights, she forced herself to change again and think of work.

Had she done a good job with Lee? Would he manage outside? How many more years would she want to spend inside a prison, locked in for up to eight hours a day as effectively as the men? She actually drove past the prison and half wished that, like everyone else on the quiet residential streets, she didn't know what went on inside. It was painful to picture the men, doubled up in their small cells, built a hundred and fifty years ago for single occupancy. They had made a mess of their lives and some of them had done terrible harm. But they dreamt about their girlfriends, their children, their mums, like anyone else. So many of them had been addicted to something or other and would probably get hooked again once they were out.

Lee might make it. He'd educated himself over his years in prison. There was a job lined up, a charity to help him in the first few weeks. Drink had been his problem, not drugs. He wouldn't mess up.

When Martha arrived home, she found three messages on her landline. The first was from the police, announcing the arrival of the search team at eight a.m. the next morning. (Would they be able to detect Max's presence – past presence?) The second was from the prison, informing her that Lee would be released the next morning. The third was from Eve who must have rung as soon as she'd left, saying how much she loved her and relied on her. Yes, thought Martha, and she sighed as she added to herself, And I love you too.

Then she went upstairs to change the sheets on both beds.

Max lay with his arm flung protectively over Eve. He didn't want more and neither, he assumed, judging by her attitude earlier, did she. She slept restlessly, moaning slightly, turning towards him and then away. Before she closed her eyes, she'd whispered, 'I'm glad you're back.' This was unusual, a recognition of the situation that in normal times neither of them dared.

Although he was back, present now in her bed, naked beside her, one day he might have to leave again. He had allowed her to claim him, but never all of him.

He withdrew his arm as she turned again. Perhaps it was too heavy. They lay side by side.

Side by side, their faces blurred,
The earl and countess lie in stone,
Their proper habits vaguely shown
As joint armour, stiffened pleat,
And that faint hint of the absurd –
The little dogs under their feet.

The earl and countess were holding hands, that was the point, across eight centuries – although later Larkin had come to believe that was the invention of a sentimental Victorian restorer.

One day he might go back to Alison. He thought nostalgically of her sunny blondeness, the down on her cheeks. He'd left her precipitately because of Dan. And now Dan's pale, questioning face took over. They were all thinking of Dan. Why had gone? Where had he gone? Most important of all, who was he? Who was – is Dan? *My father, my father* . . . He mustn't sink into the terrors of the imagination.

Alison's image was untouched by his pain. She had her own grief but it was not his and his was not hers; they could have come together in denial.

Aroused by these thoughts, he touched Eve's hip tentatively. She'd always had the softest body, skin more like thick cream than milk. Martha's skin was as pale and translucent as skimmed milk but he didn't want to think about her.

He suspected that Eve was awake but unwilling to admit her desire. She might think it inappropriate. As if sex had anything to do with appropriate behaviour! Even in their worst times, their desire for each other had never failed.

He stroked her hip with his fingers and slowly she turned towards him.

CHAPTER EIGHTEEN

Dan woke up with a lightness of being. He hadn't dreamt of Ru. Ru hadn't reproached him. Ru hadn't reminded him of their unfinished stories and called him to follow.

He opened his eyes and the limo was filled with silver greyness so he assumed the sun hadn't yet risen. In fact, only one eye fully opened; the other felt squeezed by a weight above it. Slowly, he allowed himself to remember Vinny and the Marmite jar. Marmite was supposed to support, not threaten life, he thought, pleased with his irony. He'd done what he'd planned, survived the night. He stretched cautiously, looked out of the fugged-up window at the green world outside. He thought of Si and decided that the old man would have survived too.

All the same, there was another day ahead, no food, Vinny on the warpath, and he hadn't even tested his wrenched ankle. Maybe it was time to go home. No way to ring them now.

He shivered a bit as he pushed open the door. The air didn't feel the same as it had on other mornings; the sun had risen but was mostly hidden behind streaky clouds. On the other hand, his ankle bore his weight well and he noticed a banana Vinny had overlooked lying half under the car. He ate it quickly and drank some water. He picked up the Marmite jar, unscrewed the lid and stuck his finger in. You couldn't blame the jar for a mean dude turning it into an offensive weapon. He licked his finger clean and repeated the process.

A little way from the limo, he saw the two fossils he'd brought back from the wall that first day. They'd have made good missiles if he'd been thinking that way. Gingerly, he touched his face. Wouldn't mind seeing how much of a Frankenstein's monster he looked. Raw steak was the classic remedy, but if a steak had come his way, he'd have eaten it – raw or not. Probably there'd be a mirror above the front seat.

Moving to the car, and about to open the door, he stopped and looked upwards. There it was, a single buzzard this time, making its weirdo mewing. Perhaps because of the clouds it was lower than usual so Dan thought he could see its sharp black eyes and hooked beak. There was no wind and it hung, still and watchful, in the sky.

Dan turned away from it, pulled open the door and eased down the flap above the windscreen. Only too clearly his face was mirrored back at him. Worse than he'd imagined. Very swollen, dark purply red. Somehow it hurt more when he could see how bad it was. He remembered Si telling him that a buzzard picked on the injured or vulnerable as his prey. No wonder it was hovering overhead. Just kidding.

He shut the door and set off for the stream – less evidence of problems there. A phrase came into his head: *man's inhumanity to man*. Vinny certainly fitted the bill.

His face looked even worse mirrored in the water, a cool wind rippling the surface and distorting his features even more than they were already. He was also cold, for the first time since he'd left home.

He thought about home: Eve obsessed with her losers. Why did she bother? Not a home. He thought of his bed. No, thank you. At night Ru visited him, pleading, imploring, whispering: 'Come on, Dan, Danny. Come and join me – we get on better together. Don't leave me all alone. I'm not blaming you for running away but I'm waiting, Dan, friend, my only friend. I *need* you.'

Need! Dan jumped up abruptly, hurting both his face and his ankle. Vinny had picked on him for going on about 'need'. He was right. Need was sad, pathetic. Ru didn't need him. He was dead. He, Dan, didn't need home. A book or two or three would have been nice. Just got to remind himself he was living life, not reading about it. He'd spent too much time altogether on people who didn't exist. Anyway he wouldn't want anyone to see him like this. What a performance he'd get from Eve!

What he did need, if he were to carry on, was money. He began a hobbling run back to the car. Eve might have some use after all. What had she called it? 'Panic money'. Over-dramatic, naturally. Three very small rabbits ran across his path. They were in a panic, all right, white tails bobbing as they headed one way and then back, putting up a pheasant as noisy as a creaky door, which made them run even faster.

Dan stood still and pointed a finger at them. 'Bang. Bang. Bang.' A streak of sun came over the hill opposite him and surrounded him in its glory.

He walked back more carefully, content now he'd remembered the money. He pictured Eve putting it into an inside pocket of his backpack when it was new, not quite sewing the note in but pushing it down into a small pocket he hadn't even noticed. Vinny wouldn't have either.

Dan strolled casually. Really, his ankle was fine. It must be very early still if the sun was only just coming up. He would pick up the money, take anything worth keeping and make for the station. Maybe he'd take a train to the seaside. Or to Wales. Martha and he had camped in Wales. Near a castle. They'd climbed the battlements and stared at mountains shadowed by fast-moving clouds. Then it had rained and they'd rushed down, laughing.

Martha decided she could let herself get up now. She had lain awake all night. What had they done to him that he had run away? When she'd woken up her cheeks had been wet with tears – she, who never cried. All of them loved him. They were all distraught, none of them yet accusing another. That would come. They were still hoping he would walk through the door.

Instead it would be the police who would walk through her door and she, like a murderer, had cleaned her house of evidence. Max was tucked up with Eve. They were a normal, loving family. Why had Dan needed to go?

'Max,' Eve whispered in his ear, 'I'm getting up. Do you want a cuppa?'

Max groaned. His black hair flopped on the white pillow as he turned his head but without opening his eyes.

Eve felt her energy increased by his languor. She would go to work. It was what she was best at: motivating young people with problems. Max could play the strong male holding the fort.

*

Dan thought he might be starving unto death. *Starving unto death*, he said to himself, like a boy in a concentration camp. He'd just finished a book about that. Limbs like matchsticks and stomach protruding so the belly button turned inside out.

It had taken him hours to walk to the station. Although the sun had been partly swallowed by clouds, it was warmer than ever and he was soaked with sweat. He'd drunk all his water and thrown away the bottle. He was coming into civilization. One part of him was sad, the other just a bit excited. The eyelid of his good eye twitched. He thought he had a blister on his heel. He definitely had a blister on his heel – and his ankle was killing him. The last couple of miles had been along a road. Cars again. People.

What most excited him was the idea of the station's café. He'd seen it on his way through. Seemed like weeks ago. It was a strange place, perched up on stilts, an old signal box, he assumed. The station was strange too. That was why he'd got out of the train from London there, outside the town in what had seemed the middle of nowhere, almost was.

He thought with a kind of romantic nostalgia of those first days in the limo, Si and the wall – he had the smallest fossil in his pocket as a reminder – but he had to move on. Even aside from Vinny. Adventurers move on. Anyway, he was starving.

He could see the station ahead now. He hadn't imagined seeing it again but he was glad now. Cars were parked but no one seemed to be around. That was good. There'd been a toilet on the station. Maybe he could tidy up a bit there.

The café was at the other end of the station, perched up like a look-out post. He climbed the wooden steps holding on to the handrail like an old man. The glass door was shut; that was all right until he saw the notice 'Closed'. He leant his head against the window, his stomach flapping as if a bird was in there.

Something moved behind the glass. He peered harder and there was a girl with a spout of blonde hair sitting behind a counter reading a magazine. He knocked on the door and, calmly as anything, she put down her magazine and came out from behind the counter. She stared at him, frowning, then came closer.

'What do you want?' Her voice had the same drawl as Si's.

'Food,' shouted Dan.

'Can't you read the sign?'

'Please,' said Dan, 'I'm starving,' which wasn't a figure of speech.

The girl came closer, frowned some more, before very slowly opening the door. Dan tried not to fall in on top of her.

'You're a mess, aren't you?' She sounded more reproving than sympathetic.

'My mate head-butted me.' Clever line that. Marmite had been his friend before Vinny'd got hold of it. Dan looked greedily at the cakes and sandwiches.

'Funny sort of mate. Should be locked up.' She made her leisurely way to the counter, while Dan thought that if Vinny was to be believed he'd already been locked up eleven times. He didn't take his eyes off the food.

'You've interrupted my coffee break.' The girl settled herself behind the counter and took up a mug. 'I put up that closed sign because I like to have my break in peace.' She paused. 'Not that anyone comes at this time of day. Between trains. Story of my life.' She laughed as if she'd said something funny.

'I'll have a doughnut.' Dan's mouth was watering. He'd never believed that really happened before.

'Don't you want a cooked meal? You look like you could do with it. Sleeping rough, are you?'

'Camping.'

'Not a Boy Scout with the matches, then.'

'I'll have a doughnut now.' Dan thought that clever-talking girls were the worst sort. Then he had the sugar and jam in his mouth and he had to sit down in case he fainted with the deliciousness of it. Intravenous heroin.

'Go on. Say you'll have the cooked day-long breakfast – sausage, bacon, tomato and fries. I'm so bored here I could die. Have it for me!'

Recovering slightly from starvation and ecstasy, Dan watched as she swung her long arms above her head and groaned in mock-misery. At least, he assumed it was mock. 'OK,' he said, 'just to please you.' Which was a lie. A cooked meal sounded just fine, as long as he could keep eating while she was making it. 'I'm taking another doughnut.' He spoke to her back because she had turned to go into a smaller room.

Dan ate the second doughnut to the smell of frying and the girl's commentary, shouted above the sizzling and prodding. 'My mum made me take this job. First day out of school and she had me out of the house. Doesn't want me cramping her style, that's what I think. It's not as if they pay me much here. They said I should think of it as "work experience" and getting my foot on "the ladder of the service industry". There's not even anyone to serve most of the time. And as for industry, it's never been my favourite word. Want them flipped?'

'Sorry?' Dan stared stupidly at her sudden reappearance. She was pretty, he saw, her cheeks reddened by the cooking, her eyes bright.

'Eggs. Flipped.' She made a motion with her pointed fingers. She wore green nail varnish.

'No. As they are.' Dan felt comfortable. Not happy, but comfortable. He'd been happy out on the hillside with Si. His thoughts and his eyes converged on a wire holder in which newspapers were stacked. A bit of a headline stuck out from behind another paper: LOCAL PENSIONER . . . It must be a long headline. Dan sprang up and pulled out the paper. He read it standing: LOCAL PENSIONER IN DRAMATIC HELICOPTER RESCUE.

He sat back in his chair and read the story. Si was in hospital. Alive, although in a critical condition. No one knew who'd phoned the police. An *unknown hero*. There was a photo of Si, much younger, strong and handsome.

'Those papers are free.' A large plate of fries was dumped in front of him.

'Thanks.' Dan put aside the paper. Now he was not only comfortable but happy. *Happy*, no other word for it, the unknown hero stuffing his face with a plate of fat chips.

The girl rattled the edge of the paper. 'See this rag. There's only pensioners or little kids in it.' She settled on a chair nearby. 'You noticed? The world's crammed full with pensioners and babies.'

Dan was concentrating on his food.

'My name's Maria, incidentally.' She paused interrogatively.

'D-Denver,' said Dan.

'Cool.' He could see he'd gone up in her estimation.

'How old are you?'

'Sixteen.'

'Same as me. Finished with school, then?'

'Sort of.'

'College. You're from London, aren't you?'

'Mostly.'

'I might go to London. Train to be a beautician.' She leant towards him. She wore a sleeveless T-shirt with a low neck and, although she was slim, Dan could see the curve of her breasts above a coloured bra. Girls didn't usually talk to him. She must be very bored.

'Well, Denver, what are you going to do today?'

Just a pity she was so curious.

'Myself, I fancy hopping on the train and going for a swim in the sea.'

Immediately Dan knew that was exactly what he was going to do. He wasn't going to tell her, though.

'Got to go while the weather holds,' continued Maria. 'It's going to break. Has to be storm level after all this heat. Do you like heat?'

'Yeah,' said Dan.

She surveyed him critically, as if by feeding him he'd become her responsibility. 'You could do with a wash. You know that?'

'Yeah,' repeated Dan.

'I'll tell you what. I'll give you the key to the Gents. There's a basin in there and paper towels. Better than nothing. Where're you camping, then?'

'At the farm.'

Maria laughed. 'As if there's only one farm round here. This whole place is farms, pensioners and babies.' She sighed theatrically.

Dan began to see a certain likeness to Eve. He shifted on his chair. 'I'd like that key.'

'You'll have to bring it back, mind.'

'Isn't it for public use?'

'You're public, aren't you?' Maria laughed. 'It's for private public use. They don't like it getting dirty or being used for other business.'

'Oh.'

While Maria went to find the key, Dan rolled up the newspaper and put it in his backpack. He added the fossil from his pocket and got out the 'panic note' – twenty pounds. Typical of Eve to go over the top but useful under the present circs.

Maria came back with a key and handed it over with some ceremony. 'Freedom of the lav.'

Dan looked at the label. 'Why does it say "greenhouse"?'

'To confuse people.' Maria gave the laugh he was beginning to see was her trademark. 'I don't know. Maybe it's recycling. That's the other thing that goes on round here: recycling. People – I should say pensioners – go down to the dump to throw out their stuff, and while they're at it, they pick up a whole lot of new rubbish. My mum found a brooch she thought was diamonds. She had her arms waxed and her hair colour refreshed ready for *Antiques Roadshow* but before they even came she knew it was rubbish, just like I told her. Turned black . . .'

Dan was standing now, keen to leave. He got to the door, followed by Maria who gave him a pile of paper napkins. 'Don't expect you're over-endowed with tissues. Back here with the key, remember.' She looked at the clock on the wall. 'You'd better get a move on. There's a couple of trains due. You haven't paid either.'

'Sorry.' He held out the twenty.

Maria stared at the money as if she didn't recognize it and then at him. Daylight came through the glass-fronted door. 'You're never sixteen?'

'It's my birthday.' He should have said, 'Mind your own business,' but he'd just at that moment remembered that it actually was his birthday. Fourteen today. Another celebration.

'Your birthday!' She seemed gob-smacked by this news. She reeled backwards, waving aside the note. 'Can't take money off you on your birthday. Not with your mate doing you over and every-thing. You know, you really need to learn how to have a good time, especially on your birthday.'

Dan was taken aback by her fervour. On the other hand, not paying was good news. 'Thanks, Maria. I'll try.' He opened the door, got out on to the steps. He turned back at the bottom and she was standing there, watching and waving. 'Happy birthday!' she shouted, before turning round the sign on the door and going inside.

Would he have wanted a sister like her? Dan walked on to the platform, which was still deserted, and found a freshly painted door marked GENTS. Before going inside, he noted the train timetable above his head. Two were due soon, one going to Weymouth in under ten minutes. He unlocked the blue door and went inside.

CHAPTER NINETEEN

Martha was having a meeting with Gerry, her supervising officer. Exhaustion and anxiety made her aggressive. 'I should have been informed sooner than yesterday that he was going.' They were talking about Lee. 'I've been working with him for two years.' She knew Gerry was aware this was an exaggeration.

'You care too much.'

'I'm a professional.' But was that true? Martha was surprised by Gerry's lack of sympathy. She'd told him about Dan. She felt her face flushing as she remembered that she had told Lee, too, about Dan. How unprofessional was that? A lonely single woman off-loading her problems on the most inappropriate person she could find. If anyone discovered it, she could be sacked. Perhaps that was why she was so upset by his leaving – nothing to do with his chances of survival in the big world, rather her own personal, selfish failure. He was a murderer, give or take, and she'd told him about Dan. She supposed she should be glad he wasn't a paedophile.

'You're a good officer.' Gerry sounded kinder. Perhaps he'd picked up on her feelings of panic. She who prided herself on her self-control.

They were sitting in a glass cubicle on one of the wings. Outside, men were coming back to their cells for bang-up before the lunch break. The noise was very loud, not from the men, who were mostly quiet apart from an occasional shout, but from the slamming of the doors and the officers' jangling keys and yelled commands. Martha no longer felt a sense of threat in the scene but today was different. Everything felt threatening.

'I'm sorry.' She tried to smile at Gerry in a calm way, although it felt like a rictus. 'I'd better be off. Overseeing dinner.' She stood up.

But she had to talk to someone. 'Ever had the police search your house?'

'No fun, I'd guess.'

'They did it this morning. It felt like a raid. They got into everything.'

'You're lucky. They don't often take the trouble.'

'I wouldn't know.'

Gerry heaved himself to his feet. He'd got heavy recently. Job taken its toll. Some got into exercise, others got heavy. Martha knew he was looking forward to retirement, pottering to the pub, to his allotment. He'd nearly done his time.

Martha tried a new tack. 'I still think Dan will come back. It's only four days. He probably needed a break.'

'Our kids looked after each other. Wife and I never knew the half of it.'

'Yes,' agreed Martha, without conviction, wondering what that had to do with an only child.

As she walked down the landing, hand on keys to stop them jangling, she recognized she was beginning to link the two who had gone so suddenly from her life: Dan and Lee. A young boy and an old lag. She knew it was ridiculous to think that their fates were in any way similar. Lee, after all, quite aside from his age and regrettable past, had been let out to a bail hostel. He would be tracked, have to follow rules of behaviour, times to check in. He could not contact her, nor she him, but she would know if he broke the rules, absconded, disappeared truly, not just from her life. Why did she fear that? Feel almost as if by telling him about Dan she had set him up?

Telling herself that these thoughts were the hyped-up product of a sleepless night, Martha forced herself to stride briskly to where the food was already coming off the trolley. Immediately, she was confronted by a practical issue: where were the special portions for the three Muslims on her wing? It was a relief to find herself on familiar ground.

Eve wondered at herself. She was dazzling. She was dazzling the kids: they were falling before her charm and inspiration like ninepins. Where did she find the energy? It was a miracle but she'd take credit for it.

She'd given them a scene, a Shaw play, *Saint Joan*. Impossible. Out of reach. Off the drama-school wall. So talky, alien, unemotional. It would kill them but she'd pull them through. She'd prepared it at four in the morning, Max asleep at her side, the bastard lover. She loved him, of course.

'Use the vowels, Ibou.' This was absurd but so real, so important. 'Vowels clipped by consonants.

'Gather round. Gather round.' She'd give them a lesson in grammar. None of them had a clue what she was talking about. If she wasn't careful they'd give her the fuck-you treatment and retrieve their mobiles, turned off and lined up on a ledge. But that was the thrill. She could do it.

'Aaaaw. Ooooh.' The thing was, she didn't mind making a fool of herself. She did in real life, weepy and tragic, but here she was queen.

'Miss!' Carla was playing Joan. She looked great, holding her bulk with dignity.

'Yes?' She said yes as if accepting a question was permissible but that was because she was so strong and she didn't have to answer it. Cleopatra didn't answer questions, or Churchill, once he was in power (because we mustn't be sexist), but her kids needed answers. Now and again.

'My nan's sick. I've got to go early.'

Always those other chaotic lives. No wonder they couldn't concentrate. 'No probs, Carla. Now let's do a run-through.' Two lots of five, one to watch, one to play. Keep them on their toes.

The Dauphin, Charles, was played by Brendan. Brendan was from Ireland with bright orange hair, which she knew he hated. ' "You all think you can treat me as you please because I owe you money, and because I am no good at fighting. But I have the blood royal in my veins." '

'Spot on, Dauphin. Petulant. Sulky. But beware consonants.' They hated so much about themselves, expectations so far beyond execution, that it was no wonder they flipped out and gave it all up as a bad job. She knew about it because she'd been like that herself: 100 per cent ego, confidence nil. How do you put the two together? How to explain that life was boring, one foot in front of the other? But she didn't believe that either. Of course she didn't. That was why she did her job, showed them they were something special. Finding success was another thing altogether but she wasn't going to put them off with reality checks on that one. Acting cocked a snook at reality anyway.

Ibou was playing the Archbishop. 'Come, come! This will not do. My Lord Chamberlain: please! Please! We must keep some sort of order. And you, sir: if you cannot rule your kingdom, at least try to rule yourself.'

'Archbishop, you're awesome.' He wasn't awesome, a chunky black boy who'd only just learned not to clutch his trousers in awkward situations, but he had something: an intensity, a smile, a deep, rounded voice. When did anyone call him awesome? Now he glowed.

La Trémouille was played by Andy, an undersized boy with a large head who wanted to avoid attention. 'Rot,' mumbled Andy, reading from the text.

'It may be one word but draw it out, Trémouille. It won't eat you. Come on, all of you. More energy. Energy!' She was merciless for their own good.

There were so many accents here. Jamaican, Jamaican-British, Irish, Polish, Kenyan, Albanian, Turkish, Czech, south London. She couldn't pinpoint them all. Crazy, really, added to a play where all the characters were French. But she liked it. Gave so much life to the proceedings. She wouldn't be mourning the demise of the Queen's English. Not like Max. No time for her family now. Max was a poet – or so he used to say.

'Now we'll mark out the movements. Who's got the chalk? Who did I give the chalk to?'

They were like babies, really, ready to giggle or cry. That cringing boy – what was his name? She must get to him. He was the Albanian. Albanians were supposed to be fierce. He was as pale as a newborn mouse and scarcely spoke above a whisper. She must get to him, bring him out. Maybe she'd make him play Joan to-morrow. Not this class. Tomorrow. Tomorrow's task planned today. It gave her such pleasure to think she could do this. Martha never understood.

'La Hire, how about kneeling? Too hard for you, too dirty? Oh, my, aren't we choosy . . . Well, get a chair, then, and we'll try that.'

The floor was marked with their positions. They were a bit noisy.

Even Cleopatra had to tolerate a bit of noise; the common rabble or Enobarbus rambling on about her beauty.

'Now, there's just time for a run-through from each group . . . Hold your book down, Joan, and try to remember you're a saint.'

How they enjoyed a reason to giggle and mock! But not a 'fuck' for the last half an hour. Although she had no argument with a fuck in its place. Strange the way she and Max had never had a problem on that front. She'd lost her respect for him. That was the problem.

Max drank his third cup of tea in a row. He'd made them for the police search team but they'd declined. They were quick, thorough and polite. All the same he could see they'd thought it a waste of their highly trained time. They'd been more sympathetic at first but when their accompanying PC, the man on the case, Ronnie to his friends, revealed that the missing child was fourteen, they'd nodded nonchalantly. 'He'll come back.'

Everybody said that. But what if he didn't? What if he was dead or injured or drugged or kidnapped? Every day Max imagined more specific monstrosities. Eve and Martha talked about such things, he knew, but stopped when he was around, as if he needed protecting or, more likely, because they didn't want to share their feelings with him. Male rape had always held the horrors for him. Some women seemed to enjoy anal sex, but he wasn't convinced. Once Eve had caught a hint of what was almost a phobia. She'd laughed at him and teased him about being a closet gay. 'Your worst fears are always your greatest desires,' she'd gloated triumphantly.

Unlikely: he'd never found men as interesting as women for sex or anything else. But now his phobia or desire or whatever it was had hooked on to Dan's disappearance, producing disgusting images in his imagination.

He must get out of the flat, visit the library again where Dan borrowed books. The day before the girl at the counter had pretended to, or really did, remember Dan and said she'd check in case anyone else had noticed anything different about him or his borrowings, or if he'd been with anyone unusual. With almost too much sympathy, she'd said he was always so quiet, so, you might almost say, 'bookish'.

Eve and Martha were right to go to work, forcing him, however, to stay at home – waiting for what? News from the police, a sighting, Dan's return. Next Monday, a week after he'd left, they'd promised to put Dan on the missing-children film site, shown on buses, among other places. On Monday, Max would go back to work. Do something useful. It was not like Dan to be the centre of a drama. It didn't make sense.

CHAPTER TWENTY

Dan ran out of the Gents and jumped on the train just before the doors closed. It was a very small train, only two short carriages. A couple of women with young children chatted to each other before stopping to stare at him. In another corner an old man read the *Sun*. Dan remembered Maria's remark about pensioners or babies. Maybe they were going to the sea as well.

The food and the wash had made him feel stronger but he supposed the women stared because he looked so bashed up. He stared back and they started chatting again. One of the babies began to cry.

He realized he was still holding the key to the Gents. *Tant Piss*. Good joke that. He went out of the carriage and pulled down the window on the door. The key flew out like a bird. Sorry, Maria.

'Got a ticket, have you?'

The ticket collector took him by surprise. He was red-faced and sweating. They stood together by the door and the open window. It was cooler out here.

'I need to buy one.' He produced his twenty-pound note. 'Weymouth one way. Child.'

'I can see you're a child,' which was good news – sometimes people didn't, 'and I can see your money, but what'll I do for change?'

Peanuts? Not his responsibility, was it?

'Most people have cards, see, so I don't carry much change. Sure you've got no change?'

'Not a penny.' It was my special panic money, he could have explained.

The ticket collector seemed perplexed. He took some coins out of his pocket and looked at them for several seconds. 'There's nothing for it,' he pronounced eventually, 'you'll have to travel free. This is your lucky day.'

'Actually, it's my birthday,' said Dan.

'There you are! Got your face celebrating, did you?'

'Ha ha,' laughed Dan, obligingly.

The ticket collector moved away a few steps before returning. His mind moved nearly as slowly as the old man's – rescued Si, front-page news Si.

'Now, if someone gets on in the next four stations and gives me some change, I'll be back. You understand that?'

'It's only fair,' agreed Dan. 'Birthday or no birthday.'

'Just the job. Birthday or no birthday,' repeated the ticket collector, and this time he went off altogether.

Dan went back to his seat and settled as comfortably as he could, considering the pain in his face. Outside, the summery countryside drifted by. His days in the limo seemed a happy dream until spoiled by Si's illness, then wrecked by the nasty, violent Vinny. He craned his head upwards to look at the sky and see if the buzzard was on his trail.

He began to think of home – except it was hardly a home: it was where he had a bed and kept his books. Thursday, his birthday all day. Eve would be out showing off to her 'challenging kids'. Max would be driving around the countryside, pretending to make up poems. Perhaps their paths would cross. Perhaps there was a book-shop in the seaside town and he'd suddenly see his big, handsome dad coming out. On the job. 'Hi, Dad,' he'd say, just to get the reaction before disappearing in a puff of green smoke, like a panto-mime villain. That was a fun fantasy. Although it was true: he'd headed west because he knew it was his father's beat. It was not that he wanted to see Max, more a reproach for never taking him along. Some dads were proud of their sons and wanted to be with them.

The train stopped at a station. Behind the platform, someone had created a garden, shrubs, white-painted stones and the statue of a horse – or it might be a dog or even a rabbit.

Martha would be in prison, doling out points for good or bad behaviour or whatever she did. Maybe it was just locking or unlock-ing doors, although she'd once told him she'd been trained to hold down a man three times her weight. That was to encourage him with his martial arts.

They all had their stories, that was the thing. All he did was tick the box: son, nephew. So he needed a story too. That's what he was doing, he needed to remind himself, making a story. No one had said it would be easy.

The train stopped at another station, red-brick and as severe as the other had been romantic. There was a row of terraced modern houses, out of place in this deep countryside. He'd send a postcard, the responsible thing to do. On his birthday. They might be worried on his birthday. Not that they'd get it on his birthday. What he should have done was left them a note. Suppose he was angry at the time. Looking back. At the time he'd just felt excited.

The noise of the train was making him sleepy. He didn't mind sleeping now that Ru seemed to be leaving him alone. His face still hurt but he was getting used to the pain. It didn't frighten him any more. He leant the unbattered side of his face against the window; it was smooth and warm.

'Here we are, then. Hop off quick or I might yet find that change.'

Still half asleep, he obeyed the ticket collector and stumbled off the train. It was very hot on the platform, which was crowded with what looked like holidaymakers: families, mainly, more babies but also several groups of younger people carrying backpacks.

It was funny that when there was no one around he didn't feel lonely at all, but when he was surrounded by people he immediately felt alone, almost forlorn. *Forlorn and palely loitering* – wasn't that one of Eve's quotes, or something like?

The station was clearing. Soon everybody who knew where they were going had gone. Dan continued to loiter. He peered out of the station a few times but there seemed only a road, some shops and a few houses. What he wanted to know was the direction of the sea.

A group of two men and a girl were behaving in much the same half-hearted way. They were arguing too. At least he couldn't argue with himself. The girl broke away and came over to him while the men stopped arguing and watched. She was pretty, with hooped earrings and a diamond nose stud. She didn't look much older than him and dirtyish, as if she'd been sleeping rough too.

'Know where the sea is?'

One of the men behind her sniggered. They weren't that old

either, but older than the girl. One of them, mixed race or it might have been sunburn, wore matted dreadlocks nearly to his waist. The girl had dreadlocks too, but they looked prettier on her, just to her shoulders and with a few beads interwoven.

'That's what I was wondering.'

'Fuck me. The sea's gone missing now.' The girl laughed. Her teeth were small and white and her eyes green. Like a kitten's. She seemed glad to be talking to someone other than her companions. 'Who bashed your face?'

'I ran into a wall. Not. My mate lost his cool.' He was beginning to almost believe the story.

'So you've split and now you're on your own.' She looked over her shoulder. 'Come along with us. Might stop those two going at each other all the time.'

'What about the sea?' She couldn't be serious about him coming with them. Just like that. A girl like her wanting him along. He found his heart jumping and knew his face had flushed, although it was probably far too many odd colours for her to notice.

'I grew up on the sea. The sea is cold. Beaches are good for business, though. We're looking for a squat and that's the directions: head for the sea, left along the front, third left and second right.'

'*University Challenge*, here you come.'

'Competition kills.' The girl laughed. Dan was reminded of Maria in the café. Girls were so much more relaxed than boys.

'So what's the story, Freya?' shouted one of the men. They didn't look dangerous, like Vinny. Funny how easy it was to tell that sort of thing – probably the result of growing up in London. They were kind of weedy-looking, despite their deep tans, not the sort to throw a Marmite jar in anger.

'I've got a guide dog,' called Freya, flashing a look at Dan. 'Ask someone,' she mouthed.

Girls were bossy, too, but he liked Freya, the dimple when she smiled and her little teeth and a feather stuck behind her ear. He asked at the ticket desk and a weary man laughed at him. 'No one's ever had problems finding the sea before. Turn left and it's right there in front of you. Behind the clock. You'll be wet enough without the sea in an hour or two,' he added. 'Storm's coming.'

'Storm?' repeated Dan, stupidly. So that was why he felt so hot.

'Think deluge,' said the man in the ticket desk. 'I'll have a lot of cross holidaymakers heading for home.'

'I suppose.' Dan walked away and joined the three backpackers.

'Mel and Abe,' said Freya, nodding at the two men, who didn't respond so Dan didn't know which was which.

'D-Dino,' said Dan.

'You Italian?' asked Freya, interestedly.

'Real name's Donald.'

'As in duck-head?'

'As in duck.'

'Hey, Dino.' Her diamond stud flashed.

They walked off together. It was still early afternoon but the clouds massing up ahead made it seem later.

'When we hit town, I need to buy a few things.' He should get that postcard. And a stamp. And find a postbox. It didn't seem easy.

'Your mate rob you too?'

'Most things. Had a bit of money hidden.'

'Arsehole.'

They walked on amicably. It was almost too hot to speak.

In front of them Mel and Abe, Abe and Mel, were bickering in a desultory way about the squat. Fucking this and fucking that. About a friend who stole their dope. Dan stopped listening. A droplet of sweat rolled down the side of his face into his bad eye. He brushed it gently away.

'They said at the station there's going to be a storm. Big rain.'

'That's why we need this squat. Hunker down. Music. Smoke. Chill.'

'Sounds good to me.'

'Yeah. If those two would shut up. A woman needs a man like a fish needs a bicycle.'

Dan looked again at the two men ahead. Their huge backpacks made them look like giant tortoises. Nothing dangerous there.

A fat drop of rain fell like a stone on his hand. 'Wow. Look at the size of this.' He felt another cold drop on his head.

Freya glanced across. 'No time for fucking shopping, I'd say.'

'Yeah! There's the sea!' They were walking faster now but Dan stopped to stare at the great expanse of ink blue water below a wide sky rolling with black and purple clouds. It split suddenly, with a streak of garish lightning.

133

'Coming, are you, bughead?' shouted Freya, over her shoulder. Dan hesitated. He was tempted to stand there and let the storm deluge over him. But on the other hand there were Freya's green eyes and a place to go and another world outside the shops and summer crowds he could see along the promenade. Forget postcards. He didn't want to be alone with all that rubbish.

'I'm with you.' It was a no-brainer, wasn't it?

PART TWO
Searching

Four Weeks Later

CHAPTER TWENTY-ONE

Eve lay in bed. Downstairs she could hear Max and Martha's voices and Ronnie's, their policeman who was supposed to be helpful. He wasn't, although she supposed he tried. She wanted to teach him how to pronounce 'liaison'.

A few days ago she'd moved in with Martha. Her bed was in the spare room, very neat and calm. Max insisted he didn't mind. He was back at work, trailing round the country and spotting Dan once or twice a day, so he said. Once a young tree had turned itself into their son, like some reverse of classical mythology. They were all more than a little mad.

She had been, or at least felt, fairly sane during the weeks she had taken her kids through their paces. They were a great bunch, and all of them had kept out of trouble the whole time they were with her. Word got around, of course, that her son had gone missing. Some of them went out on the streets looking for him, asked for a pic. She hadn't given them one. Keep things separate, that was always the best policy.

The moment she'd done the final show – a triumph, no exaggeration, even had an agent there – said her goodbyes, sadly said her goodbyes, everything had exploded. Imploded, maybe. She'd hit the bed and dissolved into a sheet of tears. Martha had said, in a probably non-mad comment. 'You thought he'd be back before the end of it. That's how you kept going.'

Looking back, she couldn't understand how she'd kept going. Every day out to the school, every evening expecting to find Dan at home, penitent, perhaps. Routine and expectation. She'd had those. Now she had nothing. Worse than that, an empty bedroom.

So she had moved in with Martha. Not very logical, perhaps,

when Max was being so sympathetic. But Martha had looked after her all her life.

She'd promised her not to cry at today's meeting. 'Your tears would get in the way of information,' she'd said. Quite cruel. When had mothers not wept for their missing sons, starting with the Old Testament, Rachel weeping for her children and *would not be comforted because they are not*? She remembered that line because their father, the vicar, used to quote it, although it was his wife who had died. Her mother. And she didn't believe Dan was dead. She felt the tears now, ready to torrent down her cheeks.

King Lear had something to say about weeping. Could she remember? She'd always had perfect recall for Shakespeare. *No, I'll not weep.* That was it, after some mention of *women's weapons, water-drops.* Yes, this should stem her flow and more was coming now: *No, I'll not weep/I have full cause of weeping, but this heart/shall break into a hundred thousand flaws/or ere I'll weep.*

Well, it was too late for that sort of talk in her case. Anyway, Lear went totally mad, as Shakespeare intended.

'What are you doing? Eve, what are you doing?' Martha was standing at the door in what Eve thought of as prison-officer mode.

'Trying to find behavioural tips in Shakespeare.'

'But you're not dressed!'

Eve didn't blame her for her exasperation. 'When do they arrive?'

'Five minutes. One's rung and cancelled already.'

They were a group of Dan's classmates – hardly friends, it seemed – who had agreed to talk about Dan. Detective Constable Aberdaire – Ronnie – who seemed to have joined the family, had encouraged the exercise. Most had been interviewed before but not as a group. Some had been on holiday.

The word 'exercise' propelled Eve out of bed. It was possible some of these kids would attend her drama classes next year – the GCSE course. Panicked, she went into the bathroom and peered at herself in the mirror. A challenge indeed. Blotchy, swollen skin, pinprick eyes, bulging mouth, dark roots. Lucky Max that she'd left his side.

She reminded herself she'd always liked a challenge. She went to find her makeup bag and laid out clothes and jewellery on the bed. She was a person of artifice. All actors were. Artifice came to save her.

Martha wanted to weep at the sight of the children grouped nervously in her small room. Not her style to feel so emotional. She had produced every chair in the house but still Ronnie, Max and an attendant granny stood while two of the children sat on the floor. They were young enough to make it look natural. That was what undid her. On the other hand, they seemed more mature, almost knowing, than she remembered. Probably, in her anxiety, she'd been sliding Dan down the age scale, ever more vulnerable.

'Thank you all for coming.' This was Ronnie – excellent Ronnie, big and fair and kind. Sometimes a bit too kind. They had agreed he should lead the discussion.

Eve sat on a chair. Martha wondered if anyone else noticed how odd she looked, dressed in mauve and black with lacy mittens and a shawl. Probably she was in character, possibly appropriate to the occasion. Dickens, perhaps, although Martha didn't know the books well enough for identification. Did Little Nell have a mother, for example? Truth to tell, she'd never enjoyed Dickens, disliking the obvious drama and sentimentality.

'It's now over a month since Dan went missing and, unfortunately, neither the police nor the family are any nearer knowing why he left or where he went to. Many of you have already talked to the police, some in the early days, others, who were on holiday, more recently. A couple of you have only just been contacted. It doesn't matter which category you fall into . . .'

Ronnie was long-winded. Martha sighed before assuming an alert expression. Why did she think nothing would come of this meeting?

Max stood by himself at the door. Normally she avoided looking at him. She glanced now and saw how thin he'd become, accentuating his height and brooding romanticism. Presumably nobody much was feeding him. They seldom talked directly so she had no real idea how he was managing.

'So we want you to remember the last few days or even weeks of the school term . . .' Ronnie continued comfortably – too comfortably, as if he were talking of a lost computer or a pair of trainers '. . . anything about Dan, odd things, ordinary things, anyone he met, anywhere he went.' He was right to sound comfortable. No point in scaring the children. Make them feel at home, relaxed, memories floating freely.

'Anyone want a drink?' asked Martha.

Ronnie frowned. Not so comfortable. 'I think we'll get started first.'

Eve, fixed to her chair, held up a quivering mittened hand. All eyes turned to her. 'May I speak?' Her voice was pitched to understated tragedy.

Martha tried not to think these thoughts. Eve had collapsed and knew only one way to get herself together.

'I only want to say, thank you – thank you.' Eve paused. 'And please do not hold back. Secrets are why Dan left.'

Everyone looked dumbfounded at this. What secrets did she mean? Or was it just a figure of speech? A Dickensian utterance of doom. Eve had shut her eyes. She'd lost a lot of weight, too.

Ronnie took over again. There were seven children, four boys. A girl spoke first. She sounded confident. She asked, 'Why has no one appeared on those television appeals? There's one in the morning, every day, my mum says. Police involved and everything.' Her round blue eyes in her sweet young face looked accusingly at Ronnie, who hesitated. Martha could see he was programmed to draw out useful information from shy youngsters, not to face inquisition. All the children stared at him.

What a difference there was between them! Some as full-grown as adults, girls with large breasts and makeup and boys with broad shoulders and shadow moustaches, others still utterly childlike with baby noses and little feet. It was an age on the cusp, Martha realized, and in the month Dan had been away he could have crossed the line into adulthood. Yet, as far as she remembered, his voice had scarcely started to break.

Ronnie's answer when it came was firm. 'The programme hasn't been running over the summer. However, we didn't want to organize a television appeal too soon. We hoped Dan would return,' he continued, with serious emphasis, 'as he left, of his own volition, taking food, some clothes, money. It was summer holidays. Now we're more worried and we're planning a television appeal very soon but you're just as important, Dan's friends.'

There was an awkward silence when he finished, as if, Martha wondered, the word 'friends' had hit the wrong note. It was not clear that Dan had friends but perhaps these were as near as any – a boy he rang up if he'd forgotten his homework, a girl who walked with him to the library. One of them, Pete, had been to the cinema with him a couple of times.

Pete had come with his friend, Jake. Pete was little and Jake was large but it was Pete who spoke first. 'He said to me he never slept.'

'What do you mean?' asked Ronnie, puzzled. The problem with boys, you could see him thinking, was that they wouldn't get out of bed.

'He never slept,' repeated Pete. He was a mousy boy whose mother would have admired his soft brown eyes. 'He hated nights,' he added, more vehemently.

Martha noticed that several of the children were looking in a disguised kind of fashion at Eve. Mothers are expected to know about their children's sleeping habits. But Eve, gave no indication of hearing Pete's remark, let alone reacting to it.

'He liked reading at night.' This was Max, his deep voice cutting through everything that had been said before, yet his tone was defensive.

Martha wondered what he knew. When she and Dan had last camped together, Dan had slept well. Admittedly that was over a year ago.

'Thank you, Pete,' said Ronnie, briskly. 'Does anyone know if Dan was seeing a new friend outside school?'

Various views were given on this. Jasmin whispered, 'He liked going to the park,' but, on being pressed, thought that he went on his own and fed the ducks, which caused subdued derision. Jake explained at some length that he'd tried to encourage Dan to join an out-of-school football game but he'd only turned up once and his boots hadn't fitted. Imran gave his opinion in a statement he appeared to have learnt by heart: 'Dan was a quiet boy, not easy to know but he wasn't disliked or liked. In a class of thirty-five, you can't know everybody anyway, but he didn't seem upset or unhappy. He wasn't bullied.'

As the conversation became more relaxed, the children cutting across each other with little memories or anecdotes, none with much point, Martha began to pick up on an edge of grievance, as if they felt they were being wrongly accused of some share in the responsibility for Dan's disappearance. So they, in turn, accused him: 'Why didn't he join in? Something was wrong with him. He had problems.' But none of them had the faintest idea what. Neither could they conceive of any real drama attaching to someone so modest and unassuming.

This should have been a comfort, Martha supposed, but it seemed only to deepen the mystery. The meeting was a waste of time. Yet that first boy's comment, dismissed by Ronnie, echoed with her: 'He never slept'; 'He hated nights.' Why would a boy who feared the night run away from the reassurance of home?

Eve watched Martha prepare to leave for work. She was in her prison uniform, always a shock. Max had gone already, saying nothing. What was there to say? The kids knew nothing. She'd wanted to tell Max that the reason she couldn't live in their flat was nothing to do with him but because of Dan's bedroom, empty and waiting. She couldn't bear to be near it any more, herself empty and waiting. At least here in Martha's house, she didn't listen to every noise or movement. She was surprised, however, and saddened by Max's haggard appearance. She'd half assumed (and feared) that he'd find a woman to look after him.

'I'll be back late,' said Martha.

' 'Bye.' Eve frowned bitterly. Now that her life had stopped, she hated the way other people went on with theirs. Martha had always been secretive. She'd only told Eve she was about to marry a few weeks before the event, and when Adrian had been given his death sentence, it had been weeks before she passed on the news. It did not make her a cold person but now Eve was aware of her detachment as a fault.

Max and Martha stood on the noisy pavement together. By chance their cars were parked close by each other. Ever since the heatwave had broken, the weather had been cool and unsettled, gusting winds throwing up dusty litter and sharp rain flattening it down again. Max watched Martha brush away a few drops of rain as if they were flies. It was odd to see someone quite so pale in late August. He supposed there wasn't much opportunity for sun-bathing in a prison.

'It's kind of you to have Eve,' he said.

'She's used to me supporting her.' Martha looked at her car. 'How are you managing?'

He remembered she didn't like standing on the street in her prison uniform. How should he answer her question? Briefly, of course. Truthfully? 'I can't believe I won't see him. Find him.'

'So you look?'

'All the time. Last night I went to the West End. It was disgusting.'

'Yes, it is.'

'The things I imagined were disgusting.' He watched her face closely and she took a step away.

'We all do that.'

He let her go but she turned back at her car. 'I'm hopeful about the television appeal.'

'Yes,' agreed Max, not telling her how much he dreaded the idea.

'Mostly I try to concentrate on my work.'

Max wondered why she would think he might care about that. His thoughts had room only for himself and Dan. Sometimes, while walking in the streets or, more often, in his dreams, he felt as if he was searching for his younger self: the sensitive boy growing into a man who had been bludgeoned by the noise of marriage and the battleground of fatherhood. But maybe the simpilicity and hopeful creativeness that he remembered was as insubstantial as Dan was turning out to be.

Curiously, those children trying to dredge up memories of Dan had made him seem even more distant. There was no consolation in understanding that it was not just the family where his connections had been tenuous. Children learn behaviour from their parents.

CHAPTER TWENTY-TWO

When Martha was told Lee had absconded from the hostel, she wasn't as surprised as she should have been. 'Has he any money?'

'Not sure.' The governor looked at his notes. 'You never really know, do you?'

'True enough,' agreed Martha. She thought of Lee, his watchful tightness. A part of her was even pleased he'd got out of that horrible hostel. He was a loner; maybe better if he was allowed to make his own way. She'd heard he'd had two changes of probation officer even in the few weeks he'd been out.

The governor stood up. 'I'm sorry about your nephew.'

Everybody knew and more people would know the following morning. 'We're recording a television appeal that goes out tomorrow. His father and I. His mother's too upset.'

'Good luck with it,' said the governor, dismissing her a little pompously.

It was odd, thought Martha, as she walked back to her wing, that Eve had declined the opportunity for a starring role on nationwide television. Camera, lights, makeup. She knew it was a mean, unworthy thought but living with Eve was not easy. Love had to be allowed to let off steam – or, rather, bile – now and again, even if it was only to herself.

The appeal was very short. Max was surprised. He and Martha had been in the studio an entire morning. The producer, an attractive woman in her forties, had flirted with him, reminding him of the effect he had on women – even now when he felt half a man. An approach would not have been obvious to anyone else. After all, he was a grieving father whose son had disappeared, but the signs were unmistakable to him. She'd hung over him and adjusted his mike herself.

Martha had been their spokesperson, hands shaking, he'd noticed, but voice firm. No photogenic tears from her. That was why Eve had backed down. She'd explained to him in one of their few intimate conversations, 'I've no appropriate public face to call on.' She'd never wanted to reveal her private self.

Now all three of them sat together in the flat, watching the programme in which their clip was playing. Eve had insisted they did this in their flat rather than Martha's house, Max suspected, because she was hoping for a call from Dan. It had made him so sad that he'd poured himself a large gin and tonic, not usually his preferred drink. Eve joined him and they stood together, understanding each other for once as Martha fiddled with the video machine; she was going to record the appeal.

So, there it was. Short. Impossible not to watch himself, although the man on the screen felt like a stranger, powerless and mostly silent. That wasn't so strange.

'We know Dan left from London but he had enough money to travel and so far, despite posters and Internet photographs, there have been no sightings.' This was the presenter, very, very young and trying to subdue a natural performance bounce into something more appropriate. He had not subdued his hair, however, which stuck up in cheery spikes over his round head.

Then Martha: 'Dan, if you see this or anyone tells you about it, please come home. Your parents and I are very anxious. At least make a telephone call, either to home or the following number . . .'

More information followed before he had his say, 'Eve and I . . .' The producer had tried to cajole him into calling her 'Mum' or 'Your mother' but she was always 'Eve' to Dan. 'Eve and I are waiting for you.' This was true. Every second of the day. 'We have your birthday present.' Also true. He'd put the books on Dan's bedside table with a note in case he should return when the flat was empty. 'We love you, Dan.' That had been hard to say. He had suggested poetry. *Love is not love/Which alters when it alteration finds.*

Poetry always said things better. This time the producer had bothered to explain why he was so wrong as to be ridiculous. She hadn't said so but she'd felt it, her gleaming, ambitious eyes trying to fix on his. 'We're attempting to touch the hearts of our viewers. It's their help we need. If they don't care, we'll get no information. If you say the word "love" directly into the camera, believe me, they'll care. If you recite poetry, they'll switch off, if not literally, in their hearts.'

So there it was, on air, 'We love you, Dan,' drawing in the hearts of the nation.

When the appeal had flashed by, Martha turned off the television presumably before another, perhaps more deserving, case – a pretty little girl or a disabled child – was given air space.

Immediately the phone rang. Eve lunged for it, tangling herself in the wire and hitting her knee on the table. 'Yes?' Her voice had the husky hopefulness of a child, not a mother.

It was Ronnie. Max could hear his kindness down the line and, as Eve began to sob, Martha took the phone. Eve stopped sobbing long enough to hiss venomously, 'Get him off, can't you?'

Martha finished her conversation hurriedly. Nobody said anything. Max wanted to say, 'Be sensible, darling' – but he hadn't called her *darling* for years – 'do you really think Dan will be watching this programme? The best we can hope for is that someone sees it and recognizes him and then they'll call the number given out on the programme.' But being sensible had never interested Eve and, just now, you couldn't blame her.

The telephone rang again, and again Eve snatched it up. 'Yes?' This time she handed it instantly to Martha. Max gathered it was some kind of cousin expressing solidarity. Martha was polite but didn't talk for long. 'Yes, we will.' It seemed that they were to let this random cousin know of any news. Odd.

The phone rang a third time and Max decided to answer it. 'Hello?' It was a mother from school, perhaps Chinese by her accent, saying how shocked she was. Why would she say that? She seemed to want to tell the story of her son who was in the year below Dan. Max found it hard to concentrate. Eve was sobbing bitterly and Martha crossed the room, making a lifting-cup-of-tea motion. It seemed this mother wanted sympathy: a year ago her son had died. So dulled was Max by the continual pain of Dan's absence that it took him a moment to register the words. A boy had died, a friend of Dan's, although in a lower class. 'He came to me,' said the mother, very softly, 'your son. He was so very sorry, he told me. I was happy that someone told me that.'

'Dan was—' Max corrected himself, '—is a kind boy.'

'Yes. You see, my boy kill himself. Very terrible. With a rope.'

Max fought a strong urge to cut off this woman whose suffering was far greater that his own. Was it his duty now to bear the burden of other people's horrors? He nearly said that Dan had never told him about Ru but that would have been cruel because it would show that the boy's suicide had not been important to him. He had cared enough to try to console the mother.

'I'm so very, very sorry.'

'Yes. My only boy.'

In one more second, Max thought, it would become unbearable. He would scream or sob like Eve. Actually, Eve was making herself another drink.

'So I wish you better luck for your boy.' The woman was ringing off and he hadn't even taken her name. But he didn't want her name.

'Thank you. Thank you.' Leaving the phone off the hook, he went to Eve and put his arm round her. She leant against him.

Later that evening, Martha let herself into her house. It was cold and dark. Eve had decided not to come back with her but to stay with Max. Maybe she hadn't liked the look of Max and Martha together on the television. She would have to become used to being alone again. After Adrian had died it had been very difficult for a while, particularly returning to what she knew would be a continual emptiness. Then she found, if she allowed in the sadness, it dissipated of its own accord and she could get on with her life again. The habit remained, squaring up to the realization that she was alone, just for a few minutes now, before carrying on.

Eventually, she went to the telephone. There was only one message and at first she didn't recognize the caller. 'It hit me just like that when I saw you. Made sense.'

A stranger who'd seen the appeal. But how did he have her telephone number?

'You'll know I'm not reporting in. No point. I can do it my way for a bit. Help you out.'

Lee. It was Lee. Martha, who was still standing, sat down abruptly.

'I'll take my chances on recall. I know a few tricks how to find people who go missing. Got your number off a letter you left around.

Your boy won't be hard to find. It's getting close when the shit hits the fan.'

The message ended. Martha stayed where she was. Lee sounded more confident than anyone she'd heard since Dan had disappeared. Had she set him this task?

CHAPTER TWENTY-THREE

Ronnie made an urgent telephone call to Max or Eve but neither was at home to receive it. He decided not to call Max's mobile so he left a message. It was better he got the news when he was at home rather than driving. Last time they'd talked Max said he was like the Flying Dutchman – which had made no sense so he'd adopted his all-purpose sympathy look. He never lost his sympathy for the suffering endured by the families he dealt with. They came in all shapes and sizes, but the suffering was the same and often progressed in the same way: disbelief, anger, terror, despair, endurance. Dan's family was at the despair stage. Maybe the news would give them some hope. Hope could come at any time.

Eve knelt in the dim church with her eyes fixed on the prettily painted face of the Virgin Mary. Pink and blue and gold. She hadn't thought such statues existed any more. Her father, the vicar, would have been horrified to see his daughter worshipping at painted idols. Because that was what she was doing, worshipping at the Holy Mother's feet and begging for forgiveness and help. The idea of forgiveness had come to her from her childhood. Since growing up she'd thought about it as little as she'd thought about religion. But she understood that you've got to be worthy to receive help and it was fairly clear that worthiness hadn't been her life's aim, so far.

It was also fairly clear why she was risking her father's ire (worse, if beyond the grave) by approaching Mary rather than Jesus or His Father, of which the vicar would have approved. He had not been at all High Church. Mary was a mother, Mother of Jesus, Mother of God, and the Holy Ghost presumably, since they were three in one. A mother was a mother was a mother, and she was a mother too.

And she'd lost her only son. Surely Mary would look kindly upon her, even if her belief had come on her suddenly at a time of trial. But that was human nature, wasn't it? And she was genuinely trying to admit to her bad behaviour – 'sins' was a step too far at the moment. You never knew, though. In her own way she was praying. One of her memories of her mother included the words, 'Be careful what you pray for or you may get it.' It had always seemed mysterious to her because obviously you wouldn't pray for something you didn't want. Eventually her mother had explained that we couldn't always know what was best for us. For example, in the present situation, Dan might be having the best time in his life and it would be wrong therefore to demand his return, however much she wanted it. So, the point was to put yourself in the hands of God or Jesus or Mother Mary and let them make the decisions while humbly indicating your preference.

These were the sort of things Eve mused about while she knelt, sometimes for more than an hour, in front of the painted statue.

She hadn't told either Max or Martha about her visits, not because she feared their disapproval (although Martha would certainly be surprised she'd found her way into a Catholic church – it just happened to be nearest) but because she needed her own private world. Martha might think it was role playing, and/or self-dramatization in a new area. But she would be wrong.

Eve clasped her hands together, not in supplication but in sheer intensity of emotion. This was the first time she'd looked into her heart. She felt on tiptoe, on the edge of a journey.

'Do you need any help?'

Eve started violently and opened her eyes. She'd seen him before, a priest or a verger or whatever he was, appearing for a moment out of the shadows of the church and then disappearing. Now she saw he was small, balding, unassuming, standing in front of her with a cheerful, enquiring air. 'No. No. Thank you. I'm just going.' She looked for her bag and the priest (she noted his collar) stepped back. Her communing with the Blessed Mother Mary, Mother of Sorrows, didn't need a go-between.

'Of course.'

'I'm not a Catholic, you know!' Why had she blurted that out just as he was leaving? She was not only not a Catholic but not a believer either. She should have said that.

'Ah.' He approached cautiously, as one might a wild animal.

They stared at each other, although the dim light meant neither could see the other clearly.

'Actually my father was an Anglican vicar.' It occurred to Eve that she was telling him these things to avoid the thing that mattered.

'The two churches are very close.'

'You don't mind me coming, then?' Of course he didn't mind her coming – he was probably thrilled to have a daily worshipper even if she was outside the flock. It felt polite, however, to get his permission. Her father had talked of '*my* church'.

'Please,' said the priest. He hesitated, once again the wary animal trainer, before asking hesitantly, 'You have a particular affection for Mary?'

'I don't know,' said Eve. She clasped her bag close to herself. 'I am a mother.' Now she really did want to leave. She stood and he deferred to her, moving away.

'The church is unlocked all day.'

'Thank you.' She rushed away, swiftly down the aisle where, despite her emotion, she noticed several people had gathered as if there was to be a service. She must avoid this time of day in future.

Max arrived home earlier than usual and picked up Ronnie's message. He was surprised to find Eve had gone out and waited for her return. At first he was exhilarated but gradually he became more doubtful. Hope brought a new kind of pain.

When he heard Eve's key in the door, he felt his heart beat harder and faster. 'Eve!' he called out. It was a cry of warning. In the few days since the television appeal and Eve's move back into the flat, he had developed an entirely new sense of protectiveness towards her.

She came in quietly, dressed all in black. He wished she wouldn't do that, as if they were already in mourning. Once he asked her why she did it, not every day certainly but many, she'd told him it reflected her mood. She'd paused, eyed him gravely, then added, 'As one day you read a poem by Lorca and another by Duffy.' It was the first time in years she'd referred to his passion for poetry except in disapproval.

'Eve. Come and sit down.' She sat away from him, silently. 'Ronnie rang. There is news.' Although her expression of calm didn't change, tears sprang out of her eyes and rolled down her cheeks.

Max looked away, shocked that her tears were so close to the surface. He would have liked to hold her hand. He cleared his throat. 'A CCTV camera on Waterloo station has shown Dan there on the morning he disappeared. Soon they will know which train he boarded. It's the lead the police have been waiting for. They plan to rerun the appeal next week with this information.'

'Can I see the film?' Eve's voice was scarcely above a whisper.

Max hadn't thought of asking this. 'I'll call Ronnie.' He stood up and came over to Eve. She had stopped crying. Instead she was trembling all over. He couldn't believe how small she seemed, like a bird too fragile to be comforted. 'Can I get you something?'

She didn't answer. He wondered vaguely, as he had before, about doctors and soothing pills. She'd always taken Valium but perhaps now she needed more. Or perhaps they'd put her into a dream where he could not reach her.

'So there might be more news now. Any day.' She was still whispering.

'I suppose so.' He fought against the restlessness that drove him every day to look out for Dan. He could still do his job, but only just. 'Trains from Waterloo station travel to the south-west. To my area.'

'Yes. Yes.' She stood up in an agitated manner. 'When can we see this film? I must see it. I can tell so much from it.'

'I'll ring Ronnie now.' But Ronnie was not there. Max kept his eyes on her as he left a message. He was frightened for this new person she'd become. He wanted to ask Martha if she'd been like this after their mother's death but he and Martha were not speaking unless it was unavoidable. He'd overheard her telling Eve that she had problems with a prisoner.

'I've always hated London in August!' said Eve, with a sudden, vicious energy. She got up and, with shaking hands, poured herself a large gin and tonic. This was routine. This was all right. Max didn't worry even if she knocked herself out with it and went to bed. Eve had always liked to drink in time of crisis – usually holidays or over weekends. He needed to believe she still had a sense of self-preservation.

*

It was two hours before Ronnie rang back. Eve had drifted up to bed, placing her trust in Max, so he hoped, although, just as likely, she'd drunk herself into the calm of irresponsibility.

Max immediately asked if he and Eve could see the film but Ronnie spoke about 'enhancement' and 'technicalities' and 'due process'. He was guarded in a way he hadn't been before as if the arrival of hard information had given him new powers and a need to be treated with respect.

'Eve is very keen,' persevered Max. 'I think she feels she will learn about his state of mind, which might help with working out what he was up to.' Actually, he thought, Eve just wanted, needed, to *see* him.

'I understand. We'll get the film on television too. It's our first breakthrough and I'm hopeful we'll pick him up buying a ticket, even going through the barriers and getting on a train. There're cameras everywhere. Even if some of them don't work. It's going through the film that takes time.'

Max felt irritated by his confident cheeriness. 'But people *do* disappear.'

There was a pause as if Ronnie was running through his repertoire of positive answers to this bit of negative thinking. Max realized that he was finding it very difficult to adjust to the chink of light in the blackness he'd become accustomed to. Since Ronnie still hadn't spoken, he added quietly, 'Just keep us informed. Everything.'

'Of course.'

After he'd put the telephone down, Max contemplated drinking himself into a stupor like Eve. The trouble was that alcohol 'enhanced' – to use Ronnie's word – his imagination. What he most needed was to speak to someone. Without thinking further, he dialled Martha's number.

'Yes.' The voice was strange, not Martha's clipped efficiency.

'Martha?'

'Oh, it's you.'

'You didn't sound like yourself.'

'I've been getting funny calls. You know.'

'Heavy breathing?'

'Not exactly. Are you all right?'

'Have you heard the news?' He explained about the CCTV camera and everything that might follow. At the end he said, with the kind of appeal in his voice that few women had resisted (past habits die hard), 'Can we meet? I need to talk to you.'

The pub was old-fashioned and dark, which suited Martha who would have liked to be invisible. But she needed to talk too, perhaps more than Max. He was late and she'd already drunk half her lager.

She put her hand to her eyes as a man pushed open the door from the outside and walked towards the bar. In a second, he had become Max, then Dan, then Lee. He was none of them. This was happening often, as if these images, running through her mind on a continuous loop, looked for a physical body to inhabit.

Lee had rung her several more times, always at night. She'd reported this to the prison, Probation and the police, just as she should, and they'd offered to intervene or change her number or, since they were looking for him, tap her calls. But before they could set up any of this, she'd told them he'd stopped ringing. They believed her. She was a good, responsible officer.

No wonder she imagined she saw Lee. Very probably he was stalking her. Very probably he was drinking again.

'Hi.'

Max looked as if he'd been standing in front of her for more than a moment. He was wearing a dark green shirt, his face was thin and his black hair long. She tried not to think about when they had been naked in bed together, his urgent body pressed against her. 'Hello, Max.'

'Would you like another?' He indicated her glass.

'Not yet.'

She watched him go to the bar. His shoulders were hunched and when the light fell on his hair, she saw it was streaked with grey. This was reality.

They sat opposite each other across the small table but neither looked in the other's face.

'I'm sure we'll hear more tomorrow. Perhaps even which station he travelled to,' said Max. He drank a lime juice cordial and soda thirstily. 'I can't help thinking he had a plan, somewhere he was going or someone he was going to. The police keep asking me questions. Right from the beginning I couldn't answer them.'

This loquacious person was unlike the Max of before Dan's

disappearance. Perhaps his attractiveness to women had disinclined him to make an effort or reveal much beyond the monumental packaging.

Martha, of course, she told herself, knew more of him than that, but this man seemed edgy, volatile, unstrung. 'How is Eve?' she asked.

'Drunk. Asleep. Coping the best way she knows.' Max stopped speaking and lay back in his chair for a moment, then leant forward and said, with even more passion, 'This is my time of trial. Even a few days ago when we were mouthing those platitudes in front of a gawping nation – or, more likely, an uninterested nation – I hadn't taken it in. Dan's disappearance is the most important thing in my life. Nothing – nothing equals it. I used to think of myself as a poet. Not just because I'd had a few things published but because that was the way I thought. My head was full of words, images, ideas. Mostly other people's. Writing a reasonable poem was the ultimate challenge. Now you could put me in the *Oxford Book of Verse* or make me Poet Laureate, Nobel-prize winner, none of it has any meaning. Most probably never did. My life had no point. No point at all. Pointless job. Pointless women, pointless vanity, pointless books. But what I can't see is how I was so stupid. I had Dan under my nose. Why couldn't I see him? Why couldn't I see him until he wasn't there? Call that ironic? You tell me. Oh, God.' He stopped abruptly.

Martha thought he might cry. She felt both deeply sorry for him and very far away. She would hate it if he cried. Hate him too. Men like him shouldn't cry. 'Dan's disappearance is changing us all.' She could hear how cold her voice sounded. There seemed no way she could tell him her story but that was why she'd come. She had to make the effort. 'I'm getting another drink.' He didn't look up as she went to the bar.

'I'm sorry.' He greeted her return more calmly. 'I warned you I needed to talk.' He managed a smile. 'I don't want to land Eve with too much.'

But he didn't mind landing it on her. Yet now that he was stronger, she felt his attraction again. 'I'm glad I was here to listen.' How formal they were!

'Thank you.' There was a longish pause as if now he'd spoken he wanted to leave, before he decided to make an effort. 'You're still working, aren't you?' In the past he'd never showed much curiosity about her work – unlike most people, who longed to worm out juicy details of murderers and rapists. She used to enjoy spoiling their fun: 'They're ordinary people. Like you and me,' she'd say. 'Just that things went wrong for them.' Max's lack of interest had been a relief but his questioning now gave her the opportunity she needed. 'I told you about the funny calls. Well, it's an ex-prisoner.'

Max looked up at her, his extraordinary blue eyes making her catch her breath. She forced herself to notice the red veins and the bags below. There was dandruff on his dark shirt. 'Is he violent?'

'Oh, no!' she answered quickly, almost shocked by the question.

'So, you're not afraid?' He seemed to relax as if violence was the only thing to be afraid of.

'It's more complicated than that.' Of course he was a violent man, but that wasn't what frightened her. She saw that Max was only slightly interested as if the smallest part of his mind was reserved for things not to do with Dan and his own situation. Now was the moment to tell him Dan was involved but she already knew she was going to funk it.

'I suppose you've told the police.'

She could see how hard it was for him to imagine the police spending time doing anything other than search for Dan. And what could she say that made any sense? 'A lifer prisoner has made it his mission to find Dan, a lifer who killed a man with a broken bottle among others, and although he is not a paedophile, he is not thought suitable to visit his own fourteen-year-old son.' How could Max react in any way but to scream, 'Lock him up!'?

'The police know. Police. Probation.' Martha sipped at her lager. She never drank in the week but since she was breaking all her rules of engagement, she might as well break this too. Pity she wasn't enjoying it. She pushed away the glass. 'How's Eve?' she asked, before remembering she'd asked earlier and he'd answered, 'Drunk.'

'Actually, I have faith in Lee – that's the ex-prisoner's name. I've worked with him for two years. I think he's had a lot of bad luck. He's educated himself while he's been in prison. He understands himself and he understands the world. He deserves a new life.' She paused before adding, 'He's tough, too.'

'So why's he ringing you?'

This was sharper than she'd expected. 'I suppose I'm a sort of home base.' Whatever had she meant by that? Luckily, Max didn't ask.

'I'd better get back to Eve.' He looked at her. 'I feel protective.' A message here. 'It has to be worst for the mother.'

'I'm on the early shift. I should go.'

They both stood. 'They may want us back on television with the further news.'

'Yes.' Martha bowed her head. Her sense of aloneness felt like a physical pain.

They walked out together and parted on the street. After he'd left, Martha stood for a moment. It was neither cold nor warm, no stars in the sky, no wind, few people. She was unwilling to go back to her empty house.

'Martha.' The voice came from behind her. She didn't want to turn, as if all decisions were beyond her. 'No worries. Trust me.'

She turned and Lee was there, her height, her build; they were alike. Brother and sister.

'Let's go in here.' They stepped together into the pub.

CHAPTER TWENTY-FOUR

Lee didn't seem like a man who was living rough. He was clean-shaven and his hair was smoothly cut. He wore a cotton jacket with several pockets and flaps. He looked younger than he had in prison. Martha was surprised.

'This shouldn't be happening.'

'No.'

They sat at the same table she'd been sitting at with Max a few minutes earlier. She felt she could see their shadows still there, he so big but bowed in defeat, she upright and defensive. She had been defending Lee.

'I assume you're not drinking.' Her voice was that of a prison officer but she wasn't in uniform and he wasn't in her control.

He didn't answer but went up to the bar and came back with what looked like a double whisky for himself and half a lager, which he pushed towards her. One of the conditions for his release was no alcohol.

'You know I'm better out than in.'

She thought briefly. 'I believe so,' she agreed wearily. 'But you shouldn't harass me.'

He sipped, not gulped, his whisky. She guessed he was estimating how far he could go with her. 'Is there more news about Dan?' It was only Dan that interested him.

She sipped her own drink, more than she'd drunk for a long time. Had he been spying on Max and her, that he knew what she'd been drinking? He would have recognized Max from the television appeal. A feeling of recklessness made her cheeks burn. 'They've identified Dan on CCTV at Waterloo. The day he left. Soon we'll know where he was going. Probably we'll be back on TV.'

'What was he like, your nephew?' He looked at her attentively. In prison he had seemed removed, as if he wasn't willing to accept where he was or the grounds on which any conversation took place. He was very present now, alarmingly so. Although his manner was deferential, she felt his will was stronger than hers.

'Dan was quiet, thoughtful. Liked books more than his computer. A loner. Didn't find it easy to make friends. No trouble at school. None at home. Sometimes we went camping together. He liked that. Being in the countryside.'

'So it makes sense that he left the city?'

'I suppose so.' She thought of Dan in the countryside. His pale face peering curiously at the dawn. One year they'd camped by a lake and in the evening birds had flown in from all corners of the sky. Dan had been entranced, standing with his arms outstretched till she'd called him Saint Francis and told him to come and eat his beefburgers before they got cold. One warm day he'd spent the entire afternoon lying under a tree waiting for a woodpecker, as he informed her, that he'd heard tapping. Perhaps she should have thought of this before but their camping trips had been short and widely spaced. Essentially he was a city boy, born and bred. And, after all, just because he'd left from Waterloo, it didn't mean he hadn't headed for another city, Southampton, Basingstoke, Exeter.

'If I call you tomorrow, will you tell me the news?'

'I'm on early shift.'

'In the afternoon, then.'

'They'll pick you up long before you can get on Dan's tracks.'

He didn't answer but went and got himself another double. He didn't bring anything more for Martha who'd only half drunk her first. She didn't want to know where his money came from, where he was living or how.

'I must go.'

'Yes.' He stood for her. Again Martha was aware of their similarities. They stood eye to eye, arms straight to their sides, no intention of shaking hands. In fact, a salute would have felt more appropriate, as if they were members of a secret cadre on a mission. That was fanciful. She walked away quickly, aware she'd taken a step into the unknown and not sure why, but determined not to regret it.

*

Eve whispered to Max, in the dark, 'I had a dream.'

Max, who'd been drifting in a foggy sleep, woke fully and put out his hand to reassure her. He met a crumple of cloth. In the past, they'd both slept naked but lately she'd taken to shrouding herself in loose garments and shawls, protection, he assumed, against the dangers of the world rather than against her husband. Nevertheless, he'd taken to wearing underpants in which he felt constricted and slightly absurd.

'Was it a bad one?'

'I'd give it six.' She turned over and he smelt the heat of her body and the fumes of alcohol. It was not unpleasant.

It seemed unfair to Max that at times of real trouble, the imagination or the unconscious, whatever it was, heightened horrors further during sleep. A couple of lines came into his head, '*Thou hast been called, O Sleep! The friend of Woe, but 'tis the happy who have called thee so.*'

'What?'

He must have spoken aloud. 'Nothing. Try to sleep. It'll be light soon.' More lines of poetry came into his head. '*I see the waves upon the shore/Like light dissolved in star-showers, thrown.*' That was Shelley from 'Stanzas Written in Dejection' near Naples. When Max had decided only poetry could express the world, he'd learnt twenty or thirty lines a day, so that the language of poets filled his head. He supposed it had been natural to progress from that to wanting to join them not just in the learning but the creating.

Eve had loved him for it. They would lie together, usually after making love, while he recited poetry and sometimes inserted lines of his own. He won a point if she didn't pick it up. Often she lay with her head on his chest because she liked the rumble of the words, feeling them go through her body. Poetry had bound them together.

When had it changed and his poetry become private to him? Probably when he became conscious of failure. Not Eve's fault. Poetry had turned into a barrier between them.

'I'm going to make tea.'

She groaned a little and turned away from him.

He sat in the kitchen and wondered what Dan was doing at this precise moment. He had done this so often that it was no longer a completely painful exercise. Occasionally his mind even conjured up a few seconds of hope: a young boy laughing, not totally like Dan, taller and stronger, surrounded by new friends. Sometimes he was declaiming. When had Dan ever declaimed? These were small antidotes to the worst imaginings.

Max sipped his tea and hoped that his son was sleeping quietly. When he'd been very young, he'd sucked two fingers.

The priest approached Eve more decisively. She spotted him through her wet eyes and her wet hair and her wet mind. Perhaps she had summoned him to succour her. She could do with succour. Tears continued to fall.

'May I sit with you?'

She nodded, although she wasn't sure she wanted him close. He didn't sit very close and, apart from rather heavy breathing, possibly asthmatic, he was silent. It seemed polite to try to stifle her sobbing. Which was a relief, really, because when these fits of crying took hold of her, she found it difficult to stop. What was the point after all? She might as well drown in her tears.

She glanced at him sideways. He was leaning forward, praying, she assumed. But that wasn't much use to her. It was nice of him, all the same, for an unbeliever. People were nice to her, not just priests. It was a pity it was all such a waste. Nothing was of any use except Dan's return. She managed to stop herself crying again.

'Would you like a cup of tea?'

This was a bit of a surprise. Surely priests wanted people in church, not drinking cups of tea. Perhaps she embarrassed him, lowered the tone of the church. Had she told him her father was an Anglican vicar? She couldn't remember. At least it would prove to him that she was church-trained, not likely to scream or vomit or pee. Actually, she didn't have the energy for grand gestures. 'Thank you.'

She followed him out of the church and through various corridors into a large room, bright by contrast with the church. She thought what a fright she must look and wondered whether still being self-aware meant she was not yet at rock bottom or whether it was merely the actor's reflex, reaching for the lipstick on her deathbed.

The priest busied himself with the kettle before turning. 'My name is Father Louis Henderson.'

'My name is Eve.'

'Then you must call me Louis, or Father Louis, if you prefer.' He turned back to the kettle and the teabags, the mugs and the milk.

Eve felt exhausted by everything that went into making a cup of tea. She did prefer Father Louis, even Father, singly.

A woman's head, dark and smooth, peered round the door. 'Good morning, Father.' So she preferred 'Father' too. Perhaps all women could do with an extra father or two.

'God bless you, Helen.'

The woman withdrew her blessed head.

'I expect you're busy,' said Eve, as Father Louis brought the mugs of tea to the table. It was extraordinary to consider anyone else even in this minimal way.

'I always try to have tea about now. Do you take sugar?'

Eve wondered whether he would ever ask her a question. She suspected not, so to get it over with she swallowed a gulp of tea and said, 'My son has been missing for over a month.' It could have been decades, a lifetime.

'So you're praying to the Mother of God.'

'There's nothing much else to do. But I'd say I was more sitting in her company than praying.'

'And does it bring you comfort?'

The first question. 'No. But I don't blame her because nothing could.'

Outside the door two voices started a discussion. The priest stood up. 'I'll leave you for a moment.'

When he had gone Eve drank her tea and was aware of enjoying it a little. Recently only alcohol had given her any pleasure.

The priest was gone for some time, long enough for her to finish it. But she felt no inclination to move. When he came back he was less calm – in fact, quite harassed. 'I'm sorry. Something's come up. I'll have to go. But stay as long as you like. Helen may come in to sort some flyers, but please stay.'

Eve thought someone needed him more than she did. 'Thank you for the tea. You didn't drink yours.'

He smiled ruefully. 'My fault for not grabbing my chance.' He went to the door. 'God bless,' he said, half under his breath – presumably in case she didn't fancy it.

Eve sat on and soon Helen appeared, carrying two boxes of papers. 'Sorry to disturb you.'

'Not at all.'

Eve watched her as she set to work; a flyer had to be put into a leaflet. She knew she should offer to help but her fingers were weak and shaking so she kept them curled round her empty mug. Helen's head remained bent over her work. She had a contented smile on her face and after a while Eve noticed she was wearing earphones. Sacred or profane? she wondered. Music from the church, a motet from Mozart, plainchant, a grand Haydn or, de Victoria mass, or easy-listening to keep her cheerful – Piazzola, Abba?

Her father, the vicar, had not liked music but some ladies had set up a compilation music loop inside the church, which they switched on for festival days. The effect was curious, magnificent choir turned down to a background level of mellifluence.

Helen looked up. 'How about a cup of something?' This was not an offer but a request.

Eve was startled. No one had asked anything of her for weeks. She was tempted to say, 'How can you expect me to boil water, open a jar, measure out coffee granules, find milk, sugar' – all the palaver she'd watched with respect when executed by Father Louis – 'at a time when my son is missing, perhaps kidnapped, abused, tortured and/or dead?'

'Don't worry. I'll do it.' Helen stood up.

The tears were coming again: she could feel them bubbling under the surface, powerful springs ready to burst out into the daylight.

'I'm sorry,' she said. And at least she didn't cry.

'Would you like another cup?'

Liking had nothing to do with it but she accepted another as an excuse to stay anchored at the table. Probably Helen was only a few years younger than her but she felt a gap as wide as youth from age, as happiness from sorrow.

It took Helen another half an hour to finish the leaflets. Eve was amazed at the speed she worked. She piled them neatly into the two boxes, before sitting back and looking at Eve with clear hazel eyes. 'Father Louis's wonderfully sympathetic, isn't he? I was very down. Boyfriend gone. Job gone. Self-respect gone. So he told me to come along and make myself useful.'

'Gone,' repeated Eve. She could have smiled at the simplicity of the word in Helen's mouth. She wondered vaguely if the priest had left them together so Helen could be an example of turning unhappiness into practical use.

'Do you have a job?'

'I'm a drama teacher.' Eve produced this definition with a sense of disbelief. Since she'd finished her summer course, work had not entered her head. Yet quite soon she was expected, contracted, to take up her usual role as head of drama in the school – Dan's school. However had she managed to shut this out of her mind? Even now it only agitated her in a distant way.

'A drama teacher!' Helen sounded as surprised as her. 'At least teachers don't get sacked.' She looked at her watch. 'Time for my walk. Father Louis's prescribed exercise. Want to come?'

Eve saw she was obedient, energetic and insensitive. On the other hand, maybe she was trying to remove her. She rose reluctantly. 'I'll come out with you.'

They left by the church again, Helen genuflecting obsequiously (in Eve's eyes) as they crossed the altar. It gave her a twinge of pleasure to stay strictly upright and notice that Helen had noticed.

They walked down the centre aisle and parted outside on the steps where the sun had heated the stone walls. Eve felt faint and didn't reply to Helen's goodbye. Dan had left in a heatwave. Martha had said, 'Not so bad for sleeping out,' and Eve had been angry. Now her sister's views didn't affect her.

Eve tottered slowly along the hot pavement heading for a café. She was as determined not to return to her flat as usually she was determined not to leave it.

She sat outside. The café was quiet, too early for lunch; only one other person was at a table, a young man reading the *Sun*. He wore heavy dust-covered boots, dirty jeans and a T-shirt. The skin of his arms was sunburnt and on one there was the start of a tattoo, subject unrecognizable as it disappeared under his shirt. She couldn't see his face clearly.

It was a result of her obsessional thoughts, Eve knew, that she felt absolutely certain that this random stranger could give her a clue to Dan's whereabouts. She changed her table so that she was nearer to him. The sun and the tension were making sweat prickle on her scalp.

'Excuse me.' Speaking released a little bit of tension. She could understand now those deranged women who cut themselves and watched the blood trickle with relief.

The man hadn't looked up or appeared to hear. 'You might be able to help me. I'd be so grateful.'

He lifted his head, stared at her with wide grey eyes. He spoke a word or two in a language she recognized as Polish. But if he didn't understand English, why was he reading the *Sun*? She peered over and saw a photograph of a topless woman. 'Sorry.'

She moved back to her original table and began to watch the passers-by. There were not too many but enough for her imagination to work on: a scrawny old man with a beard became Fagin with a stable of young thieves. A bosomy middle-aged woman turned into a generic ex-prostitute with connection to slave traders. A young African man with a bit of a swagger and a gold chain transformed into a drug-dealer with a successful sideline in boy prostitutes. It became a kind of game in which Eve dressed up the worst in theatrical clichés, hoping to undercut their power. She ran the risk of properly frightening herself.

A boy came past: tired, sad eyes, long unkempt hair, scuffed trainers. She thought he was speaking to himself until he came closer and she noticed the earpiece. He must have been nineteen or twenty. Not like Dan, however much he'd changed. She sat back and tried not to look any more. But from under her half-closed lids she saw a thin man advancing, walking stiffly, head bent as if in pain, and he reminded her so strongly of Dan that her whole body tautened with instinctive recognition. Yet at the same time she knew this wasn't her son: he was too tall, too dark, a man, not a child.

'Eve.'

'Max.'

He sat down beside her and ordered a coffee. She felt he was pleased to find her in the café instead of holed up in their flat. She wondered when she would tell him about her visits to the church. She wanted them to be close but didn't yet fully trust him.

'Ronnie's been in touch,' said Max, after finishing his cup of coffee as if he needed strength. 'I was in the office so he caught me. He's got some more news. He wants to come round.'

'Ah,' mouthed Eve, and found herself giving an odd, fish-like smile, as if a welcome guest had been proposed. It was amazing how many levels and different kinds of pain there were. Every time she confronted one, doing her best to survive whatever anguish it brought, another appeared, charging down from the horizon, ready to spear, squeeze, shred or pummel her heart.

'It's nothing bad, Ronnie said.'

'Ask him to come here.'

'Here? You mean here?' Max looked up at the sky helplessly as if Eve had set him a difficult problem. They were both like that, she thought sympathetically, only half their minds able to focus on ordinary practicalities. Or perhaps it was strange, even unnatural of her to want to hear news about Dan in a public place. Perhaps it was inappropriate or even against police rules. Perhaps they had to sit on their sofa drinking cups of tea made in their own kitchen.

'Do you remember,' she said, 'the advice given to a lover trying to break off an affair? Take her to a restaurant and she won't be able to cry.'

'But this isn't bad news, so Ronnie told me.' Max's voice had a despairing note, despite his comforting words.

'Emotional anyway,' said Eve, looking at his face properly for the first time. If anything, the haggardness made him even more striking.

'I'll give him a call.'

While Max called, Eve went inside and found the Ladies. She peered at herself in the round mirror, whose frame was decorated with coloured pieces of glass. She put on red lipstick, black eye pencil and mascara. She brushed her hair and tied it back. The room was very small and smelt of a particularly disgusting air-freshener promising Wood Perfume but more like rotting toadstools.

She glanced once more into the mirror and stepped out to face the music.

Max was standing up to spot Ronnie's arrival. Not that there were any other cafés on the street. Actually, he was avoiding the tragedy of Eve's face. He hoped Ronnie wouldn't be too ebullient. Ronnie was fine but he was strong and confident with a nice wife and two young daughters. Max half believed, because everything now related to Dan (how had it been when he was just their son?), that Ronnie had been chosen for their case because he was only a father of girls. Here he was now, with his sturdy, slightly rolling walk. *Shoot the messenger.*

'Hi, Max, Eve.' Ronnie lowered his bulk into a chair after first taking off his jacket and hanging it on the back. 'Hot!' He pulled out a handkerchief and wiped his face. He was a gingery sort of man whose face reddened easily.

Max was hot too, sweat under his arms and down his back. He thought with longing of damp green grass, gentle reedy rivers overhung by trailing willows.

'Not to beat about the bush, we've traced Dan to the ticket office, buying his ticket, single, and to his destination.' He paused.

Max saw Eve couldn't speak. Her skin was ghostly pale against her black-rimmed eyes. 'Where?' he asked, but he thought despairingly that all this information was more than a month old.

Ronnie named the station and Max, shocked, rose to his feet. 'I go to that town often. It's on my beat.' He felt outraged, insulted. How could this be true and, if it was, why had he not known it – felt Dan's presence instinctively, if nothing else? It was the town Alison inhabited.

Ronnie was soothing. 'We don't know if he stayed there. It isn't a big place. More likely he left immediately and went into the country-side. A local search team has already been alerted.'

'I want to be there.' Max felt both childish and defiant.

'I'm sure they could do with your help – leafleting, posters, jogging people's memories.' Max felt an absurd gush of relief that there was something he could do.

'And we're negotiating with the TV chaps for another interview.' Ronnie looked at Eve. 'I suppose your sister's working today?'

'Yes,' said Eve. Max knew she had no idea what Martha was doing. 'I think I'd be strong enough to do the TV bit this time,' continued Eve. She peered at Ronnie in a kindly, gracious way, as if he'd invited her to a pleasant evening out.

There are no precedents for any of this, thought Max, and he quoted to himself, *Heaven stops the nose at it, and the moon winks.* Eve used to ask, with a mocking giggle, 'Penny for your poem.'

'Do you know anyone in the neighbourhood?' asked Ronnie.

'No.' Max thought of Alison, her sunny looks untouched by the sadness of divorce. 'No,' he repeated. 'I take orders from the book-shop, that's all.' He began to feel an irrational anger with Ronnie's calm good sense. 'Did anyone see him get off the train?'

'We don't know. They'll look at the CCTV footage as soon as they can.'

'Soon,' said Eve. 'I need a drink.'

'Or lunch,' said Max.

Eve looked at him disapprovingly, before relenting. 'At last we can do something.'

'Yes,' agreed Ronnie, although he frowned as if suspecting criticism.

'I'll go back to the office and see if I can take the rest of the week off.' Max wondered if Eve planned to come, too, and a crazy picture came into his head of them picnicking in the fields as if on holiday.

Eve watched Ronnie and Max stand, each with an urgent, determined air. She thought that men were unreasonably cheered by a task in hand. It was why, she supposed, they liked being soldiers and wars were fought.

After they'd gone, she wandered back to the church and her place in front of the Virgin Mary. This time she was uninterrupted so she was able to submit a lengthy plea in which she offered Mary the new information and advised her she 'could do with it what she wilt'. This form of words came to her from somewhere and she liked their modesty. After she finished her supplication she sat on in a hazy stupor (she had not had her drink but neither had she eaten) and only got to her feet when an insubstantial presence lit two candles on the altar, which she assumed to be the prelude to a service.

Taking a last look at the painted but kindly face of Mary, she seemed to notice a new expression, a weary anxiety such as she often felt, although without the usual overlay of pious resignation. For the first time she remembered that Mary and Joseph had also lost their son at about the same age as Dan. They had searched for days, increasingly desperate. They had found him, of course, preaching to admiring elders in the temple. When Mary reproached him, he had answered, as far as Eve could remember, 'Didn't you realize I must be about my father's business?' A cruel reminder that he was only theirs during his childhood.

Eve sat forward and covered her eyes. If Mary had needed a harsh lesson in the limits of motherhood, how hard was it for her? Pulling herself together, she admitted the comparison was absurd and probably sacrilegious. Nevertheless, she felt slightly comforted. Understanding your son is not always so easy.

As she left the church for the second time that day she remembered she hadn't asked Ronnie about viewing the CCTV. Maybe she wasn't strong enough, or maybe she'd watch it when it was shown on television.

CHAPTER TWENTY-FIVE

Lee was waiting for Martha in an alley that ran beside her house. She felt annoyed, frightened and excited. She'd just received a message from Ronnie on her mobile, giving the name of the town where Dan had left the train. She wanted to sit down and think about it quietly.

'You shouldn't be here,' she hissed, her heart beating too fast. 'I can turn you in any time I want.' He came closer, and again she was struck by something similar about them. She hadn't felt this in prison, or perhaps she'd translated it into the special care she gave to him. Then it had been her job. Now her job was to hand him over to the police or Probation. Her mobile was in her pocket.

'I want to know the news.'

'You're stalking me.' But upping the ante like that wasn't going to scare him. His intentions were fixed. She turned away from him and opened the door to her house. She knew he'd follow. Now she'd crossed a whole other line. Like the first time she'd slept with Max. Her memory produced this link without her willing it and she closed it down quickly. 'Five minutes,' she said. It was madness but her cheeks flushed with pleasure.

They sat in her living room. He was clean and composed. He didn't seem to take any note of their surroundings. His colour had improved so his eyes seemed paler. Although his hair was grey, his eyebrows and eyelashes were dark. She told him the name of the station and that it was a smallish town. 'His father goes there on business,' she said.

He thought about this. 'So he's in the countryside?'

'Probably. Where are you living?' she asked him.

'With a friend.'

A friend. A girlfriend?

'He'll get me a car.' A friend with money, then. 'You don't have to worry about me.' He stood up, smiling. 'Lots of us make friends inside. We know we'll need them on the out.'

Martha thought of reminding him that, in her two years as his personal officer, he had never told her he had useful friends to welcome him back into the world. She had pictured him alone, scarcely surviving in a grim hostel. She was sure she'd not invented this but had been led there by him. Of course the friend (or friends) might not be the sort you declared when discussing matters of resettlement.

'It's a pity you didn't name your friend as your place of residence.' She stood up too. Facing him, she felt a simple animal desire to make him want her. She led the way to the door. He went out quickly, without looking back. He really had been with her for only five minutes.

Max went to a specialist shop in Covent Garden and bought an Ordnance Survey map for the area, including the town where Dan's train had arrived. Then he decided to spread his search further and bought six more. They were surprisingly expensive and he surprised himself by noticing it. How could money be relevant?

He'd always liked maps, the secrets captured by a code; narrowing and widening, the broken lines, dots, mini trees, the circles of tiny arrows indicating tumuli, ancient camps, earthworks and castles.

He wanted to spread them out and imagine where Dan might have gone but he was afraid of doing it in the flat and upsetting Eve. Previously he'd have headed to Martha. Instead he returned to the office and found a desk belonging to an absent colleague. She was a woman and there was a photo of her happy family, which he laid face down.

He'd hardly spread out the first map before Stan, a newcomer to the sales department, joined him. He had thick blond hair and plenty of confidence.

'Going for a hike, are we? Or plotting new bookshops in the field?' He laughed.

Max looked up at his friendly face. He felt such an insurmountable barrier between them that it didn't seem possible to tell him the true story. 'Always plotting,' he agreed.

That didn't satisfy Stan. He bent over the maps. 'West Country, I see. Just look at those names.' He began to read out a litany of villages: 'Toller Porcorum, Haselbury Plucknett, Hardington Mandeville, Winford Eagle, Queen Camel, Charlton Mackrell, Melbury Osmond, Compton Pauncefoot.'

Max realized he couldn't stand any more of this steamroller squashing his dreams. He'd pictured Dan at Melbury Osmond. He muttered, 'Forgotten something,' refolded the map and left the office. In the corridor he met his boss, an imposing man with a large nose and a slight stutter. 'Any n-news?' Russell asked.

His sympathetic question caught Max in a different wave of emotion. He put his hand to his eyes.

'Here, come into my office.' Head down, Max allowed himself to be led. 'Sit down.'

Still clasping the maps, his link to his son, Max sank down gratefully. Being on the road so much, he was seldom in the office, but he trusted Russell and, as he recovered himself, he became aware of the working bustle outside, which, combined with the protective calm of Russell and his office, gave him a sense of security. He thought that what he dreaded most was those hours alone with Eve in their flat.

'They've traced Dan as far as Sherston Abbas.'

'On your beat,' Russell acknowledged.

Max explained he wanted to join the police search there and perhaps further afield. Once more he unfolded the map and laid it on Russell's desk. He was beginning to see it as a kind of board game, with Dan the only piece. In his daytime imagination, Dan was always on his own. At night he was joined by the horrors.

'You d-do that,' said Russell. 'If you can take in a few bookshops, so much the better.'

Max made an effort to feel warmed by his consideration. 'You've been very kind.'

'We all feel for you.'

That must be true because he hadn't been much use to them over the last month and was now proposing to be even less. He didn't want to leave the office but at least he could prolong his visit by getting his briefing for the next week.

'I once met a man called Winford Eagle.' Russell tapped the map.

'I always assumed his p-parents came from the area.' He paused. 'Our novelists should look here for their names.'

Max did his best to smile and, soon after, left the office. Sticking a pin in the maps, or choosing a village name suitable for a man, might do as well as careful planning.

Martha's home seemed cold, despite the warmth of the evening. It had been Adrian's house, already established when they met. He was a clever, successful solicitor who had told her from the start that he didn't want children. 'I'm not the dad type,' he'd said, 'neither to you nor to little kiddies.' He was twenty years older than her, wiry and taut and very sexy. Perhaps he'd married her as combination of mistress and housekeeper. She was willing enough.

His hobby was philosophy and in the evenings he'd sit reading Descartes and Kant, Wittgenstein and Sartre. He'd inherited some money and he also enjoyed playing the stock market. Looking back, she couldn't quite remember what she had done while he had pursued his interests.

She'd thought it ironic that for all his philosophical insights – *Only rare human beings achieve a heroic life* was one of his favourites – when he had discovered he had inoperable cancer, he had taken it as a personal attack and made no attempt to subdue a bitter rage. He was stoic, though, no complaints about his physical unravelling, just fury about his early death.

After he had died she'd packed up his books of philosophy and driven them to a local Oxfam shop, an action she later regretted, as one or other appeared regularly in the window – a huge tome by Sartre featured particularly often. Perhaps there was not much call for philosophy in Brixton. But she'd felt saddened and disloyal. In the end she'd bought the book herself and tried to read it. She'd even copied a passage out and stuck it on her fridge: *Freedom entails total responsibility, in the face of which we experience anguish, forlornness and despair; genuine human dignity can be achieved only in active acceptance of these emotions.*

Possibly it had spurred her into leaving her office job and training for the prison service. She had wanted to be engaged in something difficult. She'd started running more seriously at the same time.

Martha picked up the phone and dialled Gerry's number at the prison. 'I'm not doing well,' she told him. It was his job to sort her out.

'This McLeish stuff's got to you?'

'McLeish?' Naturally, he'd used Lee's surname and why would he think that he was her problem? She'd assumed that he'd assume the tragedy of a missing nephew was upsetting her.

'He'll turn up. In cuffs. It's hard when you've worked closely with someone and they let you down.'

'Yes,' agreed Martha, as her best option. There was a pause. 'The police have traced Dan out of London.'

'It's taken them long enough.'

'Yes,' agreed Martha again. Gerry's blandness, which she'd previously taken for sympathy, now seemed a sign of inert insensitivity. Definitely not one of Adrian's heroic *Übermenschen*. She didn't know why Adrian and his philosophy were sticking around in her mind.

'What time are you in tomorrow? We've got a new challenge for you.'

'Midday.'

'Put on your gladrags. This new lad's twenty-six, in for GBH and signed up for the Open University. Thinks he's clever. Thought he'd suit you seeing as how you went to uni.'

'A long time ago,' said Martha. She remembered the first time she'd met Lee. He'd been determined to study too. It struck her that she'd always been a bit frightened of him, his pale, implacable eyes and slim, hard body. His Glaswegian accent had made her nervous of not understanding him. He'd said he wanted to study law but, of course, it hadn't happened. 'You're in the wrong prison,' she told him.

'I didn't put myself here,' he answered, which was true and not true. As so often, she'd let him get away with it.

After Gerry had rung off – rather suddenly, she could hear an emergency siren in the background – she made herself a cup of soup and wondered if tonight would be the night Max or Eve would ring. When she accepted that they wouldn't and that, in the new order of things, she didn't want them to, she wondered if she should give up on the Prison Service. Gerry was right. Lee had upset her to the extent that she'd broken all the rules. Sensibly, she should resign before she was thrown out. Oddly, she didn't find this idea worth considering. What would be, would be. She was glad Lee was on the out.

CHAPTER TWENTY-SIX

Max drove slowly along a narrow country lane. The hedges were tall and heavy with late-August weariness. Behind them trees rose, cutting out the sun, although sometimes he glimpsed the brightness of fields beyond, corn stubble or yellowing grass. When the road dipped, he entered a tunnel bounded by walls of sandy rock with dark branches laced overhead.

He was surprised that this was the way to the station – mainline, as it served trains from London as well as cross-country services. He'd timed his own arrival for half an hour before Dan's train would have arrived so that he could do a bit of a recce and then watch (in his imagination) his son stepping down from train to platform and making his way in one direction or the other. He knew what Dan had been wearing, the bag he had carried; it shouldn't be difficult to picture him and take the same steps.

He had considered whether to catch the train himself but he needed a car in the area.

The station surprised him again with the sparseness of its build-ings, amid widespread railway tracks, with only a small ticket office and a little further away what looked like a converted signalbox. He'd been prepared for the station to be out of town, odd but not unusual in rural areas, but the quiet, lackadaisical atmosphere was unexpected. After he'd parked the car and reached the platform, there was no sign of uniformed staff, indeed of anyone at all. The loudest sound was a robin singing from a wall.

He supposed he'd arrived with his head full of drama, which made this tranquil scene doubly disturbing. Wild flowers, mostly dry and bleached, grew between the tracks. He walked slowly along the platform, noting signs for Gents and Ladies, headed towards the bridge which crossed to the other side of the tracks, then diverted up some iron steps to the signal box, which, as he'd guessed, had been converted to a café. The door had a sign saying CLOSED and it was dark inside so he retraced his steps.

Now there were several people on the platform and a taxi had arrived outside. He went to the ticket office where a uniformed man was selling tickets to a small queue of people. Deciding to talk to him afterwards, he returned to the platform.

The weird, even spooky peace had gone, and in the brightness of early afternoon, the atmosphere was normal, cheerful. A family with several small children was creating a lot of noise while the mother tried to stop a toddler making a dash for the tracks. Vaguely, Max clocked that they must be heading for the sea with a towel half falling from one bag and a red plastic spade in another. But he was more conscious that they were from another world to which he felt invisible.

He looked at his watch: five more minutes to go. He tried to imagine Dan's face at the window: pale, fearful? Or excited by taking such uncharacteristic action? Neither seemed quite right.

At last the train, much bigger and noisier than he'd expected (but when had he last travelled by train?), came quite fast into the station. Absurdly, the sight made him want to burst into tears as if it really were bringing Dan towards him. Recovering himself, he watched as people struggled with the heavy doors, from inside or out. Only a handful of people got off, two middle-aged women, one with pink hair, an elderly man with a stick and a young man who, for a moment, made Max stare. He must get a grip. This was a stocky boy of about twenty with a heavy backpack and another bag. From his cropped hair, a soldier on leave.

All the same he followed his progress off the train, along the platform and out through the station. At the door, he stopped, looked right and left as if he were expecting someone. In another moment an old Mercedes saloon appeared driven by a woman who poked her head out of the window and called, 'Jack, over here! Sorry I'm late.' The boy went over quickly. Mother and son were smiling, happy to see each other.

This simple scene caused Max so much anguish that he ducked back inside the dimness of the station where he stood catching his breath. The other passengers passed him and soon he was alone.

'Can I help you?' It was the man at the ticket counter. When there was no answer, he pulled down the blind and came out.

Max knew he must speak to him before he disappeared again. Slowly, he explained why he was there. The man listened carefully, his smooth pink face with rather long sideburns, nodding at intervals. Each word Max spoke was painful to him.

'Yes. I know about your son.' His voice was business-like but softened by a West Country accent. 'The police were here earlier. Asking questions. They said they'd be bringing posters as soon as they've printed them. They seem to be taking it seriously.'

Max swallowed. 'Were you able to tell them anything?'

'Not for the date they mentioned. But unless someone is buying a ticket, I don't see much of anyone.'

'He's just fourteen. Tall for his age.'

'So the police said. I'll try to think.' The man looked at his watch. 'I've got to signal a fast train through.'

Just before he left, Max thought of something else. 'Was the café open then?'

'The police asked that too. "No" is the answer.' He started moving away. 'We have a job getting someone to work up there.' He continued speaking over his shoulder. 'Did have a girl round then but I checked and she came a few days later and then only lasted for a week. Said she felt like a stork in a nest. Spoilt rotten, kids, these days.' He hurried away.

The station reverted to its previous tranquillity. Max wondered whether Dan had stood as he was, unsure where to go next. It must have been a beautiful sunny afternoon too, with several more days before the heatwave broke. Whatever he did, he should walk, as Dan had done.

The exit road sloped up steeply and then he had to decide whether to take the road he'd come in on, which had skirted the town before turning into the countryside, or the road to his left, which seemed less frequented.

He walked left. The air was hot but the sun had disappeared behind a row of featureless grey clouds. Small black storm flies hovered round his face, keen, it seemed, to enter his nose or mouth. More ordinary flies gathered above his head. The road climbed steeply upwards. He had eaten nothing that day and felt very hungry.

After a while he stopped. The high hedges had gone and he could see more of the surrounding countryside, although the steep-sided hills and pockets of woodland obscured any real overview. He was surprised, however, how much there was of it, the town firmly behind him now and only the occasional farmhouse or small group of houses visible. Most of it was farmland but it seemed undomesticated, almost wild.

This was Thomas Hardy country, the ancient land that had defeated Tess d'Urberville and mostly tortured but sometimes consoled Hardy's heroes and heroines. He'd always preferred Hardy's poetry. *An aged thrush, frail, gaunt and small, / In blast-beruffled plume.*

Max sat down on a pile of stones. A spit of rain landed on his hand. He wiped it off and flapped at the flies. Soon it would rain and he had no shelter. He felt both distressed and foolish. How could he hope to find Dan by wandering round the countryside like a disoriented hippie?

The whole expedition was just a sentimental way of satisfying his own needs. Much better to return to his car and drive to the police station. He put his hand into his pocket to check for the car keys and instead felt his mobile, reminding him that he'd promised to call Eve the moment he arrived at the station. That had been nearly two hours ago.

He called their flat, and when there was no answer, from there or her mobile, felt guiltily relieved, although possibly he should have felt anxious.

It was beginning to drizzle, teardrops condensing in the warm air. He took one more look at the countryside and noticed how many tracks led off the road. More would be hidden by curves or woodland. If he'd been Dan and he'd come this way on a beautiful day, with food enough for a picnic, he'd have turned off on one of them, probably leading away from the town and the railway line. He would suggest this to the police. On the other hand, his son might have gone into town or even not got off at the station, whatever ticket he'd happened to buy.

Max was fairly wet by the time he reached his car, although the rain had stopped and an unconvincing sun reappeared.

'Excuse me.' The man from the ticket desk came out to Max. 'Can I offer you a cup of tea?'

'I was going to the police station.'

'They'll be serving tea there I've no doubt. I'm sorry I was rushed earlier. One person for a whole station doesn't stretch far. My name's Harvey and I'll help any way I can.'

'Thanks.' Max's walk had sobered him but it had also steadied his nerve. 'I'll be back after I've checked in. Is the police station in the middle of town?'

After detailed directions, Max drove away. His shirt had already dried but he combed his hair before entering the station, a large modern block set back from the road. He needed to look respectable.

The police had been expecting him and, as predicted by Harvey, tea, in polystyrene cups, flowed freely.

Max was glad he'd made his own abortive attempt at a search, otherwise this bonhomie might have made him impatient. After introducing him to 'our team', which included PC Sue Broomhill, a pretty, dark-haired girl, Detective Chief Superintendent Tim Southey, 'Call me Tim', led Max to a map on the wall. He guessed it was a composite photocopy of the maps he'd bought but spreading as far down as the coastline. Max had forgotten how close the sea was. His publisher's-rep beat didn't cover the coastal towns.

'We're taking your son's case very seriously, as you see,' said Tim. 'Given his history we rate him as a highly vulnerable misper.' There was a slight emphasis on 'we're' as if he thought the London lot had not taken the same view.

Perhaps he was right. It was the first time Max had heard the description 'misper', as if Dan had entered a new category that allowed more buttons to be pressed on his behalf. In London he'd been Dan, a teenage kid gone missing, perhaps ready to pop right back into view after a period of becoming invisible in the city's busy streets. Only recently had the intensity increased.

'Do you know the area?' asked Tim.

'Yes. The town, that is. But Dan – he'd nearly said 'the misper': somehow it suited him as if he'd been one even before he left – 'has never been here.'

The super looked at him with kindly eyes. He was a small, fit-looking man with a narrow, balding head neatly shaved. His white shirtsleeves were rolled up to his elbows, displaying well-muscled sunburnt forearms. 'Have you considered the options?'

The accurate answer would have been 'no' to *consider* but 'yes' to *imagine*. There was no option, however horrific, joyous or unlikely, that he hadn't imagined, but as for *consider*, his mind had never been cool enough for that. Lately, he had been picturing Dan's smile – he'd not been a light-hearted boy, not a 'fun-loving' or 'life-enhancing' character, as most parents described their missing kids. But when content or appreciative or simply engaged in something he enjoyed, a book or a TV programme, he had a wonderful slow, happy smile. Yes, he could be happy.

'I've tried,' said Max, as a compromise.

'Quite.' Tim looked sympathetic. He began to explain what they were planning to do and Max understood the reason for his question: despite the 'misper' category, much of their searching was not for a living boy. He was thankful that he had persuaded Eve to stay away.

'We'll fan out from the railway station. As well as police, not just from here, but from all over the county, we have volunteers from the fire and ambulance services, plus some local citizens we can trust. Nobody likes to think of a child disappeared.'

He had become a bit pompous, the tone of a general reviewing the troops at his disposal, but Max felt immense gratitude, verging on hero worship, for this man of action who really cared.

'At the same time we'll be making enquiries through the town. Sue.'

Sue stepped forward and produced, with something of a conjuror's flourish a sheaf of posters on which Dan's face was reproduced, looking to Max's misty gaze – or perhaps it was the photo that was misty – like St Veronica's image of Christ on her cloth. Although he'd given the photograph to the police in the first place, he could scarcely bear more than a quick glance.

'Thank you,' he said, and Sue gave him a kindly smile as if she understood how difficult it was to look on his missing son's face.

They were all staring at him now as if he should say more than 'thank you' – perhaps words of encouragement like a king to his general. 'When does it start?'

'Posters and enquiries as of now. Search at seven a.m. tomorrow.'

Again they turned to him and again he could think of nothing to say.

'I'm so grateful.' They looked down modestly. 'I'd like to take the posters to the railway station.'

'Of course. First, we do have a few questions.'

This was his punishment: questions about Dan's personality, his habits, his friends. It was a test he failed every time, any useful information he might have, blocked by the indisputable fact that he'd been living with his wife's sister (let's be honest, *fucking* his wife's sister – even if that wasn't the main plan) when his son had chosen to run away. So far, no one had rumbled this snippet of which he'd been totally unashamed at the time. So far, it was written on no files, fact sheets or computer printouts. Without even discussing it, he, Eve and Martha had wiped out those two weeks from recent history, particularly Dan's recent history.

'Let's see if we can find an empty office,' said the general, dismissing his troops.

King no longer, Max followed him obediently.

Eve cut short her time in the church. She had agreed to a visit from Yvonne, a fellow teacher at school, who had rung every few days since Dan's disappearance. She was a clever woman who managed her job plus being a single mother of two daughters who were also at the school, although older than Dan. She was in line to be deputy head and, quite probably, head. She might be coming purely out of kindness or as a representative of the school.

Eve forced herself to recognize this and bought a packet of biscuits on the way back to the flat. The shop, a small supermarket, amazed her by its loaded shelves and garish packaging. Shopping had also disappeared from her life.

It was another grey, hot day, oppressively so, and the effort of tidying the living room and laying out the tea things made her sweat and tremble. She brushed her hair half-heartedly and found a clean shirt. She had to trust that one day all this effort would have a meaning again.

'Come in.'

'I'm sorry I haven't been before.'

Eve guessed Yvonne was speaking for the sake of it; the reason she hadn't been before was lack of an invitation. Probably she was trying to disguise her shock at the change in Eve.

'I'll bring in the tea.'

When she returned Yvonne was leaning back against the cushions on the sofa with her eyes half shut. Perhaps she was tired too. But she shot upright quickly enough. 'I hear you've got a bit of a lead.'

Strange how news spread. Maybe the police kept better contact with the school than she realized. 'Yes. Max has gone to the country today. He's there now.' She could say this calmly because, after all these weeks of nothing, it seemed an unbelievable idea.

'You decided not to go?'

'There's to be a police search. I suppose it's easier than searching London.'

Yvonne frowned. She had a square, comfortable face that didn't frown without reason. 'I wish we could have helped more. We were all so impressed with your bravery in carrying on your summer drama course.'

'Bravery or madness,' said Eve, thinking there was denial, too, which might amount to cowardice. 'We both felt helpless.' She decided not to add 'guilty' because Yvonne, in the nicest possible way, might report back and reports could be used or distorted. 'What's the worst thing that's ever happened to you?' she asked instead.

She expected Yvonne to say her divorce, after her husband, an IT engineer, had left her without warning for a younger colleague. In truth, she didn't want to know anything about Yvonne's life.

'My parents split up when I was six. Nothing's been as bad since. I thought my world had ended. In a way I was right. The security I'd believed in had gone for ever. After that I had to make my own world. I don't expect I'd have done half the things I have without that early trauma.' She smiled at Eve. 'You might say it did me good.'

Eve thought you scratched anybody and found unhappiness, although Yvonne's message was of the 'stuff happens' variety. A son disappearing off the face of the earth couldn't be put under that heading.

'I'm so sorry,' said Eve. A comparison of troubles never made much sense but she looked at Yvonne now and saw that her face was less solidly square.

'I've been thinking about Dan,' said Yvonne.

In a second all Eve's new sympathy evaporated and she was in angry panic mode. What could Yvonne think about Dan that she hadn't thought a thousand times? This was just the reason she hadn't wanted to see anybody and allow the oxygen of other people's views to fire up her pain.

'Do you remember, last year,' continued Yvonne, inexorable, 'that boy, the year below Dan, half Chinese, who committed suicide?'

'Someone else mentioned him,' muttered Eve, who felt like gnawing her nails and tearing her hair. Did she really have to discuss someone else's tragedy?

'I think Dan was very affected by his death.'

And why not? Eve gave Yvonne a barely disguised vicious look. Her face seemed to have re-formed into a square. What good would it do to know that Dan had been upset by the suicide of a younger boy? Would that spring him from whatever entrapment he'd fallen into? Entrapment. An undernourished wild animal caught in the teeth of an iron trap.

'I don't mean to upset you,' said Yvonne, as Eve stood, nervously twisting her hands together. When Eve realized what she was doing, she sat down again, using actor technique to raise her head and steady her knees. Yvonne mustn't see her go to pieces.

'Have you seen a counsellor?'

Eve didn't blame her for the question. The Virgin Mary was the nearest to a counsellor. 'I have one on offer,' she said. The thing to do was to grasp the nettle. 'Thank you for telling me about Dan. I remember now' – she did – 'the boy's mother rang here. She said he'd visited her so I'm sure you're right.' She took a deep chest breath. 'We've had to recognize that Dan was distressed for some reason. Maybe this boy's suicide, so tragic, was part of it.'

She stopped speaking and gave Yvonne what she trusted was a bright, positive look – well, if not exactly positive, at least sane.

'You've always been strong,' said Yvonne. (Could she mean this? thought Eve distrustfully.) 'I so admire the way you deal with the difficult kids in school and even more the courses for the children at risk. You seem able to level with them so that they get involved and hold the line so that they do what you want.'

It was true. Eve remembered with amazement the bold charismatic woman she'd been. 'Thank you,' she said.

As if on cue, the telephone rang and it was Max. At once she was thrust back into reality.

'No hard news,' he said at once. But she had to talk to him. Yvonne was already rising weightily.

'Ring me back in five.'

Yvonne said kind things as she left. Afterwards Eve could hardly remember but was fairly certain the word 'sabbatical' had been thrown in.

Max put up six posters in the station. He feared this might be excessive but Harvey was encouraging: 'People walk past five and the sixth catches their eye.' After a while he was able to pretend that the sad boy's face had nothing to do with him.

Max crossed the bridge to the other side of the track and stuck one on the shelter there. Harvey and PC Sue Broomhill who had accompanied him, chatted on the other side. He looked around him. A wide patch of uncultivated ground behind the shelter was covered with a thick tangle of brambles laden with large blackberries. The westerly sun glowed on their lustrous blackness. Max curbed an inappropriate urge to savour one in his mouth. What would Harvey and Sue think if they saw a man, devastated by the loss of his son, enjoying a fruit of the earth? The conjunction of the lost son and the fruits of the earth had biblical echoes and he felt the twitch of a poetic idea, quelled almost at once by the sense of futility and exhaustion he'd become used to.

He started back across the bridge. He would call Eve, then look up Alison and suggest they had supper together.

CHAPTER TWENTY-SEVEN

Martha found a message on her landline. 'The police are all over the place, plus the dad, but the kid's off over the hill. No worries.'

She felt a mixture of guilt, fear and satisfaction. Lee knew what he was up to and he was reporting back to her. So Max had gone into the countryside to join the search. Since he hadn't mentioned Eve, she must have stayed in London. A wave of habitual protectiveness had her reaching for the phone before she recalled that things were not like that now.

She went upstairs slowly, undoing the buttons of her white uniform shirt and wondering, without quite wanting to know, why Lee had no worries.

Max woke up on Alison's sofa. He'd been dreaming of sex so it was a relief to remember they'd not made love. All the same he shouldn't have stayed the night. If Eve found out she would, understandably, not believe the truth. On the other hand, if past behaviour still held (not certain) she would say nothing.

The trouble was that both he and Alison had drunk far too much – neither used to it but grabbing at the freedom it gave to pour out their troubles. Never had Max done such a thing with a woman before and absolutely not without sleeping with her.

She had told him about her cold-fish husband (now ex) and her passionate longing for children. He had told her – reciting at length both his own poetry and others – about his ambitions and disappointments. They had not talked of Dan beyond her promising to check with her staff whether any of them had seen him in the bookshop. She hadn't. She'd looked at the photograph and looked at Max and said nothing.

'Good morning.' Alison came into the room. She was already fully dressed with makeup smoothing out her face and a pink shine on her lips.

'Hi.' Max, lying like a battered teenager in T-shirt and underpants, watched her with awe.

'Coffee? Tea?'

'Coffee, please.' Sometimes his mother had offered him coffee in bed but only if his dour father was out of the house. He knew he should get up, wash, prepare for the day, but last night he'd decided not to start out with the police search party at seven a.m. His watch was still on his wrist. Seven thirty. Maybe they were off already. Were there to be tracker dogs? Helicopters? He hadn't asked. In fact, looking back, he'd asked very little.

Alison came in with a mug of good coffee and a plate of toast.

'I'm afraid I took refuge in poetry last night,' said Max. 'Sorry. You must have been bored out of your mind.'

'You listened to me too.'

'I'm glad.'

She pulled up a chair and they drank quietly, not quite facing each other. As he revived, he thought that he could pull her on to the sofa and stroke her golden skin and feel the warmth and sweetness of her enter his body.

'I'll be off in a moment. The accountant comes in at eight this morning.' She paused. He crunched toast. Crumbs dropped on the sofa. 'You're joining the search?' Her face paled with the words.

'Yes. You've been very kind. If I stay another night, I'll find a B-and-B.'

'Or a hotel. There're some very nice ones in town.' She seemed sad now, the motherly efficiency slipping.

'I'll keep in touch,' he said, to cheer her up – perhaps to cheer himself up also.

'There's a clean towel in the bathroom. Blue.'

'Blue,' repeated Max. It struck him that awkwardness after a night not spent making love was as great as awkwardness after the fiercest physical intimacy.

'I'll be off.'

After she'd gone Max rang Eve, who told him about her dreams and didn't ask him where he was. He wondered if she understood that this was the day their son's corpse might be discovered. Her dreams had not been unhopeful: a fountain changing colours in rainbow sequence, a fox smiling with tender eyes – not very convincing but when were dreams convincing?

He lay a little longer. The flat was quiet, in a courtyard off one of the main streets of the town. It was modern, he supposed, although as they'd staggered in from the pub, he remembered heavy stone and medieval-style arches. Just as he was thinking of moving, his mobile rang.

It was PC Sue Broomhill, a cheery soul, who at this moment delivered a nasty spasm to his guts, threatening to bring back the toast. All she'd said was, 'Is that Max?'

'Yes. Max here.' He swallowed. He thought he didn't want to be lying on Alison's sofa when he heard bad news. Then he thought, more calmly, that they couldn't have discovered anything yet.

'Someone's walked into the police station and we thought you might like to come down. Not bad news,' she added.

'The misper poster. Yes,' he said, 'I'll be there.' He got ready quickly. No way to shave since he'd left his overnight bag in the car and didn't fancy his chances with Alison's delicate pink razor. He stared briefly at his greyish black bristles and hollow eyes – old-fashioned convict material.

Outside, the air was cool and fresh, clouds and sun, and enough wind to project the weather either way. He decided a walk would clear his head, although probably, now he was out of the flat, he was putting off receiving news, even if not bad, that might threaten his equilibrium – and there was a silly word. When did he last have a glimpse of *equilibrium*? It had scooted out of sight as completely as Dan.

The youth was ill at ease in the small room. He shifted about from one foot to the other, held one arm, then the other, rubbed his face, snorted and made a noise in his throat as if he wanted to spit.

Max thought he seemed rancid and furtive and untrustworthy, and hated the idea that he might know something about Dan. He also looked quite strong and was handsome in a small-eyed way, with tattoos snaking out of his T-shirt up his neck.

'This is Vince Streatham, who thinks he met Dan. He saw the poster last night.'

'Do you mind if I sit down?' Max was having trouble stopping his legs shaking.

'We'll all sit down.' Sue drew forward three chairs. Max sensed she didn't have much time for Vince either – although she'd called him in so she must believe he had something to tell them. Vince seemed even more uncomfortable sitting down, his arms alternately on his thighs or on the arms of his chair, before he let them hang loosely as he slumped backwards in a poor imitation of a relaxed pose.

'Vince is in a bail hostel in town,' said Sue, 'but sometimes he takes a walk into the countryside.' She looked at Vince as a schoolmistress encourages a pupil of doubtful ability – or intention. At her waist her cell phone exploded into sudden talkative noise, although not comprehensible. Max was reminded that the drama in this little room was the calm at the centre of a widening circle of police activity.

'So, did you see my son?' he asked, unconsciously making fists of his hands.

'I came in here freely, didn't I?' Vince's voice was a self-justifying whine but Max sensed he reacted more easily to his aggression, however disguised, than to the policewoman's attempt at cajolement. His small eyes gleamed as if he knew their sort and was equal to them. 'Suppose there's a reward, then?'

Max almost smiled. He was glad to think the worst of him, this boy who had seen Dan and told no one. He no longer doubted he'd seen him: it was too obvious he had something he thought he could sell.

'No reward,' said PC Sue Broomhill.

And yet, thought Max, I'd pay anything to get Dan back. Sue began to lecture about the duties of a citizen and, more sensibly, about the good he could do himself. He was on parole, wasn't he?

Max felt his wallet in his trouser pocket and saw Vince note the move. He sent vibes, *I'll see you right*. He watched Vince catch them.

'I could take you there. No distance in a car.'

'Hold it.' Sue spoke into her phone. She summoned DCS Tim, the general, and told him that she had information that might affect the search. He agreed to hold it. As far as Max could understand from one side of police-speak, there had been a certain confusion over timing and place for troops mustering so a further wait was no problem.

'Was he all right?' Max turned to the youth, daring his heart to take the strain.

'Sleeping in my car, wasn't he? Luxurious accommodation. I told him so.'

Max wanted Sue to say something like 'Begin at the beginning,' but instead she said, 'Whose car?'

'My car. Not exactly mine.'

'You don't have a licence, do you?' She picked up a folder from her lap. 'Car crimes, it says here.'

'This car's in a field, isn't it? A limousine, in point of fact.' His expression was injured and self-righteous.

Max's increasing hatred of him began to spread to Sue. Why did it matter what this revolting creature had done in the past? 'Do you mean my son was sleeping in this car, this limousine?'

'I'm not saying any more, am I?' He gave Max a meaningful look. 'I'll take you there, though.' He smirked at Sue. 'To show I'm a decent citizen.'

'Just a moment.' This time Sue left the room – to make arrangements, or so Max assumed.

The moment she'd left Vince became much perkier and confidential. 'We understand each other, you know what I mean?'

'Yes,' agreed Max, who despite his loathing would have showered him with money there and then if he hadn't feared they might be bugged or watched.

'Mind you,' added this new egregious Vince, 'he wasn't there long. I saw him off, see.'

'What do you mean?' Max tried to control his voice but clearly Vince got the drift.

'Nothing. Nothing. Sooner we get there, sooner you'll see.'

Max stood up and went to the door just as Sue reappeared. 'We've got wheels,' she said.

The wheels were on a marked police car, complete with uniformed driver. Sue put Max in the front and got into the back with Vince.

'Aren't you going to turn on the siren, then?' he asked.

No one answered so he muttered under his breath. His directions, however, were perfectly clear: to the station, past it, left, right and carry on. Max wasn't at all surprised when they took the road he'd walked the day before: it had felt right at the time. All the same he was glad he'd turned back. Today the weather had settled into a cool cloud-and-sun day, and he was supported by the police, by this official car, by whatever evidence Vince could produce or they could find.

'Left here.'

The first lane they turned into was tarmacked but they soon abandoned it for a much narrower track, which showed the occasional remains of a hard surface but was now mostly rubble, grass and earth.

'This is it?' said Sue, gripping Vince's arm.

'What do you mean? I'm telling you, aren't I?'

Max was surprised by just how few miles it took to enter wild countryside. They were in a valley but steep hills, roughly grazed by sheep, rose on either side of them.

'Lots of deer out here,' said the driver, who hadn't spoken till then.

'Nice one.' Vince grinned. 'Bang, bang, and venison meat for dinner.'

'You're a country boy, are you?' Sue sounded disbelieving.

'My dad was before he moved to town. A right crack shot he was. Trained by the best gun-slingers in the British Army.'

Max thought, This unpleasant youth has a father of whom he is proud. He suspected Dan had taken no pride in his father.

'How much further?' asked the driver. 'Playing havoc with my suspension.'

'Next corner,' said Vince.

The next corner looked like any other but Vince got them all out of the car and walked towards a wooden fence in the field on their left. A flurry of small birds started out from the hedge and flew away, leading Max's eye to something white further into the field.

'There she is!' flourished Vince, like a conjuror.

'So at least this part of his story's true,' said Sue to Max, as Vince hopped over the padlocked gate and bounced across to the white car, as if greeting a friend.

It was a limousine all right, about the most incongruous sight you could imagine. Although Vince had made it clear Dan was no longer there, Max felt a kind of terrified hopefulness he'd forgotten possible. He gasped for breath.

By the time they caught up with Vince, he had a back door open and stood by it like a chauffeur. 'Be my guest!'

Sue and Max peered inside. It stank, disgustingly, of damp and pee and a straggling plant that had come up through the floorboards. Nettles were growing in through the other window.

'Not a place I'd choose to set up camp.' Sue withdrew hurriedly.

'You calling me a liar? It was nicer then, nice and dry, weeks ago, wasn't it?' He tapped Max on the shoulder. 'Your boy was well set up here. Comfy sofa-bed, drinking water from the stream. Pure enough to bottle. Make your fortune.'

'How do you know?' asked Max. 'Why should I believe you?'

'Because I watched him, didn't I? Not that he knew. He liked it here. And why not? When I made the introductions, we had this limo in common, we got on. We had a bite together. Mates.'

'I thought you said you saw him off.'

'A manner of speaking. It was my car, wasn't it? He picked up on that. Fair's fair.'

'So he left?' said Sue. 'Can you put a date on it?'

Instead of answering, Vince put a hand into his pocket and pulled out a piece of paper folded many times into a small square. With a crafty, estimating expression, he smoothed it out and Max saw Dan's face.

'Went missing the twenty-fifth of July so he was probably gone from here three or four days later.'

Max's doubts rose again. The whole thing could so easily be an invention. Ignoring the others, he began to search the area, car first, putting his fingers down the sticky seat, across areas where a snail had left a mucous trail.

When he came out, Sue was on her phone, but he ignored her, bending over the grass, feeling for any sign of Dan.

'Don't worry, sir,' said Sue, who hadn't called him 'sir' before. 'We'll get Forensics in.'

He straightened slowly. He felt immeasurably old. He looked at the police officer as straight as he could manage. 'Is this a murder inquiry, Officer?'

She touched his arm gently. 'Misper. But we like to be sure.'

Although Max felt Sue now wanted to leave and hand over the site to the professionals, he continued his search. Near the back wheels of the cars he found a fossil, an ammonite, round and beautiful.

'He found that!' crowed Vince, who was following Max.

Max laid it to one side, rethought and put it in his pocket. He found the remains of two banana skins and one squashed banana. Again Vince commented, 'He had those in his backpack.' But how could Max know if there had been bananas in their flat when he wasn't living there?

He started walking towards a decrepit barn up the hill but immediately Vince shouted, 'He didn't go there,' as if they were playing a child's game of hot and cold, cool, warm, hot, hotter as you got close, closer. They used to play it with Dan when he was small. Vince had caught him up, came up to Max. He smelt his sweat and smoker's breath, although so far he hadn't been smoking.

'See me right? Right?'

Max felt for his wallet, extricated three notes and, with their backs turned to the police, handed them over. He said, 'There could be more.' Then when Vince had put them away, Max asked, 'How was he?'

This seemed to throw Vince. He juddered from foot to foot, clasped his hands together then behind his head. 'Friendly.' He looked over a shoulder, 'We shared a spliff, didn't we?'

'What do you mean?' Max was back to wanting to hit him, kill him if possible. 'Dan was a child.' He amended it quickly. 'Is a child. He didn't do drugs. He's just fourteen, for fuck's sake.'

Vince visibly relaxed, almost smiled. 'Fucking me, are you? That's nice. Where I come from a ten-year-old is up for a bit of action.' He began to walk away, before bending down and picking up something from the grass. He rolled it in his hand as if it was a ball. 'If you want healthy living, you'll be glad to hear he brought his Marmite with him. Here. Catch!' He threw the object.

Max let it drop on the grass at his feet, then thought, Forensics, and picked it up. He caught up with Vince. 'Was he physically OK?'

'Happy as sunshine. Just come back from a bit of a walk when we got chatting. You would have been proud of him.'

Max watched him jeering and cheating. He raised his eyes to avoid the sight and saw the sky had cleared, lighting up the whole valley. It was very lovely, very peaceful. This horrid, druggy, on-the-make boy seemed to him a modern version of the serpent in Paradise. Dan couldn't have been happy once Vince arrived.

'Do you know when he left?'

'She already asked me that.'

Max felt in his pocket. Sue was beginning to walk towards them. He handed over two more notes quickly.

'Morning after I saw him.' He gave the day.

'And where did he go?'

'How do I know? I wasn't there. I don't know where he came from and I don't know where he went to.'

'He came from the station.'

'So chances are he went back there.' Vince had his eyes on Sue who was only a few paces away. 'Can I go now, Miss?' he called, in a mix of cringe and defiance.

'You stay just where you are. I've got half the UK police driving over just for the pleasure of speaking to you.'

Max admired the fire in her youthful blue eyes.

'I've had the third degree from him, haven't I?' Vince pointed at Max accusingly.

Max walked away without saying anything. In a way he was surprised he'd had free access to the Serpent. He walked quickly, crossing the track and heading for a stream. He could hear the water spraying over rocks with a delicate, cheerful sound. He reached a small waterfall when Sue caught up with him.

'Someone's cut the brambles away,' he said. He saw something glinting in a bunch of nettles. He bent down and picked out a penknife. If the nettles stung he didn't feel it. He handed the knife to Sue. 'Dan's. A present from his aunt.'

Sue nodded. She gave him a moment before she touched his arm. 'They've contacted me from the station. We've heard from a member of the public. An old man. Not well. His carer phoned in. Saw your boy same time as Vince. It all hangs together. Apparently, he saved the old fellow's life.'

'What?' Max shook his head in bewilderment.

'I know. True, though. He had a heart-attack out here somewhere and your Dan phoned in for help. He was airlifted. Made front-page news in the local paper.'

Max tried to take this in. At a time when they'd been out of their minds with worry in London, Dan had been saving someone's life down here. Front-page news. 'This was day four,' said Max, 'and Dan still had his mobile.'

'So it seems. We can check.' Sue frowned. 'Didn't London check his mobile?'

Max thought back to those first few days but they were blurred and he couldn't remember the time-scale of any action taken. 'Too late, I suppose.' He went over to the stream and, crouching, let water trickle over his fingers. 'We did a TV show later and his picture went on the Internet but no one picked it up from down here.'

Max cupped some water in his hands and drank from it. 'Vince is right about the purity.' He pictured Dan leaning over like him, with the sparkling water dripping through his fingers. It was just a little consoling.

Sue's mobile was being noisy again. 'We're on his tracks now.'

'Yes,' agreed Max. Then he thought that they knew something about three or perhaps four of the forty-odd days Dan had been gone. Eve would know the exact number. 'I need to telephone my wife.'

'I'll be in the car.'

The trick was to provide Eve with a sustainable level of expectation – which sounded as ridiculous as it was.

CHAPTER TWENTY-EIGHT

Martha's new special responsibility was obese, which was unusual for a prisoner.

'You've got a long spell left, Morgan.' Why wasn't he in a Welsh prison? 'How do you plan to spend it?'

'Keep my head down, Miss.' However violently dramatic his crime, she could see he was a dull man, dull in brain, dull in body. She pictured Lee and felt a flash of excitement.

'I see you're down for the anger-management course.' It was hard to believe anger could surface out of so much blubber. 'Didn't you do it at your last prison?'

'Half, Miss. They shipped me out then.'

How had he squeezed into those tiny compartments in the van? She tried to feel more sympathetic. Obesity was a sickness. Probably fed chips as a kid and now had to deal with high cholesterol, diabetes, mockery.

'We'll soon have you sorted. Any questions?'

His questions were written down on paper, which showed a level of intelligence. Also, they contained many references to his partner, his child and his family. He was not unloved, apparently. He didn't deserve her derision or patronage.

On and off for the rest of the day, Martha wondered when she'd given up the idea of romantic love. Had it been when her mother died and her inconsolable father had taught her that nothing lasts? Or when she had married Adrian, knowing he was no story-book hero? He'd died too, of course, but that was not the point. Or had it been when she'd fallen for Max and, recognizing its corruption, still allowed him to have sex with her? He'd never made love. His love was reserved for Eve or his mythical poetry.

The only pure love was for a child, thought Martha, as she drove home. She'd loved Dan. The problem was that Dan was not her child, and it seemed that if Lee didn't keep her in the picture, no one else would.

There were no messages on the answering-machine, not even from Ronnie, who still counted her as one of the family.

Eve lifted the receiver to phone Martha. She had to tell someone about Dan's reappearance. That was how it felt to her, as if he'd fallen down an *Alice in Wonderland* hole and now emerged into the real world. OK, it was only the start of the trail but he was real again, no longer the distorted victim of her imagination. Moreover, he was a hero, had saved an old man's life. It was extraordinary, unbelievable. Beyond words.

Max had been still gasping when he rang back to say it would be on the nationwide six o'clock news. Now everybody in the country would be looking for Dan. Eve put down the phone again. No need, after all, to ring Martha. She'd see it on the TV or someone would tell her. Better to hug her hopefulness to herself and wait for Max to tell her more.

Max had been called back to the railway station. A girl had been found who'd worked briefly at the station café. Her dates might coincide with Dan's departure – if, indeed, he had departed, and departed by train. All options were still open, as the general, Dectective Chief Superintendent Tim Southey, informed Max over the telephone. They were holding Vince, now known at his insistence as Vinny, for questioning.

When Max arrived at the station, once again accompanied by Sue, with her talkative mobile at her waist or in her hand, he felt as if he was part of the shooting of a movie. There was even a camera, following the TV interest after Dan had been designated 'a hero'. There were crowd scenes, actors and gangs of 'best boys', 'chippies' and 'grips'.

'She's arriving now.' Sue looked up from her mobile. 'Name's Maria Rockway. Remembers a boy on that date.'

Max was led into the waiting room, painted a murky shade of green. Max could see at once that the girl, Maria, was enjoying the attention. Even though the press was being kept away, she was giving a high-octane performance. 'I just want to help!' she repeated.

'Hello, Max.' Tim came towards him and clasped his hand in a comforting way. 'Glad you could make it.'

As if, thought Max, he had something more pressing in his life.

'We wanted to talk to her on the spot.' He walked Max over to Maria. 'This is Dan's father.'

'Dan?' The girl looked momentarily confused. 'He called himself Denver. Cool name.'

'We'll see about that.' Tim was reassuring, the director getting the most out of his actors. 'Why don't you begin by taking us up to the café.'

'Not locked, then?' Maria, quickly recovered, gave Harvey, the station master, a challenging look.

'I've got a key,' said Harvey, dourly. Maria was obviously not on his list of favourites and Max remembered what he'd said about the spoilt young.

There were far too many of them to get up the stairs to the café. The procession included station workers who'd come from nowhere, uniformed and non-uniformed police, local people, presumably part of the aborted search party – if it had been aborted, Max wasn't sure (were they still dredging rivers? He didn't want to think of that) – recently arrived passengers carrying bags, and various journalists, photographers and cameramen.

Near the front as they climbed the steps, Max looked back and saw, beyond the trail of people, four or five police cars parked at odd angles, two with their lights still revolving, flashing. Film set, he told himself, knowing that the idea helped to keep the reality at bay.

Harvey unlocked the café and he, Maria, Tim, Max, Sue and a couple more police went in. They were crowded together in the small room.

'Where's my mum?' Maria cried out suddenly, as if realizing the seriousness for the first time and needing protection.

A panting, large-bosomed woman, done up perhaps for the cameras but perhaps in everyday flamboyance, was handed up to the café, then the door shut again.

Max felt himself lose his breath as he had when he'd first seen the limo. Had Dan been here? He looked properly at Maria. She was slim and pretty, a head taller than her mother but favouring the same bright colours and low-cut T-shirt. She was a drawn-out, younger version.

'Tell us what happened?' asked Tim.

Max liked that simplicity. He trusted Tim.

'I couldn't forget him, could I?' She gazed round as if they'd understand her point.

'Go on, Mai,' encouraged her mother.

'His face, I mean.' She hesitated.

'You recognized it from the poster,' suggested Tim.

'I did or I wouldn't be here, but there's many as wouldn't. Black and red and blue, all swollen, one eye shut and that dirty. I shouldn't have let him among food but I felt sorry for him, do you know what I mean?'

As she looked around again, once more as if searching for support, Max saw in others' faces his own shock. 'Are you saying he was injured?'

'His face. He said it was his mate. Head-butted. He limped a bit too.'

'Maybe it wasn't Dan.' Max heard his voice, croaky and gruff like an old man's. Nobody reacted.

'After you'd let him in, what happened?' Tim asked calmly.

'He was starving!' The girl swung her blonde ponytail in a way that was almost flirtatious. 'He stuffed his mouth with doughnuts, then I cooked him the full English. Wolfed that down too.' She pointed at one of the two small tables. 'Sat there.'

'Then what?'

'I told him he could use the Gents and gave him the key. Never brought it back like he promised.' She paused, flicked a quick look at Max. 'Suppose he's been murdered?'

Tim stepped closer to her. 'This is a missing-person investigation, Maria.'

'If you say so.' She shrugged and Max, trying to control his pain, noticed the mother shrugging her large shoulders in exactly the same way.

'Did he tell you anything more about himself?'

The girl tried to remember. 'He said he was camped on a farm and, oh, yes, it was his birthday. Sixteen, he said, he was, like me. Seemed younger.'

Tim turned to Max enquiringly.

Instead of screaming, Max nodded. 'It was his fourteenth birthday.'

'Knew he was younger.' Maria looked pleased with herself, before her expression softened. 'All in all, glad I gave it him free.' She glanced at Harvey. 'Hadn't any change for a twenty so I gave him a birthday present. I felt sorry for him. Got himself in trouble, hadn't he? and didn't look like the sort who could stick up for himself. You know what I mean?'

'Are you saying this young man had a twenty-pound note?'

'A twenty. That's right. Useless to look for change in this dump.'

Again Tim looked at Max. They both knew about the twenty pounds Eve had put in Dan's backpack. There was no doubting his identity.

Max thought he couldn't take any more. His son had appeared, battered, starving, and this girl had taken pity on him.

Doubtless, the police would soon find that he'd got on a train to somewhere or other. In fact, that was the best-option next stage. But he needed to go, rest somewhere, think what to tell Eve.

He held out his hand to Maria. She'd given Dan a birthday present. 'Thank you for helping him.'

'That's all right. He was OK. Had a chat, didn't we? Told him I might come to London.'

Max staggered away. He felt Sue guide him down the stairs. The sun was brilliant in his eyes, blinding him after the dim little room.

She put him into the car. 'What do you want to do?'

'I don't know.'

She took him back to the police station and led him to an empty room. He felt safer there. A young policeman brought him tea and biscuits.

After a while he decided to go back to London. He couldn't talk to Eve over the telephone. Anyway, he needed to get off the film set.

Eve and Max were sitting side by side on their sofa, holding hands while they watched the late-night news. The combination of more information and Dan's status as local hero – Silas Chaffey had been interviewed from his bed – had turned his loss from a private tragedy, one of many, to a public event. Outside the building a little group of reporters waited to get a photo of Dan's parents. A newspaper had offered a not inconsiderable sum for their story.

Eve and Max were hunched and close together, like two old people in a bus shelter.

'I can't take it in.' Eve turned to Max when the item on Dan finished. 'It's all happened so quickly.'

'There's a long way to go.' Eve's simple hopefulness astounded him. His mind still raced with the day's events. On the drive back he'd suddenly realized that Vince, now Vinny, had very likely been the one to batter Dan. His anger was so violent that he had had to pull over and take long breaths. For several minutes, he wanted to turn right round and beat Vinny to a pulp. *He'd given the man money.* Only the knowledge that Eve was waiting had stopped him. He had always thought of himself as a pacific man.

Ronnie had been in the flat when he arrived, explaining things to Eve. At least that task had been made easier. 'I'll be going west tomorrow,' he'd told them, 'so I can keep you informed.' His young, pudgy face wore the grave look that Max had come to know.

'I might go back myself,' Max had said. 'I've got a few more days off work.'

Ronnie had nodded understandingly and Max had given him Brownie points for trying, even though it was a ridiculous idea. He was merely doing a job, with natural human sympathy thrown in.

'Have you eaten anything?' In the last day or two Eve had shown signs of wanting to look after him, or at least check that he was looking after himself.

She sat in the kitchen while he made a sandwich and ate it. For once she didn't have a drink in her hand. 'Was it terrible?'

'Yes.' What else did she want him to say? If only from a distance and on film, she'd seen the insalubrious white hulk of the limo that had been Dan's home. She'd seen the café and the girl who'd talked to him. Luckily, Vinny was in police custody and out of bounds. Presumably, others had suspected his involvement in Dan's wounded face.

'You're very tired.' Eve put out a hand to him. It was a slightly theatrical gesture but he believed in its truth.

Martha walked restlessly round her living room. She knew she was losing it and there was no one to talk to, except an ex-prisoner on the run. Halfway through the day she'd shouted at a prisoner, screamed at him to get out of her fucking way and fuck off back to his cell. Now she could scarcely remember what it was about – a telephone that wasn't working and he'd moaned at her. She'd been way out of order, right over the top. Worse still, another officer had been there, not interfering but sure to report back.

Perhaps she would take time off. That was it. She had a week's holiday left. She sat down and thought about the television news she'd watched earlier. It all made sense and soon they'd know where he'd gone next. Quite possibly Lee already knew. Lee was like a tracker dog, sharp nostrils, head down, lean and fit, not to be put off the scent. The scent came from his own son, up there in Scotland, out of reach, but it didn't make him any less dangerous. Dangerous? Where had that word come from? All he was doing was trying to help find her nephew. If anyone was in danger it was Lee himself.

CHAPTER TWENTY-NINE

Dan had gone to Weymouth. The police suspected it and the press was certain. They both agreed on the train Dan had taken – a cross-country line where trains only stopped at a few stations, three of them request.

'What do you mean "request"?' asked Eve. Ronnie was on the telephone doing the explaining because Max had decided to get on the same train that Dan had apparently boarded. This continued man-of-action approach seemed out of character to Eve but everyone was changing roles. How was she managing without Martha, for example?

'The train only stops on request.' Ronnie had modified his 'informing' voice to his 'sympathetic, patient' one. He was right to think she needed it. 'They're small places, in the middle of nowhere.'

'So he might have got off in the middle of nowhere?'

'Unlikely. We're checking. The guard on duty that day is being interviewed as we speak.'

The night before, Max had told Eve his sense of being on a film set. But he hadn't commented that the star was an absent hero. Eve knew that both she and Max were playing avoidance games. Dan had taken a train to the middle of nowhere. It was far too frightening to face squarely. Instead they talked of 'progress'.

Now Ronnie was reassuring her that if Dan had gone to Weymouth, the search would be intensified: leaflets to cafés, passers-by, amusement arcades, B-and-Bs, campsites, empty houses.

Eve was grateful for his positive approach, which sat on top of grim forebodings. It did seem that tracking Dan's movements had suddenly become much easier. But all this train stuff, she reminded herself, had taken place more than a month ago. She went to a drawer in the kitchen and took out a picture calendar. It was turned to

August. There was a Klimt painting – a woman elaborately gowned and coiffured in gold and red and blue. Three-quarters of the numbers had been slashed through. She counted them, then turned back and counted the numbers slashed through on the preceding month. The police hadn't yet tracked Dan out of July and into August.

Max had managed to shake off Ronnie and Sue and get on the train by himself. He wanted to enter Dan's skin as he travelled, bruised and battered, towards the sea. He was certain he'd aimed for the sea: it was what he, Max, would have done.

Over-sensitive to his surroundings, he was startled by the train's constant hooting, a derisive sound that mocked his sadness. It was some sort of explanation, he supposed, when the guard, a bulky, jovial man, remarked to no one in particular, 'A better train today, haven't broken down, haven't killed anyone.' He paused and looked directly at Max. 'A couple of years ago we had a wild boar on the platform. Scared us silly.'

It was true that the small train sped through woods and fields, often unseparated by fences. In the same way, stations had no barriers or bridges from one side of the track to the other.

After four or five stations, at each one of which Max imagined Dan getting out and discounted it – one was too close to a farmhouse, another to a newly built estate – they stopped at a bigger town, the last before the sea. But it was impossible Dan would come so far and not stay on to the end of the line. The train pulled out, following the edge of a cemetery spreading up the hill. Disturbed by the sight of a stone Christ, arms wide and welcoming, Max moved impulsively from the right-hand side of the train to the left.

It was there he caught his first view of the sea, a wide curve of deep blue. It disappeared in a few seconds but he felt galvanized for their arrival, almost immediately, at the station. *Welcome to the Jurassic Coast*, announced a large sign.

Others had already been welcomed. Beyond the holidaymakers coming off the train, Max saw three or four uniformed police and several people who could have been journalists. On the wall behind them, he caught sight of a row of Dan's posters. He looked away hurriedly and, extracting a peaked cap out of his pocket, pulled it down over his eyes. He wanted to search alone.

Martha tried to be angry. Gerry had just told her she was being given sick leave. He'd said the stress level of prison officers was a given and she had this nephew business on top of it. He'd been patronizing, might as well have patted her head and said, 'There, there.'

'Less running, more eating and resting. You need strength for this job.' Secure in the knowledge he was helping her, he clasped his mutton-chop hands together.

Martha managed to walk away without yelling. Gerry was respecting her, not criticizing her, she tried to tell herself. She supposed she should be glad that no one had spotted her with Lee and she hadn't been sacked. The really sad truth was that she was desperate to speak with Eve. All these years she'd believed Eve was the one who needed her and now the boot was on the other foot. Perhaps it always had been. She'd just been kidding herself that Eve was more vulnerable and couldn't survive without her care. After all, if she'd really felt that, she'd hardly have let Max into her bed, would she?

More likely, she hated Eve; was jealous of her husband, her child, her looks, her career. 'I hate you, Eve.' She tried saying it aloud but the effect was paltry, unconvincing. She didn't hate Eve. They were too closely wound together for that. She just wanted to talk to her.

Eve lay on her bed. She could no longer keep at bay the knowledge that Dan had been attacked. Before, she had suffered from her imagination; now it was reality. That girl, Maria, who had given him a birthday breakfast, had described his face as 'a right old mess'. He'd explained it as falling out with a mate, which didn't ring true.

Eve passed her fingers over her own face: smooth, uninjured. Her son's face was broken and disfigured. She, his mother, hadn't been able to protect him.

She pictured Mary kneeling at the foot of Christ's cross. Without true belief, she prayed to Mary for some of her courage. After she'd run out of words, she leant over for her Valium and a glass of water.

This was the belief of modern life, she thought, and swallowed the pills, then the water.

After a while, either the prayer or the pills took effect and she fell into a light doze.

CHAPTER THIRTY

Weymouth was dazzling. A strong wind blew in from the sea, rippling the water and casting shadows from fast-moving clouds. The noisy traffic along the esplanade, the crowds of people, the garish colours of elaborate iron seating along the front, painted statues, amusement arcades — old and new bundled in together — confused Max. The contrast was too great between this and the unchanged, empty countryside he'd come from.

He remembered that Weymouth had been a seaside resort for two hundred years, visitors drawn by the wide, protected bay and the sandy shore. People came to enjoy themselves, have fun with lover or girlfriend. He pictured Dan: thin, limping, knocked about, alone. Where would he go?

Slowly, Max made his way to the tourist office. This is where adults come, he thought, not children, but he went all the same. It was a modern box placed on the front. The wind was gusting sand up from the beach. Holidaymakers sat in blue- and white-striped deck-chairs, some corralled by multi-coloured windbreaks. Stalls surrounded by plastic chairs sold hot dogs and fizzy drinks. Further along, a roundabout sedately twirled wide-eyed horses and children.

The police had already been to the tourist office. Dan's sad face stared out at him from two walls. What was he going to ask that the police didn't already know? Yet he went up to the desk. 'I'm doing some research,' he said, 'and wonder whether you could point me to the more deprived areas of the town.'

The young man at the desk looked at him seriously, seemingly unsurprised by what must be an unusual request. He called over a colleague and they conferred before producing a map. One area, they informed him, fitted Max's description. They might have been directing him to a recommended hotel or restaurant.

Max felt immensely tired. He found space among elderly men and mothers with pushchairs and sat down on one of the ornate benches. As so often in the last days, he was extremely hungry but without the will to do anything about it.

Behind him, traffic roared, around him people passed in groups, beyond, the restless waves blew in with the wind.

His mobile rang. He could hardly hear Tim above the racket. This was not how he'd imagined it for Dan.

'The guard remembers Dan. He had to wake him up to get him off at Weymouth. He remembers the face.'

'Yes,' agreed Max. It seemed that Dan's battered face had made him memorable. Not an obvious fact to share with Eve. He wondered how Dan would look a month on. Once more like the boy in the photo? 'There was a gang of police on the station.'

'Questioning. Observing,' said Tim. 'I'm on the road now. Where are you?'

Nowhere, thought Max. They agreed to meet at a Chinese restaurant on the front. Tim, it seemed, was hungry too.

Max, who'd so wanted to be alone, felt his spirits lift a little – enough to phone Eve before setting out for the restaurant. 'Dan definitely got off the train here,' he told her, enthusing his voice with good-news energy.

Eve scarcely responded. 'I'm drugged up,' she mumbled. 'Please be careful.'

What use was there in him being careful?

He rang off and, as if her lassitude spurred him on, walked briskly to the Victoria Pier, as directed by Tim. It was a brightly lit building next door to an amusement arcade in the middle of the main esplanade. It struck Max as the sort of place where boys at a loose end might gather and, even though Dan was more library- than arcade-oriented, he went in. Like a documentary about the sad habits of modern youth, there were a dozen or more boys, most wearing shorts, some with backward-turned caps, all obsessing over sparking, flashing, churning machines. As Max watched, one boy punched the face of his machine several times, ending up with a simulated (luckily, for the health of what brains he might have) head-butt.

Max left hurriedly. There was no way he could have identified Dan with those pathetic boys. As he entered the Chinese restaurant – more café, he now saw – he remembered his own youthful surges of lust, rage, yearnings and despair. Women and poetry had provided an outlet. *My love as a round wave/To hide the wolves of sleep/And mask the grave.*

What did Dan have?

'You found it all right, then.' Tim had come in with Sue, Ronnie and another detective.

Max, who'd been staring out of the window at the crowds moving along the pavement, turned. He looked at the array of police and wondered whether they minded moving in groups or pairs, or at least seldom alone. They all sat down with him, scarcely fitting round the small table, but everywhere else was full, even though it was half past two. Perhaps holiday-makers kept no particular hours for eating.

'Best Chinese on the coast,' said Tim, picking up the immensely long menu, like an eager student getting first sight of an exam paper.

In the end, he ordered for all of them. Max wondered vaguely what the other diners made of their group before he returned to his pavement-gazing. At some point, presumably, Tim's attention would turn from Chinese food to Dan and train guards.

They were waited on by a middle-aged Chinese man who ordered waiters to their table assiduously. One plate after another appeared, until a side table had to be brought.

'No beers on duty,' Tim touched Max's arm, 'but would you like one?'

'Not now.' The truth was he'd lost his appetite too, but he had begun to understand that this performance was not just about food. Tim and the owner knew each other. As the restaurant cleared for what Max suspected was a brief interlude, Tim invited Mr Ho to join them and produced one of the Dan posters.

'These boys.' The owner pursed his lips and sighed a little. He wore large glasses, and his face, below a bald pate, was round and smooth. He could have been any age.

'This is Dan's father.' Tim indicated Max.

Mr Ho gave him a deferential bow. 'I'm sorry.' He put his hands together. 'So many lost boys.' He took the poster and studied it. 'Your boy is young, sir?'

'Just fourteen.'

'Mr Ho's reasonable prices and excellent cuisine attract many young people,' commented the detective. 'So, you don't recognize him?'

'Difficult always. Boys change, although I estimate he cannot yet grow a beard.' He seemed prepared to giggle at this witticism but since no one else reacted, he became serious again. 'I'll show it to my staff.' He stood.

Tim gave him his card. 'Any time,' he said. 'This is a boy we want to find.'

Max looked at the uneaten bamboo shoots, shrimps and seaweed on his plate. What happened to the boys they didn't want to find?

As they were leaving, Mr Ho reappeared. 'The staff do not recognize. I'm sorry. But they will watch out.'

'Thank you, Ho.' The 'Mr' seemed to have gone and Max realized no bill had been paid. They emerged into the windy sunlight.

'A bit of a rascal?' surmised Ronnie, knowingly.

'Under suspicion, our Mr Ho. Drugs on the premises. Might be more than that. He knows he's under threat of closure. He's had a good business for thirty years, even stood for councillor once – didn't win, of course. But he's greedy. That's always the trouble.'

Ronnie nodded even more knowingly and the young detective, who'd hardly spoken, was sent off to get the car.

'We can sit in it,' Tim told Max, 'while the others do a bit of pavement pounding, ask questions, get the word about.'

Ronnie obviously didn't consider this his job description and got into the car with them, sitting in front.

'In short,' said Tim, 'the train's guard confirmed everything Maria told us. Strangely, Dan didn't pay for a ticket any more than he paid for his breakfast. I'm beginning to think your son's got financial acumen.'

Max smiled wanly.

'So I expect you'll want to hear what happens now.' He began to talk of phone lines and mobile police centres and local informers.

Max wound down his window and breathed in some gusty sea air. He thought of Dan on the train, the boy punching the machine, Mr Ho's smooth face. 'What about Vince – Vinny?'

'In terms of the search, he's over. Right.'

Max didn't know if that was 'right'. Surely Dan might have said something.

'He's still in custody, remember.'

Max stared at Tim. This stranger held Dan's life in his hands. He was part of a machine that might or might not be efficient. He made up his mind. 'I think I'll leave you to it. I'll have to take the train to pick up my car.'

'You do that. Any news, you can be sure we'll be in touch.'

Max let Ronnie walk with him. Maybe his large affability would tranquillize his nerves. The police knew where they were going next but what about him? Was it his place to wander around Weymouth as he had at the beginning in London?

Ronnie and he walked briskly. Ronnie wore his uniform and heavy shoes, like a man who knew exactly where he was going. When they arrived at the station, where there were more police and more reporters, he took Max's arm protectively. Max put on his cap again and they sat in the waiting room until the arrival of the next train.

A group of youthful backpackers sat opposite them, a girl and two men. One, mixed race, had long dreadlocks; they all looked sunburnt, dirty and unhealthy. On and off the two men argued, using 'fucking' as if in a most-frequent word competition.

The girl, pretty enough and with a modified form of dreadlocks strung with beads, didn't take part, but hissed once, 'Wankers,' and a bit later, 'Losers.' Then she added, as if to herself, 'A girl needs a guy like a fish needs a bicycle.'

Max glanced at her and then away. He had the odd sensation that she'd said it for him.

'Modern youth,' commented Ronnie, under his breath.

'Not keen on the police presence?' suggested Max, also in an undertone.

Ronnie shrugged. He was police, after all.

Max felt in his pocket for a folded poster of Dan he carried there. Perhaps he should show it to this trio. They didn't look as if they were the type to read anything stuck up on a wall or volunteer information, if it came to that. He could have done it for the girl – she had an appealing face, wide mouth, small nose with a diamond stud – but he didn't have the courage to go through the pain of an explanation for two such obvious louts.

'I'll leave you now,' said Ronnie, standing up.

Max looked up vaguely surprised. 'You're not coming to London?'

'Not today.'

*

Lee rang at about ten. Martha, half asleep in front of the television, felt something like an electric shock to her system. They were connected, she'd always felt that, and now he'd connect her to Dan.

'I'm here,' she said.

'I guess you know where I am.'

She'd forgotten the cool sharpness of his voice.

CHAPTER THIRTY-ONE

Martha put on her tightest jeans, filled a backpack and went to the station. What else could she do? She thought Lee, whether he meant to or not, had given her enough clues to track him down. If she failed she would make contact with the police. She was still a member of Dan's family, although now she didn't know if she was chasing Dan or Lee.

Lee had talked about a squat where Dan had lived for a while. It was a centre for drug-users passing through. Was Dan a user, Lee had wanted to know.

The train started almost as soon as Martha got on. She sat on her own at a table for four with her backpack beside her. Her head felt clearer than it had for weeks, perhaps even years. The loneliness she suffered in her house had turned into a powerful freedom. She was glad, too, that she'd chosen to travel by train. Gerry had told her to rest.

She pulled out a daily newspaper from her backpack. It was bulky with supplements on business, sport, technology, jobs, education, travel, but she headed for the news pages. Although she hadn't been consciously looking for it, she was unsurprised to read a paragraph in the News Round-up under the heading, *Boy Hero Last Seen in Weymouth*. It continued: 'Daniel Budden, fourteen, who saved the life of a pensioner after running away from his family, has been tracked as far as Weymouth. The police say they are pursuing all leads.'

Martha knew Weymouth quite well. She and Adrian had walked in the area during the early days of their marriage. She hadn't told Lee this. She'd recognized the part of the town he was talking about. Lee thought Dan had moved on, but he wasn't certain where yet. He was sure Dan was alive.

*

Martha was again unsurprised by the posters advertising Dan's disappearance, but the crowds of young and old, all dressed however inappropriately in holiday gear, reminded her that the walks with Adrian had taken place in the spring when the town was relatively empty, the woodland paths still decorated with bluebells and cow parsley, the coastal paths bright with fresh grass. It was hard to believe they'd had those good times.

Martha was strong. Backpack comfortably secure, she strode off directly away from the sea. A single policeman who'd been about to stop her stepped aside.

The day, which had been dull, broke open and a hot sun emerged, propelled by a strong wind. The road she followed was filled with cars, nose to tail in both directions; she heard noisy engines, noisy people and noisy radios. They were heading, she assumed, for the sea – it was still quite early in the morning – or maybe they were just driving round and round enjoying themselves.

She carried on past a KFC takeaway, a garage, a roundabout, into a large open car park, under one bridge and over another, which crossed an area of inland water. Without slowing her pace, she walked up a steep hill. There she paused. The only bench was taken by three old drunks so, still standing, she let down her backpack on the pavement and took out a bottle of water.

To her left was the entrance to a wildlife trail that led round the outskirts of the town. She and Adrian had taken it once. Today a couple was emerging with a very small dog on a pink harness and lead.

Martha put away her bottle and carried on. She was not so certain now. Window-boxes and bright front doors told her she hadn't reached the area she was looking for.

Eve opened her eyes and saw Max slumped against the bed. He appeared to be kneeling, arms spread wide. The image of supplication reminded her of herself at the foot of the statue of Mary. She raised herself on an elbow. 'What is it, Max?'

He looked at her and his eyes were red and puffy with tears. 'I'm so sorry.'

'What do you mean? Is there something you haven't told me?' What had happened to her man of action, her knight in armour?

How could he revert so quickly? There was only one thing he might not tell her. 'Have you had a call?' She shook his shoulder but her grip was weak and his bones were heavy.

'No. No. Nothing.'

She looked at the bedside clock. Midday. She must have slipped into sleep when Max had got up. Last night when he returned from the search he'd not been like this.

'I'm sorry for what I've done to you and for what I've done to Dan.'

Eve was almost aghast. Neither of them was good at talking like this. They'd slipped apart from each other silently, harbouring for safety's sake (or so they thought) unvoiced resentment and criticism. Now he was throwing out that delicate balance. 'It's not only you, Max.' She whispered it softly, half hoping he might not hear.

He reached up and took her hand. They were both shaking, as shy and nervous as young lovers.

'Don't kneel.' She sat up and gently pulled him towards her. They sat side by side. She put her hand on his forehead and touched his wet eyes. She wondered what she could offer him. 'I've been on my knees too.' He put an arm round her but said nothing. 'I've been praying.'

'For Dan's return?'

She was surprised by how easily he accepted this. He couldn't know it had been a private act, shutting him out from her strongest emotions. 'Do you think it's stupid?'

'If it comforts you, it must be good.' He paused, then turned to her with sudden intensity. 'Why did you never ask me, Eve?'

With a terrifying sense of vertigo, she knew what he meant. She looked at his face. It was almost a relief that the tears had made it swollen and ugly.

How to answer him? *Why did you never ask me?* Because when you were first unfaithful, I was young and angry. Because I'd been taught not to ask questions by my father – or was it by Martha, her finger to her lips, 'Sssh. Don't ask Daddy'? Their mother, once dead, must never be mentioned. Bad things were best kept hidden.

But Max was her husband. She could do what she liked. 'I was cowardly,' she said. What should she have said, 'Who are you sleeping with now, darling?'

'I thought it meant you didn't care.'

'And that made it all right?' She might have been cowardly but he was the one who'd humiliated her.

'You treated me like a child. You patronized me.'

'You were behaving like a spoilt child!' Her voice was raised but the repetition of the word 'child' echoed sombrely. 'With the first girls I hoped it would stop. Would you have stopped if I'd asked?'

Max moved slightly away from her and looked down. 'I don't know. It was a habit. I thought it was all right because I didn't love them.'

'All right for whom?'

'All right for us. For you and me.'

Eve thought of the calls she'd had over the years, the girl called Rosanna who'd had an abortion. 'I *should* have asked you,' she said painfully. 'I thought poets were special.'

Max gave a strange croak of a laugh. 'I thought you didn't care.'

'Perhaps I should have been praying for us.' Eve put her hands up to her face and said softly, between her fingers, 'It's not too late, is it?'

'I love you. I've always loved you.' He sounded despairing.

'But if I asked you never to leave me again, could you do it? If I said, "I love you, Max, and I admire you and I respect you", would you still trawl for bright-faced strangers with compliant young bodies?'

'I love you, Eve, only you.'

She knew that part was true, had always known it.

There was nothing more either of them could bear to say.

Max got carefully off the bed, like someone recuperating from an operation, and went into the kitchen.

Eve lay listening to him making tea or coffee and it seemed the first comforting sound she'd heard for years. Before her mother had died, her life had been filled with comforting sounds: her mother in the kitchen carelessly forcing the toast to pop up; the cows in the fields surrounding the village where they had lived – cows and lambs in the spring and birds all the time. Birds in London were too distressed to be comforting, confused about daylight hours and always fighting their corner among armies of pigeons.

She tried to remember if she and Max had ever thought of living in the country. It was possible he'd wanted it. She'd been excited by the city and she felt her mother would have approved. She'd been a bold, forthright woman who'd married a too introspective, clever man. In the evening she'd turned up the volume on recordings of Brahms and Schumann and Tchaikovsky so that the speakers vibrated angrily. When she died, their father had thrown away all her CDs. At least he could have given them to Oxfam. At the time she had thought it a sign of love.

Max brought her coffee and a plate of biscuits on a tray. Tenderly, he helped her settle against the pillows. She sat up and ate a biscuit to please him. They were circles iced in pastel shades, children's biscuits. She must have bought them when Yvonne came to tea, wishing to placate and elicit sympathy. She ate another and Max seemed pleased.

'I think I'm going to leave it to the police for a bit,' he said. 'They've really gripped it now.'

'I can hardly get out of bed.' She lay back and her hair fell lankly round her. She could smell its oiliness.

'My feeling,' said Max, carefully, 'is that he's alive but needs help.'

Eve felt her heart jump. Previously she would have reacted to such a statement – pointless, after all – with angry terror. Now she nodded. 'And the worst thing of all is we can't help him.'

'Why don't you get dressed?' said Max. He tried to smile. 'We'll take a picnic to the park.'

Eve looked out of the window with surprise. But he was right: it was still summer out there, when people unfolded a rug on the grass and lay back looking at the sky instead of their ceilings.

'Yes,' she said. 'We can do that.'

CHAPTER THIRTY-TWO

Martha suspected that squats were the same the world over: the dirty sheets hanging over the windows, the discarded armchair with the burn hole in the seat, the door smashed open by police or impatient user and poorly mended. The only question was whether this was the one where Lee believed Dan had hung out. The story was not going to be pretty, he'd said, however it turned out. Dan had got in with a bad crowd.

He'd said it in the same laconic way he said everything, but Martha knew it was a warning. If she and Eve (or, indeed, Max) had been speaking she'd have passed it on to them, softened a little. They should not expect their son returned to them as he'd left. Martha had briefly worked in a young offenders' prison but found the boys' brutal carapace too hard to take. A month wouldn't have done that to Dan but he couldn't be the same.

A wind sweeping up behind her rocked the door slightly and she realized it was unlocked, in fact slightly open.

She went in cautiously with the tread of an experienced prison officer – not quite a policeman because she was ready to back out. It was immediately obvious the place was empty. The smell was overpowering, of dirt, sour food, cigarette smoke, sweat, as if it had only recently been abandoned. In the middle of the mild, bright day, it was a suffocating, depressing place, reeking, finally, of despair.

Martha hung around for a bit longer, trying not to imagine her nephew sleeping in one of the filthy beds, and to hide from herself that she was expecting Lee to turn up at any minute. She also resisted her housewife's urge to find a plastic bag and throw in all the old cartons, needles, plastic forks, tissues and worse. Instead, she went to the door and sniffed the clean air.

Lee was coming up the hill. She had never seen him at a distance or in the open before, except that once outside the pub, in the dark. He had a cocky, slightly rolling walk, with a compact body tilted forward, giving a sense of aggression. His head was rather small for his height, accentuated by his tightly cut greying hair.

Martha was immensely attracted to him. The thought passed swiftly through her mind that she would give up the prison service for him. Although he must have seen her, he gave no sign until he was within a couple of metres when he raised his hand in acknowledgement.

A large cloud, passing overhead as they met, put them in shadow.

'The birds have flown.' Lee pushed the door with his fingertip. He seemed unsurprised to see Martha.

'I went inside.'

'Not a pretty sight.'

'I've seen far worse in prison.' He'd guess she was referring to prisoners on 'dirty protest', faeces spread across a cell's walls or their own bodies.

'You've lived.'

Martha wanted to ask him if he'd seen Dan but she suspected the answer was no and she didn't want to hear it on this doorstep. 'Is there a pub around here? I need to sit down and get something to eat.'

'OK.'

He led, always a half-step ahead. She thought how hard prison must have been for him where the prison officer set the pace.

The pub was unprepossessing, painted a dark blood colour both outside and in. It was called, inappropriately, the Sailor's Rest. A selection of smudgy prints of eighteenth-century sailing ships was lined up along the walls. The solid wooden table they sat down at was decorated with an interlocking series of glass rings – beer spillings, Martha felt certain. There was no one else inside.

'They do food?' she asked doubtfully.

'They have a microwave, like everyone else.'

A tall, pale girl, probably Polish, came over to serve them. 'Hi. You're eating?'

Lee nodded. Martha guessed they knew each other, perhaps the reason he'd brought her here.

'Lasagne or fish?'

'Do you have any sandwiches?' asked Martha.

'Sorry.' The girl looked at her curiously. She had an intelligent, sly face, with a wide forehead and almost lashless blue eyes.

'Lasagne,' said Lee.

'A large packet of crisps.' She thought that as he'd survived on prison food microwaved lasagne would be a treat, but there was no need for her to pollute her digestion.

Lee followed the girl to the bar. They talked there together for a few moments. She had a graceful figure with long legs, and Martha felt a stab of jealousy.

Lee came back with two beers. Martha hadn't wanted alcohol but she sipped it all the same. She was becoming more nervous about what he had to say to her.

'I saw a policeman at the station.' She spoke without looking at him.

'There're police all over. The power of the media. The boy's a hero.'

'Have you seen him?' It was not so much a question as an exclamation of distress.

'I told you, he's not here any more.'

'But he was in that squalid place?'

'Yes. I've asked Agnes to sit down with us. She's from the Czech Republic.'

Martha took a gulp of her unwanted beer. Agnes. So what did Agnes have to say?

The lasagne arrived, lank in the middle, crisp at the edges. With it came Agnes who duly sat down. She turned to Martha. 'The girl, Freya, came for work. Nice girl but so intent – "intent", is that a word?'

'Intense,' said Martha.

'A pretty girl. Hair in little plaits. Seventeen, eighteen, nineteen. I like her. We talk. Although her fingernails. Ugh.' Showing expression for the first time, Agnes grimaced.

Imagining bitten to the quick, blackened, or even torture, Martha asked, 'What do you mean?'

'Filthy.' She pronounced it 'feelthy'. 'Old feelth. No good for working in the kitchen. Ugh,' she repeated.

'I see.'

'And who came with her?' prompted Lee.

'Two men. I not like.' She shrugged.

'And who else?'

'Boy. Too young. He drink Coke.' Dan didn't like fizzy drinks, except Fanta. 'Are you sure it wasn't Fanta?' Martha saw Lee giving her an odd look. 'Dan hated Coke.'

'He drink Coke. His name not Dan.'

'He called himself Dino,' commented Lee. 'So Freya did work here?'

'Weather bad so her business on the beach bad.'

'Business?' Martha was surprised.

'She braid kids' hair. She liked doing that. Once I saw. Dino on the sand by her. He liked the kids too. Sad boy. His face very hurt.'

Martha felt her heart give a nasty jump. Sad boy with a hurt face. She'd helped to create that. 'He's my nephew,' she said.

Agnes nodded. 'Freya worked evenings at the bar. Sometimes. Come and go. Then two days ago my manager throw them out. Those men bad. Too much drugs. Chop off their hands and throw them in dark prison.'

'What?' Agnes' last sentence had been produced in the same calm tones she'd used all along, except in relation to dirty fingernails. Martha looked at the girl's hands: they were definitely attached to her wrists and perfectly clean.

'And Dino?' Lee leant forward. He'd already pushed away the half-eaten lasagne. 'When did he go?'

'Before. He found a new friend. I don't know what. These people, they are not responsible. Why they not work? Study?' Now there was more colour in her cheeks.

'Do you know where they went?'

'No.' She half closed her eyes as if disguising a lie. 'Maybe festival. Always festivals. Going, coming. I told Freya, "You get out of it quick," but she was angry. Said I not understand. She a traveller. Well, I know travellers we call gyppos in my country. Stealing-type people. I tell you she intense. Tell me about another life, free life. But I see drugs and dirty nails. I feel sorry for her so she goes off angry.' Now Agnes's eyes flashed and she waved her hand in the air.

Martha heard a door open behind her and voices.

'Customers,' said Lee.

Agnes stood up.

'I work.'

'You've been kind. Thank you,' said Martha, but she thought that the girl was hard and unfeeling, set in her own convictions, made in another, crueller country.

Outside the pub, the dark cloud that had shadowed Martha and Lee's meeting had collected others round it so that the sky was bulging with rain about to fall.

'You set this up,' said Martha. 'How did you know I'd follow you?'

'Because you believed I'd find him.' Lee walked her towards a car, an old Mercedes saloon. They both got in. 'Because you wanted to be with me.' He leant across and kissed her. His mouth was hard and confident, not quite painful.

When they parted, Martha sighed with a mixture of sadness and relief. 'Where can we go?'

He turned on the engine and began to drive. The rain suddenly battered the roof, exploding on the windscreen, pouring down the side windows. Martha shut her eyes for a few moments, and when she opened them they were pulling up outside a small brightly painted hotel, typical of seaside resorts.

PART THREE
Coming Together

CHAPTER THIRTY-THREE

'You're not a bad kid, quiet company, but I need my space, see.'

Dan heard Zeppo's voice in the kind of misty way he heard everything now. Zeppo was going to chuck him out. Was that what he was hearing? So, Zeppo was chucking him out. Not important, broth. He knew they were in Brighton but that didn't seem very important either. They'd come in Zeppo's van, swaying round corners, boxes shifting in the back. Zeppo's worldly goods. Zeppo's book too, *Biography of the British Marx Brothers*. Piles and piles of paper stacked against half a Honda. That sounded good. Half a Honda. *Half a Honda and no cheese*. Freya's sort of words.

'You listening, man? Don't go off in one of those dreams.'

Dan thought Zeppo's voice was kind of comforting but he didn't feel any need to respond. Zeppo's paper book was filled with words. Word after word, line after jiggling line. Bad moment once. He didn't want to think of that. Freya and him smoking dope in the back, lying on something soft. Zeppo and the others off somewhere.

'Hey, D. Dino.'

What was it with his mind? Coming up with memories he didn't want. Bad trip. Freya called it bad trip. Comes with living. Bad trip when the words come off the paper, rising up like corkscrews, skewers, gimlets, knives. Then the paper comes up too, towering above you, shaking down below a killer cascade. He had to stop this. What was it reminding him of? He'd remembered in the end: poor little Alice cowering under a pack of cards. *Alice on wonder-speed*.

'Hey. You listen!' Zeppo, real name Mike, was shaking his shoulder now, finger talons clutching his flesh and bones. He supposed he should have known not to go with him. Freya had warned him. 'Zeppo will dump you when it suits him. He's got a bad history. Don't say I didn't tell you. He calls himself a traveller but he doesn't understand the first thing. He'd work behind the counter of a bank if it made his life easier. He doesn't understand capitalism kills.'

Freya always talked big after she'd had a smoke or two. *Capitalism kills. Women for peace. Make trees not stumps.* He liked it. All of that belief. It made him feel happy, although that might have been the shit, dope, weed, skunk. Freya's eyes were speckled like an egg, with huge pupils like cats'. *Every day is Earth Day.*

'Don't smile at me, you stupid fucker. I'm turning you out. So, walk. Enjoy Brighton!'

Not that she looked at him that way. Probably guessed his age. Said sex was a free currency. *Property is theft.* Even had sex with Zeppo. Despised Zeppo but had sex with him. Man, were there things he'd learnt! Not a little boy any more. No sex, though. Not yet. Freya's nose was a little pink round the diamond stud.

'Get off! Get off, can't you?' There was no need for Zeppo to hurt him. Smacking his head like that wouldn't do his brains any good. Start up one of his headaches. He'd have to get up.

'Go! Go! Go! You fucker!'

Zeppo was big. Could do him harm. Big as his dad. Who was not the hitting sort. Not the hugging sort either. Not him.

'I'm going. Can't you see? If you keep whamming me, how do you expect me to move?' Funny, he'd always thought of himself as a bit of a coward but when Zeppo launched into him he didn't even duck. The blows landed, all right, but it was like there was something in between. His brain didn't feel the pain. Saw the results after, though. Bruises like spaceships.

'I'm out of here.' He'd never liked the room. No Freya. 'Just looking for my backpack. Lay off, man.'

He didn't like looking at his backpack. So battered and dirty and empty and hopeless. He didn't know why he still had it. But he grabbed it all the same. It did have the fossil. That belonged to another life. Once he'd put Freya's hair-braiding kit in it. Ribbons and bands and beads. Sitting on the beach, he'd felt best ever. Watching her fingers fly over a little child's hair. Funny all that braiding on fair hair, brown hair. Very little black in Weymouth. Freya said colour was in the eye of the beholder.

'Out! Now! Out!'

It wasn't so bad on the street. Steeply sloping, though, which was hard on the feet. *Heavenly shock absorbers.* That was one of Freya's sayings he couldn't connect with. Surely Heaven was above and Hell below. Anyway, she was a Buddhist.

Halfway down the narrow street, Dan found a bench and sat on it. He put his backpack carefully under his feet. Although it contained no history, it was his past. *The past is another country* – but that wasn't Freya. She didn't like talking about what she called *unalterable inevitables*. She liked big words. She said childhood made her puke.

Mel and Abe had told him they'd picked her up in Cornwall. They never said where, but he pictured a cave and rocky cliffs sprouting with wild flowers and a turquoise sea, with bursting white crests to the waves, and fishing-boats bobbing around with nets and jars. *One raindrop raises the sea.* Another of her favourite lines. Maybe Freya had learnt her hair skills at the knee of her net-making fisherman's-wife mother. All romantic shit, of course. She'd probably grown up on an estate. Once, she'd said Cornwall was the most deprived area of the UK – *United Kids Limited* – and if she thought politicians were anything but *buttercup wankers* (mysterious, that) she'd stand for the EU – *Eggs United*.

He loved her, that was the point, so that his knees knocked and his hair stood on end and his teeth chattered. *Knickerbocker Glory.* That was what she'd said when she was up there with the stars. On speed, Es, anything she could get hold of. *Knickerbocker Glory.* She'd scream it sometimes in the night. Not tell him why in the morning but he could guess. There wasn't much privacy in the places they stayed.

You wouldn't think Mel or Abe worth Knickerbocker Glory but she was high then, too. She didn't allow him on anything but the skunky-type dope, said it fried growing brains, and that was how the trouble had started.

Dan looked up at the sky, puzzled for a moment. Why was his face wet? Little-boy tears? No, man. Just rain.

Martha was stretched out on a blue-and-white-striped deck-chair on Weymouth beach. The day was warm, rather overcast, and she lay with her eyes closed. She tried to remember how she had felt about Lee when he was in prison – or told herself she felt. Protective. Her job had been to help him overcome his offending past and settle into a productive, non-criminal future. As if words like this could ever get near someone with Lee's history. He would always be dangerous, even if he didn't break the law.

Martha bent forward to untie her trainers; she pushed them off her feet. Her toes wriggled in the sand. After the night in the Prince Regent B-and-B, her whole body felt sensitized. There had not been much sleeping in the pink-and-white floral bedroom with the frilly lilac lampshades.

In the morning they'd hardly spoken. It seemed she was destined to be with men who thought sex was something she gave without asking for intimacy: no small-talk or flattery, insincere or even sincere. Maybe it was what she wanted, felt safer that way. Yet she had felt Lee's gratitude for services rendered. She smiled to herself in remembrance. They both had needs.

They'd not breakfasted together. He'd left not telling her where he was going but saying he would be back. That was enough, even more than she'd expected. She knew he was looking for Dan, guessed his connections were drug-related. On her way to the beach she'd bought the local newspaper. It was under her deck-chair now; the headline read *Missing Boy Hero in Weymouth*. There was a picture of Dan, the same one as on the poster.

Lee had said Dan had already left Weymouth so he had to track him further. With the police and the papers and, doubtless, television too, although she hadn't seen anything, it was impossible to believe Dan wouldn't be found now, even without Lee's help.

She allowed herself to fantasize about Dan, returned and healthy, she and Lee spending a celebratory week in Weymouth. They'd do childish things: go to the funfair, shoot down a water slide, screaming like lovers in bad movies; swim out to sea, holding hands, then turn round to admire the curving esplanade with its elegant hotels; lie kissing on the beach like happy people did. She'd never had any of that – Adrian had been too old, too unromantic – and Lee was even less likely to take part in such silliness. But she liked day-dreaming, still smelling the salty tang of sex – or maybe that was the sea. She didn't care. For once she'd be foolish.

In an hour or two she'd find a café to eat, sit outside, batting away the seagulls like any other tourist. She wouldn't read the newspaper under her deckchair, she'd buy a *Guardian* and tut-tut at the state of the government. She definitely wouldn't telephone Eve, who would be furious if she knew where she was. Max might be around somewhere, but he was too introspective to notice anything, let alone his wife's sister. That was what she'd become.

It was possible now to admit how badly he had behaved towards her, as if Lee's toughness had stiffened her sinews. She, had been weak, lonely, self-deluding. She, who had always prided herself on her strength. She owed Eve an apology but she wouldn't give it. Eve owed her so much from their childhood and she'd stopped trying to make Max happy. She'd lost her regard for him.

Strange how love can depart, slowly or abruptly. If Max came and sat on the empty chair nearby, her heart would stick to its regular beat, set to another clock. She would look at him fondly, perhaps, a strikingly handsome man who was suffering. She imagined his soulful blue eyes, his craggy face and his thick dark hair; she imagined his long legs stretched out as he read poetry in his wonderful deep voice, but nothing excited her. He was her brother-in-law. She felt sorry for him. As well as furious.

Still lying in the deck-chair, she continued to plan her day. After she'd visited the café and become bored with the piped music and her neighbours who had too many overweight children and favoured tight T-shirts exposing too much holiday-pink flesh, she'd go back to the pub, the Sailor's Rest. Agnes would be there, which was a pity, but she guessed that was where she and Lee would meet again. She needed quiet time to prepare for that.

'Excuse me.'

At her feet, a boy of five or six was collecting his ball which had bounced on to the side of her deck-chair. She hadn't noticed. She looked down at his solemn eyes and sturdy body in Arsenal shorts. He was so polite. Dan had been a polite boy, self-effacing, although not particularly keen to please.

'Don't worry.'

The boy ran off, giving a wild war-whoop as if to exonerate himself from too much good behaviour.

A policewoman stood in front of Dan. He must have shut his eyes for a moment because he hadn't seen her approaching his bench.

'Can I help you?'

She was young, with a shiny, friendly face. Freya called policemen pigeons because they shat on you from high up. Guess this applied to policewomen too. Before he could think of anything to say, she sat down beside him. 'Having a rest are you?' She said it in a kindly, not too curious way, but Dan saw the danger.

'Yes. Waiting for my mum.' He paused, then added, to make it seem more real, 'She's always late.'

'I need a rest too. Community police always get extra walking.'

'Suppose.' Dan wondered if they were pigeons too. Probably. Freya hated all authority figures: she said they were *vampires sucking the lifeblood out of ordinary people*. She said she'd die if she couldn't live the life of the traveller. She'd told him he might become a natural traveller too. He'd been proud. It had made what happened later much worse.

'On holiday here, are you?'

'With my mum and sister.' Why bother to give himself a dad?

'Dad working, is he?'

She was turning out to be curious after all. He stood up slowly and picked up his bag. 'Got to go.'

'Take care.'

As he walked down the hill in the direction of the sea, he felt his legs shaking as if they might give way under him. He'd been comfortable on the bench, even in the rain, until that pointless pigeon had come to spoil it. Now he had to think where to go. Plus worry about the pigeon being on his tail.

He still had the fiver Freya had given him. He'd go down to the beach, take a burger with him. Throw stones into the sea, watch the ripple effect. He could do that for hours. But Brighton wasn't like Weymouth. It felt like he was back in a big city – the last thing he wanted. Maybe he should nick the food and keep the money for a train – not that he'd get far. A bus, then.

Vaguely he remembered the bright times with the old man building the wall. It seemed like a dream. Now and again he took out his fossil just to remind himself it really did happen. He'd saved the old man's life too. He'd lost the newspaper that had told the story. It'd blown away on some beach or other and he hadn't had the energy to run after it.

Freya had taught him the reality. He knew what the world was like now. No silly, childish dreams. You had to look after yourself. He could, too. Which reminded him – not that he'd ever really forgotten – he had a package in his pocket. And Zeppo had one fewer. Clever, that. Zeppo was a creep even if he had given him a lift. He was a real thief, too, not just someone who *took what he was owed from the capitalistic society*. Which was what Freya and he did. She earned too. Zeppo did nothing, except write what he said was a masterpiece. No, thank you very much. Freya said writers were vampires too, or was it parasites when he'd asked if she wrote because she had such a feeling for words? She'd been insulted, or acted like it, saying slogans were the only words worth considering. *God is short for Goddess.*

The rain was coming down more heavily now, flattening his hair into his eyes. He pushed it away and, as he looked up, saw a vision of turrets, bulbous domes and spires, a bit Disney but, to his hazy mind, beautiful too.

Ru would have liked it. Funny to be thinking of him now when he'd been gone for weeks, not even visiting him at night. He'd told Freya about him, first person he'd ever told: that was because he loved her and she cared. He knew she cared. At first she'd not understood, said Ru couldn't have been a true friend if he was calling on him to take a long dive into the night. Told him that was Ru's dark night, not his. So he'd explained what had happened and how he'd run away. She'd said, 'Guilt trip, man. Shake that off. If a boy's hanging like you saw, he's dead. Dead, dead, no retrieval, you know what I'm saying?'

Maybe it was what she'd said that did it, but Ru stayed away after that. Other dreams when he smoked, but not Ru. So he told her Ru didn't seem to be around and she was nice and said that was because he approved of their life, and him being with them. But it was after that she'd cut down on his smoking. Told him about frying his brain. Well, as he saw it, his brain felt better fried. He told her so and they rowed after that. Not seriously, at the start.

Dan walked in the gardens of the palace, because that was what it looked like, but even more beautiful and exotic. He knew why it had reminded him of Ru because they had often talked of places they'd prefer to live. Ru had some pictures of old Chinese palaces, with little bridges over sparkling water, willow trees and elaborate buildings. Sometimes there was a lady with a parasol. Ru said in China there were still places like that, although only used for tourists. Sometimes he said he was descended from Chinese emperors, but Dan knew his dad came from Barbados or somewhere and was long gone and his mother was small and shrivelled, not at all like someone descended from an emperor. Once Ru had shown him a heavy green seal with a red tassel and told him it was his inheritance, but Dan hadn't believed him. He'd seen seals just like it in the Chinese junk shop down the road.

All the same he enjoyed Ru's stories set in China; he had a much harder life than Dan so he had to go further in his dreams. Dan had thought himself lonely – an only child and busy parents, no real friends at school – till he'd met Ru. At school Ru put off people because he was so small and shy – even the teachers didn't try to understand him. Home was just as bad, with his mother working in some takeaway noodle place at night and cleaning in the day. Ru said she'd quarrelled with all their relatives because of going with his dad. Some of them were illegal, too, but she and Ru had passports. Ru said she was so proud of their passports she would have framed them, if she'd had the money. She never talked of China, only kept those pictures.

Man, Ru's life had been *so* sad. No wonder he'd got out into dreams, then out altogether. Just wish he hadn't been there to see him. Whatever, Ru shouldn't have come back to haunt him, that was the truth.

CHAPTER THIRTY-FOUR

Martha, in her deck-chair on Weymouth beach, was asleep, but not altogether asleep. She knew that her mouth was slack, that she was snoring a little and that it was raining. She was part dreaming, part thinking about her life. She dreamt of her mother, eternally young; Her mother's face had been round and rosy, more like Eve's – or Eve as she used to be – than her own. Her father was the grey-faced skeleton in the hospital, an ancient man (although not old) reproachful and bitter to the end. It was her problem that she had taken his reproach personally as if a mere daughter could do anything to help when all the centuries of religious conviction he'd continued to espouse had left his heart cold.

She had no time for religion. She expected no help from anyone but herself, which was a source of pride. She even smiled a little and slipped further into sleep so that the sea's waves, a rhythm of forward and backward of which she'd hardly been aware, became part of her own pattern of breathing. She sank down physically, her thin body flat on the hammock of the chair.

A shadow crossed her, then a man. He stood in front of her for several seconds, looking down, negligent as if he didn't really care, waiting for her to wake. He judged his presence would rouse her but in fact it was only his voice.

'Bought a ticket, have you?'

The light was behind him. The rain had passed and he was dark against the shimmering sea and sky. For a moment Martha, the fearless, was afraid.

'Lee?' It might not have been Lee. It might have been anyone, including a man collecting money for use of a deck-chair.

'Hey, Marth.' He crouched beside her. Now she could see his face.

'Hey.' He had come to find her. She was surprised. And his face was alive in a way it hadn't been, even when they made love; then, he'd been fierce and determined. Now he was transfigured and she knew it couldn't be for her. 'What's happened?'

'I talked to him!'

Martha pulled herself further upright. Dan! But did he care so much for Dan? She said nothing.

'She let him come to the phone. Won't let me see him. Don't blame her for it. The kid's accent, fuck that, we could hardly understand each other. Gave us a good laugh.'

Paternal joy. She'd never seen his face with colour lighting the neutral beige, his eyes no longer opaque and pale. She was pleased to feel happy for him. He had brought the news to her and he was a man not accustomed to sharing. 'I'm so glad for you.'

'It's a start.' He settled back on his heels and then, in one quick movement, slid down to the sand and stretched out on his back.

Almost before Martha had realized it, he was asleep. She bent over to look at him, withdrawn from her again. But she was used to that and could manage.

Overhead, two seagulls wheeled and cawed, occasionally swooping low enough for her to see their sharp eyes. The beach was very full now, the noise level higher in every direction, including a carousel of painted horses that played the same three tunes over and over again. For one of the songs, lines came into her head, *Many a promise is broken . . . It's a sin to tell a lie.* It seemed odd to have such mournful words attached to a cheerful childish tune but she certainly knew it from somewhere – her own childhood, perhaps.

It struck her uneasily that perhaps Lee would lose interest in Dan now that he was talking to his own son, whose name she didn't know. She reminded herself that the police were on the job – there was an officer now, threading his way among the holidaymakers, handing out leaflets. Photographs of Dan? Even from a distance she could see he was taking his bonding-with-the-public skills seriously, bantering with each person he approached.

She wondered if Lee should take evasive action – a prisoner on licence in serious breach of his parole conditions. But they didn't have a photo of him and probably no one very much was looking for him, particularly in Weymouth. She glanced down at him, prone on the sand, utterly vulnerable, and thought that no one should mistake vulnerability for innocence. This was a man who'd smashed a jagged glass into a friend's face.

Working in the prison, she was used to carrying two pieces of often contradictory information about the men there: their history, sometimes containing horrific acts of violence or abuse and their present behaviour, in most cases normal. Outsiders, she knew, including police, retained the image of a killer as someone visibly dreadful, as if being 'a murderer' was a constant state.

While she wondered why she'd always found it easy to approach even the toughest cases as fellow humans instead of 'monsters', the uniform continued to approach. As if drawn by a magnet, he stood in front of her holding out what was indeed a photo, *the* photo, of Dan. He was a young man, not as cheery as she'd decided from afar, too hot with all his gear.

'Thank you,' she said, as if he'd given out a promo for a new curry house. She caught him giving a longing look to the promenade behind her, as if meandering along the beach was not the sort of policing he appreciated.

A slight movement near her feet made her look down. Lee had opened his eyes. His stillness had become taut. She imagined him leaping at the policeman, from prone to active in one. But that was ridiculous.

The policeman moved on; his heavy shoes disturbed sand, which flurried round Lee. Specks flew across his face.

Martha shut her eyes for a moment. How much of her life had she spent waiting for men to be angry?

'Fancy a Chinese?'

She got up slowly, resisting an impulse to kiss Lee, who stood in front of her. He shook off the sand like a dog shakes off water.

'If you want.'

'Did I say? Your Dan's gone to Brighton.'

The park, with its fantasy domes and pinnacles – Disney crossed with culture – was beginning to make Dan's head spin. He wanted to open the packet he'd pinched from Zeppo. In Weymouth, Zeppo had visited the Chinese – funny that, Chinese like Ru, well, half of Ru anyway. Zeppo had been excited when he'd got back, hopping round the room, driving everyone mad. That was what had started

Freya off – Zeppo going on about a special trip and she rattling on about 'bourgeois investment in self' and telling Dan that, special stuff or not, it wasn't for him.

Man, he deserved this package.

He'd come back round to the gateway, sort of like he imagined the gateway to Heaven, all carved and curled. Reminded him of something. He looked up and a raindrop sploshed right into one of his eyes. *One raindrop raises the sea.*

The bushes and flowers were a bit blurred – the water in his eyes plus the way everything seemed to be these days. Nice, soft focus. The grass was bright, though, separated by a little hooped fence to keep you off – rules even in Heaven, then. Anyway, he wanted a bench, something hard under his bum.

Somewhere there was music, not far away, a sax. Perhaps it was inside his head. He'd have liked to play a sax. Never told anyone that. Eve would have been too pleased and Max wouldn't have cared. He had told Ru.

There was a bench right next to something tall and pink and flowering, the flowers as big as faces. He didn't want them turning into faces. Maybe he'd move to the next bench.

Better. Wet, but better, next to yellow flowers that looked like staying the same. He felt the package in his pocket.

Freya had said a boy like him should go home and sort himself out. She said he was lucky to have a mum and dad who treated him with respect. 'Respect' was one of her words. He didn't argue with her. He never could.

Abe had made fun of him most of the time. They were at it when Zeppo came back, smirking with the deal he'd done. Freya'd said you could never best the Chinese when it came to dope and he, Dan, believed her. Zeppo got the money from selling and thieving. He was high most of the time, though he slid down the scale when he had to drive. Said it showed he was a 'recreational user', not an addict. The others had hooted with laughter.

That was how it had started. The bad night. They were all smoking. Zeppo too. Keeping his packages for later. For himself. Not into sharing, Zeppo.

Somehow they were at the sea. No idea how they'd got there. How we'd got there. Tagging along, high as any of them. Night-time but warm. Sweating. The waves so loud they were breaking his eardrums. Must have been close to the water. Black as the sky. No lights reflecting anywhere.

Why were they there? Why were they anywhere? Mel started repeating over and over, 'All-purpose soluble plant food.' Nobody knew why. Perhaps he was challenging himself. He found the words difficult. 'Soluble' got him stuck each time. Drove them all crazy.

Dan's thoughts drifted back from that dark night on the beach to his present surroundings – the wet bench, the dripping yellow flowers, the gilded palace rising out of the grey afternoon sky, the escape he had from it all secure in his pocket. He was in no hurry now. Anyway, he'd have to find a straw or a piece of paper from somewhere, from a bin probably. He'd seen Zeppo sniff often enough. And the others when they could get hold of the stuff. 'A lifestyle choice', Abe had called it, which had made Zeppo laugh. 'You think you've got style, dickhead?'

He'd grown to dread Zeppo's laughter. On the beach, it had begun like a kind of game. Tossing up sand in little fountains of light. Light from somewhere out of the black. Then they were scooping and throwing, hearing a little hiss as it hit the waves. They weren't lying down any more, the sand wet, like a wet fish in their hands, slapping on the ground, plopping into the water.

He'd been giggling – at least, he'd heard laughter, high-pitched, angry, ugly, no joke. The first lump of sand hit him in the back, the next in the face and after that it was wet fish slapping him all over. Mel and Abe cackling like maniacs, throwing too, although he didn't know then and he didn't know now.

He wasn't giggling any more, screeching with fear and hatred, while they were falling over with laughter. He could see them now, crawling about like animals.

So he'd run towards the sea and someone or a gull had screamed and screamed. The water was cold and heavy. He tried to launch himself on it like a boat, turn on the engine and speed away, the only sound the waves thrusting back and forward, bursting over his head so his eardrums rattled.

He couldn't remember . . .

A naked figure, hair wild like Neptune's, pulling him by his neck, yelling, 'Fucker – cock-sucker' – no, it can't have been Neptune.

He lay on the beach, sodden to the sand, and the naked man was not far away with Freya, who was still screaming – it had been her

237

screaming earlier – but he didn't want to hear. How did he know what the screaming meant?

He remembered the light coming and the four of them like wet sacks on the sand, the sea far away, Zeppo still naked, his legs over Freya; she was half dressed.

He must have slept again. There was only Freya when he woke. She had her back to him, sitting cross-legged, looking out to the horizon. Meditating. His head split and gonged like it needed some-one to bind it up. A big white bandage to hold it together.

Behind him, he could hear the other life beginning, the cars, the people, like there was a glass wall between them. Anyway, there was no one so near the edge of the water.

He must have made a noise because she said, without turning, 'You could have died, Dino.'

He tried to think what she meant. He thought one of her lines went, *Death is a bourgeois invention*, but he wasn't sure and, anyway, his out-of-action head was unlikely to produce words.

'You've got to go home.'

If she'd just said that it might have been all right, even though his head hurt and she had her back to him so he couldn't see her beautiful cat's eyes. Her back was beautiful, too true, straight and supple. She could sit cross-legged and put her head right down on the floor. He'd seen her sleep like that. Or meditate. You could never tell which with Freya. Sometimes she was made of china like a Buddha and sometimes she was silk.

That morning she was china or bronze or silver steel. Something smooth and hard that didn't do soft things any good.

'You don't fit in here,' she said. 'You're not one of us. So now you must fuck off.'

She was so final – her back was so final because she still hadn't turned round – that he stood up, almost without thought, like a soldier obeying commands and said, quite simply, 'OK.'

Then he'd walked away, legs like rotten rubber, all the way back to their house.

Zeppo had been packing up, Mel and Abe asleep.

'Where're you going?' he'd asked. All he was thinking was that Freya had told him to go home because he wasn't one of them, making him an outcast, cast out. She hadn't been angry, that might have been better, just decided.

238

'I'm moving on,' Zeppo had conceded eventually.

So he'd packed up his own bag, which hadn't taken long because he didn't have anything to pack, and tagged along with Zeppo. It was the only way he could think of getting back at Freya. Going with Zeppo wasn't going home.

Zeppo made it clear he didn't want him but he didn't stop him climbing into the van either, as if it didn't make much difference whether he was there or not.

Freya was the only one who'd cared and she'd turned on him. Fuck you, too, Freya.

CHAPTER THIRTY-FIVE

'Brighton?' Martha ran her fingernails down Lee's naked arm. The muscle was hard even when he was relaxed. They'd eaten at a noisy Chinese place, returned to the Prince Regent B-and-B and gone to bed.

Lee had shown a little more tenderness, which she suspected was about his son. She still didn't know the son's name. Perhaps he didn't care enough about her to confide it. 'Brighton?' she repeated. 'Do the police know?'

'Not yet.' He rolled over to face her. 'Do you want to tell them?'

She thought about that. So far, Lee had been a step ahead but he still hadn't found Dan. 'Should I? What do you think?'

'He's keeping bad company. If it was my lad, I'd want to find him.'

What was Lee playing at? Of course she wanted to find him. She'd thought of nothing else for nearly two months. Not true. She'd thought of Lee. 'What's your son's name?'

'Braveheart.'

If that was how he wanted it. 'What would I tell the police?'

'That he went to Brighton with Zeppo.'

'And if they ask how I got this information?'

'Tell them that Chinaman tipped you the wink.'

'I see.' Martha watched Lee turn away from her again. He would go up to Scotland, she thought, try to persuade his ex-wife, if that was what she was, to let him meet 'Braveheart'. He'd be picked up at some point and have to serve out his sentence. She was nothing to do with his plans. He was moving on.

'Lee.' Yet there was nothing to say. 'So, you think I should approach the police?'

'It's up to you.' He rolled back again and touched her body, her breasts, her sex.

She thought he was saying they were quits: he had given her Dan, she had given him her body. She wanted him again, even more now that she knew he'd leave. In the morning she'd go to the police.

Max and Eve sat together, as they did everything. They walked together, talked together, were silent together, slept together, although they didn't make love. They felt safest close. They had weathered the first storms apart and they knew the difference.

When the phone rang, however, only one of them could answer it. Max let go of Eve's hand reluctantly. Eve looked at it lying in her lap and thought they had become like an old couple, although he was stronger, more able to face reality. She had given in to a kind of willed Alzheimer's in which she wanted to forget, not to remember.

The telephone rang several times before Max picked up the receiver. Eve noticed his whole arm was shaking. She looked lovingly at his long, wiry frame, the bend of his shoulders, his fine, beaky nose.

It was a man's voice on the line. She could hear his intonations, no words. She guessed it was important but her Alzheimer's wouldn't allow her to make connections. She even shut her eyes so that she couldn't see Max's expression. He would tell her.

She was surprised when he put down the receiver and, instead of coming directly to her, went into the kitchen. Perhaps he thought she was asleep but even her Alzheimer's wouldn't let her sleep.

'Max!'

He came back with two cans of Coke and some crisps. No alcohol, these days. He opened the tin with a little spurt of bubbles before handing it to her.

'They're getting nearer.'

'What do you mean?'

He took her hand. Both their hands were chilled from the Coke. 'A girl came into a police station. In Devon. Or maybe Cornwall.' He paused, apparently confused by his failure of memory. 'It was the detective inspector who'd phoned.'

Eve waited. *They're getting nearer.* Like a game. She realized she no longer dared believe in Dan's reappearance. This news could mean anything. She did believe in Max so if he told her they were getting nearer, as he just had, then she would go along with it. She squeezed his hand and watched his frown clear a little.

'I'm trying to work out what it means.'

'Tell me.' She wanted to help him. That was all.

'This girl. A traveller, I think he said. Whatever that might mean.' He paused again and drank some Coke.

'A gypsy?' suggested Eve, and thought it was as if they were doing a crossword puzzle.

'That kind of thing. She came in to tell them that she'd been with Dan for quite a long time. In fact, they'd only just parted.'

Eve felt herself become very still. She felt her protective Alzheimer's shredding away. She had an image of flesh bleeding. She needed to find a voice to ask the question or Max might not tell her. 'Was he all right?'

They were squeezing each other's hands so tightly that she could feel her fingers swelling.

'I think so. But this girl, Freya, was worried about him.'

'What do you mean, "worried"?' She was coming out of her trance and into agonizing life again. Sleeping Beauty woken by the kiss of a prince was filled with terrors. At least, she'd always thought so. Secretly. In the days when she was brave, she didn't admit it. 'Please, Max, tell me everything.'

He looked at her and she saw that his blue eyes were filled with tears. She wanted to cling to him with every part of her. 'It's not so bad,' he said. 'This Freya told the police who he was with, which was why she was worried.' He paused, frowning, again apparently bewildered by the disjointedness of his memory. 'Oh, yes. Oh, yes. She told them where this friend . . .' he hesitated, '. . . this man was going. Almost certainly.'

Eve held her breath and felt her face whiten.

'Brighton.'

'Brighton!' A wail. Air pouring out of her lungs. *A handbag!* Brighton!

'Yes. I can't take it in.' He seemed to want to loose his hand, probably to pace around the room, but she wouldn't let him.

'Can we go there?' She who hadn't been anywhere, who'd lain on her bed or crawled to a statue of Mary or clung to Max, suddenly felt a huge thrust of energy. Brighton was an hour by train. Jack

Worthington was found in a handbag at Victoria Station, on the Brighton platform. She must stop her mind whirling about. She knew Brighton. If Dan was in Brighton, he wasn't missing any more and she could go there (with Max, of course) and bring him home.

'The police are going. Will go. Have gone. I'm not sure. It's late.'

The time seemed of no importance to Eve. Actually, it hadn't for days. Weeks. Once she'd stopped teaching, time had lost any meaning. Now she glanced out of the window and saw it was dark. 'What time is it?'

'Night time.'

'You want us to wait till morning?'

'In the morning I'll ring Ronnie. Get more details. Work out how we can be involved.'

After all, Max had chased after Dan. All those weeks when he'd walked through London streets. She'd hardly noticed then his coming and going. Then he'd dashed to the west, taken the same train as Dan, followed in his footsteps. If Max said wait, she must wait.

Her mother had taken them to the panto in Brighton. It was not so far from where they lived. She'd loved the Ugly Sisters most; one used to undress himself – she was played by a man naturally. He pulled off his stockings first, striped, spotted, flowered, stocking after stocking, on and on and on till the audience were screaming and shouting in wonder and encouragement. Then he'd started on his skirts or, rather, petticoats first, scarlet, lacy white, flounced yellow – he'd found a squeaky duck when he was taking that one off. She'd howled with laughter till Martha had told her to stop showing off. But she hadn't been. She'd just loved everything about it. The stage transported her. Probably Martha had been jealous. Nothing ever transported her. Nothing she talked about anyway. Yet they'd been so close.

A year or two later, she'd badgered their father into taking them back to the same panto. What a disaster that had been. The Ugly Sister was still there but now she was old enough to notice the lewd jokes or perhaps they'd got dirtier. Their father had made them leave. He was wearing a dog collar, of course, as he always did. Looking back, she didn't blame him. Martha did, even though she'd never been that keen on panto. She'd whispered, 'Mean old bastard.' So shocking Eve had never forgotten the words. That had dried her tears, all right. Martha was tough. Where was Martha now? Another missing person.

'Max?'

'Yes.'

'This is good news, isn't it?'

Why was he hesitating? A responsible girl had been with Dan all this time. She might be a gypsy or a traveller but she'd gone to the police when she saw the poster. She must have cared about him.

'I think so. In the morning we'll know more.'

Again she was surprised by a thrust of energy, enough this time to propel her out of her chair to a standing position in front of Max. 'Why shouldn't we go to him now?'

'We don't know where he is. Brighton's a big city.'

'But what if he needs us?' It was the first time she'd dared shout those words.

Max bowed his head. She could hardly hear him. She wished she couldn't hear him. 'We should have thought of that before.'

CHAPTER THIRTY-SIX

'Kubla Khan'. That's what this place reminded him of. Dan, who was lying on the bench now, opened his eyes and peered through the dusk. Max used to recite it to him when he was young and couldn't get to sleep. He couldn't remember much, though – *pleasure dome* and *caverns measureless to man* or something like that. Dreamlike, as he felt, lying in the drippy, greenish evening.

He'd got his head down when a seagull came swooping over him. Didn't like birds, not since those buzzards. Could say seagulls were the downside of the sea.

Seemed to be evening so he must have been asleep. Suddenly worried, he sat up and felt in his pocket. No, the package was still there. He supposed he was putting off using it, like a child hoarding his sweets. He'd done that, hiding a bag of liquorice allsorts behind the books on his shelves, pretending it was because Eve wouldn't approve, although really he was hiding them from himself. He'd always liked secrets.

He was a whole big secret now! No one in the world knew where he was. He shifted uneasily. He wanted to like the idea, just as he had all that time in the countryside. That was before he'd met Freya. He'd been a child then.

'We're shutting the gates now.'

Dan jerked round, heart pumping painfully. It was an unthreatening man, old, dull-faced, but he felt threatened. How had he crept up on him so he hadn't heard a thing, coming out of the shadows like a ghost?

'Dusk. We close at dusk.'

He'd felt safe on the bench, cut off from the city. 'OK. I'm going.' He stood up and took his bag. Freya and the others had taught him about moving on. 'If you do it quick enough, without making a fuss, people don't see you.'

He'd asked, 'What do you mean? Of course they see you when you're there, right in front of them.'

'It's because they don't want to see you, sucker,' Freya had answered. 'So you give them the chance. We're part of the other. No one wants to recognize *the other*.' She'd given the words a ghouly quaver. 'Makes them nervous.'

'Why would we make them nervous?' Dan wanted her to say more. He felt it would explain why he'd felt invisible sometimes, at school, at home, on the street, anywhere, actually.

But she'd got on to the time she'd sold the *Big Issue* and how humiliated she'd been. 'Like you weren't part of the human race. Not that I wanted to be part of their idea of the human race,' she'd added scornfully.

Freya was protected by scorn and obstinacy and hatred, probably. If he'd been older, he'd have protected her. Not that she wanted that. 'I'm on my own,' she'd say, eyeing Mel and Abe or anyone else in her orbit, her diamond stud winking, her beautiful, green eyes bitter and baleful.

He'd thought she'd made an exception of him. But he'd been wrong.

The old man followed him as he walked out of the gardens. Maybe he could see him after all or maybe he only saw a shadow. A ghost and a shadow, you could laugh at a thing like that.

The noise outside the garden was hideous. He'd feared as much. His heart was pounding again as if he was being stalked, although no one looked his way. The shops were closed mostly, their windows glaring brightly, the cafés were like wide-open mouths, posturing at him as he passed. He needed to be somewhere else quickly or he'd get really panicky, like he did sometimes. He'd told Freya and she'd started on at him about too much dope so he'd said he'd always had feelings like that but she hadn't believed him. Then he couldn't remember whether it was true. Nobody seemed very keen on looking at their past.

He reached a wide road jammed with cars. Where were people *going*? Then he realized there was nothing behind the stream of cars – no buildings anywhere. It must be the sea. The idea entered his head like dawn, making a hopeful space.

He walked purposefully. Not many people went to the beach after dark. Till that last time, beaches had been a place of refuge. They'd been to a festival on the Isle of Wight once, whole droves of stoned people singing to the waves. Spectacular, man. Not exactly a refuge, then, more like a recreation ground. *Fan-tas-tic*! That was what they'd sung, over and over, as if it had a special meaning. Sometimes it sounded like *fan-ta-stick* or even *fanta-stick*. Freya said, 'Words have no meaning.' He'd tried to ask if she meant no fixed meaning but she'd told him to 'cool your fucking overworked mind'.

How he missed Freya! He shouldn't have run away from her. Running away could become a habit. They'd met Zeppo at that festival beside the sea, another sea, although Freya might have known him before. She said everything that goes round, comes round, particularly when you're travelling.

Perhaps at this very moment she was sitting on the beach, meditating just like when he'd left her. When she'd told him to go.

Dan crossed the road. Trouble was, this sea had a great mass of lights sticking out into it. A pier. Brighton pier. Just what he didn't want. He could always walk along the sea front in the other direction, keep the lights and noise – music, too – behind him.

'Hey. Yo. You.'

Dan didn't stop. He knew that voice. Why did he get involved with men who had big images – or wanted to have big images? Zeppo must have followed him over the road. Vinny with the Marmite jar was the first in a line. He could still feel the pain above his eye. Gave him headaches. Freya had said he'd cracked his skull. 'Stay away from dickheads like that,' she'd said. Then along comes Zeppo.

A hand clamped tight on his shoulder before falling away again. He wasn't stoned, that was the trouble, or he wouldn't have cared.

He turned round warily, took in the wavering figure. 'You kicked me out.' If Zeppo had noticed his thieving, he might as well shove himself under the waves and get it over with.

'Yo! Hey!' But Zeppo was staggering. There was enough light from the esplanade for Dan to see that his eyes were unfocused, his face gone smooth and round like a dough ball.

Dan began to run slowly, but faster than Zeppo – or, at least, he couldn't hear any steps behind him. He needed to get down to the beach; it was darker there.

There was a walkway coming up now. He glanced round in time to watch Zeppo's legs give way. He sank to the ground like melting jelly. Just a blob on the paving. Dan thought about going back to kick him but, first, someone might see him and, second, luck like this didn't hold. Also, he'd never kicked anyone. Best to get away as far as possible as quickly as possible.

The beach was different from Weymouth's or any other he'd seen. In one way it was remote enough, well below the road, but there were stalls and shops and cafés, paved play areas and the brightness of the pier, like a funfair, still on his left.

At least there weren't many people where he was and the shops were mostly closed. He carried on walking, headed for where there was darkness. He speeded up past a café playing loud music, then slowed again. Ahead, one section blazed with light; a whole lot of boys – big boys, bigger than him – were trying to throw a ball into a net.

Disoriented, Dan watched them jump and run for a few minutes. They shouted at each other, 'Get it! Go now!' This wasn't the deserted space he needed. He stared into the emptiness on his left to check that the sea was still out there somewhere. He turned and walked towards it. The wooden slats and stone slabs under the thin soles of his trainers changed to pebbles, sliding, rubbing against each other.

At last he heard the sound of the sea, the same everywhere. It was quiet tonight: the rain must have tamed it. He liked the way the waves rolled over the water as it was sucked out backwards. Maybe he'd sit at the edge like Freya, cross his legs and meditate.

Instead he remained standing, swaying a bit, peering into the darkness ahead and making sure he cut out the garish pier, further away now but still bright. He cut out the music too.

'Freya,' he said, out loud. The sea joined everything, everywhere, everyone. 'Freya.' He remembered reading about lovers far apart in different countries who spat into the sea as a way of linking to each other. He moved nearer to the water's edge and had a go. But his mouth was too dry to work up much spittle and then his trainer got soaked by a fast-crawling wave. So he thought of throwing something in – a stone or something. Maybe the fossil he still carried everywhere. Put it back in the sea where it came from. It was small enough to be tumbled along with the tide and taken out to sea.

So he got his bag open and found the fossil, sat it in his hand like a ball. He would be sad to lose it but all in a good cause. He threw it as far as he could, not very far, and he nearly lost his balance in the process. When he heard the splash, he called, 'F-r-e-y-a!' in a long drawn-out romantic sort of voice. Crazy, man, if anyone had been watching. He didn't care.

He moved away from the edge of the sea. Didn't feel like getting out his package yet. Anyway, he'd forgotten a straw so he'd have to go back to one of those cafés. Find a bin. It was raining again and, even in the darkness, he could see the pebbles gleaming. What he needed was a bit of shelter. Just as he thought that, any quiet was blotted out by a police siren nearby – *The pigeons having their fun*, Freya would have said. Sometimes she got up and danced to the noise, waving her arms and making faces like she was in an African war dance. He guessed the police had something to do with the past she didn't talk about.

The siren stayed quite close for a longish time, then was joined by another. Ambulance, perhaps. At last the whole lot went away, receding along the coastline.

Slowly, picking his way unsteadily over the stones, Dan walked along the sea's edge, always further from the noisy pier and the cafés and the shops. Looking inland he could see mostly black under the road, although above there were still cars moving busily. That other world.

He was stopped abruptly by something hard sticking out of the pebbles, like an iron girder but attached to nothing. Screwing up his eyes, he saw a couple of others out to sea, and further into the water, what looked like the skeleton of a huge dinosaur rearing from the waves. So, was he hallucinating or what?

He turned inland hurriedly and soon found himself facing locked doors and overflowing rubbish bins. In the third he found two cans with straws sticking out of them. He imagined children using them, little pursed lips sucking up the sweet stuff. He felt a moment of nostalgia for his own childhood but with no real emotion. All his feelings were bound up with Freya. Always had been from the moment she'd summoned him on the station at Weymouth. Like Jesus calling his disciples. What was it she'd said? Something about defending her against the two fuckers she travelled with? Not quite the New Testament.

The happiest time in his whole life had been sitting beside Freya on the beach as she plaited little kids' hair with beads and coloured thread, feathers and shells. She did it at festivals too and there the boys came forward as much as the girls, although they usually chose just beads. It was quite an art. First, she separated out a strand of hair – not so easy if it was curly – and pulled it though a piece of circular cardboard with a hole in the middle. Then she put in the decorations – the kids chose them at the beginning – and when she'd finished, she'd cut off the cardboards. The kids went mad for it, running off to show their friends, some as young as three or four.

Freya loved children. She said they hadn't been contaminated yet by our decadent society. Once on the beach they'd stood for ages watching kids riding donkeys up and down a little track in the sand. They'd wanted to ride the donkeys, too, but they weren't allowed. Too old, too big, the donkey woman told them. Pity.

Freya said she felt more in common with a six-year-old than anyone, although by that age she'd already lost her innocence. Although *lost* wasn't the word.

He'd never dared ask her how she'd lost (or something else) her innocence because he guessed it was horrible and she'd have told him if she wanted him to know. He suspected she thought he was innocent and that was why she'd tried to protect him. She'd never let him tell her he loved her. But he thought she was pleased all the same. Perhaps it was because he *was* innocent. True enough, sad to say, on the sexual front, but not in other ways. Ru's death had taken away any innocence he might have had. That and his dad whisking off to Martha whenever he needed a break. Actually, he didn't think *innocent* meant anything much. Except maybe in Freya's case. Which he didn't know about.

Mostly he believed Freya absolutely. She was his lodestar, his love, his eternal beauty.

Once she'd fallen asleep in his arms – too much drugs – and as he'd looked down at her pale face, something burst open inside him and he'd felt his whole body would explode with love. More than that: wonder, ecstasy, euphoria, not words he'd ever thought about a girl before.

The sex part was there too, of course, but not at that moment. It was like . . . Well, funnily enough, he'd once asked Abe what coke did to you and he'd described something like that. The whole world being lit up by a fireball of feeling, everything perfect, clear, easy. *Knickerbocker Glory!*

How could he have left her? Even if she had told him to go. Ever since, he'd been lost, wandering, night time all the time.

As he thought this he noticed one of the doors that led into places under the road was not quite shut. A padlock dangled from a chain. The door had an arch above it, which somehow made it look like a cave. Just the place for someone licking his wounds.

Not that he was totally miserable, with the package in his pocket and the straws in his hand. Abe had said, 'It's like all the bad stuff gets shot away in the biggest jerk-off on earth.'

He'd got good at jerking off in the last few weeks so this was the next stage, wasn't it? But he didn't want Abe's voice in his head so, as he pulled the door carefully open – there just might be someone inside – he pretended Freya was coming in with him, close at his side, perhaps with a finger to her lips, whispering, *Sssh.*

With her at his side it was easy to feel his way round in the darkness. Boxes, that's what was in there, a bit of rubbish too, but no scurrying rats. Nothing bad. Not like that fox-smelling place they once bunked in.

'Let's make armchairs out of them,' Freya suggested in his ear. Even though she yelled *capitalist comforts are for cunts*, she was good at making things special. Once at a festival when they were in a tent on their own, smoking dope, she'd said, 'It's like we're in a desert with the nomads, stopped at an oasis. Listen up, dude, can you hear the camels snorting outside?'

So he'd said, 'I'm your sheikh,' and she'd fallen about laughing, which was good, if not the best reaction. Sometimes she was more like a child than him.

It was that night he'd told her about Ru. The sheikh let's-pretend business had made him think of the limo in the field. Told her all about it and she'd really got off on the idea. She'd pictured them driving through the countryside and waving to the peasants. He'd kept saying to her, 'But it doesn't move,' and she'd answered, in her magic-mysterious voice, 'It'd go like a rocket with me behind the wheel.' She'd said she'd drive it to Glastonbury and Stonehenge and give all those ravers an eyeful. They'd been giggling together like a couple of kids. Then they'd come down a bit and he'd remembered some of the not-so-good nights in the limo and he'd told her about

Ru. The dreams. He knew she liked talking about dreams, which she called FIS, First Indicators of Stress. Nightmares.

He'd told her about how he and Ru had become mates. Two outcasts, well, outsiders. Then he told her about Ru hanging himself, broke down in the middle of the story like a baby. Told her he'd run away from the sight of it. She'd held his hand – he could feel the print still – she'd said death wasn't the worst thing if someone was unhappy. But when he'd got on to the nightmares, she called them straight off 'the haunting'. She said that wasn't fair and no wonder he'd tried to escape them.

He'd thought then of telling her about Max and Martha but he didn't want to seem a no-hoper and, anyway, it was almost a tale of everyday life, if you believed what you saw on the TV. Besides, it was bound up with his feelings about Martha, which weren't quite right, and he didn't want to mix those up with his feelings for Freya, which were absolutely right.

Dan sighed into the darkness. Even though he'd left the door open, very little light came in from outside. He'd put the straws on a box near him and now he took out the packet and opened it very carefully. It would be a terrible shame to lose such magic dust. Once Zeppo had gone on a bender – drink this time – and recited a list of drug names. *Base, basuca, Aunt Nora, beam, belisha, blast, blizzard, blow, blotter, candy, Charlie, dream, froofroo, frisky, hooter, jelly jam, rock, snow, wings, witch, whizzbang, zip . . .*

They'd recited them together once, then over and over.

Those were only a few of the names. There were many, many more. It was Zeppo's party turn, his big face turning red and his eyes bulging. Once he'd done it in a group and a guy had struck up with a guitar as if he was accompanying a song. Some song! *Song of Songs*, someone had shouted.

Dan opened out the packet and broke off an end of a straw. He realized his heart was beating very fast, like the time he'd been bullied into jumping off the high diving-board.

He thought, It's so dark, a man mightn't find his nose. Which, all things considered, present circumstances being what they were – that was, the *stuff, hooter, jam, jelly* being so especially special – would be a pity.

He still hesitated a moment, thinking, What if Freya really disapproved? But she couldn't, not when she used it herself. She just thought he wasn't ready for it, but he was, and doing it, even the stealing from Zeppo, would prove it.

Of course he'd go back and find her, tell her she was his queen, his bright star, his only light and hope.

Bending close to the box, Dan positioned the straw and began to sniff up the white powder.

CHAPTER THIRTY-SEVEN

Martha woke to find Lee gone. Although his exit fulfilled her expectations, she put her head into her hands and gave way to despair. This was a rare event and she allowed it to last only for ten minutes or so. Nor did she permit tears or any other show of grief. Nevertheless, she asked herself the eternal questions and came up with no answers. He had been important to her, not just the sex. Perhaps she had thrown away her career for him. After a while she decided to believe that it was just possible, although remotely, that he would return to her. He was, after all, alive.

Smoothing her body to remind herself of his caresses, she slid out of bed. It was surprising that he had got out from so small a room without waking her. But, then, he was used to a cell, often shared with a cellmate.

She put on a robe from her bag, then went into the corridor and down towards the bathroom. But the door was locked, with sounds of showering inside. This repulse, which felt like the greatest humiliation, nearly undid her. She stood outside for several minutes, facing the pale mauve walls, hoping that anger would join her in her loneliness. It would have been a relief to give a karate chop to the door or jump at it with her feet. She was trained for that sort of thing.

Slowly, she went back to her bedroom, noticing on her way a print of two piglets looking at each other approvingly. It was called *First Love*.

Back in the bedroom, she immediately spotted the note stuck behind another picture, this time of two little girls in a wheelbarrow. Although she had read its short message at first sight, she took it down and studied it. 'Don't forget the police.'

She had forgotten the police. Lee had written in capitals. Many residents of Her Majesty's Prisons used capitals either in preference to lower case or because their education gave them no choice. She suspected Lee was suggesting urgency. It was the closest she would get to a love note: concern for something that concerned her.

She'd worn her watch during the night and now she saw it was still only seven thirty. What seemed like a long time ago, special-family-policeman Ronnie, of the sympathetic nature, had told her to call him at any time. His number was in her mobile. She replayed in her mind what Lee had told her to say.

First she'd ring Ronnie, then she'd go for a hard run. Remind her body of who was really boss. Later she, too, would go to Brighton.

Max called Ronnie at eight o'clock. 'Have you heard the news?' Max asked. On and off throughout the night, he and Eve had discussed it. Eventually, at six, Eve had packed a bag. Max had watched as she put in one of the birthday books from Dan's bedside, a sweatshirt, clean underwear, a packet of chocolate biscuits, a banana and an apple. He couldn't remember her ever packing for Dan before but he presumed she must have when Dan was small.

'I suppose Martha called you,' said Ronnie.

'No,' said Max, bewildered. He did not want to think of Martha. Eve was sitting so close she might easily have heard her sister's name. Ronnie had what was commonly called an 'open' voice (to match his 'open' face) which meant it held no hint of irony or doubt and made him particularly easy to hear.

'Martha called me just now. She's acquired some information.'

Max hesitated. He didn't want to acquire any information from his sister-in-law. All acquiring from her was in the past.

'I have just spoken to the detective superintendent,' added Ronnie.

'He phoned me last night,' said Max. He now wished that he'd rung the detective himself but it had been impressed on him in the early days that Ronnie must always be his first point of contact. How obedient they all were!

Eve pulled at his arm. 'What is it?'

'Nothing,' he told her, and said to Ronnie, 'We understand Dan is in Brighton.'

There was a pause before Ronnie agreed. 'That appears to be the case.'

'We're planning to go there ourselves,' said Max, 'but Brighton's a big place.'

Eve was becoming restive. After filling the bag, she'd dressed with great care, quite unlike her habit over the last few weeks when she'd flung on anything, often including what she'd been wearing in bed. Retaining her actorish attitude to clothes, this morning she'd dressed, consciously or not, as a good mother. Her hair was smoothly tied back, her clean shirt neatly buttoned above a flowery skirt. Both were quite a lot too big for her. She sat by Max with her bag on her lap and an expectant expression on her face.

'There are complications.' said Ronnie.

'Complications!' Max felt outraged.

'The Drugs Squad have become involved.'

Max didn't repeat the words 'Drugs Squad' because he hoped Eve could avoid them, but they made as much sound in the air as bell clappers. 'We're planning to take a nine o'clock train,' he said, mostly for Eve's benefit. He felt that they were not going to get help. He even felt, with the beginning of an almost certainly unreasonable bitterness, that they had never had real help, that this was a new era, when Eve and he would join in finding the son they had so disastrously lost. Complications. Drugs Squad. What could this have to do with Dan? He was, after all, a retiring boy of just fourteen.

Then he remembered his visit to Weymouth and the feeling of powerlessness.

'Perhaps I should go with you,' said Ronnie.

'Yes,' said Max, 'Where shall we meet?' A rhyme came into his head: *Bye, baby Bunting/Daddy's gone a-hunting/Gone to fetch a rabbit skin/To wrap the baby Bunting in.*

'You catch your train,' Ronnie was back to being comforting, 'and I'll be in touch.'

When Max had rung off, he hugged Eve, then picked up his own bag, although he couldn't remember what he'd put in it – nothing useful, he felt certain.

They stepped out of the flat bravely and, in both their minds,

256

although neither dared voice it, was the simple prayer, Let us come back with Dan.

Martha's run had not helped her mood. The seagulls had been offensive and her legs heavy. Now she was releasing her feelings in anger towards an inoffensive official in the Weymouth railway station, which did little for her morale.

'That's the timetable,' he repeated, for at least the third time, on this occasion accompanied by a muttered 'I didn't make it, you know.'

'I know some other fool did it,' began Martha, before managing to moderate her harridan tones. But the official, having reached his tolerance limit, closed the book and turned away. It seemed that to get from Weymouth to Brighton you had to take at least three trains, none of them remotely connecting, or return to London and start again.

Lee would have gone back to London before heading up to Glasgow. Already she had created a shadowy aura of the past around him. She was used to being alone, she told herself and, with an air of resignation, she went to buy a strong coffee and wait for the next train.

It struck her, as she did this, the station crowded with departing holidaymakers, most frazzled by early starts and inharmonious family relations – whining, moaning, out-and-out screaming from the babies – that the police presence, so evident on the day before, was gone. Her talk with Ronnie had been brief and she'd assumed it was fresh news she'd been bringing him, but perhaps the police had already known the scene had shifted from Weymouth to Brighton. Since this would make Lee's contribution unimportant, she didn't want to believe it. She wanted to trace his hand in future events, even if he had become the past.

She walked meditatively out of the station – the London train wasn't due for half an hour – and stood with her carton of coffee. Almost at once a police car drove up, as if to contradict her previous deduction. The sun shone brightly into it and she saw Ronnie sitting in the back seat. He hopped out, removed an overnight bag from the boot and walked briskly towards the station. Then he saw her. 'Martha!'

'Ronnie!' It should have been funny. Actually, it was. Martha felt herself on the verge of hysterical laughter. When she'd rung him earlier that morning, she'd pictured an official man in a grey London office. Here, despite his exit from a police car, he was like a man on holiday, no uniform, no concern.

Unavoidably, they moved into the station together. Behind them, the police car drove away, lights flashing, siren wailing. Martha frowned irritably.

'I assumed you were in London,' said Ronnie, and Martha saw he was making an effort to recollect his more sober self.

'I thought *you* were there,' said Martha. They reached the train barriers and she added, 'I'm going there now.'

'So am I.'

Neither looked enthusiastic that chance had made them travelling companions. They stood on the platform together. After the rain the day before, it was clear and fresh, but neither felt like commenting on the weather.

'It's strange to see you out of your uniform.'

'I'm hoping to get out of it altogether soon.'

'A detective, you mean?'

'Hopefully.'

Martha reflected on her own wearing of uniform. There was a bond although she felt protected by her black and white.

'I've been staying overnight with my family. They're holidaying in Weymouth.'

'What a coincidence. But without you?'

'I should have been with them.'

He meant, presumably, that his holiday had been buggered up by Dan's appearance – near-appearance.

'I'm sorry.'

At last the train came in. Making up her mind, Martha turned sharply right. 'I need to catch up on sleep.'

Ronnie raised an arm in salute. It struck her that she liked him better as a family man than in his uniform, striving to shoulder other people's burdens. Perhaps towards the end of the journey, she would go and find him, confide that she, too, was heading for Brighton – surely his destination – and ask him what he expected to find there. Would Dan really be waiting at the end of the rainbow?

The train was crowded but eventually she found a window seat and shut her eyes. She'd expected to think about Lee, her gain and loss, but instead she considered Eve and tears bulked her eyelids. She'd never wanted her to suffer. Until Dan's disappearance, they had spoken every day, often more than once. Their love and closeness had been so strong that it had made Max incidental, or so she'd thought. Eve had talked of him with disparagement, disappointed by his lack of success and his fatalistic acceptance of his daily round. After all, she, Martha, had been one of a string of women he'd slept with. Eve didn't even bother to mention them, except, very occasionally, in passing. Once she'd said, 'I could never understand what Max saw in Swindon until I read a letter from a girl called Ruth.'

After this was all over, she would find Eve and face the music, if music there was to be faced. As she drifted into sleep, she heard the rolling of drums and the slapping of cymbals.

'I love you, darling Max.' Eve felt the approbation of the Virgin Mary as she plighted her troth, as if she and Max had been given the chance to start all over again. 'We will never, ever be parted. For everything that has gone wrong in our lives, I blame myself. I am a weak, tawdry sort of person, overblown and self-indulgent.' Her simple declaration of love was in danger of becoming a confession or even a speech.

They sat together on an almost empty train. Eve was glad they had decided against driving. Max's car had taken him into his other life while the train was anonymous and easier to imprint with their new beginning.

'We will grow *old* together,' she said, in the same impassioned voice. She knew they shared a sense of sudden ageing, as if they'd gone from the selfish restlessness of adolescence and the sense of an infinite future to the certainty of death. In fact, they wouldn't *grow* old together: in the most important respect, they were already old.

Even their physical change told them so, the angularity as the flesh fell from their bodies, their stillness, their watchfulness.

'We'll find him,' said Max.

He was right. It was all about Dan. She was guarding herself against the unimaginable worst, making Max a protection, taking on old age as a cloak against youthful suffering. Nevertheless, her love for Max was real and their twin ageing was no invention.

'I love you, darling,' she repeated, perhaps too loudly because the train had stopped at a station and a passenger entering stopped in her progress through the carriage long enough to glance or even stare at the couple so intensely together.

Eve was shocked to find herself wondering what the elderly woman, grey-haired with a small pullalong case, saw. Would she never rid herself of the sense of an audience, even at this, the crux of her life?

Max had bought a newspaper on the station, which he unfolded, carefully so as not to disengage Eve's arm wound into his. She loved him for it but, trying to follow his eyes across the page, found she could not concentrate.

Instead she looked out of the window where the loveliness of the countryside disturbed more than it soothed. Dan had bolted to the countryside, like an animal bolts for its burrow. It reminded her of the title of the novel that had haunted her as a teenager, *Gone to Earth*. Perhaps it had been a prediction. Dan had preferred unknown ground to his home and turned himself into a missing-person statistic. Could any of them bear such a load of guilt when there'd been no beatings, no abuse, no poverty?

She knew because she'd been told by Ronnie that, when Dan reappeared, there would be family counselling, questions about why he had left. You couldn't engage a police force and not expect to be accountable.

What would Dan say? Would he bring accusations of neglect and lack of love? Would he brand his family dysfunctional? What humiliations lay in store? Would she be judged no longer suitable as a teacher? She didn't want to be thinking this way. She wanted to be directed only towards Dan's safe return.

Trying to turn her thoughts, she saw the station that had been nearest to her childhood home flash by. She didn't want to think about her childhood either but it struck her that, by a horrible coincidence, today was the anniversary of her mother's death. She wondered if Martha had remembered. Usually they spoke to each other on the day.

'Max.' He turned to her at once. She would spare him more sadness. 'Only twenty minutes left.'

They were to meet Ronnie in a hotel on the front but not till midday.

PART FOUR
Holding On

CHAPTER THIRTY-EIGHT

The marble pillars were stout and strong as a giant's legs; they were angrily mottled, too, as if his circulation wasn't too good. Eve tried to look past them at more kindly sofas, of which there were many. She hadn't imagined Ronnie's suggested meeting place would be such a grand hotel, literally called The Grand.

She and Max had stood outside with the sea behind them and stared up at the elegant façade. Max had pronounced, regretting it as he spoke – she could hear it in his voice – 'This is where those IRA bombers blew up some Conservative MPs.'

Since it was still only ten thirty, they could have gone for a walk – it was a bright day – but they were both exhausted and the idea of a coffee in comfort was too tempting.

So now they stood in the entrance, overawed and unsure. Above the first sofa, which Eve targeted, hung a portrait of a large and disapproving Victorian lady.

'I'm not sure I can wait here,' she protested.

'Don't panic.' Max gripped her arm.

But she *was* panicked. What were they doing in this weird place when Dan was outside somewhere? Ever since they'd heard the news of his whereabouts, she'd had a desperate sense of haste, yet it was so matched with ignorance and lassitude that no action seemed possible, increasing her frustration and impatience. A line had played in her head: *Grief fills the room up of my absent child* . . .

'I'll sit here.' She chose a sofa under a glass dome above the stairwell. Feverishly, she counted seven floors of elaborately railed staircases. She imagined the glass dome crashing down between them, splintering over their heads. The sense of risk helped a little, as if it brought her closer to Dan. He was 'at risk', a phrase that previously had made her impatient. 'I wonder if we can drink coffee sitting here.'

Max was still standing, peering round unhappily. He took a step towards an open doorway.

'You go.' She tried to smile. But if he went, she'd be on her own and that would be unbearable.

He led her to a glass conservatory at the front of the hotel. It was quite full and stuffy. Eve fixed her eyes on the world outside while Max ordered coffee. Beyond the pavements and the road, the sea was a greenish-blue wash, deeper than the sky.

'What's that?' Once the waiter had gone, she took Max's arm again.

'What?' He narrowed his eyes against the glare. Wrinkles spread nearly as far as his hairline, now lightened with white threads.

She pointed. 'That black skeleton in the sea. Like a prehistoric animal.'

'I don't know.'

'It's horrible.'

An old woman, alone at the next table, lifted her hand. 'Excuse me interrupting. That's the remains of the West Pier. Gutted by fire. Two fires, actually.'

'Oh, how sad!' Eve tried to control the tears, always so ready to burst from her eyes.

'Criminal, more like.' The woman, who had seemed warm and friendly with her shopping bag and cardigan, suddenly reminded Eve of the Victorian lady on the wall.

'Thank you,' said Max, politely, and the woman, with pursed mouth, turned back to her table.

'Do we have to feel anguished about city piers now?' hissed Eve, tears repressed.

'You started it,' said Max, and they both stared out gloomily at the burnt ribs and limbs poking out of the bright sea.

Ribs and limbs, girders and struts. It sounded like the start of a song. 'I'm sorry,' said Eve. 'I'll be more together after my coffee.' It was nearer a wish than a promise.

Max looked at his watch. 'We've still got an hour.'

They weren't just waiting for Ronnie. They were waiting for an outcome. They were waiting for Dan. Despite everything, they still hoped that Ronnie would come from between the giant's legs with

Dan at his side, just as they'd last seen him (except they hadn't really seen him), diffident, thoughtful, their child but hardly yet a person. They'd assumed there would be time to get to know him.

Martha and Ronnie walked along the sea front together. Disconcertingly to Martha, he was now wearing his full uniform. He must have changed in the train's loo, an odd image, particularly with such a big man. He was explaining his appointment with Max and Eve.

'They may not want to see me,' said Martha, and checked Ronnie's reaction.

'I'm sorry.' He seemed unsurprised as if his training encompassed problems within families. In fact it was silly to think it would not, since missing children were all about dysfunctional families.

Martha felt herself sagging, confidence falling. 'It might be better if I stayed away.'

'Whatever.'

Had he really said, 'Whatever'? Maybe his thoughts were still with his happy holiday in Weymouth, where he should have been disporting himself with his well-balanced daughters. 'I think I will come.' At least he didn't say, 'Whatever,' again.

Eve and Max had moved from the stuffy conservatory to one of the sofas where a fan whirled lazily overhead and a large potted palm gave the impression of shade. She had turned her back on the Victorian lady and Max had disappeared to ask whether the canned music could be turned down. They had just admitted to each other that they were petrified about what was to come. Eve felt hot and cold by turns and feared she might be sick. She sized up the capacious brass jar in which the palm stood as a possible receptacle.

When Max returned with Ronnie and Martha in tow, Eve began to shiver violently. Max sat down beside her and took her hand.

Martha muttered something about coffee and headed for the conservatory. She hadn't even said, 'Hello.'

Eve's concentration on her potential to vomit gradually changed to contemplation of her sister's iniquities. Interrupting Ronnie, who was sitting at a slightly distant armchair, she hissed to Max, 'What's *she* doing here?'

'I don't know.' Max looked at Ronnie, who shook his head with a serious but meaningless expression.

They sat in silence, apart from the music – it hadn't been reduced. At this precise moment an arrangement of 'One Enchanted Evening' was playing. Ronnie had already explained he was waiting for further information, even instruction. His radio was prominent on his wide chest. They would all know when there was further news.

'What did you mean about the Drugs Squad being involved?' asked Max, mildly.

Before he could answer, Martha returned with a cup of coffee. 'Do you mind?' she asked, over Eve's head.

Eve felt a wave of violent colour pump her up. 'What do you think? And on the anniversary of our mother's death too!'

Martha hesitated, obviously unsure how she should take Eve's response. Eventually she sat down near Ronnie. 'I'm sorry.' Her tone was clear but humble.

'So you should be!' Eve felt her still just-contained rage might cause a stroke and kill her. She wanted to be a viper with a poisonous tongue long enough to spike Martha to death. Let her die! Despite Max's controlling hand, she stood up. She felt her hair tumbling down her shoulders like Medusa's – not just one snake now but a multitude, all striving to reach out and strike her faithless sister. 'It's you.' She could hardly choke out the words so great was her mounting hatred. 'It's you who's caused everything. Why do you think Dan ran away? Why? You cowardly piece of shit!'

'Eve.' Max tried to grab her back. Ronnie looked enquiringly at his shoes, which, as it happened, were not police issue but a casual holidaying pair.

'And you too!' While shaking herself free, Eve spared a quick vituperative glance for Max. So far her voice, although intense, had been a snake-like hiss but now it rose in volume. There was a reception area at one end of the room and a long bar at the other. In both, heads turned their way.

Sensing an audience did nothing to deter Eve. On the contrary, it encouraged her actor's adrenalin, far preferable to the previous sad petrification or pathetic fears of vomit. She took several steps towards Martha. 'You're a lying, traitorous worm! Not an honourable snake. A worm. A worm in the bud. Pretending to be loving and kind but actually a slimy destroyer. A slug!'

As Eve took another step forward as if she might physically attack Martha, Ronnie stood up and placed himself in front of her.

His shielding bulk enraged Eve further. She began to move from one foot to the other in a kind of dance. She felt more alive than she had for weeks. When she and Martha were small, before their mother's death, they had used to fight, scratching and biting, often in the bath, which they shared, so that the effect on their naked skin was dramatic. Their mother had called them 'kittens' and reminded them to sheathe their claws. She understood that they loved each other but their natures were so different they had to fight.

Suddenly darting round Ronnie, she made a lunge at Martha, who cringed backwards in her chair. Eve tried to grab at her hair, which was short and slippery, then at her shirt. She screamed, 'I hate you! I hate you! You've stolen my husband. You've stolen my son.'

Ronnie was about to detain her – in a humanitarian-conscious arm-lock, perhaps, for which he'd been carefully trained, as had Martha – when a voice spoke from his mobile. Other training took precedence and, head bent attentively, he abandoned the situation and walked away quickly to find a quieter space.

Max took his place but he was half-hearted and both women knew it was not his role to interfere. He was nothing like a policeman. Yet once there was no impediment between her and Martha, Eve's energy flagged. Although Max could not stop her, she was aware of his presence close behind. They loved each other.

'It's not all on one side,' said Martha, flatly, as she ducked an ineffectual swipe from Eve. She was still sitting so that Eve had to bend to reach her.

Meanwhile a responsible-looking woman, who wore the tailored suit of a manager, approached them from the reception area. Ronnie stood by one of the pillars listening to his mobile. Management must have thought it strange that a policeman had so little control over his friends, if that was what they were. Several coffee drinkers in the conservatory, including the old lady who cared about the West Pier, stood at the doorway, attracted by the noise. 'What a rumpus!' she commented with satisfaction. Her neighbour nodded in agreement. Before this, how dull and hot they'd been!

'Call yourself my sister!' shouted Eve. But despite her heated

269

mind and body, she was thinking how little there was to say. This was all theatricals about another time. She wanted Max. She had forgiven him. They were together. Soon she might even feel sorry for Martha.

'Sisters.' The old lady nodded knowingly.

'Excuse me,' began the responsible woman in the suit.

No one paid any attention. Ronnie was coming towards them with purposeful steps.

Eve gasped and turned into Max's arms. Martha swivelled round so she could see the expression on Ronnie's face. The assistant manager – the manager didn't work on Sundays – stepped back without entirely removing herself.

No one spoke as Ronnie resumed his place in the armchair. Martha, trying to gather herself together after Eve's onslaught – it was like her to do it in public, not that she could blame her for anything now – admired the policeman's calm. It was easy to tell he had difficult news to impart. She had been in such situations herself and recognized the task he had set himself: *Inform, sympathize, contain and control.* Someone had once told her that. It was far better to think of such things than to think of Dan. Or to look at Eve's stricken face. Or even Max's tender protectiveness.

'The news is not good, I'm afraid.'

She had forgotten that – *Prepare, inform, sympathize, contain and control.* What a lot he must do. Was he himself prepared, she wondered, when he'd eaten cereal that morning with his loving wife and cheerful daughters? Actually, he'd need a cooked breakfast to sustain that mountainous frame.

'Dan was found earlier this morning. Unfortunately, he's now in the Intensive Care Unit of the Royal Sussex Hospital.'

He's alive! Martha amended her thoughts: He's alive at the moment.

'Why?' Max's deep voice sounded in the large room.

Martha became aware of the faces peering from the conservatory. They couldn't have heard Ronnie's measured tones, but Max's agonized single word had stirred their hearts.

'I'll explain on the way.' Perhaps Ronnie, too, had become aware of the audience because suddenly he was active in shepherding them out of the hotel. It was wise, not least because Eve looked on the point of fainting or being sick.

'A car has been sent for us.'

They huddled on the steps of the hotel. It wasn't a car: it was a white police van, with darkened windows. It reminded Martha of the kind of transport used to transfer prisoners to and from court or from prison to prison. It made her think of Lee, on his way to his son in Glasgow, or so she presumed. He was lucky: the person he loved most in the world was well. He was lucky: he had someone he loved most in the world.

Ahead of her, Max was leading Eve towards the van. She seemed dazed, unaware of her surroundings. Ronnie half lifted her in. Then he turned back.

'You should come too.' His face was kind. He had always been kind.

'After what went on in there?' Martha turned a little towards the hotel and caught a glimpse of curious faces. She muttered, 'They must think we're being arrested.' Then she asked, 'How bad is he?'

'Cocaine overdose. Eve will need you.'

Martha considered. The light dazzled and a wind was blowing in from the sea. She, who prided herself on her toughness, shivered in a frightened way.

'Come on, then.' Ronnie took her arm and led her towards the van, almost as if she was Eve.

CHAPTER THIRTY-NINE

Max held Eve close but his eyes gazed out of the window. The hotel, with its pompous grandeur, was a place of death, he thought. As the van did a U-turn, he saw the skeletal remains of the pier and that, too, was a place of death. *As flies to wanton boys are we to th' gods – they kill us for their sport.*

'Is he dying?' Eve's whisper was so soft he could hardly hear her.

'I don't know, my darling.'

Ronnie had said he would explain on the journey but he sat near the driver and said nothing, and they could not bear to ask.

'Where's Martha?' Again he could hardly hear.

'She's behind us.'

'She should be here. She's his aunt.'

'I'll tell her.'

After that they were quiet while the van raced along the sea front to the hospital. After a few minutes the siren was put on.

Just before they arrived, when the van had turned inland and was going a little slower, Eve asked, 'What was the music you brought to the hospital when Dan was born? I keep trying to remember and I can't.' He saw that tears were pouring down her face.

'Elgar. *Serenade for Strings*.' He'd been crazy for English music then, and English poetry, Ted Hughes, Larkin.

'I cried with happiness.'

'We both did.' It had become a tradition. On each of Dan's birthdays he'd played to her a piece of music. He could remember the year he'd stopped. He'd just discovered the Scottish composer James Macmillan, a man not much older than himself. He'd brought home 'The Gallant Weaver', a song based on a poem by Burns. Dan was five or six at the time and he played the exquisitely moving music (or so it seemed to him) to a chorus of violent imitations of car and tractor noises. Eventually he'd asked Eve to shut Dan up. Instead, she'd screamed about it being his birthday and he, Max, being a loser and why couldn't he be a poet like this Macmillan was a composer? The car noises had got louder and louder and he'd left the flat. Happy birthday.

The van went up a ramp into a parking space in front of the doors to A and E. As they got out, Max had a curious sensation of being suspended in space, everything around him light and airy. He raised his eyes and saw the sky, and, far, far below, the sea.

'In here,' said Ronnie.

Max took a deep gulp of air as if he might never breathe again. He noticed as he put his arm round Eve that she seemed to be bent over as if she was an old woman. Behind them he was aware of Martha. Perhaps she could be a source of strength.

The floor was blue, then it was purple. Then, although Eve didn't raise her head, she was aware of blue dolphins jumping along beside her. Then they were at the lifts.

Max's voice said, 'What's wrong with him?' What a question! Eve knew there would be no answer. Poor Max. When they saw Dan, they would know.

The lift took a long time coming. Gratefully, Eve felt a dreamlike quality entering the surroundings. It enabled her to run a few happier pictures of Dan through her mind. When he was four or five, he'd become obsessed by the bird house at the zoo. He'd stand watching for as long as she let him, lifting his arms like wings, fluttering his fingers, sometimes laughing as a bird landed on a branch near him, sometimes shouting, 'Look, Mum, look!' That was before he'd called her Eve.

The lift doors opened and they joined three people already inside. Two women wore white coats with badges. Eve read 'Magda Evans' and repeated the name to herself, like an invocation, 'Magda Evans, Magda Evans, Magda Evans.'

A doctor met them, Dr George Soueff. He was very handsome with dark curly hair, perhaps Egyptian. Eve wanted to trust, even love, him. He led them through doors that needed his pass to unlock them, and into a windowless side room. Everywhere had become very cold.

'Please sit down.' His hand, with long, slender fingers, indicated a row of green plastic chairs. They sat obediently.

'May I?' Martha looked at Eve enquiringly. Eve saw she wanted to sit in the chair next to her and wondered why she'd asked. She needed her sister beside her. She took her hand in her own icy fingers. Max held her on the other side.

Ronnie chose a chair at the end.

Max said, 'Are you looking after Dan?'

Eve held her breath. If she held it long enough the news would be good. She thought Martha was holding her breath too.

'Yes. I'm part of the team. Mr Sawyer will be along in a moment or two to talk to you.' Dr Soueff looked at them calmly, like a man who has nothing to hide.

None of them said anything and Eve decided she would save some of her love for Mr Sawyer. Then, as Dr Soueff took a step towards the door, a ghastly fear squeezed her guts. 'Is he alive?'

Dr Soueff hesitated. His face was grave. 'Yes. He is certainly alive. Mr Sawyer will be here shortly.'

'But I have to see him! I have to see my son!' Now she had breath to scream. Max and Martha were holding on to her, pegging her down like a balloon straining for lift-off. 'Please. Please.' She was subsiding, forcibly.

'I'm so sorry.' The doctor's face seemed less handsome, more human. 'I'll go and look for Professor Sawyer.'

Now he was 'Professor'.

'Thank you,' said Max.

The doctor went and Martha whispered to Eve, 'He's alive.'

Eve squeezed her hand but at once a new ghastly fear made her whole body shake. Tears ran down the side of her face. 'Yes. He's *alive*,' she mouthed, wanting Martha to understand without further words. Dr Soueff's face had been grave. In what state was he alive?

As mad as the vex'd sea, singing aloud, crowned with rank fumiter and furrow weeds . . .

She must have murmured aloud the last word or two because Max gave her a queer, knowing look. At the beginning they'd hardly known the boundary between their lives and poetry.

She was struck by a horrible idea, that she'd blamed Dan for destroying all that. But she hadn't! No. It was impossible.

'Don't, Eve.'

What was she doing that Max was telling her to stop with such solicitude? Pulling faces, stretching her eyes, pursing her mouth? She and Max were at fault. A child could never be at fault.

Blessed Mary, forgive us our sins. Please. Or should that be addressed to God? In a minute she might scream again.

Professor Sawyer was standing before them. He'd entered so quietly, an unassuming man without any stage presence. Eve was judging him as an actor, noting his small, pointed nose, his large ears, wide, thin mouth, high cheekbones, black eyes. He was fit and trim, but would she be able to love and revere him? Maybe she could trust him.

He introduced himself, shook hands, distinguished between mother and aunt. Eve noticed that Martha was a strange blotchy colour and so very thin. When had she become so thin? She was also wired. As if she'd come back from one of her ten-mile runs. She'd crossed her legs and one of her feet bounced in the air.

'May I sit down?' The professor's voice was pleasant, better than his looks. He wanted to be on a level with them. Was this a good or bad sign? Eve put her hand to her heart, which was beating so fast and hard that she could see her blouse moving. She'd used to think it an entirely theatrical gesture. Theatre. A surgeon performs in a theatre.

'Dan is in a coma,' said the professor, calmly. 'He's in a critical state but that doesn't mean we've lost hope. Not at all. Despite everything, he's a strong boy.'

Despite everything. Despite everything.

'He was picked up unconscious. He'd inhaled a large dose of what was probably very pure cocaine. In simple terms, this raised his heartbeat so high that it caused a stroke and unconsciousness. We're now keeping him artificially unconscious until we find out the condition of his brain.'

This was too hard. Eve stopped listening. She looked at Martha and Martha looked back. She would listen and note. She was the older sister and good at such things.

Max said, 'Can we see him now?'

He was saying it for her, Eve knew that. He understood too. How lucky she was! She didn't deserve such luck.

'Yes. You'll be shocked by the medical array but just go in and sit by him quietly. One at a time. At the moment he is heavily sedated. But the time will come when we lift the sedation and then you'll be very important. Get used to him now. You have a role to play.'

All this Eve listened to and understood. She nodded and felt just a fraction better. She could see it in Max and Martha's faces too. They would have a role to play. That was what the professor had said.

'Shall we go in now?' asked Max.

Eve didn't recognize his expression. He was leaning forward and everything in him seemed to be concentrated on that movement, like the prow of a ship cutting through water. He had to go to Dan first. They were all longing, they were all guilty, but Max needed to be first.

'You go,' she said, and Max turned, surprised. She thought there were tears in his eyes. How could he be beautiful at a time like this? Perhaps she had been jealous of his beauty.

'Come with me,' instructed Professor Sawyer.

The walk-on part of Dr Soueff appeared suddenly. 'There's a bigger waiting room. With a coffee machine. That sort of thing.' He escorted them and Professor Sawyer escorted Max, and now Eve miserably regretted her moment of unselfishness.

She and Martha found themselves beyond the locked door in an indecipherably shaped room with one stained-glass window depicting the sun plus rays. How could she have allowed herself to be separated from Max? And she had to wait again.

'I'll get us coffee,' said Martha.

'Do you think Max will stay long?'

'I don't know. I suppose he might.'

'I'll sit. *Like Patience on a monument.*' It was a phrase the sisters had often used in their bored teenage years. Vaguely, she recalled her outburst at Martha. So pointless and irrelevant, it now seemed.

Ronnie came into the room and Martha offered him a coffee too. They stood together at the machine and said things quietly to each other. Eve sat facing the inappropriate sun in splendour. She clasped her hands together and tried to take regular breaths. Quite soon she shut her eyes, but she didn't sleep. Her images were all of Dan, flashes of memory she'd forgotten until this moment: his first day at nursery school, his eyes huge with trying to understand what was happening to him. She was the one who'd cried. One evening he'd discovered an unknown cupboard in their flat behind a sealed panel. He must have been about ten and claimed it for his own space, as if it was the entrance to Narnia. He'd always liked mystery, she realized now, or escape.

She felt Martha's hand on her shoulder. 'He had been with an older man. A dealer. They found this man first. Yesterday evening. He wasn't as lucky as Dan.'

Eve didn't open her eyes. She didn't want this kind of information. Martha should have known. 'Thank you,' she said.

Martha looked down at Eve and felt the familiar surge of love, helplessness and fury. She had been going to tell her where Dan had been found. It was sheer good luck that a man had gone to his lock-up under the road early that morning. But she must let Eve deal with things her way. How could two sisters be so different? Yet Eve had been able to surprise: letting Max go in to see Dan before her. It wasn't that she was scared; cowardice was not one of her faults.

'I'm going out for a little while.'

Martha turned round to Ronnie and thought that she'd miss his solid presence. They'd been lucky to have someone like him. She felt ashamed of her behaviour on Weymouth station. 'You've been so good to us all.' A shocking idea struck her and she followed him out of the door. 'You might be able to help me with something.' Did she truly want to go through with it? Would he find it too strange when she was surrounded by family tragedy? But he was a professional like her.

'Of course.' Ronnie's face took on a new level of sympathy. Probably he thought it was something to do with Dan. Well, in a small way, it was.

'It's to do with my work.' She hesitated.

'I see.' Just a touch of surprise.

'One of the prisoners I've been working with was recently released on parole. A few weeks ago he absconded.' Was she acting out of revenge or self-protection? She should care about her job. What else did she have? He might be sent back to the prison where she worked, although it wasn't very likely. Would she want that?

'I see,' repeated Ronnie, looking as if he wanted to leave.

She could stop now. Maybe she was acting in Lee's own best interests. That was a joke. 'I saw him in Weymouth.' She hesitated.

'Yes?' enquired Ronnie. 'You think he's still there?'

Martha sighed, felt herself pulling back from the brink. 'Most unlikely. In fact, thinking about it more clearly, there's no point in doing anything at all.'

'Fine,' agreed Ronnie, seeming relieved, if bewildered.

Martha returned to sit beside Eve, staring with shut eyes at the glass sun. She, too, stared, although with open eyes. She pictured Lee walking up the hill towards her in Weymouth. She'd admired the swing of his liberated stride. In the end it was the police, not him, who had found Dan. But he had cared.

CHAPTER FORTY

The professor began talking to Max as they made their way to Intensive Care. 'Essentially, he has had a stroke, which means, as you know, blood has flooded his brain. It is probable that there was some weakness there, maybe linked to an earlier injury to his skull, although a very high dose of cocaine, or cocaine cut with some poisonous substance, could have caused it. Was your son a user before he left home?'

'No,' Max answered quickly, the shame stabbing so painfully he stood still. 'I don't think so.' He looked down. 'We've had to accept we know very little about our son.' He thought, And if he dies, we will never know.

'Unfortunately the man he was with didn't make it, so he can't tell us. I understand some girl was in touch with the police. Would she have any information?'

'I don't know,' said Max, who couldn't even remember the girl's name.

'The body itself gives us important data but a little additional information can be useful. For example, it might be helpful to know whether, as I suspect, this was Dan's first time on cocaine. We're running all kinds of tests, which will give us some answers.'

'Perhaps the police can pick the girl up,' said Max.

'Yes. I'll make your request.'

Max stared at Professor Sawyer. They were about the same age; in the crowd, where he, Max, would always stand out, the professor would be an insignificant man, but here in the hospital he was the conductor of life and death. Did he have a son as well? Loved and cherished?

'Are you ready to go in?'

He wasn't. He wanted to ask about the coma, how long it would last, how much was a medical decision. Most of all, he wanted to ask about Dan's chances. But Professor Sawyer, whose time was important, had opened the door and he must follow him.

Yet when Max saw Dan lying there, the medical interventions obvious, as he'd expected, it was not the horror of this that overwhelmed him but rather the wonder of having his son back in the same room, under his eyes. His absence had been so terrible, the endless weeks of not knowing, the nightmares of his imagination so horrific, that this sad sight filled him with something approaching joy. In tune with this he allowed himself to believe that all would be well, that Dan would be returned to them so that they could have a second chance. Tears of hope fell from his eyes.

Professor Sawyer, who thought he understood a father's feelings, patted his shoulder consolingly and pointed to a chair.

'May I touch him?'

'Go ahead.'

Max sat down. He would kiss Dan when they were on their own.

'Sister Aru will keep an eye on things.'

The situation was more frightening with the doctor gone. Max tried to concentrate on his son's peaceful face. The moment of physical contact seemed important but, having been unaware of his tears, he was surprised to put a finger to his own face and find it wet.

Keeping his eyes all the time on Dan as if he might vanish again if he looked away, he dried his face as well as he could with his fingertips. Then he leant over his son. He was thin, very thin, bruises and dirty marks on his face and neck. His hair was long and also dirty. He wanted to take his whole body into his arms and cradle him as if he were a baby. He longed to swaddle and comfort him, give him his own strength, but all he could offer was a kiss.

If only he could kiss Dan into life. But the boy was no fairytale princess. Despite everything, the skin of his forehead was young and taut. But what was behind the skin, inside the skull?

Never taking his eyes off his son, but still without kissing him, he sat down again. Had Dan ever been in love? By the time he, Max, was fourteen, growing up in a small town in Northern Ireland, he'd often been in love. At least, girls had loved him, claiming him as their own, telling him, with bossy certainty, that they loved each other. They quoted from pop songs when he was already reading Shakespearean sonnets, happy to be wanted, secure in the knowledge of his superiority. He would go to university in England. They would stay behind. He would never be their husband. But in England he'd met Eve.

Very slowly, feeling like an ungainly giant in comparison to the flat figure on the bed, Max stood and bent. The forehead seemed the place to imprint his fatherly blessing, his hopes and encouragement. *Love is not love which alters when it alteration finds.* It was what he'd wanted to say on the television appeal. Even as he felt the truest love of his life, a line of someone else's poetry was the only way he could express it.

He could never and would never write such a line. He had staked his all on poetry and only become its humbled servant.

He sank back into the chair. In front of him the pale face with its beautiful closed eyelids was unchanged, neither forgiving nor unforgiving. He claimed nothing. He had never claimed anything.

'Dan. Listen to me. I love you.' He spoke aloud, with emphasis, leant forward urgently. He would make it true. 'If you live, I will love you for ever and I will show you I love you.' He forced out the plain, honest words, which held not a glimmer of poetry. 'Please, don't die. If you can help yourself, please, I beg you, don't die.'

'I can't wait any longer!' For the last few minutes Eve had been wandering round the room, fixing for a few seconds in front of the stained-glass sun or the coffee machine, then moving on restlessly.

'It's awful,' said Martha. She, too, found the waiting unbearable. Possibly Max was watching Dan die and had forgotten about them. A man's connection to other people was so tenuous, she thought, even if they were wife, sister-in-law or lover. 'I'll try and find a nurse.'

'Yes. Yes,' agreed Eve, grasping Martha's shoulder as she had Max's before he left.

They both moved to the door but were stopped by three sad-faced women in saris and, behind them, Ronnie, returned from wherever he'd gone.

'Apparently you left this in the hotel.' He handed a bag to Eve, who looked so bewildered that Martha took it for her.

'We're going to ask to see Dan,' said Martha.

Suddenly Eve snatched the bag. She undid the zip and, with

shaking hands, began to pull out the things inside. She threw them on to the floor. 'They're for Dan,' she cried. 'A sweater, food, a book. But how can he use them if he's in Intensive Care?'

'I see,' said Ronnie, and gently took the bag and Martha helped pick up its contents. 'I'll look after them while you visit Dan.'

'Thank you,' said Martha. Eve's behaviour reminded her of a prisoner driven either to silent despair or unexpected violence. 'We'll both go.' Martha took her sister's hand and they walked out of the door together.

Max's concentration was broken by a light touch on his arm. 'Your wife would like to come in now.'

'My wife. Of course.' How long had he been here? But it was painful to be escorted out by this nurse, however long he'd been. He wanted to stay near Dan for ever. He wanted to sleep under the bed. I love you, Dan.

'Max!' Eve took hold of him the moment he'd passed out of the quiet room and into the corridor. He tried to respond but his heart was still with Dan. 'Is he . . . ?' She didn't finish the sentence. She clutched at him. 'Please come in with me.'

'You know it's not allowed.' Max hugged her then and kissed her cheek, and whispered to her that Dan was alive and she was strong. She clung to him for a moment, then stepped free and passed through the door.

Max watched her and wondered if he could wait for her where he stood, but a nurse shepherded him back to the waiting room where the three women in saris sat in a dignified row and Martha stood drinking coffee. She looked at him questioningly.

'I don't know. He's still alive.' She used to be his port of call in a storm.

'Coffee?'

'Thanks.'

They took their cups and stood on either side of the rising sun.

'It all depends on Professor Sawyer, I suppose?' Martha still had a questioning look on her face.

Max noticed for the first time that her eyes were large and dark, her nose long and her mouth wide and thin. She was like Dan. The whiteness of her skin was familiar.

'He didn't tell me when they'll bring him out of his coma. Perhaps it'll be days.' He pictured Dan lying peacefully in his bed and feared for a change.

'I see. We might need somewhere to stay.'

Max tried to contemplate this idea. 'I suppose so.'

'I'll make enquiries. Maybe the hospital has facilities.'

Max managed to say, 'Yes,' before he turned away. He threw his empty cup into a bin and went into the corridor. After a while he forced himself to re-enter the room. 'I'm sorry,' he said.

'I know.' She was holding yet another cup of coffee. 'We all are.'

He kissed her cheek and turned to go outside again, but his way was blocked by Dr Soueff whose handsome figure vibrated with suppressed urgency. Max felt himself shrink and go pale. He steadied himself on the door jamb.

The doctor went past him and said something to the first of the Asian women, who reacted with an eerie wail. Max began to shake.

All three women hurried past him, with Dr Soueff behind. He murmured to Max, 'Never buy a motorcycle.'

Max half ran to the lift, but since it didn't come immediately, he found the door to the stairs and ran down seven floors. He retraced the purple lino and the blue lino until he could fling himself into the open air. He stood there breathing deeply.

'You all right, mate?'

Vaguely, Max saw an ambulance man putting aside a cigarette to look at him with concern.

'Yes.' He walked away until he was staring beyond the city, outward to sea and sky.

How would Dr Soueff summon them when Dan was being told to enter the world again? What news would he bring? What would he murmur out of the side of his mouth? Would Eve scream in disbelief? Would he?

CHAPTER FORTY-ONE

Eve, Max, Martha, Ronnie and Detective Superintendent Tim Southey sat in a side room in a small hotel in Brighton. The owners obviously liked colour because the carpet was whorled in bright patterns, the chairs were upholstered in blue stripes and the wallpaper was a mauvish trellis where a few birds plucked greedily at darker mauve grapes.

It was a room fit for agony, thought Eve. But she thought it listlessly and without rancour. All her energy was saved for Dan, lying unchanged in the half-world of Intensive Care. Today might be the day when it was decided he should come back to them. No longer be missing. They'd expected it yesterday. Each of the five days he'd lain there.

In that time Ronnie had left them for London, accompanied by Martha, who had collected clothes and other things they needed. Now they'd returned with this detective. Eve eyed him warily. He looked very fit and eager. 'I wanted an informal meeting,' he was saying – as if informality or formality made the slightest difference to anything. He began to talk about drugs, a case they'd been working on, the role played by someone called Zeppo, an unlikely name. 'I hope I'll have your co-operation.'

Eve twisted in her chair. Her new thinness made her uncomfortable. She thought she totally understood people who starved themselves to death. How could she eat when Dan lay in a state of un-being? Although, she tried to remind herself, he was being fed through tubes.

'. . . this afternoon so I wanted to give you a little warning. It goes without saying that she can't see your son unless the family give permission.'

Eve began to take more notice. She whispered to Martha – Martha who was so strong, so helpful, so self-effacing, 'Who's she?'

'The girl who was with Dan, who told the police where he was.'

'And why would we want to see her?' Eve realized she'd raised her voice and that the rest of the room was listening.

'None of you has to see her,' said Ronnie, 'but Professor Sawyer thought she might have useful information. Medical information.'

'And she's part of the police investigation,' added Martha.

'Oh, yes,' said Eve, indifferently. She put a hand over her eyes. 'When are we going to the hospital?'

'Soon,' said Max. He held Eve's hand but turned to the policeman. 'I'd like to meet her.'

'Here, at two? Or would you prefer the station?'

Eve made an effort to concentrate and understand why Max wanted to talk to the girl. 'What's her name?' she asked.

'Freya.'

She must not be separated from Max. 'Let's meet here.'

'I'll make the arrangements.' The policeman rose. 'Can we give you a lift to the hospital?'

'Thank you, no.' Max rose too. He was still impressive despite his gaunt, numbed look.

They knew the short walk to the hospital as if they'd been doing it every day of their lives. Past the Audrey Emerton Eye Hospital, crossing the road to the old hospital, white-painted and dated 1887. Turn left up the steep hill to the tall modern block housing A and E and Intensive Care. The first day there'd been journalists outside the door.

It was a penitential pilgrimage, which culminated in the meeting with Dr Soueff. 'What news?'

'No news.'

But today was the day, certainly. Early this morning they had started the process of withdrawing the drugs. Today the walk would be even more a procession of preparation, a prayer for hope.

Eve still prayed but in a more general way. She'd recited to Max: *Hail, Holy Queen, Mother of Mercy, our life our sweetness and our hope . . .* He'd said it sounded like poetry, then asked her sadly how he could be included. He was a Protestant from Northern Ireland and didn't believe anyway. So she'd said she was an Anglican and didn't believe either and they'd pray together to some higher unspecified being. She didn't give up her private prayers to Mary, however. *We who are sinners plead for your pity.*

CHAPTER FORTY-TWO

Freya felt like a bird of paradise among these mournful middle-aged middle classes. Didn't they get it that tragedy happens all the time? To everybody. Irrespective. The trick is to face it out, create your own vibrations so nothing can destroy you. Where are their feelings, man?

Dan needed life to draw him back to life, not long faces and self-pitying mumblings. How she hated all that! They'd tried it on her when things were bad, police, social workers and the like, trying to drag her down to their level of grim and grisly. She'd known better and kicked them in the teeth as soon as she was old enough.

You wouldn't catch her mourning for what Zeppo 'might have been' or some other meaningless jargon. He had been what he was, not very nice, not very clever, despite his posing as a writer.

It was different with Dan. He was a kid. Kid brother, whatever else he'd dreamed of making it. Never thought he was sixteen.

She'd dressed up for him. Spent hours the night before weaving magic into her hair, spells of blue beads and turquoise feathers. Round her neck more beads, in the colours of the chakra, the colours of a rainbow: green for the heart, that was in the middle, red at the bottom to earth him solid, plus a black basalt stone she'd bought at Glastonbury from a sacred mountain in America. In her backpack she had a crystal too and oils from a wise woman, Christy, in Cornwall. She'd even got a CD. Dan wouldn't stand a chance, man, once she got to him.

Trouble was, these dull ghosts had to give her permission to get to him. She'd done her bit already with the doctor and his sidekick, who wouldn't let her go. That was another story. Now they'd brought her here to the family. What a joke! 'Give them something they don't know,' the pigeons who shat from on high had said to her.

'So what *do* they know?' she'd asked. He'd smiled, understanding well enough. A kid doesn't run away from a knowing mum and dad. They didn't know him when he was with them so why should they be told things when he goes?

But she would tell them all the same, because she wanted to see Dan. Fair's fair. *One raindrop raises the ocean.*

'Thank you for coming.' The father must have been a bit of a raver. Check out those eyes. Not so drab, Freya girl.

'That's OK. I'm sorry about Dan.' Which was his mum, then? The blonde with brown roots and saggy boobs or the skinny dark one, who looked like Dan. Must be her.

'This is Dan's mother, Eve, and his aunt, Martha.' Wrong, then.

The wise old woman had said, 'Dan must want to come back. The way things are he'll run away again, if he can.'

'It's so very kind of you to come.' His mum. Surprising voice, deep and vibrating. Suddenly she was over, grabbing her arm, staring into her face. 'We need help. Very badly. We can't help Dan but you can.' Near tears.

Freya withdrew a bit, although this Eve didn't let go of her. Big eyes staring at her, appealing. Reminded her of Dan after all. Too right she was more likely to help Dan but they had to do their fucking bit too, didn't they?

'We blame ourselves,' said Max, giving her a sober eyeful.

Too right again. But they weren't quite what she'd thought. Not trying to control their emotion, after all. More open. More suffering. There's a word. Served them right – them and their sort. Freya glanced quickly at the aunt, Martha. She was different, more uptight.

'I don't know about blame.' Freya spoke to the mother. 'Doesn't do good in any direction.'

'We want him back!' cried Eve, dropping Freya's arm and turning to Max. 'But we don't know how.' Her voice descended to a whimper.

Freya remembered Dan had said his mother was an actress or taught acting. It figured. 'I guess it wasn't just you.' Freya hadn't meant to be consoling. They didn't deserve to be let off the hook. Ever. Although, as she thought this, she remembered old Christy saying her attitude was what would call Dan back. No mean thoughts or he'd not think it worth his trouble. Got to be on her best behaviour, then.

'What are you saying?' It was the first time the aunt had spoken. She sounded aggressive.

'He told me things.' The room went very quiet. She hadn't meant to sound heavy but she could see they were taking it that way. She forced herself to go on. Usually expectation made her run. 'There was this friend. Died. Kind of haunted Dan.' As she spoke, she remembered Dan's face as he'd told her this – honestly she hadn't been listening too well. *Puff, the magic dragon*. She felt tears, hard and sharp. She should have paid more attention.

'Haunted?' repeated Max.

'Yeah. Like a ghost. Frightened him so much he didn't like to go to sleep. The weed helped him there. Chinese boy or something. Topped himself. I don't know. Dan got involved or what. He felt guilty. Anyway, this boy came at night and told Dan he needed a friend out where he was. All lonely. Dan felt sorry for him. Guilty. He hated him too.'

Freya stopped talking. She really didn't know much about this stuff. Didn't want to make up things. Point was, Dan hadn't told his mum and dad, who were doing all this sorrowing now. They could have dealt with it.

'There was a half-Chinese boy called Ru, younger than Dan, who committed suicide,' said Max. He put his arm round Eve.

'That'll be him, then.' Freya heard her voice sounding nonchalant, as if it was all sorted. Well, she'd given them someone else to blame, hadn't she? Not that they looked less shattered. His mum had her head in her hands, her whole body shaking. Someone had to take a grip. 'Can I go and see him now?'

She'd earned that right, hadn't she? Like the pigeons had said, 'Give them something and they'll give you.'

The mum didn't look up. 'Yes,' Max said. 'Thank you.'

Now, he was some man. Freya stood up, felt her beads dance on her shoulders. She pulled her backpack off the chair, started to go, then turned. 'Don't mind if I play him a bit of music, do you?' Music would do for everything, candles, scented oils. She even had a piece of silk for him to feel. Christy again.

Max nodded and Freya left the room. Outside a policeman waited.

Martha watched her go. Girls like that sent her crazy. Those filthy, matted dreadlocks made even more ridiculous by all the bits stuck in them. Only stupid white girls thought they could ape a black man's culture. All the same, she cared about Dan, you could see that. It struck Martha that she should accompany her to the hospital.

'Shall I go with her?' They made decisions together now.

'Good idea,' Max answered.

Martha hurried out of the room. She was glad to escape from the ugly claustrophobic hotel. She caught up with Freya. 'I'm coming with you.' The policeman with her said, 'Fine,' but the girl frowned and hitched her backpack higher as if it were a shield. She was holding it on one shoulder but it was large and obviously heavy and should have been on her back.

'Here. Let me help.' Martha took hold of the other strap.

The girl let her, but unwillingly. She smelt of oils and dirt and girlish sweat. The backpack was filthy but decorated with embroidered flowers, patterns and a zodiac sign. Gemini. They shared the same star sign.

'That's one big bag.'

'I'm used to it.'

It was clear she didn't want to talk. Martha couldn't blame her. Dan was why she was here, not his family. But she'd told them about this boy – they should have known about him already: Ru's mother had telephoned them.

Martha's thoughts veered off the subject. That morning she'd had a call from the prison. Lee had been picked up in Glasgow the day before. Gerry had thought she'd like to know, even though Lee wouldn't come back to their prison. She wondered whether Lee had managed to see his son. She hoped so. One day she and Lee would meet again. What shameful self-pity had made her even think of turning him in? Although he wouldn't have been surprised.

'How are his mum and dad coping with the good-bad news situation?'

Martha jumped at the policeman's voice. For a moment she didn't understand what he meant. It must have shown on his face because the policeman – she couldn't remember his name, there'd been so many – added, 'Finding your missing son and maybe going to lose him again.'

'To death, you mean.' She enjoyed the uncomfortable expression on his face. She was not doing well here, she knew. Bad thoughts led to bad behaviour. There was no real role for her. Even though Eve had forgiven her and pretended to need her sisterly comfort, she really looked to Max. She could organize things for them but that was about all.

She should get back to work. Sort herself out. Decide if working in prison was still the right place for her. Freya was striding on ahead, every now and again turning her head to check she was on the right path. Her swinging, beaded hair, garish backpack and skinny legs in tattered jeans spoke of defiance and bravery. Martha, who had wanted to deride her, found a sort of admiration growing. How did a girl like her survive? From the West Country, by her accent, no middle-class trustafarian games. Probably something bad she'd left behind. The next thing. A girl living on the edge. She herself had never dared be that.

But what a trio they were! The bullet-headed policeman (she'd do him an injustice), the coke-head hippie and the bitter prison officer.

'I once knew the mother of a misper – her son gone since he was eleven – who bought him a present for his every birthday, and he'd been away ten years.' It was the policeman trying again. 'Yes. Wrapped each present up, with ribbons and a tag, to dearest Sammy on your twelfth, thirteenth, et cetera birthday. When I left the unit she was planning a big twenty-first party. I half expected her to buy him a car. She was convinced he'd be back, that was the thing. Mothers are like that. Never give up.'

'Did he?' Against her will, she was caught.

'What?'

'Come back?'

The bullet head retracted regretfully. 'Never heard any more about it. Probably not. Of course, there might be a body years later.'

'Check,' agreed Martha, hoping to shut him down. But the uniform gathered steam again. Clearly, he lacked listeners.

'The point was this mother was a believer. Said she believed God was looking after her son and God would bring him back when the time was right. She packed up the parcels not because she'd gone crazy or desperate but so he'd see that she'd kept in touch with him. Had some religious text she quoted all the time.' He paused to think.

But now Martha really had had enough. Besides, they'd arrived at the hospital. Freya stood waiting at the doors, facing them, not like the rest of them who stared out to sea like a diver taking a last gulp of air. She was directed, that girl.

Freya was feeling the pressure. She'd have liked a soothing joint. That was a laugh. What joker, if it came to that, had put dolphins dancing along the hospital's corridors as if it was a play centre for kiddies? She remembered again what Christy had told her: 'You've got to be in the right frame or he won't want to come back to you.' She'd done right by Dan's mum and dad but this one with her was difficult, with her tight, closed face. They were all guilty, that was the point. They'd all messed up Dan one way and another, herself included, if she was honest. But she understood him and he, poor, deluded sod, loved her so, stands to reason, he'd come back for her. Or not.

Forget the 'or not'. Christy had kept her going over the years, more than ten now, and she'd said, 'Think positive. See off those negative vibes with sounds or smells. Sing if you can.'

That was another laugh. Her singing. 'Jingle Bells' was about her start and finish. That was why she'd brought the CD – which probably wouldn't play. Found something might ring a bell with Dan. Think positive, Frey! She pictured Dan sitting on Weymouth beach listening to the carousel music, with the little kids going round and round, all serious, like they were heading for the moon. There'd been donkeys, too. Nicely kept, no mangy leftovers.

The festival they'd been at, she'd been too spaced out to notice what music Dan liked. The doctor had just said, 'Tell him who you are. Talk to him.' She could do that, no problem. Tell him about the refloating of the capitalist bonanza. *Bikes, not bombs*. Not that she rode a bike. Never had one as a child. He'd encouraged her political rants. At least he hadn't walked away. Not sure they would bring him back, though.

They were waiting for a lift now, the policeman left behind. Got to get the good vibes going. Talk to this woman.

'Was Dan always a loner?' She wasn't so bad when you looked at her straight on. Sad. The police had told her she was a prison guard. Didn't look stupid enough.

'Yes. I guess so.' A pause. 'We all feel we didn't know him.'

'Yeah.' Talk to her. Open up. 'This friend of mine says you have to think positive to get him back. Warm up the atmosphere. You know. But I don't expect you believe in things like that.'

Freya noticed Martha smiled a little, ironic, not warm, but against herself. 'I don't know what I believe in just now.'

Building bridges, that was what Freya thought she was doing. On the other hand she didn't want an old lady's problems dumped on her. She wished those lift doors would open. But the aunt had gone silent again. She seemed to be looking at a picture pinned to the wall; it might have been a mother and child, if you decoded the arty bit.

At last the lift doors opened.

CHAPTER FORTY-THREE

Eve lay in her hotel bed. She felt closer to Dan, lying down like him. She remembered how, as a baby and against all the nurses' advice, he'd slept with them. They'd said she or Max, so big and heavy, might roll on him in their sleep. But he was their joy, their delight. How could they have harmed him? She'd fed him in bed whenever he wanted, her breasts enormous and sensitive, spouting milk as Dan sucked greedily. Max had been jealous so she'd let him suck too. Now it seemed the most sensual experience of her life.

'Max?'

He was sitting in the room, pretending to read. She couldn't really believe he was capable of that sort of concentration. If he was, she admired him for it. Not poetry, though. It looked like a guidebook.

'Yes.'

'I suppose Freya was close to Dan?' They'd discussed this already, coming to no conclusions, but she wanted more.

'She wants to help.' Max looked up with more attention. 'Does she remind you of your drama kids?'

Separate boxes. Since she'd finished the course and allowed herself to be put on sabbatical from the school, she hadn't thought once about her 'kids', as Max called them. *My* kids, as she used to call them. 'They're city, she's a traveller. Even more outside the system than they are.'

'Do you like her?'

She wanted to be honest. The truth was, she couldn't quite bear to look at Freya, let alone talk to her. She felt jealous and angry. Not appropriate emotions when your son hovered between life and death. 'I'm trying.'

Maybe she'd put Freya in her prayers. Don't expect she'd approve but that's show business. Her praying was still more of a meditation than a belief but it steadied her mind and, now and again, she felt an inkling of something greater outside her present suffering.

'You know, I saw her before.' Max, who had gone back to his book, suddenly spoke quite loudly.

Eve sat up, stared at him. 'What do you mean? When? Where?'

'On Weymouth station. I was with Ronnie in the waiting room. These two backpackers were there with a girl. Dreadlocks, stud in her nose.'

'Why didn't you tell me?' They told each other everything now.

'I didn't want to upset you. Or myself, I suppose. If I'd approached her then – I even thought of showing Dan's photo to them – we might have found him earlier. Before he took the coke.'

'Oh, Max.' There was no question of anger or forgiveness. She would forgive him anything. She got off her bed and went to sit with him.

'One more failure,' said Max.

Max had been looking at a guidebook to Brighton. Fifteen years on the road had given him a particular interest in maps, guides, weather reports. They'd formed the structure of his comings and goings – of his life, in many ways. In the last day or two, after lunch and before their second visit to the hospital, he had left Eve resting or with Martha and spent several hours walking round Brighton. Keeping up a quick pace, he covered the seafront, parks, elegant crescents and squares, the shopping centres, the harbour and the wide hinterland of terraced roads with occasional apartment blocks. Eventually he'd come out into the countryside and found himself faced by the unearthly beauty of the Downs.

It was there on a dull, breezy day when, even at this drab end of summer, the grass shone a luminous green, that he'd confronted the nasty truth of his marriage. Possibly, even probably, Eve's and his own attempts to evade the ordinary reality of existence – more to the point, of being parents, himself with his 'poetic ambitions' more guilty than Eve – had killed their son. They had always put their entirely self-centred needs before Dan's, refusing to make the smallest sacrifice on his behalf. No one had told them parenthood was about sacrifice.

They would be guilty for ever whether he lived or died. But if he lived they might have a small chance to give him something better.

Freya could see that the doctor didn't like the look of her. Dr Soueff. He was so tall and clean and efficient.

'What are you doing with all that stuff?'

They were in the corridor outside Dan's room. She'd got a candle, some oils, a bell, the silk in her pocket. She'd decided against the CD player today. 'The other doctor said it was OK.'

'You mustn't expect too much yet.' He sounded kinder now.

'I'm patient.' Which was true. She was used to waiting, doing nothing. When she was young she'd waited for things to get better. Not like doctors. Never had time. Sick people had to be patient too. Suppose that's how they got their name.

'Half an hour. Sister will come and get you.'

Everybody had to be patient. Day after day. The same hours for visiting, the same faces. The same Dan lying asleep. The doctor said he was no longer in a coma but nearer to sleeping. That was the change but it was invisible to the eye of the visitor. He looked as he'd always looked, with fewer tubes.

The doctors, if directly asked – only Max dared – were non-committal. They would know how he was when he woke up and told them. The test results were not bad, inconclusive.

Six days passed. Freya slept on the floor of Martha's bedroom. This was a concession on both sides. Martha got used to the smell of oils and incense; Freya put away her dope and put on a headset when she played her CDs. They recognized some similarity in each other.

Life of hard knocks, decided Freya, although she had no idea about Martha's life.

Brave child, decided Martha. She said, 'Let's go out and find a beer.'

'Better than a kick in the eye,' agreed Freya.

They walked out to the Bristol Bar and sat together in crusty armchairs with a view of the sea. It soon became something to look forward to, although they didn't talk much or tell each other secrets. They knew they looked out of place, with each other and with the shabbily elegant bar that was part of an old hotel. It amused them and drew them together.

'I suppose the Bristol Bar's become a habit,' said Martha.

'Only dead fish swim with the stream,' said Freya, with a grimace, but it was a friendly kind of grimace.

Max mostly walked to the Downs. It was a long walk and tired him. When he came back Eve was usually lying on the bed, unless they were going to the hospital, in which case she was waiting expectantly, sitting on a chair in the hotel's small foyer.

'I love you,' they said to each other, and tried not to believe that anything could take it away.

PART FIVE
Ending

CHAPTER FORTY-FOUR

Dan felt as if a huge, soft, heavy, furry weight was pressing on him and through him and into whatever was below him. He couldn't separate himself from it. Nor did he want to. It was in his brain too. No pain. Just something else.

Then the blackness came again.

Sometimes now the furry weight reminded him of something. Grey-brown over yellow. Dim colours had begun to wash into his head. And the grey-brown formed into shapes, which moved.

To black again.

The shapes moved to a pattern or the pattern was sounds. He heard sounds now, repeating until they held his attention. He didn't want to listen, it made him uncomfortable, but once the great weight had lifted, he didn't seem to have much choice. There were no words yet to describe what was happening to him, just the images and the sounds.

Black.

Dan saw grey-brown animals in a trail, one behind another, stepping daintily over yellow sand. Donkeys. Donkeys on the beach. He felt as if his whole body was lifting up, trying to see them more clearly. Exhausted, he sank back. But the sounds were still there. Music. Round and round and round. Three tunes. Round and round and round. He tried to listen more carefully, pick out one tune from another. But that was exhausting too.

Black.

'Dan. Dan.' The same donkeys. The same beach. Someone was calling his name. 'Dan. Dan.' He rose up to hear better. A gentle sound, mixed with the three tunes. But who was it? Safer perhaps to drop into blackness.

Oh, but the utter black was frilled with a dangerous glare, orange lightning splitting the night sky. Who was it calling? A little wheedling voice, pathetic, pitiable, wanting him, growing loud enough to drown the earlier gentle voice, the sweet music, the docile donkeys on the trail. *Dan. Dan. Dan.*

Terrified, Freya watched as Dan's eyes opened wide as if in agony and he mouthed a tortured groan. He sank back again.

It was the first time he'd opened his eyes, the first time he'd made a sound. They all exchanged notes, the family in the morning and the evening, she in the afternoon. There had been nothing. No change.

Why had Dan seemed terrified? Was it something she had done to frighten him? The fucking nurses had told her to say his name. Hurriedly, Freya turned off the CD player and sat watching him. He was restlessly turning his head. Unconsciously, she sucked her fingers.

There was another hour of her watch – sometimes she felt like a guard on duty, watching for signs, watching for the enemy. That was what Dan had seen: an enemy. Freya frowned and shook her head so that the beads in her hair clacked together.

How could she have been so slow? He'd heard Ru calling him. He'd told her Ru came in his sleep, saying his name over and over. What better chance for a shithead ghost than now when he lay in the grim and grisly half-world?

'It's Freya.' She took his hand. It was unnaturally soft and white but she was used to that.

'I'm Freya. Freya.' She whispered her name close to his ear.

The jagged lightning splitting Dan's brain slowed its sawing motion. A name like a gentle breeze calmed the sharp edges and brushed away the glare. The darkness returned to the grey that he was more used to now.

'Freya, Dan. Freya's here with you. Freya.' Freya's face was so close to Dan's that when he smiled, she wasn't sure at first whether it really was him or whether it was her, willing her smile on to him. She pulled back a little.

It was *his* smile. Oh, *Knickerbocker Glory*! His eyelids fluttered but didn't open. Then she felt a faint squeeze of her hand. The smile faded a little and his mouth moved. Only an F came out, a sound like a breath.

'Freya. Yes. Me. Here. Freya.'

Again, the smile, the squeeze of the hand. Another attempt at her name. Slowly his eyes opened.

Tears poured down Freya's face. His eyes looked straight at her, unblinking and absolutely clear. This boy had been nothing to her and now he felt like everything. Not just as if he had been reborn but as if she had too.

'Freya?'

She felt her whole body quivering. 'I'm here, Dan.'

After a few seconds his eyes shut again and she sensed an extraordinary calmness in the room.

Later Max and Eve found her there. Her manner, the dried tears on her face, terrified them. 'What happened?' they asked, in nervous, anxious voices, breaking the rule that nothing but peace must surround Dan.

'He knew me,' whispered Freya, the tears falling again although she didn't notice them. 'He opened his eyes and he knew me. He tried to say my fucking name. Then he did say it.'

Eve began to cry too and also didn't notice the tears.

'It was as if he was being reborn.' Freya faltered as she tried to explain what she'd felt. It struck her that Eve had actually given birth to him. 'You should have been here. Sorry.'

But although she apologized, her manner was of extreme happiness, almost exaltation.

All three of them stood looking down at Dan. He was quite calm again.

'The doctors said that at the moment of waking we'd be able to tell whether he was all right,' said Max quietly. 'You say he knew who you were?'

'He smiled. He recognized my voice first, then he opened his eyes. He squeezed my hand.' Freya still wore an air of wonder, quite unlike her usual air of defensive defiance.

'What did you say it felt like?' asked Eve. She'd been silent and unmoving till then, as if afraid to disturb or even undo the miracle that Freya was describing.

'I felt he was being reborn. It was something in his eyes. So clear.' Freya hesitated but didn't add that she had felt as if her life was being given a new beginning.

'Thank you.' Eve sat in the chair.

Freya thought Eve would take Dan's hand, try to get a reaction from him again, make his awakening her property too. But instead she sat bowed humbly. Her lips seemed to be moving, without any sound.

'I'll go now,' whispered Freya.

Max came out with her. 'We should tell the doctors.' He leant against the wall of the corridor. Freya saw he was shaking. 'We don't deserve this.'

Freya said nothing. She'd never found 'deserve' a very helpful word. They'd got their boy back. That was all there was to it. Now they'd have to get on with it. Sadly, she felt the almost unearthly glow of joy that had surrounded her beginning to wane. 'Martha here?'

Max didn't look up. 'In the waiting room, I think.'

'I'll go and tell her.'

As Freya walked down the corridor, she glanced back and saw, through the open door to Dan's room, Max return and stand behind Eve, his hand on her shoulder. They were both staring down at their son.

ACKNOWLEDGMENTS

Grateful thanks to my editor, Sara O'Keefe, and to her assistant, Natalie Braine, to my ever-supportive agent, Bruce Hunter, and my valued copy editor, Hazel Orme. John Podmore helped me with useful contacts in the police force and in the prison service. Sarah Dunsmure once again led me through Brighton with an expert's knowledge and Colette Prideaux Brune put me right on the chakras and other related subjects. All my family contributed in various ways; in particular my daughters Chloe Billington and Rose Gaete gave me much good advice, including drama teaching notes from Chloe. Finally, especial thanks to my husband, Kevin Billington, for encouraging my writing over so many years.